Three romances celebrating
the joys, tears and blessings
of motherhood

It's thrilling, nerve-wracking, full of
anticipation and emotions; waiting
for her own special delivery is something a woman remembers all her life.
And the lucky ones have the right
man by their sides...

Mothers -To-Be

THE GREEK AND THE SINGLE MUM
by Julia James

ADOPTED: ONE BABY
by Natasha Oakley

THEIR BABY BOND
by Amy Andrews

*First published in Great Britain 2007
by Harlequin Mills & Boon Limited, Eton House,
18-24 Paradise Road, Richmond, Surrey TW9 1SR*

MOTHERS-TO-BE © by Harlequin Books S.A. 2007

The Greek and the Single Mum © Julia James 2007
Adopted: One Baby © Natasha Oakley 2007
Their Baby Bond © Amy Andrews 2007

ISBN: 978 0 263 85826 6

010-0307

*Printed and bound in Spain
by Litografia Rosés S.A., Barcelona*

THE GREEK AND
THE SINGLE MUM

by
Julia James

Julia James lives in England with her family. Mills & Boon® novels were Julia's first "grown up" books she read as a teenager, alongside Georgette Heyer and Daphne du Maurier and she's been reading them ever since.

Julia adores the English countryside ("And the Celtic countryside!"), in all its seasons, and is fascinated by all things historical, from castles to cottages. She also has a special love for the Mediterranean, "the most perfect landscape after England!" — she considers both are ideal settings for romance stories! Since becoming a romance writer, she has, she says, had the great good fortune to start discovering the Caribbean as well, and is happy to report that those magical, beautiful islands are also ideal settings for romances. "One of the best things about writing romance is that it gives you a great excuse to take holidays in fabulous places," says Julia. "All in the name of research, of course!"

Her first stab at novel writing was Regency romances – "But alas, no one wanted to publish them," she says. She put her writing aside until her family commitments were clear, and then renewed her love-affair with contemporary romances. "My writing partner and I made a pact not to give up until we were published – and we both succeeded! Natasha Oakley writes for Mills & Boon Romance, and we faithfully read each other's works-in-progress and give each other a lot of free advice and encouragement."

In between writing Julia enjoys walking, gardening, needlework and baking "extremely gooey chocolate cakes" — and trying to stay fit!

**Don't miss Julia James's new novel,
Royally Bedded, Regally Wedded, out in March
from Mills & Boon Modern Romance™!**

PROLOGUE

CLARE took a deep breath and walked forward into the dimly lit cocktail bar. Soft music issued from the white piano in the corner, and she vaguely recognised an old number from the fifties. But she paid it no attention, heading instead for the nearest table, set low and surrounded by deep leather easy chairs designed to soothe the bodies of besuited businessmen, weary from a hard day's work in the corridors of power.

Her mouth twisted slightly. Those corridors—and the boardrooms and suites that opened off them—might demand long hours, but they also awarded a de luxe lifestyle to those who stalked them. Bespoke suits, handmade shoes, perfect grooming, and the ability to pay exorbitant prices with a flick of a platinum credit card.

As Clare approached the table, around which a cluster of suits eased back in the armchairs, a soft, throaty laugh made her turn her head slightly. A little way away, at another table, a couple sat on a sofa, drinks in hand. It was not the man who had laughed so seductively, but his female companion. For a brief moment Clare allowed herself to look. Even in the soft lighting she could see that the woman was very beautiful, with chic hair, expertly styled, and immaculate make-up. Her dress was a designer number, and clung to her lissom form. As she gave her soft laugh, she crossed her long, sheer-stockinged legs, and one elegantly manicured hand hovered over her companion's thigh.

A little stab went through Clare. She looked away.

I shouldn't have taken this job. I knew it was a mistake!

For four long years she had kept away from places like this. The world she lived in now was in a different universe. Stepping back into this lush, expensive environment was not something she had wanted to do.

It brought back too many memories.

And the brief glimpse of that designer-clothed female had intensified them.

Was I ever really like that?

It seemed impossible—and yet with her brain she knew it was true. She too, once, a lifetime ago, had been like that woman. Beautifully clothed, immaculately made up, elegant and chic.

She inhaled sharply. What did it matter that this place brought back the past? Memories she didn't want and didn't welcome. She was here simply because it was the best way she had of making the extra money she needed if her determination to take Joey and her friend Vi on holiday that summer was to succeed. Evening work was the only kind that was possible, and waiting cocktail tables in this swish new hotel, recently opened on an arterial road *en route* to Heathrow in West London, a bus ride away from where she lived with Vi, had to be a lot better than working in a pub, or in her local pizza parlour.

As for the memories its luxury triggered—well, tough. Her chin lifted. She'd have to get over it.

The uncompromising injunction resonated in her head. *Get over it.* One of the toughest self-help commandments around—and yet it had helped her, she knew, during those four long years. Years when she'd had to completely change her life—not just her lifestyle, but something far more profound. Far more difficult.

No. *Don't go there!*

That was another maxim she'd had to rigidly cling to. Don't go there—where in her dreams, her yearnings, she longed to go. Back into the past. A past that ached like an old, deep, unhealable wound.

Or, worse, don't go into a present that did not exist—a parallel universe of longing and desire that was conjured up out of her deepest places, where the choice she had made had been quite, quite different.

Well, I didn't make that choice! I chose a different way. And it was the right way to choose—the only way.

However hard the choice had been, it would have been far worse if she hadn't made it. She'd paid the price for her decision, and even to think of it was agonising…just agonising.

Her own voice interrupted her painful thoughts.

'Good evening, gentlemen—what may I get you to drink?'

Painting a bright, attentive smile on her face, she listened and nodded and scribbled as fast as she could, hoping she was getting it down right. She headed back to the bar to relay the order.

'Doing OK?' asked Tony, one of the barmen, congenially.

'I hope so,' Clare replied cautiously.

He wasn't to know that it was not just her being new to the job that was making her cautious. That the whole expensive ambience of the place was disturbing her. Threatening her with memories of a life she had once led, and which was gone for ever. At least she'd never been at this place before; she was more familiar with the classic de luxe hotels, like the Savoy in London and the Plaza in New York. This hotel was too new, too impersonal, not at all the kind that—

She spotted a customer beckoning her and hurried across, glad of the distraction. Glad, too, that she was kept on her feet without respite as the evening wore on. Her feet in the unaccustomed high heels were starting to ache, but apart from a couple of confusing moments regarding complicated cocktails she was basically coping, she thought. She was careful always to keep her physical distance from the guests, but by and large she wasn't getting any hassle.

But then, of course, she acknowledged, with part relief and partly a little pang, the closest she got to a beauty treatment these days was filing a hang nail...

But what did she care? she thought fiercely. Joey didn't give a hoot if her hair was just tied back in a utilitarian plait, or if her face was bare of make-up. All he wanted was her attention—and her love.

And he got both in infinite amounts.

Even as she thought of Joey her hand automatically went to her apron pocket. Her mobile was on, but there had been no peep from it. Vi still found it tricky to use a mobile, but she'd made a gallant effort to learn, and had faithfully promised to call Clare if Joey surfaced and was distressed at her absence in any way. But, with luck, Joey was a good sleeper now, and once he went off he was usually fine until morning.

She handed round the drinks she'd just collected from the bar, spotted another of her tables starting to disperse, and kept an eye on them to see if she was going to get a tip. The wages, like all in this line of work, were hardly brilliant, and tips were important, like it or not. Every penny counted, and every penny was going into the Holiday Jar that would, she fervently hoped, take her and Joey and Vi to the seaside in the summer.

A shadow formed in her eyes.

If fate had dealt her a different card there'd be no such thing as the Holiday Jar...

But it was no use thinking that way. She had made the right choice, the only choice.

This way, though Joey might only be the fatherless child of yet another impoverished single mother, wearing clothes out of charity shops and eking a living, that was still infinitely better than being the alternative—the unwanted bastard of a Greek tycoon and his discarded, despairing mistress...

CHAPTER ONE

XANDER ANAKETOS stifled his impatience with a civil, if brief smile at the man beside him. Richard Gardner was of the school of businessmen who considered that every deal should be sealed with a drink and an expensive meal. Xander had no time for such niceties. The investment he'd just agreed in principle to make in Gardner's company would be mutually profitable, and the details would be hammered out by their respective subordinates. Now Xander was eager to be gone. He had plans for the evening which did not include making small talk with Richard Gardner. However, he had no wish to snub the older man, and besides, his 'other business' would wait for him.

They always waited for him.

Sonja de Lisle was no exception.

Oh, she might pout for a few minutes, but it wouldn't last. Soon she would be purring all over him. He pulled his mind away. Best not to let his thoughts go to Sonja when he had dinner to get through first.

And before that a drink in the cocktail lounge while they perused the menu.

As the guest, Xander let Gardner choose where to sit, and took his place accordingly. He glanced round, concealing the disparagement in his eyes. This was not a hotel he would have chosen to patronise, but he could appreciate that it was convenient for the business park where Gardner's company was sited near Heathrow. But, for himself, he preferred hotels to have more class, more prestige—usually more antiquity. He liked classic, world-famous hotels, like the Ritz, Claridges, the St John.

Memory flickered. He rarely went to the St John now.

Like a stiletto sliding in between his synapses, an image came into his mind. Blonde hair, curving in a smooth swathe over one shoulder, diamond studs set into tender lobes, long dark lashes and cool grey-green eyes.

Eyes that were looking at him without emotion. A face held very still.

A face he had not seen again.

He thrust the image aside. There was no point remembering it.

Abruptly he reached for the menu that had been placed on the low table in front of them and flicked it open, making his selection without great enthusiasm. Snapping it shut, he tossed it down on the table again and looked around impatiently. He could do with a drink. Did this place not run to waitresses?

There was one a table or so away from them with her back to him. He kept his eye on her, ready to beckon. He could see her nodding, sliding her notepad into her pocket.

She turned towards the bar. Xander held up an imperious hand. She caught the gesture and altered direction.

Then she stopped dead.

Clare could feel the blood and all sensation slowly draining out of her body. It emptied from her brain, her limbs, every part of her, draining down through every vein, every nerve.

And in its place only two things.

Disbelief.

And memory.

Memory…

Poisonous. Toxic. Deadly.

And completely overwhelming.

She was dragged in its wake, down, down, down through the sucking vortex of time.

Down into the past…

Xander was late.

Restlessly, Clare paced up and down. She should by now be used to him arriving when he wanted to, but this time it was harder to bear. A lot harder. She could feel nerves pinching in her stomach. Every muscle was tightly clenched.

Am I really going to tell him?

The question stung in her mind for the thousandth time. For two weeks it had been going round and round in her head. And with every circulation she knew that there was only one answer—could only be one answer.

I've got to tell him. I can't not.

And every time she told herself that she would feel the familiar flood of anxiety pooling in her insides—the familiar dread.

If—she corrected herself—*when* she told him, how would he take it? Automatically, in her head, she felt herself start to pray again. *Please, please let him take it the way I so desperately want him to! Please!*

But would he? Like a lawyer, she tried to shore up her

position as best she could, mentally arranging all her arguments like ducks in a row.

I've lasted longer than the others. That has to be a good sign, doesn't it?

Xander Anaketos never kept his mistresses long. She knew that. Had known it since before that fateful night when she had joined their long, long list. But she hadn't cared. Hadn't cared that her shelf-life in his bed was likely to be in the order of six months, if that. Hadn't cared even that she'd got that fact from one of the most reliable sources for such information—her predecessor. Aimee Decord had warned her straight. The woman had been drunk, Clare knew, though it had hardly showed except for the slightest swaying in her elegant walk, the slightest lack of focus in her dark, beautiful eyes.

'Enjoy him, *cherie*,' she'd said to Clare, taking yet another sip of her always full champagne flute. 'You'll be gone by Christmas.' Her smile had almost had a touch of pity in it, as well as malice. And something more—something that had not been jealousy, but something that had chilled Clare even more than jealousy would have. A despairing hunger…

But Aimee Decord had been wrong. Clare had not been gone by Christmas. Indeed, she'd spent the holiday with Xander in Davos, skiing. Just as she'd spent the last two weeks of January in the Caribbean, and Easter in Paris. Followed by a tour of North America, taking in New York, Chicago, San Francisco, Vancouver and Toronto—a hectic schedule which had whirled her along in the wake of one business meeting after another. Then it had been back to Europe, a sojourn in Paris again, then Geneva, Milan, another brief, but so very precious holiday in the Caribbean, and back to London.

Six months—nine months. Nearly a year. Very nearly a year.

In fact, Clare knew to the day—the night!—that in three weeks it would be their anniversary. And by then—oh, please, sweet God—by then she would have more to celebrate than that.

She went on pacing restlessly. Nerves still pinching. Still running through the tangled, shadowy fantasies that might or might not prove true.

It wasn't just that she'd lasted nearly twice as long as other mistresses of Xander Anaketos. Or that he had never installed her in an apartment, as he had the others, preferring that she should accompany him on his constant travels to the continents on which he conducted his complex and never-ending business affairs in the mysterious and arcane realm of international finance. Clare knew nothing about it, and did not enquire, having realised very early on that when Xander did finally clock off from business he wanted no more discussion of it until he was recalled to its demands.

There was another fantasy, most precious of all, that had came true recently, and which she now hugged to herself with a desperate hope.

Their last time together, nearly a fortnight ago, had been different. She'd known it—felt it. At first she'd thought it was only herself, suffused, as she had been, body and heart, with the knowledge that she possessed about what had happened to her so completely and absolutely unexpectedly, and yet so thrillingly.

But the change had not just been in her, she knew—*knew*. Xander had been different too. Oh, he'd been as passionate as ever, as voracious in his desires and needs, and as dedicated to fulfilling her own physical needs, desires. But there had been something more—more than could be accounted for merely because he had not seen her for ten days and had, the moment he'd stepped through the door, tossed aside his briefcase and swept her into his arms, carrying her off to his bed even while he was removing her clothes and devastating her with his kisses, the kisses of a man deprived for too long of what he most wanted.

The flames had consumed them, as they always did, bathing them like writhing salamanders in the fire of passion. But afterwards…ah, afterwards…Clare shut her eyes, shivering with remembered emotion. He had gone on holding her, tightly, closely, fervently. His hand had slid around her head, spearing through her hair, pressing her into his shoulder, while his other arm had wrapped around her like a clamp. She had heard, against her breast, the tumultuous pounding of his heart, felt her own beating against his.

He had said words to her in Greek and then fallen silent. She'd gone on lying crushed against him, her heart so full, *so full*. Then his hand had left her waist, and his other hand the back of her head, and he had shifted to cup her head with both his hands, one either side, and she'd half lifted herself from him.

She'd gazed down into his face. The face she knew so intimately, so absolutely. Every line, every plane, every lean contour, every sooty lash, every indentation around his sculpted, mobile mouth. He'd stared into her eyes from the depths of his own dark, midnight eyes, and there had been something in the way he'd looked at her that had made her heart turn slowly over.

He'd said another word in Greek. She hadn't known what it meant, hadn't cared, had only gazed down into his eyes, her heart slowly turning over, like a satellite in space, dissociated from the common earth.

It was that look, that long, endless exchange, that she clung to now. It had become a symbol, a beacon that she was now about to test her fate upon.

He cares for me. I know he does. It's not just the consideration of a lover, the conventional courtesy of a man towards his mistress. It's more than that.

How much more she did not know, dared not hope. But there was something there—a seed, nothing more as yet, but enough, oh, enough for her to feast on!

But she must not feast—she must be frugal in her hope. And she must not, *must not*, seek to harvest it before it had time to grow, blossom to fruition.

Automatically she paused in her pacing, lifting her hand to her abdomen, and placing it there. She felt, as always, emotion welling up in her. So much depended on that harvest.

If he cares for me then it will be all right. It will all be all right.

But what if she were wrong? Chill shuddered through her.

Too much depended on his reaction. Her whole life. Her whole future.

And not just hers.

Again, in an instinctive gesture as old as time, she cupped her abdomen.

'It will be all right,' she whispered to herself.

Clare went off to the kitchen to make herself a cup of calming herb tea. The kitchen—fearsomely modern—still made her breath catch whenever she went in. So did the whole apartment—but then so did Xander's apartment in Paris, not just the one here in London, and the one in Manhattan.

She still found it strange that he seemed to have no fixed abode anywhere. Nowhere he called home.

But then, neither did she. Since her father's death two years ago she had had no home. Both her parents had been only children, and her mother had died when she was thirteen. The tragedy had thrown her and her school-teacher father very close together, and his death from a long drawn-out cancer, when she was twenty, had been devastating.

And it had made her vulnerable. Susceptible. With the death of her father she had been entirely on her own. She had gone back to college, her studies having been inter-rupted when her father's illness had demanded full-time care, but her heart had not been in them. She had gone to London, preferring the anonymity of a huge city, far away from everything familiar and painful. The casual come-and-go of city life had suited her, teeming with people, none of them important to her, or her to them. She had taken tem-porary jobs, undemanding and unimportant, her emotions completely on hold after all the trauma of her father's death.

And then, without the slightest expectation, her emotions had sprung to life again. Vividly, terrifyingly alive. Alive in every nerve, every sense, every shimmering awareness.

Because of one man. She could remember in absolute detail the moment she had first seen him.

Clare had been sent by her temping agency to cover for a sick receptionist, and on her very first day, as she was sitting behind a plush, modernist-style desk, a covey of suited men had swung in through the doors. Her eyes had gone to them automatically—and stalled.

The man at the centre of the group had been the most

arresting male she had ever seen—she hadn't been able to take her eyes from him.

He'd been tall, easily six foot, and lithe, and lean. His suit had been fantastically cut, making him look smooth and svelte and…devastating. And that was even before she'd registered the rest of him.

The sable hair, the tanned Mediterranean skin, the jaw-droppingly good-looking features.

And the eyes.

Eyes to drown in.

He had walked right past her with his entourage, unchallenged by the security guard, who had merely said in a respectful tone, 'Good afternoon, Mr Anaketos.' But just as he'd swung past her, sitting there staring at him, his head had suddenly moved minutely and brought his gaze to her. Abruptly, instinctively, she had twisted her head away…

They had gone past, and she had breathed out again, not even aware till then that she'd been holding her breath.

She had felt alive for the first time in a long, long time. As if she had woken from a long sleep…

It had been stupid, she knew, to have done thereafter what she had done. She'd been a woman rendered incapable of behaving rationally, but she had done it all the same. She had let Xander Anaketos seduce her.

And he had done it with a swiftness that had cut the ground out from under her feet. Before the week was out she had been flying to Geneva with him. How had he done it? She still did not know. She had done her best not to react to him whenever she had seen him, and even when he had paused by the reception desk to have a word with the security guard she had assiduously paid attention only to her computer screen. Yet on the day she'd been due to finish the posting, she had been summoned by phone to Xander's executive office on the top floor, where he had coolly invited her to dinner that night.

She had stared blankly.

'I'm afraid I don't think—' she had begun. Then stopped. Her chest had seemed tight. Xander Anaketos had been looking at her. She'd felt her toes start to melt into her shoes.

So she had gone.

And from dinner she had gone to his bed.

Should she have done it? Done something she had never done before—slept with a man on her very first date with him? She had. She had gone to his apartment, his bed, as unhesitatingly as if she'd had no conscious thought. But then she *hadn't* had any conscious thought about it. It had been instinct, an urge, an overwhelming, irresistible desire, that had made it impossible, utterly impossible, to say no, to stop the evening, to back away from him.

So she hadn't. She'd been able to do nothing but stand there, her whole body trembling with an intensity that she had never, ever experienced before, while Xander Anaketos walked across his vast apartment lounge towards her and slid one hand around the nape of her neck, caressing it lightly, oh so lightly, so sensuously, while his other hand slid long, skilled fingers into her hair and drew her mouth to his.

She had drowned. Fathoms deep.

Falling deep, deep into that wondrous, blissful world she still dwelt in now.

Or did she? Again, the strained look haunted her eyes again. Living with Xander was bliss—but it came with a price. She had learnt swiftly to start paying that price. Learnt it the first time she had taken Xander's hand in a spontaneous gesture of affection in public. He had disengaged and gone on talking to the person he'd been speaking to. She hadn't done it again. Nor did she ever put her hand on his sleeve, or lean against him, or show any other similar demonstration of affection. She had learnt not to do so, adopting instead the cool composure that he evidently preferred. In private he was passionate—thrillingly so!—taking her in a sensual storm, time after time, leaving her overwhelmed with emotion. Yet even in that white-out of exquisite sensation, and in the exhausted, replete aftermath as she lay limp in his arms, she knew better than to say to him what her heart urged her to say.

That she was, and had been even from their very first time together, hopelessly in love with him.

But she could never tell him. She knew that—and accepted it. He was a man who was essentially a loner, she recognised. He had made his own way in life, she knew, amassing his fortune through skill, daring and formidable financial acumen. Brought up by an elderly uncle, a professor of maths at a provincial Greek university, who had died some years ago, Xander had put his energies into his work. Clare knew that for Xander women were only for recreation and sexual pleasure, fleeting companionship, nothing more. He did not want emotional attachment. Let alone love.

But in the year they had been together he had shown no sign of restlessness with her, no sign of growing bored and weary of her. It was the reverse, if anything—especially that last, most precious time when they'd made love. She had sensed in the depths of her being that something was different between them.

She felt her heart catch again. Fill with hope again. Surely she was more than just the latest in his endless parade of mistresses who, as she had so swiftly learned, never engaged him for more than a handful of months at a time? He found it hard to express his emotions, she knew, preferring passion and sensuality—but that did not mean he did not feel them! Did not mean he felt nothing for her beyond physical attraction!

Again she replayed in her mind the memory of how he had been different last time, how he had held her, gazed into her eyes, spoken those words to her in Greek that he had never said before… And yet again came hope, searing and urgent.

There was the sound of the apartment door opening. She felt her heart leap, then quiver, her eyes going immediately to where he would walk into the reception room.

And then he was there, paused in the entrance, his figure tall and familiar, making her breath catch in her lungs as it always did, every time she saw him again after an absence.

For a second her eyes lit, and for the briefest moment she was sure she saw an answering expression in his eyes.

Then it was gone.

'Delays at JFK,' he said. 'Then the motorway was jammed.' Xander gave an irritated shake of his head and set his briefcase down on the sideboard.

Clare stood, poised in the centre of the room. He turned to look at her. For a second there was that look in his eyes again, and then it was gone once more.

'I'll take a shower, then we can go out and eat,' he said.

Her eyes flickered. 'You don't want to eat here?'

He gave another cursory shake of his head. 'I've reserved the St John.'

'Oh. That's lovely,' Clare answered.

It might be lovely—the restaurant at the St John had become one of her favourites—but it was also unusual. Usually when Xander got back from abroad he preferred to eat in.

After sweeping her off to bed…

She looked at him uncertainly. He was loosening the knot of his tie, but he made no move towards her. Instead, he headed to the bedroom.

'Fix me a drink, will you, Clare?' he called.

She headed back to the kitchen and extracted a chilled bottle of beer from the fridge, opening it carefully and filling a glass. She made her way down to the en suite bathroom. He was already in the shower cubicle, and she could see his tall, naked body dimly behind the screen through the steam. He was washing his hair and had his back to her.

She left his drink on the vanity, and went into the bedroom. If they were going to the St John she'd better dress accordingly.

She had learnt very early on that Xander did not care to be kept waiting. He was never uncivil, but she could sense his irritation. The irritation of a rich man who didn't have to wait for things, or people. Including herself. So now she simply slipped on a dark green sheath, one of her favourites, brushed out her hair and retouched her make-up. Then she stepped back to check her appearance.

The familiar svelte, classically beautiful image looked back at her—hair smooth, make-up restrained, cool and composed.

She was still extremely slim. Nothing showed at all. Yet she could feel a distinct tightness in the dress fabric that was noticeable only by touch, not sight. Instinctively, yet again, she slipped her hand across her abdomen. Protectively. Cherishingly. A soft look came into her eyes.

Oh, let it be all right—please, please let it be all right!

The St John's three-Michelin-starred restaurant was as busy as ever, but for Xander Anaketos one of the best-positioned tables was always available. It was set back, in a quieter spot, although the hushed tones of the other diners made anyone else's conversation quite inaudible.

They took their places, and Clare knew that the eyes of the women there had gone to Xander—because women's eyes always did. And so did hers. After ten days of his absence, just drinking in his face, his features, running her eyes over the high slice of his cheekbones, lingering on the way his sable hair feathered, the way the lines around his mouth indented, was bliss.

She was glad now he had not swept her off to bed. In that sensual ecstasy she might not have been able to control her feelings for him, and in the aftermath she might have been tempted, oh, so tempted, to tell him what had happened. But it would not have been the right time, she knew. His mind, when he was in bed with her, was on sex—it was natural for a man, after all—and afterwards another hunger would take precedence, and he would suddenly want dinner. No. Better, she knew, to let him eat now, relax, chill from the irritations of the flight and let his mood mellow. And then, over brandy, she would tell him. It would be perfect.

The familiar stab of anxiety came again, but she dispelled it. There was no point in doing otherwise. She must think the best, hope the best. And in the meantime she must make it easy for him to relax. So she did what she always did— was poised and composed, chatting lightly, only in answer to him, not plaguing him, giving him time to eat, to let the fine wines slip down his throat, making no demands on him.

He was preoccupied, she could see. That was not unusual in itself. The demands of his work were immense, the convolutions of his myriad deals and negotiations, investments and financial manoeuvrings intricate and labyrinthine. In the early days she had asked him about his work, for the world of international finance was completely strange to her. She'd looked a bit up on the Internet and in newspapers, to try and be less of an ignoramus, but when she'd asked him about things he'd either looked wryly at her or told her that he had enough of it all day and wanted to relax now. So she'd accepted that and changed the subject.

Her eyes flickered to him again, as he focussed on his entrée. Yes, he was definitely preoccupied, his mind somewhere else. Quietly, she got on with her meal. She was hungry. Eating in the mornings now had little appeal, but by the evening she had worked up an appetite. However, she was very cautious about what she drank—her single glass of wine was still half full, and she was only taking tiny sips from it. She hadn't made a big deal out of it, and Xander hadn't remarked on it. Usually she drank a glass of white, and then red, and sometimes had a small liqueur afterwards, while he nursed a brandy. Tonight she would make do with coffee only.

Her mind, she found, was running on. She would need to buy a good comprehensive manual, she knew, and start finding out everything that was going to be in store for her now. It was such a complicated, overwhelming process, with her body and her psyche going through such profound changes. Physically, she felt wonderful—except for that distinct reluctance to eat first thing—but that might well change, she knew, over the coming months.

Another wave of unease went through her. Her figure would change totally, obviously, and what would Xander think? She'd always been so slim, so slender. How would he take the swelling of her body? Well, she would cope with it when the time came. It was only in the last trimester that the weight really piled on, and until then, if she kept fit, as she obviously must now, she should not look too bad. Her eyes softened. Xander might actually find her roundedness appealing…

Again, hope pierced her.

The meal continued, with both of them refusing dessert, and Xander ordering coffee and liqueurs.

'Just coffee for me, please.' Clare smiled at the waiter.

She felt Xander's eyes flicker over her a moment. Then it was gone again.

The coffee arrived, with his customary cognac, and the waiter departed again. The restaurant was thinning out now, the hushed voices more subdued. She watched as Xander cradled his glass in his long fingers and swirled it absently, his eyes going to the slow coil of topaz liquid within.

She felt her pulse quicken and took a breath. Now she must tell him. It was the right moment. She must not put it off. Nothing would be gained by doing so. Yet for an instant she desperately did not want to say anything! Wanted to put it off, procrastinate, delay what she must tell him.

She opened her mouth, his name forming on her lips.

'Clare.'

His voice came before hers. Her name. Clipped, pronounced.

Slowly her mouth closed, and she looked at him. Inside,

emotions warred. One was dismay that he had spoken just as she was going to—but the other was sneaking and sly. She didn't have to tell him just yet…

Her eyes rested on him expectantly, waiting for him to continue. But there was a hesitation about him—something she was not used to seeing.

'Yes?' she prompted. Her voice was cool, composed, the way it always was—except in the throes of passion, when she cried out his name in ecstasy. 'What is it?'

Something shadowed in his eyes, and was gone. He swirled the brandy once more, then lifted it to his mouth and took a slow mouthful, lowering the glass. The air of preoccupation had vanished. There was a set in his shoulders, a tightening in his jaw. She looked at him, wondering what he was going to say to her. Wondering, far more anxiously, whether it would mean that telling him her news now would be delayed beyond this evening.

For a second longer he was silent. Then his eyes went to hers. There was no expression in them.

'I've met someone else. In New York.'

She heard the words. They were flatly spoken, his accent hardly showing. For a strange, dissociated moment she did not understand them.

Then he was talking again.

'There's never a pleasant way of doing this, but I wanted you to know how very much I've appreciated you over these last months. But it is now…' Did he hesitate again, just for a fraction of a fraction of a second? She could not tell, was blind and deaf to everything. 'Over,' he said, breathing out with a short, decisive breath.

She was sitting there. Just sitting there. Everything around her seemed to have gone into immense slow motion. As if it was not there. Was not there at all.

Her heart rate had slowed. She could feel it, slowing down like a motor running out of motion. Everything stilled inside her, around her, in the whole universe.

Her face did not move. That had stopped as well. Nor did her eyes. They were still looking at him. Just looking at him.

His eyes had a veiled look to them, and she could see his lips press together, as if in irritation. And as she went on just looking at him, because everything in the entire universe had just stopped, the line of irritation strengthened.

Then, abruptly, it was gone. He was moving, sliding his hand into his jacket pocket and gliding out a long, slim case. He placed it in front of her with a precise movement.

'As I said—' his voice still had that strange clipped quality to it '—I've appreciated you very much, and this is a token of that appreciation.'

Slowly, very slowly, as if there were lead weights on them, she pulled her eyes down to the slim jeweller's case in front of her, beside her coffee cup. Slowly she lifted her hands and opened the case. A long line of white fire glinted at her.

Diamonds, she thought. These are diamonds. A diamond necklace. For me.

He was talking again. His words came and went. She could hear snatches, as if through a thick, impenetrable fog.

'Naturally I don't want you to have any immediate concerns about accommodation. So I've taken an apartment for you, which is yours for the next month. That should give you ample time to make alternative arrangements—'

The words were coming and going, coming and going...

In strange, dissociated slow motion, she felt herself stand up.

'Clare?' His words had broken off. Her name came sharply.

'Will you excuse me a moment?' she said. Her eyes drifted to his. He seemed very far away. As far away as a distant star.

She felt for her handbag and walked away from the table. It was the strangest feeling—feeling nothing. That was what was so strange about it. Walking through a fog of nothingness.

She found the Ladies' and went inside. There was no one else there. For a moment she just looked at herself in the mirror above the row of gleaming basins.

She was still there. That was odd. She'd thought she had gone. That everything had gone.

But she was still there.

She blinked a moment. Her fingers closed around her clutch bag. For one moment longer she just looked at herself in the mirror. There was the faintest scent of lilies in the air, from the massive bouquet that adorned one of the vanity units to the side.

A sudden, hideous spurt of nausea leapt in her throat.

She turned on her heel.

The door swung open in her hand, and she was in the carpeted corridor outside. To her left was the way back to the restaurant. To her right the corridor led to a side entrance to the hotel that opened into a quiet street off the main West End thoroughfare the St John was situated on.

Her feet walked to the street door. It swung open at her touch.

Outside, on the pavement, the night air should have felt chill. But she did not feel it. She did not feel anything.

She started to walk.

CHAPTER TWO

CLARE had not seen him again from that moment to this—standing now, staring at him, as he sat in the deep leather chair, one hand raised imperiously to summon her.

It was Xander.

Xander after four years, there again, now visible and in the flesh.

It was as if everything inside her had drained out, leaving her completely, absolutely hollow.

She saw the expression change as in slow-motion across his face. Saw him recognise her.

'Clare?'

She heard him say her name, heard the disbelief in it, even though he was some way from her. Saw him start to his feet, jerk upright.

He started to stride towards her.

She turned and ran.

Blindly she pushed her way across the room, getting to the service door by the bar and thrusting through it. The staff cloakroom was just near, and she dived inside, and then deeper, into the female staff toilet, slamming the door shut and sliding the bolt with fumbling fingers. She yanked down the lid of the toilet and collapsed.

She was shaking. Shaking all over. Shock juddered through her like blows, one after another. How, *how* could Xander have walked in here? Hotels like this, impersonal and anonymous, did not appeal to him. She knew that—that was why she'd taken the risk of getting a job here. If she'd had the slightest idea he'd ever come here she would never have chanced it!

But he had. He had walked in and seen her, and crashed the past right into the present in a single catastrophic moment.

I've got to get out of here!

The need to run overwhelmed her. She had to get out, get home, get away…

Forcibly, she stopped herself shuddering and made herself stand up, walk out into the cloakroom. Her bag and coat were hanging on a peg. The bag held her ordinary clothes, but she didn't waste time changing, only yanking off her high-heeled shoes and slipping her feet into her worn loafers. She could walk faster in them.

Memory sliced through her.

That night, walking out of the St John, walking along the pavements, walking without thought, without direction, without anything in her mind except that terrifying absolute blankness. She did not know how long she had walked. People had bumped her from time to time, or woven past her, and still she had gone on, stopping only at crossings, like a robot, then plunging across when the coast was clear. She had walked and walked.

Eventually, God knew how long later, she'd realised she could not go on, that she was slowing down—as if the last of the battery energy inside her was finally running out. She had looked with blank eyes. She'd been on the far side of Oxford Street, heading towards Marylebone Road, on a street parallel to Baker Street, but much quieter. There had been small hotels there, converted out of the Victorian terraces. There had been one opposite her. It had looked decent enough, anonymous. She'd crossed over the road and gone in.

She had spent the night there, lying in her clothes on the bed, staring blindly up at the ceiling. Very slowly, her mind had started to work. It had been like anaesthesia wearing off.

The agony had been unbearable. Tearing like claws through her flesh. The agony of disbelief, of shock.

Of shame. Shame that she could have been such an incredible fool.

To have been so stupid…

I thought he had started to feel something for me! I thought I meant something to him—had come to be more to him than a mistress…someone who mattered to him. Someone who…

Her hand had slid across her abdomen, and the agony had come again, even more piercing.

What am I going to do?

The words had fallen like stones into her head.

They had gone on falling, heavier and heavier, crushing her, hard and unbearable.

It had taken so long to accept the answer that she had known, with so heavy and broken a heart, was the only one possible.

I did the right thing. I did the only thing.

The words came to her now, as she yanked on her coat.

Nothing else was possible. Nothing.

A hard, steely look came into her eyes. And what did it

matter that Xander Anaketos was out there? What did it matter? Nothing at all! He was nothing to her and she—oh, dear God—she was nothing to him.

Had always been nothing to him…

She came back to the present with a jolt. Steeling herself to forget.

Don't remember. Don't think. Just pick up your bag and go. This job is over before it started. I don't care, I'll get another one. Only one thing is important—only one. That I never, ever have to set eyes on Xander Anaketos again.

With grim resolution she walked out of the cloakroom.

He was waiting for her outside.

It was like a blow across her throat, punching the breath from her. Then, with an inhalation that seared in her lungs, she said, 'Let me pass.'

He didn't budge. His frame, large and powerful, blocked the narrow way.

He said something in Greek. She had no idea what it was. It sounded hard, and angry. Then he switched to English.

'What the *hell* did you think you were playing at? Pulling that disappearing act at the St John when you walked out on me?' There was naked belligerence in his voice.

Her mouth fell open. Then closed again. A wave of unreality washed over her, even deeper than the shock waves that had been washing over her since she'd impacted her eyes on Xander Anaketos.

'Do you know what hell you put me through?' His tone was unabated, his dark eyes flashing with dangerous fury.

Sickness warred with shock. She stared at him with wide, uncomprehending eyes. His dark eyes narrowed.

'I thought you'd been run over, killed, injured. I thought you'd gone off to someone else. I thought—'

'You thought what?' There was incomprehension as she spoke. What was he saying? She did not understand.

His eyes flashed again. 'What the hell did you *think* I'd think? Don't even bother to answer that! It took me a while, but I finally realised you'd done it entirely on purpose. To get me to come after you!'

Her mouth fell open. Then closed again. A grim, hard look came into her face.

'You really thought me that stupid? Stupid enough to think you'd come chasing after something you'd just replaced with a new model and paid off with a diamond necklace?'

His expression hardened even more. 'I was concerned about you,' he bit out.

She laughed. It was a harsh, brief sound. Then it cut out.

'Let me pass,' she said again.

There was a movement behind her, and she turned. Tony, the barman, had come through the service door, and was regarding them with a concerned expression.

'Clare—is everything all right? Why have you got your coat on?'

She turned to him.

'Tony—I'm sorry. I'm going home. I can't work here. I apologise for the nuisance. I'll phone Personnel tomorrow and sort out the formalities.' The words came out staccato and uneven.

He frowned, his eyes going from her to the tall, imposing figure of someone who very obviously was a guest of the hotel.

'Is there a problem? Do you want me to fetch the manager?' His question embraced both her and Xander Anaketos.

Behind her, Clare heard Xander's voice. The one she was so familiar with. Giving orders to underlings.

'There's no problem,' he said, his accented voice clipped and dismissing. 'I'm seeing Ms Williams home.' He stepped back, giving her room to walk by him. For a moment Clare hesitated, then walked past him. She was not going to make a scene here, in front of Tony. She would get out of the hotel by the service exit, and then head for home. She'd take a taxi. It was an extravagance, but she didn't trust her legs.

It seemed like a million miles to get to the staff entrance, and she could feel Xander's breath almost on her shoulders. She was in shock, she knew. It could not be otherwise. The past had reared up to bite her, like a monstrous creature, and she could not cope with it—could not cope at all…

As she pushed the door open and stepped out on to the pavement by the staff car park, she took in deep, shivering lungfuls of air.

Her elbow was seized in an iron grip.

'This way.'

Her head snapped round, and she pulled away from him violently.

'Let me go!'

'I said, this way,' Xander repeated with grim heaviness.

She tried to shake herself free. It was impossible. His grip was unshakable.

'Do you want me to scream?' she bit out.

'I want you to come this way. You,' he ground out, 'have a lot of explaining to do! I don't appreciate the game you played—'

The word was like a trigger in her skull.

'*Game?*' She stared at him. Four years had changed him

little. It was like looking into the past. The past that had almost destroyed her. The past that was ravening at her again, trying to devour her. Trying to swallow her up with memory of how once her heart had leapt every moment she had seen this man. Each time he had touched her, kissed her, she had come alive…

Pain lashed at her as she stared at him—but what was the use of pain?

It got you nowhere. She'd had four years of knowing that. Four years of getting over it. Moving on. She'd changed.

'Game?' she said again. Her voice was flat now, the emotion gone from her eyes. 'How can you stand there and say that to me? How on earth could you think that I was playing some infantile game? How can you possibly have been anything other than relieved by how I reacted? Do you think I didn't know you by then? Didn't know that you would never tolerate scenes? Let alone by women you had finished with. I saw you when Aimee Decord came up to you, half-cut—remember? That time in Cannes? I saw how ruthless you were to her. So when it was my turn I knew what the score was. You know,' she said, and there was an edge of bitterness in her voice she could not conceal even now, four long years later, 'you should be grateful to me. I must have been the easiest ex-mistress you've ever had.'

Abruptly, he dropped her arm, and stepped back.

'I spent days looking for you! You just vanished.'

His voice was accusatory. His Greek accent thick.

'What are you complaining for?' she flashed back. 'You'd just pressed the delete button on me. I was *supposed* to vanish.'

Xander's expression darkened.

'Do not be absurd! I had made arrangements for you. Of

course you were not simply supposed to vanish! Besides, there were all your things still in my apartment—'

Clare's head shook sharply.

'There was nothing of mine there. Nothing personal.'

'There were your clothes, all your belongings!'

'They weren't mine. You'd bought them. Look—what is this? Why this totally pointless post-mortem four years later? You finished with me, and I left. It was very simple. I don't know why you've followed me out here, I don't know why you're talking to me, and I don't know why you think you've got some sort of right to lay into me!'

Her tirade ended, and she could feel her heart pumping like a steam train. Her brain seemed to be whirring like a clock that had suddenly gone from dormant to overwound in ten seconds. She couldn't cope with this—with Xander Anaketos suddenly coming into reality again. It was like some churning hallucinatory dream that she could not believe in.

She turned away, half stumbling. She wanted out. Out, out, *out*. Just at the range of her vision she saw a taxi turn into the concourse of the hotel, towards the main entrance. She ran towards it. If it was depositing someone at the hotel, she could grab it!

A minute later, heart still pounding, she collapsed in the back of the taxi she'd claimed as it pulled out into the busy road again.

She felt sick. Like a concrete mixer on full spin.

It had been Xander—Xander. There, real, alive. Suddenly, out of nowhere, after four years—*four years*—in which her life had changed beyond all recognition.

Her stomach was churning still, shock waves turning her

into jelly, her mind a hurricane. The taxi ploughed along the busy arterial road, and headlights flashed into the car. She sat clutching her bag as if it were a lifebelt.

When the cab pulled up outside the house, she fumbled inside the bag for her purse, forcing herself to count out the right money. It was more than she wanted to pay, but she didn't care. She was safe back here again. As she walked up the short path to the front door, getting her key out, she forced herself to be calm. She must not upset Vi.

Oh, God, I've just chucked in my job—I can't tell her that! Not yet.

She opened the door quietly. Vi's bedroom was the front room downstairs, as she found stairs hard to manage these days. The door was half open, and Clare peeped inside. There was Joey, as she'd expected, cosy in a 'nest' on the floor—cushions from the sofa and some extra pillows—snuggled into his child duvet. He was fast asleep and did not stir.

For one long, long moment, Clare stood gazing down at his shadowed form. Her heart turned over, almost stopping.

No! She must not let her thoughts go the way they were about to. She knew what she had been on the point of thinking, and she must not let herself do so. Again, a seismic wave of shock went through her as she fought the acknowledgement of what she had so nearly let come into her mind.

Instead, she backed out. She took off her coat, hung it up on one of the row of pegs beside the stairs, and headed towards the back of the house. There was a small sitting room just in front of the kitchen, and then the bathroom behind the kitchen. Vi was in the kitchen, putting the kettle on for her late-night cup of tea.

'Hello, love,' she said, her voice surprised, as Clare came in. 'You're earlier than you said you would be.'

Clare forced a smile to her face.

'Yes, I thought I'd be later, too,' she said. She left it at that. She could say nothing else. Not right now. Instead, she said, 'How was Joey? He's out like a light now, I see.'

Vi's wrinkled face softened into a familiar smile.

'Oh, he hasn't stirred. Don't you worry about him. Have a nice cup of tea and sit down before you take him upstairs.'

Clare went through into the sitting room and sank down onto the end of the sofa that still had its cushions on. Vi's armchair was closer to the TV in the corner, with a little table beside it, handy for the standard lamp. The room was old-fashioned, like the whole house, but Vi had lived here for thirty years and more.

For Clare it had been a haven. Those first few months, when the life she had been hoping against hope for had simply dissolved in her hands, it had been hideous. But although homeless, at least she had not been destitute. After her father had died she had received an offer for their flat which she'd felt she should not refuse, and she'd put the proceeds into the bank. But she had known she was in no state of mind to sort out her life properly, other than drifting through casual jobs from the temping agency and living in anonymous bedsits, and the money in the bank was still her nest egg. But once she'd known she was going to have to face life as a single mother, she had had to face up to the grim fact that if she bought another flat, even if just a small one, for her to live in, then what would be left for her to live off—and her baby?

The answer had come from a charity supporting single

mothers, which put them in touch with elderly people who needed someone to help them continue to live independently in their own homes. So Clare had been introduced to Vi, and Vi had taken to her, and she to the older woman. She had moved into Vi's old-fashioned terraced house in its quiet street in an unexciting but shabbily respectable part of West London. The money in the bank yielded a frugal but sufficient income for everything but luxuries like holidays, and in place of rent she looked after Vi, kept her house for her and kept her company as well, and made her home with her. Now, four years later, Vi was family—an honorary grandmother to Joey, whom she openly adored, and a kind but bracingly realistic support for Clare.

'Here you go, love,' said Vi, making her way slowly into the room, carrying two mugs of tea. Clare took them from her, setting down hers, and putting Vi's on her little table as the old lady sat herself down in her armchair.

'You look peaky,' observed Vi. 'Was it very busy?'

'Yes,' said Clare. She was trying hard to sound normal, look normal. She didn't want Vi upset—not by the fact she'd walked out of her job, nor by something so very much worse.

No—that was forbidden. She was not to think about that. Control. That was the word. The way it had been those first awful months, and then again, when her baby had been put into her arms, and the physical reality of him had brought it piercingly home to her just what she had done.

But it was the right thing to do.

'What you'll need to do, Clare, love,' Vi was saying, 'is give your feet a good soak. Always look after your feet, I say. My gran used to tell me that. She had very bad feet…'

Clare smiled absently, sipping her hot, reviving tea. She

let Vi chat on. Vi's mind was as sharp as ever, but she liked to gossip, reminisce, just have someone to talk to. Tonight, though, Clare could hardly focus on what the older woman was telling her. All her energy was being spent on trying to block from her mind what had happened.

I can't think about it now. I'll think about it later. Tomorrow. Next week.

Never...

She had trained herself well not to think of Xander Anaketos. She'd had four long years of doing so.

But conscious thoughts were one thing to control. It was the unconscious ones she dreaded. And that night, as she lay in her bed upstairs, Joey in the little room beside her, asleep in his own bed now, it was, as it had always been, her dreams that betrayed her.

Dreams of Xander, his strong body arching over hers, his mouth on hers, his hands on her breasts, her flanks, stroking and smoothing, gliding and arousing, so arousing, taking her onwards, ever onwards, to that wonderful, ecstatic place where he had always taken her...always.

She awoke in the early hours, sick and heart pounding. The dreams had been so real, so vivid, with the horrible, super-realistic feelings that only dreams could have. Her stomach writhed, her pulse racing like a panic attack.

And her breasts, she realised with a sick horror, were swollen, her nipples distended.

She jerked out of bed, padding with bare feet down the stairs to the bathroom, feeling sick and ashamed.

The day passed with agonising slowness. She seemed to be two people. The person she always was these days— Joey's doting mother, attentive to him, responsive to him, adoring of him, and Vi's companion, bringing breakfast to her before she made her slow morning toilette, and then, after lunch, making their familiar daily expedition to the nearby park, Vi walking slowly with her stick and Clare pushing Joey in his buggy. In the park, Vi sat on her usual seat, and Joey got stuck in with Clare. First to the sandpit and then the playground, and the expedition ended with the usual ritual of taking Joey to feed the ducks on the pond. All blessedly familiar.

But she was someone else as well, she knew. Someone who was still jarring with shock, with disbelief that she had actually seen Xander Anaketos again, spoken to him, run from him…

He's gone. It's over.

She kept telling herself that repeatedly, as the other person she was went through the familiar rituals in the park.

I've got to calm down. I've got to get back to normal. I've got to forget it happened.

But it seemed so cruel. It had been such agony four years ago, to do what she had known she must—get over it, move on—but she had done it. She'd had to put her son first. And they were safe now. Secure. Familiar.

The past was gone.

Last night had been nothing but an aberration. And she had run from it, just as she had run from that hideous night when her stupid, stupid hopes and illusions had been ripped from her.

'Let's go, Mummy!' Joey's little voice was a welcome interruption from her tormenting thoughts. He lifted up the empty plastic bag that had contained the bread crusts. 'All gone,' he announced.

'Time for tea,' said Vi, and got slowly to her feet from the bench she'd been sitting on.

Then they headed homewards in a slow procession.

She had no premonition. No warning. Just as she had had none last night.

As they rounded the corner into the street where Vi's house was it was Joey who spoke first, pointing.

'Big car!'

Clare followed the direction of his pointing, and slowly her heart stopped in her chest. Outside Vi's house was parked a long, lean, brilliant scarlet monster of a car.

And out of it Xander Anaketos was emerging.

Why? That was the first weird thought in Clare's stricken brain. Why was he here? What for? What else could he possibly have to say to her, now he'd vented his spleen at her for daring not to be disposed of in exactly the way he liked to get rid of discarded mistresses?

Then, like an explosion in slow motion, she realised that it didn't matter why he had come here, or how he had found out where she lived.

Because as he started to walk towards them she realised he was not looking at her. His eyes were entirely, terrifyingly, on Joey.

Her breath was crushed from her lungs. She gave a silent, inaudible, breathless scream inside her head.

Desperately her brain worked feverishly. If she could just bundle Joey inside, without him getting close enough to make out his features...

But it was too late. She could see it. See it in the change of expression in Xander's face. See the shock—the disbelief—jagging across his features.

He stopped. Just halted where he was, in the middle of the pavement, some yards from them.

Greek came from him. Hollow. Rasping.

Then slowly, very slowly, his eyes lifted from his son and went to her.

There was murder in his face.

CHAPTER THREE

XANDER got them indoors. He had no memory of how he'd done it, or of what house they'd gone into. No awareness of anything other than the raw, boiling rage thundering through him. His mind had gone into a white-out.

Somehow, and he had no conscious thought of how, he had got her away from the old woman and the boy.

My son. Theos—*my son!*

There was no doubt about it—could not be! He could see his own features in the child's face.

And in hers—oh, he could see completely, absolutely, that she knew the toddler she was pushing along was his. She'd given birth to *his* son!

An iron will clamped down over the raging voice in his head. Control. That was what he needed now—absolute, total control. He was good at control. He had practised it all his life, from childhood with his stern uncle, who had required silence while he worked, and carrying the same discipline into his business dealings—never letting his rivals see his hand, always concealing his thoughts and aims from them.

And control, too, had been his watchword when it came

to his dealings with women. It was the reason he changed them so frequently. A rule he had bent only once...

The irony of it savaged him.

Emotion surged in him like a terrifying monster, but he slammed it back down as he marched Clare down through the house, out through a door at the back, yanking it open and thrusting her outside. There was a garden there, narrow and quite long, with a plastic sand tray and a miniature slide. There were children's toys, a ball, a push-along dog and some big colourful bricks, on the small stone-paved patio before the lawn started.

He grabbed her elbows and hauled her round.

'Talk,' he said.

His eyes bored down into hers like drills.

Her face had gone white. He was not surprised. Guilt was blazoned across it. Rage spurted through him again. The vicious, vengeful bitch! To keep his son from him! Deliberately, knowingly...

'Talk!' he snarled again.

Her face seemed to work, but not well. Slowly, faintly, she spoke.

'What do you want me to say? There's nothing *to* say.'

He shook her like a rag, and she was boneless in his grip.

'You keep my son from me and say there's nothing to say?' he demanded, fury icing through his words, his features. 'Just what kind of a vengeful *bitch* are you?'

Her expression changed. Blanked.

'What?' she said. There was complete incomprehension in her voice.

He shook her again. Emotion was ravening in him, like a wolf.

'To keep my son from me as some kind of sick revenge!'

Her mouth opened, then closed. Then suddenly she tore free.

'What the *hell* do you think you're saying to me?'

His eyes darkened like night.

'You kept my son from me because you were angry that I finished with you!'

Her face worked again, but this time there was a different emotion in it. Her features contorted.

'You conceited oaf!' she gasped at him. 'Just who do you think you are? First you think I played some stupid manipulative game by walking out the way I did! Now you think, you *really* think, that I didn't tell you I was pregnant so I could get some kind of *revenge* on you?'

'What other reason can there be?' he snarled back at her.

A choking sound came from her.

'How about the fact you'd just replaced me with a new model and had given me my pay-off of a diamond necklace, like I was some kind of *whore*?' she spat at him.

Xander's mouth whitened.

'You knew you were pregnant that evening?' His voice was a raw rasp. 'You knew you were pregnant and you kept *quiet* about it! You walk out, carrying my baby, and you never say a *word* to me—in *four years*?'

She was staring at him. Staring at him as if he had spoken in Greek.

'Well?' he demanded. His jaw was gritted, fury still roiling inside him. Fury and another emotion, even more powerful, that he must not, must *not* yet yield to, but which was driving him—driving him onwards with impossible motion.

'You're not real,' she said. Her voice had changed. 'You're just not real. You actually think I would tell a man who'd chucked me on the garbage pile, who'd paid me off with a diamond necklace, that I was pregnant by him?'

His expression stiffened. 'I did not "pay you off",' he bit out. 'It's customary to give a token of appreciation to—'

'Don't say that word to me! Don't *ever* say that word to me again! And don't even think of trying to tell me that after you'd just flushed me down the pan I was supposed to announce I was carrying your child.'

Emotion was mounting in Xander's chest.

'If you had told me, obviously I would have rescinded my decision to—'

A look of incredulity passed across her contorted features.

'Rescinded your decision?' Her voice was high-pitched and hollow. 'It wasn't a bloody business meeting. You had made it clear—absolutely, killingly clear—that I was out. You had someone new to warm your bed and that was that.'

His face tightened. 'Obviously, had you told me that you had got pregnant, then everything would have been very different.'

She turned away. The gesture angered him. He reached out for her again, his hand closing on her shoulder.

She froze at his touch. He could feel it, all her muscles tensing. Her reaction angered him even more. Why should she resist him?

She never resisted me—always yielded to me...eager for me. All that cool, English composure dissolved, like ice in heat...my heat...

He thrust the memory aside. It was irrelevant. All that was relevant now was to deal with this shattering discovery.

I have a son!

The impulse, overwhelming and overpowering, to go

now, this instant, to find the child that was inside the house, find him and—

No, he could not do that either. Not yet. Not until—until... *Christos*, he could hardly think straight, his mind a storm of emotion.

His hand dropped from her.

'As,' he said heavily, 'it will be different now.'

She was still half turned away from him. He could not see her face. He didn't care. Providing she could hear, could understand, that was all that mattered. He fought the storm inside him for control. He had been iron-willed all day. Controlled enough to instruct his London PA, very calmly, to find out the address of Clare Williams from the hotel she had been working at. Detached enough to rearrange today's schedule so that he could be free by late afternoon to drive and find her. She'd run out on him once before, vanished into the night—she was not going to do so a second time.

But the reason he had sought her out had evaporated—instantly, like water in a volcano—the moment he had realised just what Clare Williams had done to him...

Emotion whipped through him again, that white-hot disbelieving fury that had ripped through him the moment his eyes had gone to the child in the buggy she had been pushing.

That was all that concerned him. *That* was all that consumed him.

But he must control it. Giving vent to the storm inside him would achieve nothing. With Herculean effort, he hammered down his emotions.

'I want to see him.'

His voice was flat. Very controlled.

She turned her head back towards him. Her eyes were quite blank.

She uttered a single word. A word that went into him like a knife.

'Why?' she said.

Carefully, very carefully, he layered icy control over his features.

'Because he is my son,' he enunciated. Then, before she could answer, he walked back indoors.

The elderly woman was in the small, drab sitting room. It looked ancient, and so did she. She was sitting in an armchair and the television was on, with a cartoon. His son was sitting on her lap, lolled back on her, all his attention on the screen.

As Xander walked in, the woman looked at him. She was old, but her eyes were sharp. They rested on him for a second, then went past him. Behind him, Xander could sense Clare. The child did not look round.

The knife went into Xander again. He did not know the name of his own son.

'Tell me his name.'

He spoke quietly, but there was an insistence in it that would not be brooked. It was the old woman who answered.

'It's Joey,' she said. 'Joey, pet—say hello.'

Reluctantly, the toddler twisted his head briefly. ''Lo,' he said, then went straight back to the cartoon.

He must be gone three, Xander thought. I have a three-year-old son, and I never knew. I never knew…

The storm of emotion swirled up in him again, but he forced it back. The elderly woman was looking at him. She had a steady gaze. Did she realise who he was? He assumed so. He had recognised his son instantly. It would not be hard to see him in Joey, and know that he must be the boy's father.

His throat convulsed, and again he had to take a deep, steadying breath. He opened his mouth to speak, but the old woman was before him.

'Clare, love, Joey needs his tea. The programme will be over soon, and he'll realise he's hungry. I'd do something quick for him, if I were you. Eggy soldiers is always nice, isn't it?'

She spoke cheerfully, calmly, as if she were not witnessing a man discovering his three-year-old son.

She was right to do so, Xander realised. Whatever else, his son—*Joey*—must not be upset. What must be settled now would not be helped by his giving voice to fury, his emotions. Abruptly, he sat himself down on the rather battered sofa, opposite his son. He said nothing, just watched him watching the television with a rapt expression on his face, interrupted by bursts of childish laughter.

My son!

The storm of emotion in Xander's breast swirled, then gradually, very gradually subsided. But deep inside his heart seemed to swell and swell.

Clare put the eggs to boil. She got out the bread, and popped it in the toaster. She fetched some milk, and poured it into Joey's drinking cup. She set out a tray with his plastic plate with pictures of puppies on it, and started to pare an apple for his pudding. She worked swiftly, mindlessly.

She mustn't think about this. Mustn't do anything. Just give Joey his tea.

When it was ready she carried it through. The programme's

credits were rolling, and Joey had returned to the real world. He looked about him.

'Time for tea,' he announced. Then he focussed on the man looking at him. 'Hello,' he said. He looked interestedly at the man who had started his life four long years ago.

Xander looked at the child who was his. Emotion felled him. For a moment his brain went completely and absolutely blank. What did he know of children? His own childhood was so far away that he never thought of it— his father had been dead, his mother too. He had no memories of them.

Cold iced in his spine. If he had not come today, sought out the woman who had walked out into the night four years ago, his own son would, like him, have had no memories of his father…

That will not be…

Resolution steeled inside him. His son would have a father, and memories of a father, starting right now.

'Hello, Joey,' said Xander. 'I am your father. I've come to see you.'

Clare felt the knife go through her throat, and she gasped aloud. Xander ignored her. So did Joey. Joey tilted his head and subjected Xander to an intense look.

'Fathers are daddies,' he announced.

Xander nodded. 'Quite right. You're a clever boy.'

Joey looked pleased with himself.

'Clare, give Joey his tea. He's a growing boy.' Vi beckoned to her, and cleared some space on the table by her chair. Shakily, Clare crossed and put down the tray.

'Soldiers!' shouted Joey, pleased. 'Eggy soldiers.' He seized one of the fingers of toast and plunged it into one of the two eggs with the end sliced off, starting to eat with relish. Around his neck, Vi was deftly attaching a bib.

It was all, thought Clare, with a sick, hollow feeling inside her, intensely normal.

Except for one thing.

She rubbed a hand over her brow, her eyes going to the man sitting on Vi's old sofa. The man who was her son's father. This couldn't be happening. It just couldn't. Wave after wave of disbelief was eddying through her. So much shock. Last night had been bad enough, but now this… This was a nightmare. She couldn't think, couldn't feel. Could only watch, with a strange unnatural calm, how Xander Anaketos was watching his son—her son—eat his tea.

He stayed for another half an hour. Time for Joey to finish his tea and start playing with his toys. Clare washed up, trying to do anything to bring back normality—to pretend that her life hadn't just crashed all around her. She started to get her and Vi's supper ready, taking a cup of tea in to the other woman. Silently, she placed a mug of instant coffee—black, as she knew he liked his coffee—beside Xander. He gave her a long, level look that was quite expressionless. Then he returned his attention to his son, asking him about the car he was pushing around on the carpet.

'I like cars,' said Joey.

'So do I,' she heard Xander say. 'When you're bigger you can ride in my car.'

'The big red one?' asked Joey interestedly.

'Yes, that one.'

'Does it go fast?' Joey enquired, making 'vrooming' noises with his own toy car.

'Very fast,' said Xander.

'I like fast,' said Joey.

'Me too,' agreed his father.

'Can we see it now, outside?'

'Next time. Today it's too late,'

'All right. Next time.' Joey was contented. He went on chatting to his father.

All the while Vi sat and did her knitting, the needles clicking away rhythmically.

Xander did not speak to Clare until just before he left.

'I must go now, Joey,' he said. 'But I'll come back tomorrow.'

'OK,' said Joey. 'Then I'll see your car. Bye.'

Xander looked down at him, one long last look, drinking in every detail, then turned to go. Clare followed him down the narrow hallway to the front door. As he opened it he turned to her.

'If you try and run again,' he said, and the way he spoke made the hairs rise on the back of her neck, 'I will hunt you down. Tomorrow—' he looked at her, his eyes like weights, pressing into her '—we talk.'

Then he was gone.

'Vi—what am I going to do? What am I going to do?' Clare's voice was anguished. Upstairs, Joey slept peacefully, though it had taken him longer to go down than usual. He'd started talking about 'the man who said he was my father'. It was more curiosity, Clare thought, than reality. But she had been as evasive as she could without arousing suspicion.

A spurt of anger went through her—another one. They'd been coming and going with vicious ferocity ever since she'd shut the door on Xander.

How *could* he have said that to Joey? Right out—bald. Undeniable. Unqualifiable!

At just gone three, Joey was still feeling his way in using language, and Clare was never entirely sure how much he understood, how much he took in.

Now she sat, her hands wringing together, gazing hopelessly across at Vi.

For a moment Vi did not reply, concentrating on a tricky bit in her knitting. Then, without looking up, she said, 'You know, Clare, love, I've never been one to give advice when it's not asked for. But…' her old shrewd eyes glanced at the younger woman '…whatever you do, it has to be what's best for Joey. Not for you. I know that's hard. I know you came here to me when you were very unhappy, and I know you told me that Joey's dad wasn't ever going to be someone who would care about him or you, that he'd just pay money and nothing more, and wish Joey to perdition, and that wouldn't be good for any child. But—' her voice changed a little, taking on the very slightest reproving note, while still staying sympathetic '—that man doesn't seem like the one you told me about when you came here. That's an angry man, love— and not because he's found out about having a son. If he was angry for that reason, why did he stay here and tell Joey he was his dad? He wants to *be* Joey's dad, that's what.'

Clare just stared. 'Vi, you don't understand. He's not an ordinary man—he isn't a "dad" as you call it! He lives a life you can't imagine—'

She fell silent. In her mind she felt time collapse, and saw again the gilded, expensive world that Xander Anaketos moved in—where she had once moved at his side, gowned in dresses costing thousands of pounds, jewels even more—

a world as unreal to her now, when her horizons were bounded by finding the best bargains in supermarkets, by ceaseless careful budgeting and never splashing out on anything, as if he came from a different planet.

Vi shook her head. 'If he wants to be Joey's dad you can't stop him, love.'

Clare's expression hardened. 'The fathers of illegitimate children in this country have no legal rights over them,' she exclaimed harshly.

Vi gave her a long look over her knitting needles.

'We're not talking law and rights—we're talking about being a dad to a little lad.'

'I won't have Joey hurt.' Clare's voice was passionate. 'I won't have him thinking he's got a father, and then he hasn't. I won't have Xander swanning in here, upsetting him! Joey's got *me*!'

Vi put her knitting down. 'Oh, love,' she said, her voice sorrowful. 'He'll always have you. But you can't stop him from knowing his dad—it wouldn't be right.'

'But *why* does Xander care about Joey? He *doesn't* care. That's the *point*! Vi—you don't know him. He's not a man who can feel for others—I know that. Dear God, I know that. He's just angry because… Because…'

She felt silent again, her chest painful. *Why* was he so angry? She didn't understand—she just didn't. Xander hadn't wanted her, had thrown her out like last year's model, chucked and discarded, paid off with a diamond necklace. So why, *why* had it angered him that she'd disappeared just as he had *wanted* her to?

Anger warred with anguish.

Vi sighed. A long, heavy sigh, from one who had seen a

lot of sorrows in life and knew there wasn't always anything that could be done about them.

'Why not just see what happens, pet?' she said. 'You'll always do what's best for Joey. You always have, you always will.'

The hard, painful knot in Clare's breast eased, just a fraction. But she still looked at Vi with fear in her eyes. Her heart was squeezed tight, as if in a vice, painful and crushed. Emotion was inside her like a huge, swelling balloon, filling her up, terrifying her. How, *how* could it be that a bare twenty-four hours ago her life had been normal...safe? Her stomach churned again—it had been doing that over and over, making her feel sick and disbelieving. Hadn't it been bad enough setting eyes on Xander again like that last night, having the past leap out of nowhere and slam her into the ground like that?

But that had been nothing to what she had gone through— was still going through—when he had found out about Joey.

The sick feeling intensified. Oh, dear God, what was she going to do?

And even more frightening, more unthinkable, what was Xander Anaketos going to do now that he knew he had a son...?

CHAPTER FOUR

XANDER stood at the window of the reception room in his London apartment, the morning sunshine streaming in. There were no memories of Clare here. He'd moved on since then, and this apartment must be the second or even third he occupied when he was in the UK on business. It was the same with his places in Paris, New York, Rome and Athens. He didn't keep things long. He changed his cars every year or so, whenever a new model of his favourite marque came out. He changed his watches just as often, whenever a newer and better one was launched. Similarly the yachts he kept at Piraeus and the South of France.

He had no sentimental attachments to things.

Or to women. He changed those just as frequently. He always had. There was, after all, no reason not to...

But a child—a child could not be changed. A child was for ever.

Emotion knifed through him. It had been doing so regularly for the last thirty-six hours. Ever since he'd looked up in the cocktail lounge and seen, for the first time in four years, the woman who had got up from the table at the St John with a low murmur and walked out, vanishing into the night.

He saw again her blank, expressionless eyes as he told her, 'It's over.'

Christos—she was already pregnant. She sat there, carrying my son, and then walked out on me without a word. Taking my son with her.

Fury bit savagely. He turned abruptly away from the window and headed for the door. It was time to get this sorted. Time to get his son.

Tension racked through Clare like wire stringing her from the ceiling. She was standing rigid as a board in her bedroom, the upstairs room above Vi's bedroom, because it was the only place they could be without Joey hearing them from the back sitting room, where he was with Vi, while opposite her Xander stood, his back to the window, silhouetted against the light. It made him look very tall and dark.

Clare felt again that sickening sense of unreality sweep over her.

And something else, too. Something that had nothing to do with the hideous fact that Xander had discovered Joey's existence and everything to do with the way she was so stupidly, insanely aware of his devastating effect on her.

As she had always been…

No! Dear God, out of everything in this nightmare that was the last, the very last thing she must think about. Once, so fatally, she had been vulnerable to the man who stood looking grimly at her now. But that had been a lifetime ago. Once, so pathetically, she had thought she might mean something to him. But in one callous utterance he had ripped that pathetic hope from her…

He had started to speak, his voice harsh and clipped, his

accent even more pronounced than usual. Clare forced herself to listen, however much her stomach was churning.

'My lawyers are making the necessary arrangements,' Xander was announcing. 'There will need to be a prenuptial agreement, and for that reason the ceremony itself must be on a territory where it is legally binding—which is not, so I am informed, the case in the UK. Is, therefore, your passport up to date? And does my son have one of his own? If not, this will need to be expedited. You will also—'

'What are you talking about?' Clare's voice was blank, cutting across his.

'I am telling you what will need to be done for us to marry—quickly,' Xander said. His mouth tightened automatically at her interruption—and her question.

'*What?*' Incomprehension, disbelief yawned through her.

His eyes flashed darkly. 'Did you not realise that I would be prepared to marry you?'

Clare shook her head. 'No.'

Her voice was hollow.

Xander looked down at her. Had she really not thought he would do so? His gaze narrowed. Was that why she had walked out on him that night four years ago? Had she not realised that he would marry her?

Of course he would have married a woman carrying his child.

Especially—

No. He slammed down the lid on the memory. That was then, this was now.

'I would have married you four years ago if you had taken the trouble to tell me you were carrying my child,' he said tersely.

'Would you?' Clare replied slowly. 'Would you really?'

'Of course.' His voice was stiff.

For one terrible moment pain ripped through Clare. Oh, God, if she had taken that other road—the one she had refused to take, the one she had had to find all the strength she possessed not to take, not to go back to him, to seek him out, to risk telling him she was pregnant…to risk him rejecting her unborn child.

But she had assumed that he would never in a million years have thought to marry her. She would have been given an allowance, a gagging order so she could not babble to the press about any 'love-child' of Xander Anaketos, and then dumped in some expensive villa somewhere where she could raise her son as the unwanted bastard of a discarded mistress…

He would have married me!

Pain ripped again.

Agony.

Because that was what it would have been—just as much as if she had been kept as his discarded mistress bearing his bastard. The agony of being married to him for no reason other than that she had conceived his child. When all along she would have known—as she knew now, so bitterly, had known since that last, lacerating evening with him—just how *nothing* she was to him.

She looked at him now. Just as he had been able four years ago to stop the breath in her lungs, so he could still do now. The passage of four years had merely matured his features. The breathtaking impact of his masculinity still was as potent as ever.

It would have been torment to have been married to him. And there could still be no greater torment…

'So,' he continued, his voice still clipped and harsh, 'now

that you have understood that, perhaps we can finally proceed? If you pack promptly, we can be at my apartment for lunch. Please ensure you have all the legal documents required, such as my son's birth certificate, and—'

'I'm not going to marry you!' Clare's voice rang out.

'You will,' he commanded.

She took a step backwards. She could not be hearing this. She could not be hearing Xander Anaketos calmly announcing that she would marry him. Was he mad?

'Do not play games over this,' Xander bit back angrily. 'Of course we shall marry.'

She shook her head violently. 'It's insane to think so!'

Xander's eyes darkened. 'If it is the prenuptial agreement you object to—tough. That is not negotiable. You've hardly proved trustworthy'

She gave a laugh. It had a note of hysteria in it. It made Xander's eyes focus on her even more narrowly. She rubbed a hand over her brow.

'This is insane,' she said heavily. 'It's mad that you should even think of marrying me like this.' She lifted her eyes to him. 'I never wanted you to know about Joey. Never!' She saw his eyes darken malevolently at her words, but ploughed on, ignoring his reaction. 'I wish you had never found out,' she said bleakly. 'I wish I had never set eyes on you again. But it's too late now. Too late.' Her voice was heavy. Then she looked at him, her shoulders squaring. 'I won't marry you—it's insane even to think it!'

Something moved in his eyes. Something that made her feel faint. Then there was a caustic etching of lines around his mouth as he replied.

'You are saying you prefer *this*—' he gestured with his

hand, his eyes sweeping the room, which was furnished with old-fashioned furniture from Vi's younger days, worn now, as were the carpet and the curtains '—to the life you would lead as my wife?'

'Yes,' said Clare. 'If all I cared about was your money, Xander, don't you think I'd have told you I was pregnant— even if you had just thrown me out like garbage?'

His eyes flashed again. 'I did not "throw you out like garbage"! I made suitable alternative arrangements for your accommodation. I gave you a suitable token of my apprec—'

'*Don't say that word!* If you say it *one* more time to me, I swear to God I will…I will…'

She sat down heavily on the bed, and the springs creaked. Her legs would not hold her up any more.

She looked across at him. He was standing stiffly, rigid.

'Oh, go to hell,' she mumbled. 'Just go to hell, Xander. I know the law will let you have some visiting rights to Joey, and if you really insist on them I know I can't stop you. But don't *ever* think you're going to get any more. I don't want you in my life again.'

His face stilled. It sent a shiver of foreboding through her.

'But I,' he said, 'have every intention of being in my son's life. I have every intention of being his father.'

She gave a twisted laugh, cut short.

'Father? You don't know the slightest thing about being a father.'

For a moment there was a silence that could have been cut with a knife.

'Thanks to you,' said Xander, softly and sibilantly. 'Because of you, I am a stranger to my own son. I did not even know his *name* when I spoke to him!'

Clare's mouth tightened. She would not let him make her feel guilty. She would not. She stood up, forcing herself upright, folding her arms tightly across her chest. Her chin lifted.

'Well, if you're so keen to be a father, come and learn to be one. But listen to me—and listen to me well!' Her expression grew fierce. 'Fatherhood is for *life*, Xander! It's not some novelty that you can amuse yourself with or get off on self-righteously because I dared to object to the way you treated me and never told you about Joey. Don't think that being stinking rich means you can just have the easy bits and dump the rest on your paid minions! And above all—' she bit each word out '—it is *not* something you do without committing to it for the rest of your life. Because if you hurt my son—if you cause a single tear to fall from his eyes because you get bored with him, or put yourself first, or put making money first or, God help you, play with your mistresses first!—then you won't be *fit* to be his father!'

She could see anger light in his face, but she didn't care. Didn't give a toss! She glared at him, and he met her eyes with his dark, heavy ones. Then, abruptly, she spoke again.

'I can't cope. I can't cope with this. It's like a steam train going over me. The day before yesterday everything was normal. Now it's—' She closed her eyes. 'A nightmare.'

'A nightmare?' Xander echoed her words. His voice was cold and vicious.

'Yes!' Her eyes flared open again. 'I never wanted to see you again. Not for the rest of my life. But you're here—and it's a nightmare. And I can't cope with it. I just can't. I just *can't*…' She took a deep, shuddering intake of breath. 'Look—I need time…time to get used to this. I've been in shock since that night at the hotel—and I don't handle shock well. I can't get my head round it.'

'You want my *sympathy*?' Xander's voice was incredulous.

'I don't want *anything* from you!' she bit back. 'Like I said, I wish to God I'd never set eyes on you again. But it's too late. So I'm simply telling you how it is for me—too much to handle right now. And you know something?' Her eyes flashed again. 'I don't *have* to handle it right now. I don't have to do anything until you come back here with a court order for access in your hand. Right now, if I wanted to, I could phone the police and tell them you're an intruder here. So back off, Xander. Back off and give me the time I need to get my head round this.'

'The time you need to run, perhaps? The way you like to do?' His voice was silky and dangerous.

Her face tightened. 'I won't run, Xander. That would be playing into your hands, wouldn't it? And besides—where would I go? I can't leave Vi.'

He frowned.

'You can pay rent elsewhere, not just to your current landlady.'

'Vi isn't my landlady. She's my friend. And she doesn't charge rent because I help look after her so she can go on living here, in her own home. She's like a grandmother to Joey. Family. I could never leave her!'

She dropped her arms to her sides, weariness and defeat filling her. 'Look, I can't take any more right now. I want you to go. I won't run—I can't. If you don't believe me, set some guards or whatever round the house to make sure I don't. I don't care. But just go. Say goodbye to Joey if you want.'

'That is very generous of you.' His sarcasm was open, and Clare felt herself flushing. Then her face hardened again.

'Joey needs to take this slowly too, Xander. He needs to get used to you. And most of all—' her eyes were like needles '—he needs not to depend on you to stay interested in him.'

For a moment she thought she could see murder in the dark, long-lashed eyes that had once, so long ago, melted her bones.

'I don't have to prove myself to you,' he said, with a softness that raised the hair on the back of her neck. 'Only to my son.'

Then he turned and walked out of the room, down the stairs. His tread was heavy on the floorboards. Like hammers going into her chest.

She stayed upstairs in her room, standing motionless, as if wire was wrapping her round, biting into her cruelly. It seemed for ever until she heard his tread on the hall carpet and the sound of the front door opening, then closing.

Slowly, she went downstairs again.

Joey was taking one of his picture books across to Vi, but as Clare came in he looked round.

'That was my daddy here,' he announced. 'There's a daddy in this book. Look.'

He opened the book to a page showing a happy nuclear family, sitting having a meal around a table, with a baby and a toddler. It wasn't a book Clare liked—because of the nuclear family—but Joey had chosen it because it included a scene where the toddler was playing with a very impressive toy garage.

His stubby finger pointed at each person in the illustration.

'Mummy, Daddy, me.' Then he frowned. 'Baby,' he said. He looked at Clare. 'We haven't got a baby.'

Clare swallowed. 'No, but we've got a nan instead. That's a different family from us, Joey.'

Joey looked at her. 'Can we keep my daddy?' he asked.

Clare could see Vi's eyes on her. Eyes that said nothing—and knew everything. She crouched down beside Joey.

'Your daddy doesn't live in this country, darling. He travels all over the world. Lots of countries. So you won't see him very often.'

Joey's eyes clouded.

'He said he was coming back. When?'

'Soon,' said Clare. She got to her feet.

Too soon.

Her stomach churned at the thought.

Xander gave her till the weekend. He used the time to his own advantage. In a series of punishing meetings, and flights to Geneva, Milan and Paris, he got through of a formidable amount of work.

He also disposed of Sonja de Lisle. She was no longer a requirement, only an unnecessary complication.

When he gave her the news, she flew into a tantrum. Eyes spitting, language foul, she stormed out, with her suitcases filled to bursting with every garment, accessory and piece of jewellery he'd ever bought her.

Four hours later she was back on the phone to him, purring away and saying it had all been a mistake on her part, enticing him back to her, inviting him over to a very intimate dinner in the suite at the Grosvenor he'd taken for her, to ease her departure.

He hung up on her in mid-purr.

Memory sliced through him like a meat cleaver—to the time when he'd got rid of another woman from his life.

Those expressionless eyes, that very still face...

Now he knew why. She'd already known she was pregnant, and when he'd called time on her she'd decided that her revenge on him would be to keep his child from her. And she was doing the same thing in refusing to marry him. Keeping him at arm's length from his son. Anger bit in him like a scorpion's sting. And she'd had the unmitigated gall to claim it was because he was inexperienced with children—

Her doing. She kept my son from me, and now accuses me of knowing nothing about him.

Rage boiled in him. Then he quenched it. He would get his son. Joey would grow up with him. There was no question—no question whatsoever. Whatever it took to achieve that, he would do.

He picked up the phone on his desk and summoned his PA. His instructions to her had nothing to do with business…

CHAPTER FIVE

'WELL,' announced Vi robustly, 'to my mind it's just the thing to get little Joey used to you.'

Her eyes went approvingly to Xander. Clare, at the furthest end possible of the sofa, stared aghast at Vi.

'You can't mean that!'

How could Vi be taking Xander's part? How could she even be civil to him? She was being even more than civil—she was treating him with approbation. She'd all but forced Clare to take Joey out to the park with Xander today, when he'd turned up just after lunchtime on the first day of the weekend. Clare had walked in stony silence, pushing the buggy, while Xander focussed all his attention on Joey. It had been excruciating.

His arrival back at Vi's house after four days had sent her hopes plummeting. She'd been hoping against hope that he'd gone abroad, summoned by all his complex international business dealings. Yet even the few days' intermission had allowed her, she knew, to mitigate the demolishing shock that had possessed her. She'd had time to accept that the nightmare was real, that Xander Anaketos had found out about Joey—and that he wanted to be a part of Joey's life.

And Joey, it seemed, twisting the knife in her breast, was of the same opinion. His childish conversation had returned to the subject of his father time and again over the last few days, and even though Clare had done her best to change the subject, Vi, of all people, had been matter-of-fact in answering.

'He'll come when he can, lamb. Dads have to work, remember? So he's very busy.'

But not busy enough. Clare had heard his monster of a car arrive as Joey was finishing his lunch, and her heart had sunk to her shoes. Now it had congealed into cold ice. Was he insane, thinking she and Joey would go on *holiday* with him? Yet here was Vi, thinking it was a perfectly unexceptional thing to suggest.

'Yes,' Vi retorted. 'A holiday together would be just the thing. It's a very good idea.'

'I don't *want* to!' Clare exclaimed vehemently.

Vi gave her a level look. 'Joey's got a right to his father, love,' she said calmly. Her gaze went to Xander again. He gave her a slight nod of acknowledgement.

Clare was staring at Vi as if she were a traitor.

'He can come and visit *here*!' she countered.

'Well, he will, love. And he is already, and that's all very well. But Joey needs to spend more time than just an outing to the park or some playtime indoors. A holiday would be just the thing, like I say.'

'I couldn't possibly leave you, Vi. How would you manage?' Clare said desperately.

'That has been taken care of,' Xander interjected. 'Mrs Porter has been good enough to accept a minute token of my appreciation for her contribution to the care of my son over these last years. While Joey is on holiday she will be too.'

'That's right,' said Vi. 'Though I don't need thanking—Clare and Joey are family to me. But I'll be very glad to see Devon again.'

Clare felt another punch of betrayal go through her. 'We were going to go there all together! In the summer—'

'Well, Clare, love, a caravan always was going to be a bit tricky for me, wasn't it? And this hotel I'm going to is specially adapted for old people, and it's right on the sea front. It couldn't be better. And this time of year the town won't be too crowded either—nor the weather too hot for me.'

'So, do you have any more objections?'

Clare's eyes snapped to those of the figure at the other end of the sofa. Somewhere deep inside, on a different plane of existence from the one her mind was occupying, something detonated. Xander was not wearing a business suit today. He wore the kind of casual wear that looked relaxed but was, she could tell at a glance, extremely expensive. His dark blue sweater was cashmere, his loafers hand-made, his petrol-blue trousers bespoke tailored.

But it wasn't his clothes that had caused the detonation.

It was the body beneath…

The body she had once known with such sensual intimacy that if she even began to remember it would crucify her…

I don't need this.

Wasn't it hideous enough having to watch Xander with Joey—and, worse, Joey responding with increasing confidence and pleasure to all the attention from him? Wasn't that enough torment for her?

Why did her own self have to betray her as well?

There was only one cruel comfort, if such a thing were

possible in this nightmare that had engulfed her since she had come face to face with Xander Anaketos again. Only one.

That, whatever her treacherous memory might be trying to conjure back, it was finding no answering echo within him.

From him came only grim hostility and condemnation.

Be grateful for it, she thought. Be grateful he treats you like a block of wood!

And she must do likewise. It was the only way she would be able to cope.

But how could she possibly survive a holiday in his company? She couldn't. It was impossible.

'Well?' Xander's prompt came again. 'Do you think Joey would not enjoy the seaside?'

She would not, *would not* be steamrollered like this.

'He can enjoy it here, in this country. Taking him to the Caribbean is just ridiculous.'

'It's at its best at this time of year,' said Xander. 'And though the flight is long, one of the advantages of a private plane is that we can not only fly whenever we want, but there will be ample room for Joey to move about freely and be entertained. Surely you remember,' he said, and his eyes levelled at her, 'how easy travel is when you can do it in comfort?'

She pulled her eyes away. Oh, God, she remembered only too well. Remembered how Xander had taken advantage of the sleeping accommodation on his private long-haul jet.

Not that that they had slept much…

'Joey will have a lovely time,' Vi said, speaking decisively. 'And that's what's important. Isn't it, Clare, love?'

She looked speakingly across at her, and all Clare could do was feel totally, absolutely betrayed.

Xander got to his feet. 'My PA will be in touch on

Monday, and will make all the arrangements necessary—including whatever is needed to expedite Joey's passport.' He glanced at his watch.

The gesture was not lost on Clare. It was Saturday—Xander Anaketos would not be spending the evening alone. What was his current mistress like—blonde, brunette, redhead? Petite, voluptuous, tall? She let the litany run like a river of pain through her head. The one who had replaced her four years ago had been her opposite—a fiery, tempestuous Latino beauty, with a taste for flamboyant, revealing clothes. She'd seen a picture of them together in a gossip magazine at the antenatal clinic. Clearly Xander had got bored with the cool, classic type that she had exemplified, had wanted something more exciting…

She tore her mind away. Xander Anaketos's sexual tastes, both past and present, were of no concern to her.

They never would be again.

The river of pain in her head intensified.

CHAPTER SIX

'SEA!' yelled Joey, beside himself with excitement.
'There, there!'

He pointed through the car window to where a bay of
dazzling azure blue had just become visible, fringed with
vivid emerald-green, all drenched in the hot glare of the
Caribbean sun. They had landed at the small, deserted airport
of this tiny Caribbean jewel half an hour ago, and were
heading to the coast in a chauffeur-driven car.

Contrary to Clare's apprehensions about the long flight,
Joey had revelled in every moment, fascinated with the swivelling leather seats, the seat belts, the huge TV screen, the
onboard bathroom, the portholes, the cockpit, the galley,
and every other aspect of the private jet that had winged them
across the Atlantic. To Clare's astonishment Xander had
spent the time exclusively devoting himself to keeping Joey
entertained, whether by playing childish computer games
with him or doing colouring and jigsaws. It was very different from her memories of travelling with Xander as his
mistress. He had either spent flights working at his laptop
and his papers—or sweeping her back to the sleeping accommodation for some undivided personal attention.

Now he was giving her his undivided personal *in*attention. He was turned away from her, chatting to Joey, pointing out the sights of the island's landscapes.

'See those big trees, and all the round fruits dangling off them like they're on bits of string? Those are mangoes— you'll like mangoes. We'll have some for breakfast. They're very juicy and sweet. And those trees there are banana trees. Do you know something funny about bananas?'

Joey shook his head, eyes wide.

'They grow upside down. I'll show you when we're at the villa.'

Clare was staring bleakly out of her window. She'd been twice to the Caribbean with Xander. Not, thank God, to this island, but even without direct memories just being in the Caribbean was painful. Most of the time she'd been with Xander had been spent travelling with him. He had constantly been doing business. Only occasionally had he pulled the plug on his business affairs and actually had a holiday. Their two visits to the Caribbean had been such. They'd stayed at the kind of five-star boutique hideaway hotel that was written about in the Sunday newspapers with breathless awe at what money could buy, surrounded by exclusively rich and beautiful people—the men rich, the women beautiful.

But Xander had hardly treated those stays as holidays. Oh, he had kept her at his side, both by day and by night, but he had remained in constant communication with his staff and had struck, she knew, at least one business deal with his fellow guests.

How much would Joey see of him now? she wondered. It was one thing to visit Vi's house, another to live for two weeks with a little child in a secluded villa.

The car swept through an iron-gated entrance and along a gravelled drive between lush vegetation, to pull up outside a long, low building. As they got out of the car, the humid warmth enveloped her. Beautifully kept gardens, brilliant with hibiscus and bougainvillaea, surrounded the villa, and already she could see the flashing dart of a hummingbird amongst the vivid blossoms.

She took Joey by the hand and followed Xander inside into a cool air-conditioned interior, with a high, cathedral ceiling, and through huge glass doors to a terrace, beyond which Joey immediately spotted the sea again. He cried out excitedly, and tugged on Clare's hand.

Xander turned and held his hand out.

'Let's hit the beach, Joey,' he said with a grin.

Clare felt pain stab through her. It hurt to see Xander smile like that. A carefree, boyish grin. He was not a man who smiled easily.

'You'll need beach clothes, pet,' she said to Joey. 'And sunblock.'

She led him off to find the bedroom, not caring what Xander wanted. Her luggage, such as it was, was already in the bedroom the smiling maid showed her to, and it did not take long to get herself into shorts and T-shirt and Joey into swimming shorts and a top and hat to protect him from the sun. He protested over the sunblock, but she was adamant.

From the verandah on to which her room opened she could see Xander, standing by an azure swimming pool. He, too, had changed for the beach, and Joey ran down towards him. She followed reluctantly, her cheap flip-flops flapping on the stone paving. She watched as Xander gave Joey another grin, took his hand, and headed down the path to the beach.

Clare might as well not have been there.

Pain stabbed again. To be so cut out—as if she did not exist…

Doggedly, she followed the two receding figures. The moment he could, Joey slipped Xander's hand and ran down over the silvered sand into the crystal-clear turquoise water. As she walked onto the beach, Clare looked around her.

It really was like something out of a brochure for paradise. The long, low villa, set into jewelled gardens, the white sliver of beach, fringed by coconut palms whose fronds were swaying in the gently lifting breeze, and everywhere, stretching to the horizon, the fantastic brilliance of the turquoise sea. Far out, she could see waves splashing on a reef, creating the mirrored pond of the lagoon within.

But she would have given anything not to have been here…

'Mummy! Come in the water!' Joey's voice was high-pitched with excitement.

She waded in with her sandalled feet, feeling the cool water like a balm. Joey jumped up and down, then sat down with a splash.

'You see how happy he is?' Xander's voice was accusatory. 'Yet you would have deprived him of this—as you deprived him of a father.'

Her eyes hardened. 'Don't try and make me feel guilty, Xander!'

Something moved in his face. Then it had gone. In its place was a different expression.

'This isn't good for Joey. All this aggression. He'll pick up on it and it will upset him.'

Clare just looked at him. Her face was stony. How could

she possibly endure two weeks here, like this? For a long moment Xander returned her gaze, level and unreadable.

'We're going to have to talk,' he said. 'Tonight, when Joey is in bed.' He turned away, returning his attention to Joey. 'OK, Joey—I'm coming in. Prepare for some serious splashing!'

Xander peeled off his top in a single fluid movement, and without her volition Clare's eyes went to him. Her breath caught, and she was humiliatingly grateful for her dark glasses.

His body was as perfect, as fantastic, as she had remembered it. The smooth, strong-muscled torso, the broad shoulders, the long, lean thighs, hazed lightly with dark hair. As he ran down into the water past her, her eyes went to the perfect sculpture of his back, the narrow form of his hips.

Memory burned, like a wound in her flesh, vivid and excoriating. Once she had held him in her arms. Once that taut, muscled flesh had been hers to caress, hers to yield to, hers to crush herself against.

And now?

He was gone for ever. Beyond her for ever.

She turned away, heading back up towards the terrace.

This holiday would be a season in hell for her.

CHAPTER SEVEN

JOEY was asleep, his bed drawn next to hers, his teddy tucked in beside him. Jet lag had finally overcome him, despite his state of excitement at being here on holiday—and at the wonderful new addition to his life.

As Clare smoothed his dark hair gently, a heaviness of heart pressed on her.

How could two people react so differently to another one? Joey's pleasure and excitement at Xander's presence in his life shone from his eyes. While she dreaded every moment in his company.

And now she was going to have to face him again, without even Joey to dilute the hideous tension she felt.

Another round of Xander's virulent hostility to endure. What would it be this time? she thought bitterly. More trying to make her feel bad for not having told him she was pregnant? More lectures on Joey's right to a father? Or, worst of all, more insane proposals like their getting married?

At least he'd backed off on that one. Maybe even he now saw the insanity of it. Cold ran down her spine at the memory of him coolly informing her he was going to marry her—

Marriage to him would be as agonising now as it would have been four years ago. Nothing could change that...

She straightened and left the room, checking the baby monitor was on and taking the handset with her. As she walked back along the terrace she could hear the cicadas in the bushes, the occasional piercing chirrup of a tree frog, and feel the encircling warmth of the tropical night embrace her. She was still warm, even in shorts and T-shirt. She hadn't bothered to change. What for?

Who for?

Not for Xander, that was for sure.

Never again for him.

The heaviness in her heart crushed her yet more.

The swift Caribbean night had fallen. The sky to the west carried the faint remains of blueness, while in the east brilliant gold stars were pricking through the floor of heaven.

The beauty of the setting mocked her.

So, too, even more cruelly, did the beauty of the man waiting for her, in an old-fashioned steamer chair set on the lawn near the pool, his legs stretched out, a bottle of cold beer in his grip. He looked at her as she walked towards him.

She felt suddenly acutely self-conscious. There was something in the way he was watching her that had nothing to do with the way he had regarded her since their fateful, nightmare encounter in the cocktail lounge.

Heavily, she plonked herself down in the other steamer. Almost instantly one of the house staff was there, enquiring politely what she would like to drink. She asked for a fruit punch, and it was there moments later, served in a beautiful expensive glass, with slices of fresh fruit and a frosted rim. She took a sip and frowned. It had alcohol in it—rum, probably. For an instant she thought to return it, then shrugged mentally. She could probably do with some Dutch courage.

She looked across at Xander.

'Well?' she said. She might as well get this over with. 'You wanted to talk, so talk.'

For a second he said nothing. Then he spoke. 'You've changed. I would hardly have known you.'

Even in the dusk she could feel a flush in her cheeks as his glance levelled at her assessingly.

'Well, that's hardly surprising,' she retorted. 'My lifestyle's a little different,' she said sarcastically.

He gave a quick shake of his head. 'I don't mean your looks. That's understandable. I mean you.' He paused, looking at her. 'You're—harder.'

She gave a snort. 'Depends on the company,' she said. She took a mouthful of the rum punch. The alcohol kicked through her.

His eyes narrowed. 'So this is the real you I'm seeing now? I never saw it before.'

No, she thought, because I wasn't like that then. I was— stupid. Trusting. Hopeful.

Stupid.

Well, so what? That was then, this was now. She took another drink from her cocktail, and stared across at Xander.

'I thought you wanted to talk about Joey,' she demanded

He didn't like her speaking to him like that, she could see. But she didn't care. He was right—she wasn't the same person she had been when she'd been his mistress. She *was* harder now. She'd had to be. Had to be ever since the moment she'd murmured, 'Will you excuse me a moment?' to him in the restaurant at the St John and walked out of his life. Taking the marching orders he'd just handed her with brutal suddenness.

'Obviously,' he answered brusquely. 'What else would we have to talk about?' For a second, the very briefest second, there was a shift in his eyes. Then it was gone. 'Like I told you—this aggression is not good for him. It's got to stop.'

She stared at him. 'So stop it,' she said.

His mouth tightened. He definitely did not like being spoken to like that. Then, visibly, he made his expression impassive.

'For Joey's sake, I will. And so will you.'

For a moment Clare wanted to bite back that she did not take orders. Then she subsided. Joey would only be upset if he realised how much hostility there was between the two people who had created him.

'OK,' she conceded. 'In front of Joey.'

He shook his head.

'Not good enough. It's not something you can turn on and off, whenever he's around or not. It's got to be permanent.'

She just looked at him. Looked at the man who had deleted her from his bed—his life—in a single sentence. With brutal words. A man she had actually thought felt for her something that went beyond her role as his mistress.

But all he had felt for her had been 'appreciation'.

Appreciation that he had paid for with a diamond necklace.

'How the hell,' she said heavily, 'do you think that's possible?'

Again there was that brief flicker in his eyes. Then it was gone.

'By forcing ourselves,' he replied. 'Until it becomes a habit. Because this isn't going to go away. *I* am not going to go away. I'm going to be part of my son's life for ever—and you'd better accept that. This is what I propose—'

She snorted again. 'Not another insane idea like the last one, I hope?'

Again came that strange, very fleeting expression in his eyes, which she could hardly see in this dim light.

'No. For Joey's sake we behave…normally…with each other. Putting everything else aside. And we can start right now.' He got to his feet. 'Over dinner.'

He indicated the terrace, and Clare could see that the table there had been set for a meal, with flowers and napery and soft candles. Xander was looking at her. She headed towards it, rum punch in her hand, and plonked herself down, flicking her plait over her shoulder.

He took his place opposite her. It seemed a whole lot too close for Clare's liking.

'Your hair is longer,' he said.

'Long hair's cheaper than short,' she answered.

'Why do you wear it constrained like that in a…a pigtail all the time?'

She looked at him. 'It keeps it out of the way when I'm busy.'

'Well, you are on holiday now. You don't have to be busy. You can relax. Let your hair down.'

His eyes flicked over her. In the pit of her stomach Clare felt desire begin to pool.

The appearance of the steward was a reprieve, and the whole formal rigmarole of serving dinner gave her the insulation she needed. Wine and water was poured, bread was proffered, plates deposited with gloved hands. This might be a villa by the sea, but it was a silver service. No doubt.

Sickly she realised that the last time she had sat having

dinner with Xander it had been the night she had been terminated.

He had seemed preoccupied then—and with hindsight, of course, it had been obvious why. He hadn't even wanted to be there—had simply been waiting for the moment to hit the delete button on her…

She glanced across at him now. Four years ago. Had it really been so long? It seemed much, much closer in time than that.

But it wasn't—it was four years ago. Four years—and everything changed that night. Your whole life. And nothing—not even Xander Anaketos storming back to claim his fatherhood of Joey—will change it back. Nothing.

She started to eat.

It was a strained, bizarre meal. Xander made conversation. Deliberately so, she realized. Perhaps partly for the waiting staff, but also because he was following his own precepts and trying to give an appearance of normality to their dining. He talked of the island—a little of its history as a former colony, and the activities it afforded those rich enough to holiday here. Clare returned the barest replies, a feeling of unreality seeping through her.

She tried not to look at him, tried not to hear that naturally seductive timbre in his voice, tried not to catch the scent of his skin. She had to stop herself, she knew. But it was a torment.

I've got to get used to this. I have no other option. So if I'm to endure it, I must make myself immune to it. To him.

It was with a sense of relief that she felt herself yawn at the end of the main course. She pushed her chair back. The glass of wine she'd sipped almost without realising it, combined with jet lag, was knocking her out fast.

'I'm falling asleep,' she said. 'I'm going to go to bed.'

Did that slightest flicker come again? She didn't know, didn't care—was too tired to think about it.

'I'll see you in the morning,' he murmured, and reached for his own wine glass.

She left him to it and headed indoors. The cool of the air-conditioning made her shiver after the warmth outdoors.

Or something did.

Behind her, Xander watched her go. His expression was strange. His mood stranger. She had changed, all right—she was a different woman from the one he remembered. The one who had been so reserved she had refused to look at him as he walked past the time he'd first spotted her at his London offices. The one who had become his mistress without a murmur, her cool, understated beauty engaging his interest as an intriguing contrast to the sophisticated passions of the previous incumbent, whose charms had palled for him. Clare had fitted into his life effortlessly, and he had taken her with him because she'd been undemanding and ac-commodating, calm and composed—the classic English rose without thorns…

His mouth twisted. Well, that had gone, and with a ven-geance! Now she scratched and tore at him verbally, snapped and snarled and answered back, defying him and refusing to do what was best for his son. His expression darkened. Would she realise why he had brought her here? He lifted the wine to his mouth and savoured its rich, expensive bouquet. His eyes glinted opaquely.

Not until it's far, far too late for her…

CHAPTER EIGHT

CLARE sat on a padded lounger on the beach, under the shade of a coconut palm, looking out over the brilliant azure water beyond the silver sand.

She had been here a week. The most difficult week of her life. Even the days after Xander had thrown her out of his life, even when she had given birth to his child, even the nightmare of coming face to face with him again, did not compare with this.

Each passing day here seemed more difficult than the last. She tried her hardest not to let it show for Joey's sake—to be calm and normal, to conceal from him the emotions roiling in the pit of her stomach, to speak civilly to Xander so that Joey would not be upset. But it was hard, so hard.

But only for her, it seemed. Joey, she could see with her own eyes, day after day, was having the time of his life—and so was Xander.

Her eyes went to the two figures in the sea, one so small, battling with his armbands, the other tall and bronzed and lithe. She watched Joey throwing a huge inflated ball at Xander, who made a vastly exaggerated play of launching himself sideways to catch it, landing in the water with an almighty splash. Joey whooped with laughter and Xander surfaced, his grin wide, shaking water drops from his head.

Clare felt her hands tighten around her book. Watching them together sent a pain through her heart she could not stop.

Could that really be Xander Anaketos there? Playing with his little child? It was a man she had never seen before. Xander as she had never known him. A man who—pain pierced her— had existed only in her imagination, for so brief and pathetic a time, when she had hoped against hope that he felt something for her, that when she told him the news that she was pregnant he would sweep her up into his arms and declare his love for her—marry her, make them a family together…

That dream had been obliterated for ever in a single moment. '*It's over.*'

Pain stabbed again, the deepest yet. All she had was this hollow mockery—three people who looked like a family but who were no such thing…

'Mummy! Mummy! Come in the water!'

Joey's excited voice called to her. He was wading out, running across the sand to her. He seized her hand. 'Come on, Mummy,' he said, and started to drag at her.

'Your mother wants to rest, Joey.' Xander's deep voice sounded as he came up to Joey, ready to lead him back to the sea. Water ran from his sleek, bare torso, dazzling like diamonds. Clare did not want to look.

Joey's expression grew doleful. 'It's no fun resting,' he objected. 'Come on, Mummy.'

Clare got to her feet. 'Of course I'll come in,' she said. There was no point lying there, heart heavy.

Joey seized her hand enthusiastically, then grabbed Xander's hand.

'Swing me!' he commanded.

Automatically Clare raised her arm, as did Xander.

'One, two, three, *swing*!' ordered Joey.

She hefted him, and Xander did too.

'Whee!' cried Joey. 'Again, again!'

'One, two, three, *swing*!' said Clare, hefting Joey up again, and realised that she had said it in unison with Xander. Her eyes flew to his, and just for a moment, the briefest moment, they met. Then she tore her eyes away.

Emotion buckled through her.

Suddenly, out of nowhere, it seemed unbearable—just unbearable. To be here, Joey's mother and father, so close to him, with him linking them together, and yet to be so unbridgeably far apart.

'Swing me into the water!'

'You'll have to run, then,' said Xander. He glanced at Clare. 'Ready?' he said.

She nodded. They ran, all three of them, down into the water, and at the last moment they lifted him up and up, then swung him out and let him go in the deeper water. He gave a squeal of glee as he splashed down.

Clare laughed. She could not stop herself. She felt Xander's eyes on her as well, and suddenly he gave a laugh too, plunging forward to scoop up Joey.

'Throw me again, Daddy!'

Xander laughed, and tossed him once more into the water with a huge splash.

And now Clare wasn't laughing. She felt, of all things, her throat constrict and tears start in her eyes.

He was good with Joey—so *good*! The evidence could not be denied. Full of fun, laughter and, most piercingly painful of all, affection. And she knew, with a deep hollowing of her stomach, full of love. Love for Joey. His son.

And Joey loved him, too. She could see that—could not deny it. And how should it not be? He was a father any child would adore.

Memory came to her out of the years so long ago. A beach holiday with her parents. She'd only been little, how old she could not remember, but she remembered her parents, running down into the sea with her, how happy she had been…

I should have told him—I should have told him I was pregnant. I should have taken the risk and lived with it. He had a right to know, and Joey had a right to a father.

The self-accusation burned in her. Xander might not be capable of love for her—perhaps not for any woman—but he was capable of love for Joey. And she must accept it. Whatever it cost her, however cruel the fate she had been left with. The fate of knowing that all she could have was this bitter mockery—to see Xander with Joey, so warm and loving, and know that she was forever excluded.

And another torment too. One that was twisting in her day after day, night after night. For if the days were bad—when she had to watch Xander and Joey forge their new bond together, a bond that shut her out—the evenings were even worse. Because every evening, when Joey was asleep, she had to endure the ritual torture of dining with Xander.

And that was the worst of all. For the most awful of reasons.

Anguish flashed in her eyes.

Why? *Why* was it so hard? It should be getting easier, not harder! Day after day of seeing Xander again—surely it should be getting easier to endure? She should be getting more immune to him, day by day—surely she should?

And yet she wasn't. Her helpless, crippling awareness of him was increasing. It was a torment—a terror. Everything about him drew her eye—made her punishingly aware of him.

During the day she could fight it—she had Joey's presence to strengthen her. But over dinner… Oh, then, dear God, it was an excruciating torment. For him to be so close to her, a few feet away across the table—and yet further from her than if he had been on the moon.

She had tried to fight it, but it was so hard, so impossible. While she had been able to resort to open hostility it had been a bulwark, a barrier against him. But now—

I don't want to want him!

As she stared out over the beach, let her eyes run with helpless longing over his lean, muscled torso, feast on the sculpted features of his face, caught her breath as he threw back his sable head and laughed, she felt her stomach clench unbearably and knew the truth that terrified her.

She still wanted Xander Anaketos.

Whatever he had done to her—she still wanted him.

Xander lifted his wine glass and looked across the table at Clare. Turbid emotion, laced with memory, swirled within him, but he ignored it. The past was gone, over. It was the present he had to deal with. And the absolute priority right now was to achieve his goal. He would do so. He had no doubt. He had always achieved his goals in life. He would now, too—whatever it took. Too much was at stake. His son's future.

His son…

As he had done time after time, whenever those words rang in his head, he felt his heart turn over. Catch and swell with pride and love. How was it possible that he should feel so strongly? Emotion had never figured much in his life. He had had no use for it, no need of it, and he had always kept it at bay, taking whatever steps necessary to do so. Irony flickered briefly, then he brushed it aside, as an irrelevance that he could do without. And yet when he had set eyes on Joey, recognised him as his son, his reaction had been over-whelming. In an instant his son had become the overriding imperative of his life.

Every day he spent with Joey only made him more deter-mined that he would spend his life with him. And how he achieved that did not matter. Only his son's happiness mattered. And Joey *was* happy—every grin, every excited cry of glee, told him that. There was no sign, none at all, that Joey sensed any hostility between his parents.

He watched as Clare crumbled a piece of bread in her fingers. He had demanded a cessation of hostilities and she had complied. He granted her that. From the outside they must look like a normal family on holiday.

His mouth twisted. How deceptive appearances could be. And yet…

Xander's fingers tightened momentarily around the stem of his wine glass. That moment today, when they had swung Joey into the water, for a few fleeting moments they had acted in unison, as if it were normal, natural to do so. As if the appearance was, even for a brief moment, the reality.

His eyes rested on his son's mother.

Four years since she had been in his life.

She had changed, indeed. Or had she merely revealed the person she had always been, having concealed it from him when she was his mistress? He had called her harder now than when he had first known her, and with him that was true—and yet with Joey she was as soft as butter. Emotions warred within him. What she had done was unforgivable—to keep his son from him, to deny Joey his father. And yet all the evidence of his eyes, both in London and now here, day after day, was that she was devoted as a mother. Warm and loving. Affectionate and demonstrative.

A good mother.

He had to allow her that, begrudge it though he did. And for his son's sake, he had to be grateful. Even though the disparity between how she was with Joey and everything else he knew about her was so discordant.

He frowned inwardly. With Joey he saw her being someone he had never seen before. A different woman from the one he'd known four years ago. As his mistress she had always been so cool, so detached, so undemonstrative. As his mistress he had found it highly erotic—knowing that, for all her outward composure, all he had to do was touch her and she would come alive at his touch. Within seconds she would be quivering with passion. It had been a powerful fascination for him, the contrast between her public self and the private one that he could arouse in her.

That alone had been enough to justify why he had kept her so much longer than any other mistress.

For a moment his eyes shadowed, as he remembered again the moment when he had finished with her. When she had got to her feet and walked calmly out of his life. Carrying his child away with her out of spite for being discarded.

No. He set his glass down with a click on the surface of

the table. There was no point going there. No purpose in revisiting the past. It was the present he had to deal with—and the future. That was all that was important. Right now, only his son's happiness was important—and he would take whatever measures necessary to safeguard that happiness.

Whatever measures necessary...

His eyes rested on the woman who had once been his mistress, and he focussed his mind on the task ahead. She had been responsive to him then—oh, so responsive!—and neither the passage of four years, nor the splenetic anger she had unleashed on him, nor her cursed vindictiveness towards him by keeping his son from him, had changed that. He'd had proof, every day they'd been here, with no room for her to shut him out, ignore him, escape him.

Exactly the proof he wanted.

He eased his shoulders and lounged back in his chair as the staff served dinner. Opposite him, Clare sat stiffly. But her eyes had followed his movement, he knew. Surreptitiously, but discernibly. He could see her eyes following him and then flicking away, the way she didn't want to meet his eyes, the way she pulled herself away from him if he got too close. Her whole body language and behaviour with him betrayed her.

Well, that was good—very good. Just what he wanted.

Excitement flared briefly in him, but he suppressed it. In its place he forced himself to look at her with impassive objectivity.

Four years on her beauty had matured. Even without her making the slightest attempt to improve on nature by way of make-up, hairstyling or clothes, her beauty revealed itself. Beneath the cheap fabric of her T-shirt he could see the soft swell of her breasts, and her chainstore shorts could not disguise the slenderness of her waist and hips, the long smooth curve of her thighs.

He felt the shimmer of sexual arousal ease through him.

A sliver of emotion broke through the barrier he'd imposed.

Can I really go through with this?

For a moment doubt possessed him. Then he freed himself.

He would do what he intended.

For his son's sake.

Tonight was the worst yet. Clare sat, tension racking through every limb, and picked at the exquisitely presented food in front of her. It felt so wrong not to appreciate it more, but she had no appetite. Maybe too much sun?

But she knew that wasn't the reason she had no appetite—wasn't the reason she kept taking repeated unwise sips from her wine, even after she'd fortified herself with the rum punch that she was diligently handed every evening as she emerged from seeing Joey to sleep.

The reason she felt so strangely weak, so hazed, was not because of the sun. It was because of the man sitting opposite her. The man who was lifting his wine glass to his lips with a lounging grace that sent a tremor through her veins. The man whose long legs were stretched out underneath the table, so close to hers that she had to inch them away, awkwardly shifting her position.

The man whose gaze was resting on her now, with an expression she could not read.

She took a forkful of food and tried to chew it, but it was hard to swallow. She washed it down with another mouthful of wine and set the fork back on the plate, letting it be.

'You don't like the fish?'

Xander's enquiry, civilly made, but with the slightest lazy drawl in it, drew a quick shake of the head from her.

'I'm just not hungry,' she said.

'The chef will cook you something else. You only have to say.'

'No—no, thank you.'

She took another sip of wine—for something to do. She could feel the effects of the alcohol and knew she should not drink any more. Yet it seemed to give her the strength she knew she needed. She took another sip, turning her head to gaze out over the softly lit pool and the glimmering sea beyond. She could just make out the shape of the palm fronds, outlined against the sky.

It was so beautiful.

Idyllic.

Idyllic to be here, on this beautiful tropical island, with the warmth kissing her body, the softest breeze playing with her hair, the coil of wine in her blood easing through her veins.

She gazed out over the view, dim in the starlight and the shimmer of the pool lights.

Her thoughts were strange.

Unreal.

Slowly she drank more wine.

Across the table she could hear the chink of Xander's knife and fork, but he did not talk to her.

She was glad. Their stilted, deliberate conversations over dinner this last week had been an ordeal for her. Silence was easier.

She eased back in the chair, stretching out her legs, and kept on gazing out to sea. She could hear the waves, murmuring on the shore, the wind soughing softly in the palms, the soporific song of the cicadas.

Her body felt warm from the heat of the day. Warm and languorous.

She felt herself easing more in her chair, stretching out her legs yet more.

Lifting the wine glass to her lips.

It was empty.

Curious, she thought, and twisted her slender fingers around its stem, slowly replacing it on the table.

Xander was watching her.

He'd stopped eating. He was sitting there in his chair, very still. His eyes were narrowed, very slightly narrowed.

Memory hollowed within her like a caverning space, enveloping time. She knew that look—knew it in the core of her body, in the sudden pulse of her blood. Her eyes locked to his. Locked, and were held.

She could not move. Could only feel the heat of her body start to spread, like a long, low flush. Could only feel her heart in her chest start to beat with long, low slugs, a drum beating out a slow, insistent message that she knew—oh, she knew.

Xander got to his feet. She watched him, eyes still locked to his, as he came around the end of the table to where she sat. He reached down his hand to her.

And, ever so slowly, she put her hand in his.

He drew her to her feet.

For one last, long moment his eyes stayed locked to hers. And then the dark sweep of his lashes dipped and his head lowered.

His lips were velvet on hers, touching her with liquid smoothness, dissolving through her. It was bliss—honeyed, sweetest bliss—and she felt her eyes flutter shut as she gave herself to the exquisite sensation. With infinite skill he played with her mouth, and yet with every touch his kiss deepened, strengthened. Somehow—she did not know how, could not tell—his hands had folded around her, one splayed across her spine at her waist, one at the tender nape of her neck, holding her for him.

She felt herself sinking, yielding to the sensations he was arousing in her.

From touch…exquisite touch.

And, more potent still, from memory.

Because her body remembered. Remembered as if four years had never been. Instinctively, as if she had always, always been in his arms, his embrace. As if no time had passed at all. As if it had dissolved at his liquid touch.

How long she stood there, with his hands gliding down the length of her spine while his mouth gave play to hers, softly, arousingly, oh, so arousingly, she did not know. Did not know when it was that she felt the strong columns of his thighs pressing against hers, guiding her, turning her, or when his hand slid to hers, folding it within his fingers as his mouth, still dipping low over hers, drew back enough for him to start to lead her—lead her to where she could only ache to go.

She was helpless, she knew. Knew somewhere in the last frail remnants of her mind that she could not stop, could not halt what was happening to her. Could only go where she was being led, along the terrace to another door, another room, a room with a wide, luxurious bed. He was guiding her towards it, his mouth dipping to hers, tasting her, caressing her, arousing her…

And she was responding. She felt the heat flow in her veins, flushing through her skin, warming her with its soft, insistent fire. She could feel herself quickening, tightening, tautening—her body's responses feeding off him, off itself. Her breathing quickened too, her pulse beginning to beat more rapidly.

He was lowering her down upon soft sheets already drawn back by the maids, the pillow yielding as her head pressed down, his mouth still on hers.

Her hands were on his back, and as the hard muscles and flesh indented to her fingers she felt memory flood back into her head like a racing tide.

Oh, dear God, it was Xander—Xander in her arms again, Xander's mouth on hers, his hands caressing her, his strong, lean body pressing down on hers. Desire was unleashed within her, and hunger, such a hunger, ravening and desperate, to have him, to hold him, to touch him and possess him—to give herself to him.

Swiftly, he pulled off her T-shirt, and she lifted her arms to let him, and in the same skilled movement his fingers had slipped the fastening of her bra. It was falling loose, loosening its burden within, so that her breasts spilled into his returning hands.

Her back arched in pleasure as her breasts filled his grasp, and then, as his thumb teased over the instantly stiffening peaks, a low, long moan came from her throat.

How could she have forgotten such bliss? How could she have lived without it? It was ecstasy, it was heaven, it was everything she had ever wanted, could ever want. The low, gasping moan came again, and as if it had been a signal his hands went from her breasts to her waist, lifting her hips, sliding down the unnecessary covering of her clothes. And then his body was against hers. He was naked. How had that happened? She did not know, did not care—knew only that her hips were lifting to him while at her breasts his mouth was lowering.

Sensation flooded through her. The exquisite arousal of his tongue, slowly circling the straining peaks of her nipples, shot with a million darts of pleasure, making her neck arch back, her lips part.

She wanted more, and yet more. An infinity of more! Her body knew and was asking for it, craving it, hungering for it, hips lifting to him, wanting him—oh, wanting him so much, so much...

She could feel herself flooding, dewing with desire, and she could feel him, feel the seeking tip of his velvet shaft. Excitement burst through her, more intense, more urgent than ever, and she gave again that low moan of longing in her throat.

His head lifted from her breast. For one long, endless moment his eyes looked into hers. In the dimness she could not see his face, only the faint outline of his features, only the glint of light in the eyes that held hers—held hers as slowly, with infinite control, while she gazed wildly, helplessly up at him, her body flushed and aching for him, he came down on her.

He filled her completely, in one slow, engorging stroke, and as she parted for him, took him in, it was if she had melded to him, become one with him.

Her hands convulsed around his back, her hips straining against his.

He was saying something, whispering Greek words she

did not understand. She knew only that suddenly, out of nowhere, the rhythm had changed, that suddenly, out of nowhere, he was moving again within her—not slowly now, but urgently, desperately.

She answered him—meeting each thrusting stroke with her own body, clutching at him with her hands, her shoulders lifting from the pillows, bowing herself towards him, legs locking around him.

She cried out, and what she cried she did not know—knew only that she wanted him, *needed* him to hold her. He held her so closely as he thrust into her, deeper and more deeply yet, until he struck the very centre of her being. The very heart of her.

And she cried out again.

A cry stifled as his mouth caught hers, as her body caught fire from his. It sheeted through her body, white-hot, searing with a sensation so intense it was as if never until this moment had she existed.

It went on and on, flooding through time, dissolving it as if it did not exist. Burning away everything that had come between them. Emotion swept through her, overwhelming and overpowering. Filling her, flooding her.

She knew, without uncertainty or doubt, without hesitation or resistance, what that emotion was.

And as the realisation gaped through her she realised the most terrible truth in the world.

She was still in love with Xander Anaketos.

CHAPTER NINE

CLARE lay in his arms. She could do nothing else. She had no strength to move. No strength of body or of soul. She lay quite still, her head resting on his chest, his arm around her shoulder, his hand lying slackly on her upper arm, his legs still half tangled with hers.

She disengaged, her body slipping from his, indenting heavily into the mattress, as her heart-rate began to slow, her heated flesh to cool.

What had she done? What madness, insanity had possessed her?

And—more than that—what criminal stupidity had she committed?

They lay there, two people—two completely dissociated people. Lying there, flesh against flesh, hers soft and exhausted, his hard and muscled, bathed in a faint, cooling sheen of sweat, chilling in the air-conditioned atmosphere.

But she didn't care about the cold.

It echoed the chill inside her head, where her mind was very slowly repeating, like an endless replay, the same question.

What have I done? What have I done?

She went on lying there, her mind barely working, as if shut down or on standby. Because there was a program running that was taking up all her brain—only she could not let it out into her consciousness. Yet it was growing all the time, consuming more resources, more space, consuming everything she was.

She stared out blindly into the dark room.

Was he asleep? There was no movement—none—from the body beside her, only the subdued rise and fall of his chest. She waited, hearing through her bones the uneven slug of her own heart—unquiet, unresting.

Quietly she slid from the bed. He still did not move. Carefully, shakily, she picked up her discarded clothes, not finding her bra, not caring—caring only that she pulled on her shorts, pulled on her T-shirt, covered her nakedness.

And she went. Fleeing from the scene of her crime, her unspeakable folly.

She slipped out onto the terrace, the humid warmth of the tropical night hitting her like a wall. For a moment she gasped in the steamy air, as if unable to breathe, and then, swallowing hard, made her way to her own room. Inside, she ran for the bathroom.

The shower was hot—as hot as she could stand it. Washing her. Washing everything from her.

Everything but the knowledge of what she had done.

Then, like a wounded animal, she crawled to her bed.

Beside her, undisturbed, her son lay sleeping. The fruit of her folly. The folly of being in love with Xander Anaketos—for which folly she must now pay the same killing price she had paid before.

Out over the water nothing stirred—except the faint, far-off sound of the sea on the reef. Behind Xander the incessant cicadas kept up their sussurating chorus, and in the palms above his head the night wind soughed. Somewhere a lone dog barked, and fell silent.

Xander stood staring sightlessly out to sea, to the dark horizon beyond. He had waited until she had gone, lying in the simulation of sleep. Then he had got out of bed, unable to stay there longer. Pulled on his jeans and walked out here, into the darkness. The warmth of the tropical night lapped him, yet he felt cold. He plunged his hands further into the pockets of his jeans, roughly drawn on, his torso still bare, like his feet.

The coldness was all the way through him. Chilling him to the core.

He had done what he had set out to do. Achieved his goal.

He should be pleased. Satisfied.

Relieved.

He felt none of these things.

Only that he had made a terrible, catastrophic mistake.

'I've eaten my breakfast. Come and play, Daddy!'

Joey beamed invitingly. He seemed completely—thankfully—oblivious to the atmosphere at the table.

You could cut it like a knife, thought Clare, her face expressionless. She was moving like a mummy, wrapped up so tightly that she was almost incapable of moving. There were circles under her eyes from a sleepless, self-lacerating night.

Joey had woken at his customary early hour, and she had gone with him, like an automaton, to make their customary early-morning inspection of the gardens and walk along the beach till breakfast. Usually it was the time she almost enjoyed—so quiet, in the coolest time of the day, and safe from Xander, whom she would not see till breakfast. It was a time when she had Joey all to herself and could almost forget just how totally her life had changed now. How disastrously.

But this morning the walk along the beach had been torture. Hell in the middle of paradise.

The beauty of the island had mocked her mercilessly, showing her cruelly, pitilessly, with every glint of sunlight off the azure water, every curve of the emerald-fringed bay, every grain of soft, silvery sand, just how misery could dwell in the midst of beauty.

Now, as she sat at the breakfast table, she could not let her eyes go near Xander. Could say nothing to him. Could not bear to be near him. Yet she had to. For Joey's sake she had to make everything appear normal, though the mockery of it screamed at her in her head. Her awareness of his presence was like a radio tuned to a pitch that was like fingernails scraping. Every move he made, every terse syllable he spoke in response to Joey's artless chatter, every breath that came from him, vibrated in the air between them.

She was completely incapable of eating anything. She had forced down some sips of coffee through a tight, constricted throat, and that was all. Now, as Joey beamed so invitingly at Xander, she thought, desperately, Please, yes. Take him off and play with him. Go, just go—anywhere, but away from me, away from me…

'Not right now, Joey. Soon.'

Clare scraped her chair back. If Xander would not clear off, then she would. Must.

'I'll play, Joey,' she said, her voice stiff and expression-less. She held her hand out to help Joey down. But he looked at her mutinously.

'I want Daddy,' he said. His lower lip wobbled. Maybe he was not so immune to the tension stretching like hot wires between her and Xander after all, Clare realised heavily. She saw Xander press the service button on the table. A moment later the housekeeper appeared.

'Juliette, would be you be kind enough to amuse Joey for a while, please?' he said to her. His voice sounded as tense as Clare's.

Juliette gave a warm smile, and then bestowed an even warmer one on Joey.

'You come with Juliette, now. I happen to know…' she looked conspiratorial '…that it's car wash day this morning—and there's a hose with your name on it!'

Joey's lower lip stopped wobbling instantly. He scrambled down eagerly.

'I need a *big* hose,' he informed Juliette as she led him off.

Clare watched him go. He was out of sight before she turned her head back. What was going on? Why had Xander got rid of Joey?

Oh, God, he doesn't think we're going to have sex again, does he?

The thought plunged, horrifically, into her brain, and her eyes lashed to Xander's face before she could stop herself. But whatever was on his mind, that was not it. She looked away again instantly and felt relief flood through her, drowning out any other reaction she might have had to that sudden debilitating thought.

Over and over again during the long, agonising night she

had asked herself the same question—why, *why* had he done it? Why had he wanted sex with her last night?

And there was only one answer.

Because right now she was the only woman around. And she was better than nothing. There was no other reason he could possibly have had. None.

Loathing shot through her. For him, for doing that to her, and—worse by far—loathing for herself. For having been so crushingly, unforgivably stupid as to let him...

'Clare—'

Her name jolted her, and her eyes went to him involuntarily.

His face was expressionless. Quite expressionless. And yet there was something so far at the back of his eyes that she had seen once before...

And suddenly, deep inside her, fear opened up. She knew that face. Knew this moment. Recognised it from four long years ago, when she had sat in the restaurant at the St John and heard her life destroyed—her hopes decimated—in one brutal sentence.

But this time she was no longer the person she had been then. Harder. Xander had called her that to her face, and it was true. She'd had to make herself hard, or she would not have survived. Would have bled to death.

How can I love him?

The cry came from deep inside, anguished and unanswerable.

How can I love a man who threw me out like rubbish, who packed me off with a diamond necklace, who last night used me for sex because I was convenient and on hand...?

How can I love a man like that? A man without feelings,

without conscience, without remorse, or the slightest acknowledgement that he was so coldly callous to me?

I mustn't love a man like that! It debases me to do so. I thought I was free of him—I made myself free of him. I forced myself to be free of him.

But it had been in vain. Completely in vain. It had all come to nothing that night she had stood face to face again with the man she had loved, but who had never, ever felt anything more for her than 'appreciation' for her sexual services…

The whole excruciating agony of her situation honed in on her like a scud missile. Because of Joey she could never be free of Xander. Never! The nightmare she had feared four years ago had come true—she would be forced to see him, forced to be civil to him and pretend, time after time, year after year, that he could not hurt her any more. For Joey's sake she had to let that happen, had to endure it.

'Clare—what happened last night—'

He stopped, mouth tightening. She stared at him expressionlessly. As blankly as he. But his next words came out of the blue.

'When is your period due?'

'What?' Her eyes stared in shock at the question.

His mouth tightened again. 'When is your period due?' he repeated.

She stared at him uncomprehendingly.

'It may have escaped your notice,' he said tightly, 'but last night we had unprotected sex. What are your chances of getting pregnant?'

Faintness drummed through her. She could feel it fuzzing her brain. She pressed her fingers down on the table, willing herself to be calm.

Dear God, do not do this to me—

The silent, despairing plea came from her depths of fear.

'When will you know? Know if you are pregnant?'

'I—' She forced herself to think—think what date it was. With all the turmoil in her life, keeping track of her menstrual cycle was the last thing on her mind.

'At the end of the week, I think,' she said uncertainly.

He got up from the table abruptly.

'Let me know,' he said tersely, and walked away.

For one long, timeless moment Clare sat there. Then, with a strange, choking sound in her throat, she blindly pushed herself up.

She started to walk. Her legs were jerking, but she forced herself. Forced herself to go on. The lawn crunched under her bare feet, the stone of the paving around the pool was hot to her soles, and then there was sand, soft, sinking sand, and she couldn't walk any more. Her feet stumbled on stiff, jerky legs.

She sank to the sand.

Her shoulders began to shake.

Xander heard the scrape of a chair on the terrace and stiffened. Was she coming after him? He half turned his head, tensing.

He didn't want her coming near him. Didn't want her speaking to him. Didn't want her in the same universe as him.

But that wasn't possible. Because of Joey, because of his son, he couldn't get rid of her. And there was nothing, *nothing* he could do about it.

She was a life sentence for him.

He could feel the prison doors closing on him. There was no escape—none.

Emotion churned in him, harsh and pitiless.

She was heading away from him, he saw with grim vision. Walking over the lawn, past the pool, towards the beach. His eyes went to her, and his mouth tightened even more.

Christos—no escape. None!

A life sentence.

He went on watching her walk away from him, with that strange, uneven gait.

Then he saw her falter, sway very slightly, then, with a sudden jerking movement, she folded onto the sand.

He started to move.

Her shoulders were shaking. Through her body huge, agonising shudders were convulsing her. Her throat was so tight she felt it must tear and burst. She wrapped her arms around herself, pulling tighter and tighter. She would fall apart if she did not. The wracking convulsions were shattering her, shaking her to pieces, to tiny fragments.

She took a terrible, agonising draft of breath.

And then the tears came.

She couldn't stop them. They poured out of her, gushing from her eyes with hot, burning salt, choking in her throat, her lungs. She drew up her legs, wrapping her arms tightly around her knees, trying to hold herself together.

But she couldn't. The sobs shook her, raw and rasping, impossible to halt. It was the first time in four years she had cried—and now she couldn't stop.

Her hands pressed around her knees, nails digging into the bare flesh of her thighs. Head buried in her arms, her shoulders convulsed.

She could not bear it. She had reached the end now. There was no more strength in her. Nothing left in her at all.

A shadow fell over her.

'Clare?'

The voice was strange. The strangest voice she'd ever heard. But she could not hear it clearly. The sobs in her throat drowned out everything; the hot, agonising tears blinded her. Her nails digging into her legs was all she could feel, except for the convulsions of her body

'Clare?'

It was that voice again. Stranger still. She did not recognise it. It belonged to someone she did not know. Who did not exist.

The sobs went on, consuming her.

'Clare!'

That voice again, different still, and more words, words she did not understand, sounding urgent. Imperative.

He was beside her, crouching down. His hands were on her shoulders, hunched so tightly, with her arms wrapping around her, holding herself together. His hands went to her head, bent and broken over her knees, forcing it up.

A word broke from him. She did not know what it meant. Could only stare, blindly, through the tears coursing down her cheeks, as the sobs jerked in her throat, her face crumpling, breath gasping.

There was something in his face, his eyes.

It was shock. Raw, naked shock.

'Oh, my God, Clare—*why?* Why?'

It was the incomprehension in his voice. That was what did it. Her hands flew up. Lashed out, flailing. Hitting and hitting at him on the solid wall of his chest.

'You bastard!'

The invective choked from her, crippling her.

Hands closed about her wrists instantly, in a reflex action.

She struggled against his grip, hopeless and helpless, and the sobs were still storming through her.

'What do you mean, "Why?"' she choked. 'How can you say that? After everything you've done to me, you ask Why—like it's some kind of *mystery*?'

His grip on her wrists tightened, and his crouching stance steadied.

'What I've done to you?' he echoed. Suddenly, frighteningly, the expression in his eyes changed, flashing with dark, killing anger. 'You kept my son from me! Nothing, *nothing* justifies that. You've had *four years* to tell me I have a son. But you never did and you were never going to. I was going to live not knowing about Joey—*never* knowing about him!'

Her face contorted, but not from weeping this time.

'Did you really think I was going to tell you I was carrying your child? After you'd thrown me out of your life like I was yesterday's used tissue? Paying me off like a *whore*!'

His face darkened. 'God almighty, would you have thought better of me if I'd just ended it flat, without even saying thank you to you?'

She yanked her hands free, jerking back with all her effort.

'You didn't have to *thank* me for the sex. Dear God, I knew I was a fool to go anywhere near you, but I didn't think—I didn't think it was going to…going to…going to—'

She choked off. 'Oh, God, what's the use? I know what you are—I've known for four years. And last night I found out all over again. Didn't I? *Didn't I?* You were feeling randy and there was no one else around—so why not take whatever was on hand? Even if it did risk another unplanned pregnancy. You wanted some instant sex, and you took it. And don't throw back at me that I didn't say no. Because I

know what a criminal fool I was last night. What an unforgivable idiot! Just like I was four years ago. A complete fool
to go and fall in lo—'

She broke off, horrified, dismayed, wanting the ground
to swallow her. She stumbled to her feet, staggering away,
her eyes still blind with tears, her throat still tearing, lungs
heaving. Tears were pouring down her cheeks, into her
mouth, her nose was running and her face was hurting.

He caught at her hand, bolting to his feet to seize at her.
She threw him off, heading blindly to the sea. She had to
escape—she *had* to! How could she have said that? Just
blurted it out like that? How could she?

Behind her, Xander stood stock still.

Completely motionless.

Yet inside him, like a very slow explosion, her words
were detonating through him.

What had she just said?

Slowly, like a dead man walking, he followed her.

She was standing, feet in the water, her back to him. Her
shoulders were still heaving, and he could still hear ragged,
tearing sobs, quieter now.

With a more desperate, despairing sound.

He noticed little things about her.

Her pigtail was ragged, frazzling at the end. The sun
glinted on the pale gold of her hair. Her waist was very
narrow—he could almost have spanned it with his hand. Her
legs were tanned.

So many things—so many things he noticed.

He knew her body—knew it from memory, and from this
week he'd spent watching her, letting his desire for her grow
day by day to suit his purpose, his dark, malign purpose.

Last night he had possessed her body, known it intimately. As he had four years ago.

But he hadn't known her.

He hadn't known her at all.

Slowly, very slowly, he spoke.

'What did you just say?'

She started. Had she not heard him approach on the soft sand?

'What did you just say, Clare?' he said again.

Her shoulders hunched. When she spoke, her voice was shaky, raking.

'I said I hated you. I said I loathed you. And if I didn't, I should have. And I'll say it now instead.'

He shook his head. She couldn't see the gesture, but he didn't care. It came automatically to him.

'But that isn't true, is it, Clare? That's not true at all. Not four years ago when you sat at that table in the St John and I told you it was over. You didn't hate me then. It wasn't hate, was it, Clare? Not then.'

His hands curved over her shoulders. He turned her around to him. The sunlight blinded her eyes. Or something did. She stood looking at him. Hollowed out, emptied out.

'I hated you,' she whispered. 'You threw me out of your life. I hated you.'

He shook his head. Sunlight glanced on the sable of his hair. She felt faintness draining through her, her legs too weak to stand. He held her steady by her shoulders. His hands were warm and strong, pressing into her through her T-shirt.

'You didn't, Clare. You didn't hate me then. You didn't hate me at all.'

'Yes, I did. I did and I do!' Her voice was fierce, so fierce.

His thumbs rubbed on her collarbone, slow and strange.

'You gave yourself away, Clare. Just now. Gave yourself away. For the first time. The only time. Gave yourself clean away. And now I know, don't I? I know why you walked away from me never to return, not even for your clothes, your books, your toothbrush—everything you left at my apartment.'

'You should be *grateful* that I did. Grateful.' The fierceness was still in her voice, raw and rasping. 'I must have been the easiest mistress to dump you'd ever had.'

His face stilled. There was something very strange in his eyes. Very strange indeed. She couldn't tell what it was. It must be the sun blinding her. That was all it could be…

For a long, endless moment he was silent. She felt the gentle lap of water round her feet. Felt the hot sun beating down on her. Felt his hands over her shoulders, pressing down on her. They were completely still—like him.

Then, into the silence, he spoke.

'You were the hardest,' he said.

Her eyes flared. 'The hardest?' she jeered bitterly. 'You said "It's over" and I *went*! I went without a question, without a word! I just *went*!'

'You were the hardest,' he said again.

He dropped his hands from her. She felt bereft.

His face was sombre.

'I got rid of you because I had to. To save my sanity. To keep me safe. Because I was scared—in the biggest danger I'd ever been in. And I couldn't hack it.' His jaw tightened. 'When I went to New York that last time I knew I had to act. I knew I could put it off no longer. Because the danger was—terrifying. And I knew when I came back that I had to deal with it. Fast. Urgently. Permanently.'

His eyes rested on her. They had no expression in them. She had seen them look that way before…

'So I did. I dealt with it. Immediately. Ruthlessly. Brutally.'

He paused again. 'And it worked. Worked so perfectly. But as I realised that you had simply…gone…I realised something else as well.'

His eyes were still on her. Expressionless eyes. Except for one faint, impossible fragment…

'I realised,' he said, and each word fell from him like a weight, 'I would have given anything in the world to have you back.'

His eyes moved past her. Out to the sea beyond. A sea without limits. Without a horizon.

'But you were gone. As if I'd pressed a button. Just … gone. I started to look for you, to wait for you. You had to come back—you'd left everything with me. So you *had* to come back. But you never did. You just—vanished.'

'You said I did it to try and make you come after me.' Her voice was still very faint.

He kept looking out to sea, far out to sea. As if into the past.

'I wanted it to be for that reason. I wanted it to be for *any* reason that meant that you didn't *want* to go. That you wanted to come back to me—that you wanted me to come after you.' He breathed in harshly, spoke harshly. 'That you *did* feel something for me. Then—when finally I'd accepted that when I'd said "It's over" to you, you had indeed gone for ever—then…' His eyes went to her, hard, unforgiving. 'I told myself that I had made the right decision after all— that there was no point regretting it, no point wishing I had not done what I had. You'd felt nothing for me. Nothing at all. Which meant I had to move on, get over it. Get on with my life. So that's what I did. I had no choice—you were gone. So I got on with my life.'

She shut her eyes, then opened them again.

'You were angry with me when you saw me again.'

The sombre look was in his eyes again.

'I was angry with you because you'd been able to walk away from me without a second glance. With nothing— nothing at all. I was angry with you because you'd made me live with the choice I'd made. The decision I'd made. To play safe. And by playing safe to lose what I most wanted.'

He took another harsh breath. 'You. That's what I wanted. *You.*'

She looked into his eyes. 'Why?' It was all she said—all she could say.

Something moved in his eyes.

'Why?' His voice changed. *'Why?'* he echoed. 'Because I wanted you there, still. With me. Not to let you go.' He looked at her again. 'It scared me. I'd never wanted that before. Never. Not with any woman. Not even with you until I realised, that last time we had together, before I went to New York, that you had become important to me. And it scared me—scared me senseless—because I had never felt anything like that before, because it made me feel afraid and out of control—and worst, worst of all, it made me realise that I had no idea, *none*, of what you felt.'

He looked at her.

'You never showed your emotions to me, Clare. You were always so reserved. I couldn't read you—I didn't know what you felt, if you felt anything at all. That scared me even more. So I wanted out. Because that was the safest call to make.'

His eyes slipped past her again.

'I was a fool,' he said heavily. 'I made the wrong call. And because of that I lost you. And I lost the son you were carrying. The son you hid from me. And now I know why— I know why you never told me about Joey.'

His gaze shot to her again, holding her like rods of fire. 'I know why, and the knowledge kills me. And it hurts me to think what I did to you last night. Do you know why I did it, Clare—do you?'

His hands had come up again, to lie heavy on her shoulders. 'I deliberately, cold-bloodedly took you to bed last night with one purpose only—to get you pregnant. I *had* to get you pregnant! I had to. Because if you were pregnant again, then this time, *this time*, you would have to marry me. You couldn't turn me down. I'd make sure of it. And that way I'd get Joey—I'd get Joey, and he's all I wanted. When I discovered you'd hidden my son from me, the only reason I could come up with for why you'd done it was to punish me for finishing with you. The reaction of a woman scorned. And it vindicated me. Vindicated what I'd done to you, the call I'd made. A woman who could vengefully hide my son from me wasn't a woman I wanted in my life, wasn't a woman I should…care about. But that wasn't why you hid Joey from me, was it, Clare? *Was it?*'

'No.' It was a whisper. All she could manage.

'It was because I hurt you,' he said. 'I hurt you so badly that night at the St John that all you could do was walk. Run. Hide. For ever. And there was only one reason why I could have hurt you.'

His hands slid from her shoulders, cupping her face, lifting it to his so that she had to look deep, deep into his eyes.

'Why was I able to hurt you, Clare? Hurt you so badly?'

His voice was strained. Desperate. 'Please tell me—please. I don't deserve it—but—'

'I was in love with you,' she said.

For one long, agonising moment there was silence. Then, 'Thank God,' he said. 'Thank God.'

His thumbs smoothed along her cheekbones. Silent tears were running.

'Don't cry, Clare. Don't ever cry for me again. I'll never let you cry again. Not for me. Not ever for me.'

He gazed down into her swimming eyes. 'I'm going to do everything in my power, Clare, to win that love again. Everything. Because, fool that I was—that I am—fool that I have been in everything to do with you—I at least now know this. I had fallen in love with you then, four years ago, and didn't realize—refused to believe I was capable of it And I still love you. I know that completely and absolutely, because last night—' he gave a shuddering breath '—last night was my own punishment. My punishment for having denied what I felt for you—a terrible punishment. Because last night I realised, with all the horror in the world, that I still love you—love a woman who had felt nothing for me, had been able to walk away from me without a word, who had wreaked vindictive revenge on me for having spurned her by keeping my own son from me.

'But it was never, *never* that that stopped you telling me about Joey. It was because you could not bear to have anything to do with the man who had hurt you—because you love me.' His voice changed, and she could hear the pain in it. 'I've wronged you so much, Clare. Four years ago I hurt you unbearably—and I've hurt you again. I can't ask for your love again, but I will win it back—with all my being. Ah, no, don't weep, Clare—not for me, never for me!' His thumbs smoothed again, but her eyes were spilling, spilling uncontrollably, and her face was crumpling, and she couldn't stop, couldn't stop.

He wrapped her to him. And the feel of his arms going about her, holding her so close, so safe, was the most wonderful feeling in all the world, all there could ever be. He held her so tightly, as if he would never, *could* never let her go. She could hear words, murmuring, soothing, and she could not understand them, but it did not matter.

She could hear them in her heart. Know them in her heart.

And it was all she needed. All she would ever need.

Slowly, holding her hand, Xander walked her back towards the villa.

'I didn't know anything about love. Did not know that that was what I had started to feel for you. I only knew that you were a woman I did not want to lose. A woman whose cool composure seemed to inflame me with desire.'

A sensual, reminiscent smile played at his mouth, and Clare felt the so-familiar weakness start inside her.

'It got to me—every time. More and more. I revelled in the difference that only I could make in you, the sensuality beneath the surface that only I could release in you. When we were out together I didn't like you to touch me. I liked you to look untouched—untouchable. Waiting for me. Waiting for me to get you back to the hotel, the apartment, where I could finally indulge myself in doing what I'd been holding back from all evening…'

Clare looked at him. Was that why he had been like that? Not because he'd thought her out of line being physically demonstrative towards him even in the briefest way?

'I didn't know,' she said. Her voice was faint again.

He glanced at her, frowning. 'You must have known—I couldn't keep my hands off you. You must have seen that I was…losing control. And that last time—surely that last time you must have seen, known, sensed that I was…?'

Her throat tightened. Pain, remembered pain, pierced her.

'I did! I thought it meant—meant that you were beginning…that I might mean something to you. But then…' she could hardly speak '…then you came back and took me out to dinner, and I was trying to screw up my courage, to pin my hopes on a future with you and tell you…tell you that I was pregnant.' She swallowed. 'And then you spoke first.'

His hand crushed hers, tightening automatically. He stopped dead.

'*Theos mou*—that it should have hung in the balance on so fine a thread. How the gods mocked me that night. If I had only—only—'

Anguish silenced him. She lifted his hand with hers, bringing it to her mouth and kissing it as she might Joey's, to comfort him.

'We can't undo the past, Xander—neither of us can. We can only—' her voice caught '—only be grateful—so very, very grateful—that we have been given a second chance.' She took a deep, painful breath. 'I know I should have come back to tell you about Joey. I know that. I've known it all these years, and fought it. Fought it for my own selfish reasons. Because I was too much a coward to think of anyone but myself. Because I could not face letting you back into my life after you had thrown me out of it. Could not face being what I knew I must be—the unwanted mother of your son. I told myself I did not need to tell you because you would not want Joey anyway—that you would, out of common decency, pay for him, but you would not want him. And when you found out about him, and you were so angry, I knew—I knew you had a right to be. But I didn't want to admit it—to face up to it!'

She took another unforgiving breath.

'I've been punished for keeping him from you—not just by your anger, but by my shame at keeping him from you, not giving you the chance to say you wanted him, not giving Joey what I knew he could have had. A father. And by more— by the knowledge that if I'd just gone back to you, if I hadn't in my pride, my own pain and anger, kept away from you…'

'It would have been a reward I did not deserve,' Xander said heavily, condemningly. 'Not after my cowardice in not admitting to myself what I had come to feel for you, in denying my own emotions. Not after my cruelty in the way I ended it—so brutally, so unfeelingly. Even if you had not loved me it would still have been brutal. But knowing now what you were feeling as I sat there and said those words to you—' He broke off, pain in his eyes.

Clare's heart filled. 'It's over, Xander. It's gone. Don't torment yourself. Let's start again—a clean slate, a new beginning.' She paused, her eyes lambent suddenly. 'Did you mean it—about last night? That you were trying get me pregnant?'

His face shadowed instantly. '*Theos mou*, Clare—forgive me for that. I should never have—'

'But I don't forgive you,' she said. 'I *thank* you! Oh, Xander, can we have another child? Now?'

Xander caught her and swept her up into his arms. She gave a gasp, and clutched her arms around his neck.

'Joey can have a dozen brothers and sisters. And I, my

most adored one, will take the greatest, most grateful pleasure in fathering each and every one of them.'

His mouth caught hers, warm and soft and so full of love that it was like heaven in her heart. She felt her body quicken, answering with swift eagerness the arousal of his touch as he carried her off, bearing her away, striding swiftly over the grass to reach the terrace, sliding back the bedroom door with a powerful glide of his arm.

Inside, the instant cool of the room embraced them—but it could not quench the heat rising between them, the heat of passion, of desire, as they came down on the bed in a sweet tangle of limbs.

'I love you so much,' he said, gazing down into her eyes. 'I loved you then; I love you now. I will love you for ever. I love everything about you. Everything that is you. *Everything.* Except—' his expression changed suddenly, and there was a disapproving frown on his face '—this.'

He lifted the long frayed end of her pigtail and eyed it with critical disdain.

'This has to go,' he told her. 'No negotiation.'

'It's very practical,' said Clare.

'You don't need practical,' he said. 'You just need me. And I—' his fingers deftly disposed of the restraining band and then started to unplait the strands, '—just need you. And we both—' he flicked free her hair, running his fingers through the pale gold of it '—need Joey, and Joey needs us—and a new brother or sister!'

She pulled his head down to her and kissed him. Then she pushed his head back a little, so she could speak.

'Xander,' she told him, 'Joey has been with Juliette for a good long time now, and soon he's going to have finished hosing down the cars, and anyone else within range, and realise that he hasn't been swimming yet. And that means he's going to want you to take him. And *that* means—' she pulled him down to kiss him again, then let him go to finish speaking '—we had really, *really* better get on with this! Right now.'

'Oh, Kyria Xander Anaketos-to-be…' Xander's voice husked, his eyes agleam with anticipation. 'How very, *very* happy I am to oblige.'

His mouth lowered to hers, and softly, sensuously, with tenderness and desire, passion and pleasure, he began to make love to her.

EPILOGUE

THE sun was setting over the Aegean in a splendour of gold. Enthroned in a huge bath chair on the foredeck, and adorned with a very extravagant hat, Vi surveyed the scene, a satisfied smile on her wrinkled face. But it was not the gold and crimson sky that drew her approbation. It was the sight of Clare and Xander, still in their wedding finery, their arms around each other's waists, gazing out over the sea through which the huge yacht was carving its smooth path.

On her lap sat Joey, resplendent in a tuxedo the miniature version of his father's.

'Tell me a story, Nan,' said Joey.

Vi settled her shoulders into the cushions and reached for the cup of tea that wasn't quite as good as proper English tea, seeing how it had been made by a Greek chef, but was very welcome for all that. It had been a long day for her, but one that had brought a lift to her heart. Young people really could be so foolish, so blind and so stubborn—it took such a lot to make them see sense.

'A story?' she said, and took a mouthful of tea before setting down the cup carefully. Her eyes went to the couple by the rail, who had turned to each other. 'Well, let's see. Once upon a time there was a princess, and a prince fell in love with her, but he was very silly and didn't say so. And the Princess fell in love with him, and *she* was very silly and didn't say so. And so they parted. And the Princess had a baby, but she was even sillier then, and didn't tell the Prince, and so—'

Joey was tugging her sleeve. Vi turned from watching his parents gazing into each other's eyes.

'What is it, pet?' she asked.

There was a disgusted look on his face. 'Nan, tell me a *proper* story. With knights in armour. And dragons. And fast cars.'

He snuggled back against her. Vi took another sip of tea. 'Oh, a *proper* story? Well, let's see…'

She started to weave a story with the elements her charge required.

At the prow of the yacht, Xander was lowering his head to Clare, and she was lifting her face to his. The setting sun turned their kiss to gold, and Vi paused in her tale, wiping a tear from her eye. Yes, the young were foolish, blind, and stubborn—but they got there in the end.

And that was all that mattered.

ADOPTED : ONE BABY

by
Natasha Oakley

Natasha Oakley told everyone at her primary school she wanted to be an author when she grew up. Her plan was to stay at home and have her mum bring her coffee at regular intervals – a drink she didn't like then. The coffee addiction became reality and the love of storytelling stayed with her. A professional actress, Natasha began writing when her fifth child started to sleep through the night. Born in London, she now lives in Bedfordshire with her husband and young family. When not writing, or needed for 'crowd control', she loves to escape to antiques fairs and auctions.

Find out more about Natasha and her books on her website www.natashaoakley.com

Don't miss Natasha Oakley's new novel, *Crowned: An Ordinary Girl*, out in February from Mills & Boon® Romance!

To my Mum

CHAPTER ONE

SITTIFORD was pretty enough, but it wasn't somewhere you'd want to stay for long. At least it wasn't if you harboured any kind of ambition beyond the cultivation of the most perfect petunia.

Lorna Drummond reached for her handbag as her taxi pulled into a lay-by within the hospital car park. So *why* had her sister chosen to come back to Sittiford to have her baby when practically the only thing they'd ever agreed on was the need to leave?

It didn't make any sense. Not unless Vikki had experienced some kind of epiphany. She looked up and caught the driver watching her in his rearview mirror.

He swivelled round in his seat. 'You're the sister of that girl in the accident, aren't you? The one who died?'

'That's right.' Lorna reached for her purse, hiding her face with her blonde hair. 'How much do I owe you?'

'£7.40, love.' He reached out a tattooed hand to take the ten-pound note she offered, then, 'I was sorry to hear about your sister and that.'

'Thank you.' Lorna convulsively reached for the door handle, desperate for escape.

'The baby is doing all right, is she?'

'I haven't seen her yet, but I think so. Thank you. Please keep the change.' She uncurled herself from the car and shut the door firmly, standing back to let the taxi drive away.

Lorna took a deep breath and looked up at the high walls of Sittiford Hospital. Gone was the dour Victorian building she remembered, and in its place was curved brickwork and commissioned sculptures.

And up there, apparently, was her sister's baby. *Vikki's* baby. It was unbelievable. She felt guilty thinking it now…but Vikki with a baby didn't make any sense either. Her life was all about parties, new places, exciting people…

Had been about all those things, Lorna corrected silently. *Vikki was dead.* However many times she said that over to herself, she couldn't quite accept it.

Ever since that late-night phone call she'd felt like a non-swimmer in one of those wave pools. Wave after wave crashing against her. Consequence after consequence. And each one coming so fast that it was difficult to know what she should be reacting to first.

Lorna walked across the sweeping drive towards the entrance to the Rainbow Wing. The doors opened automatically as she approached, and, obedient to the sign, she paused long enough to cleanse her hands with the jelly-like hand-wash.

The heels of her shoes clipped loudly on the hard surface of the floor, and the sterile smell caught at the back of her throat. Vikki must have come back for a reason other than that she was pregnant. She'd hated this town. Hadn't been able to get away quick enough…

Was the reason a man?

Somewhere out there was the father of her sister's baby. Was he here? In Sittiford? And, if so, why hadn't he come forward? Vikki had been irresponsible, and generally feckless in the choices she'd made, but she must have known who the father was.

Surely she'd told someone? Even if the police hadn't been able to find them yet. Lorna came to an abrupt stop at the reception desk and waited while an involved conversation was translated by an elderly woman's son.

It was the strangest feeling to know the baby's father could be anywhere. The man sitting in the corner reading a newspaper. The one she'd just passed in the car park, perhaps? Anywhere. He could be absolutely anywhere.

Was he married? With other children? Was *that* why he'd not come forward yet? And, if he was married, did that mean he'd never come forward?

'Can I help you?'

Her head spun round. 'I'm here to see Baby Drummond. M-My sister—'

'Ah, yes. They're expecting you in Neonatal.' The receptionist's hand was reaching for her receiver before Lorna had time to consider what she was going to say. 'I have Ms Drummond in reception now. I'm sending her up.'

The receptionist's eyes were suspiciously glossy as she looked at her, and it made Lorna's control falter. Too much sympathy was difficult to cope with. 'You need the third floor. There's a lift to—'

'I'll walk. Thank you.' Anything to escape that caressing kindness. Lorna started towards a likely pair of double doors. 'Through here?'

'Yes. Third floor.'

Lorna pulled the door open and started up the staircase. At the large black number three she stopped to read the sign that stated Neonatal was to the left. She pushed through the fire door and walked onto a utilitarian landing.

One large window looked out on an ugly arrangement of cylindrical storage containers connected by pipes— who knew what for? Lorna stood for a moment, bracing herself for what was to come next, and emotion flooded through her.

It was all so sudden and unexpected. One moment she was living the life she'd chosen, happily immersed in academia, the next she was on a plane back to Heathrow and dealing with the death of a sister she hadn't seen in almost nine years—and seemingly expected to deal with the baby she'd left behind.

It was all so ridiculous.

What did she know about babies? Or even family for that matter? She'd spent a decade avoiding both. Lorna placed a hand on her flat stomach as though it would stop the churning inside. She was scared. She didn't *do* babies. Didn't know one end from the other.

'Not the best view,' a male voice said behind her. Sexy, deep…

Startled, Lorna whipped round in time to see the lift doors close and a man walk towards her. Tall. Scruffy… In a kind of actor-promoting-a-film style.

'Are you going in?' he asked, indicating the buzzer with a tilt of his head.

Lorna's eyes skimmed his denim-clad thighs, took in the worn leather jacket and continued on up to the too-long hair. A confident and all together too sure of himself type of male—with an incongruous pink teddy bear tucked non-chalantly under his arm.

No sooner had she thought it odd that a man like him would be carrying a soft toy than she remembered that this was outside Neonatal and he must have a baby in there…

She bit her lip. He might even be quite worried by that. He didn't look traumatised, but he might be.

And at least he was here. Showing support. Doing the best he could. Shame if his best was a pink bear. 'Yes. Yes, I am.'

'Only you need to push the buzzer or they won't know you're here.'

She raised her eyebrows. 'I was just about to buzz.' Did she really look so stupid that he thought she couldn't work that out for herself?

He was exactly Vikki's type of man. The thought slipped into her mind. Her sister had always seemed to go for the kind of man who, personally, made her feel as if her blouse was buttoned up a little too high and her make-up just that little bit too perfect.

He strode forward and pushed the red button, and Lorna had ample opportunity to see that his denim jeans clung equally tightly to his firm buttocks. There was an arrogant confidence in every line of his body. Sexual simply because of the way he moved.

She hated that. It made her feel so uncomfortable. Some memory jagged, like cobwebs on nails. *She'd seen him before.* Or someone like him?

Had she seen him in one of Vikki's photographs?

'It doesn't usually take this long to get an answer,' he said, peering through the strengthened glass aperture.

'I—I wouldn't know.'

He glanced over his shoulder and then back, as a young and harried-looking student midwife pulled the door open.

'Sister's not finished her shift yet.'

'No worries. Can you tell her I'll wait in the Bistro. Oh, and I've brought this up for Baby Drummond—'

'Why?' The question shot from Lorna like a bullet from a gun, scarcely allowing time for her to register that the younger woman had clearly recognised him.

'Sorry?'

'W-why have you brought that for my niece?' she asked, pointing at the teddy bear.

'Niece?' He turned and really studied her. He'd not done that before, and it made her feel flustered. 'That must make you Lorna Drummond. I'd never have recognised you.'

Lorna pulled a distracted hand through her blonde hair. 'Have we met?'

He held out his hand. 'Raphael McKinnion. Ellie's brother.'

Raphael McKinnion. Rafe McKinnion.

She allowed him to take her hand, feeling as though her stomach had been invaded by several hundred butterflies.

Ellie's elder brother. At fourteen she'd have thought she'd died and gone to heaven if her best friend's brother had so much as spoken to her. Now he was shaking her hand.

And still holding a pink teddy bear intended for her niece. *Was Raphael McKinnion the reason Vikki had come back to Sittiford?*

Her sister wouldn't have been intimidated by a man like Rafe McKinnion. If she'd wanted him she'd have crooked her little finger and he'd have come running. All men had. Always. Like moths around a candle.

Whereas she…found them threatening. Just about as threatening as they usually found her. Lorna swallowed the hard lump in her throat. 'And the bear?'

'Oh, that. I'm afraid you're going to find he's just the tip of the iceberg. The hospital has been inundated with soft toys,' he responded, with a swift smile at the student midwife—who melted in a pool of hormones.

Lorna felt a flicker of irritation. Nothing had changed in Rafe's life then.

'Why?' Her voice sounded unnecessarily clipped.

'Your sister's accident has been in all the local papers. It's touched a nerve, and people have responded in their hundreds.'

But not, apparently, the baby's father. Lorna felt as if a big black cloak was being wrapped tightly around her. It was trapping her, stifling her…

And there was no escape.

Everyone expected her to take this baby. But *how*? She'd never even held a baby. Not once. She couldn't do it. It just wasn't in her. A feeling of nausea surged through her.

'I'm sorry about Vikki,' he said, watching her. 'We all are.'

'Th-thank you. I…' She reached a hand up to hold her head as the walls started to close in on her. She felt so hot. Hot, and a little confused. Colours started to blur and the walls disappeared into blackness.

And then nothing…

'She's fainted.'

Lorna heard the words as though they were being spoken down a long dark tunnel.

'Rafe, fetch a chair from my office and bring it out here, will you? Let's get her sitting down and off the floor. She's going to ruin her skirt down there, and it looks like it cost a fortune.'

It didn't seem worth speaking. Lorna's head was thumping and her eyelids felt unbelievably heavy.

'Lorna? Lorna? Can you hear me?' The female voice was quite authoritative, so she opened her eyes. 'You're going to be fine. You've just fainted.' Then, seconds later, 'Bring the chair over here.'

Which didn't appear to be directed at her, so Lorna let her eyes shut again.

'Lorna?' A hand moved under her arm. 'Come on, now, let's get you up on a seat. That's it. Now, put your head between your knees.'

Strange, embarrassing, but after a moment or two the world began to steady. She was aware of small rhythmic movements across her back, and a quiet-voiced conversation happening way above her.

'I'm sorry. Really, I…' she began as she struggled to sit up.

'Take it steady,' said the voice that had been directing it all. Then the woman who owned it knelt down in front of her and smiled. 'Feeling better?'

Familiar features swam in front of her face. 'Ellie! I'm so glad to see you.' *Thank God it was Ellie.* If she'd ever needed a friendly face this was the time. In all the trauma it hadn't even occurred to her to hope her old schoolfriend might be on duty.

Ellie would know how unfair it was to expect her to take on responsibility for Vikki's baby.

'How are you feeling now?'

Terrible. 'Fine. Better,' she conceded, putting a hand up to steady her head. 'In a minute. I'll be fine in a minute.'

'There's no hurry. Take your time.'

Lorna leant forward and rested her pulsating head on her hands. *She'd never fainted in her entire life.* Slowly she sat back up. 'I'm sorry.'

'Don't be daft.' Ellie broke off from her conversation and knelt down to Lorna's level. 'I ought to call someone, but—'

'No! Please don't. I should have stopped for something to eat. That's all this is.'

Ellie bit her lip. 'Let's see how you are in a little while. After we've got a cup of tea inside you. Rafe?' She turned her head to look up at her brother. 'Can you help support Lorna? She might be a bit unsteady. I'll manage the chair.'

The hand under her elbow felt strong. Lorna took a shaky breath and then responded. The room swam a little, and she reached out to clutch at the nearest support. Soft leather was beneath her fingers, and she looked up into Rafe McKinnion's strong face. 'My bag…'

'I have it,' said a new voice from behind her…it was too difficult to work out who it belonged to.

All she wanted to do was lie down somewhere very comfortable. Somewhere dark and quiet. Somewhere Rafe McKinnion wouldn't be around to see what a fool she was making of herself.

'Tea, please, nurse,' Ellie said, putting the chair down and coaxing Lorna into it. 'As soon as you have a moment.

'I'm so sorry. I've never fainted before. I'm—'

'—having the worst day of your life,' Rafe finished for her. Lorna looked across at him and his mouth twisted. 'Don't apologise for anything. This must be very difficult for you. How are you feeling now?'

She let her hands fall back into her lap. 'It wasn't that.

I'm…' She trailed off. *Having the worst day of her life* was exactly right. In fact, she was slap-bang in the middle of the worst *week* of her life.

'Tea.' Ellie came back into her vision and handed her a cup and saucer. 'I've also asked for some toast and butter.'

Lorna smiled, though she wasn't sure how she was going to manage to eat anything. Everything had tasted like cardboard since she'd heard the news.

Strange how funny little things she'd thought she'd forgotten long ago were coming back to her. Like the genuinely good times she'd shared with her sister when they were very young…

'It should help, even if you don't feel like eating it,' Ellie said, reading her mind as she moved to sit behind her desk. 'Do you remember my brother, Raphael? Rafe, this is Lorna Drummond.'

'We introduced ourselves out on the landing,' Rafe said, moving forward suddenly as her cup tipped. 'Careful.'

She felt so woozy, but the tea was warm. Sweet. She looked up and caught the edge of Rafe's smile. He must think she was a complete no-hoper. But then he'd probably always thought that about her. Assuming he'd ever thought about her at all. Which he almost certainly hadn't.

The boffin and the sex god. There was a joke in there somewhere. Oh hell.

Lorna took another sip of tea and concentrated on bringing it down in the centre of her saucer. It was easier to do that than risk seeing what Ellie's elder brother thought of her now.

There was a brief knock at the door, followed by, 'Sister, can you take a look at Baby Benjamin? His BP is a little low…'

'I'm afraid you'll have to excuse me for a minute,' Ellie said standing. 'Just sit quietly and drink your tea. This'll probably not take more than a moment.'

The door shut behind her and there was silence.

Rafe shrugged his way out of his jacket and threw it across the back of the chair. 'It's hot in here.' Then, 'Have you only just flown in?'

'Yes.' She bristled against the implied criticism. No doubt he'd have been able to clear his desk in minutes, but she had responsibilities. Things she'd needed to do first. 'Almost.' She'd *almost* just flown in. She took another sip of tea, letting the warmth slide down her throat, and tried again. 'I've already been to the police station.'

Lorna rubbed her fingers against her left temple. She felt so tired. *So* buffeted.

'Have they given you all the details? About the accident?'

'Well, they told me they found her car in a ditch.' Precious few details, it seemed to her. They'd been more interested in asking questions.

Questions she hadn't been able to answer. She'd absolutely no idea whether her sister was usually considered a safe driver. She didn't know why Vikki might have been in Sittiford. And she couldn't even begin to speculate on whether her accident might possibly not have been an accident at all.

Guilt ripped through her, and the pain in her left temple intensified. Sisters *should* know things about one another. She should have tried harder to find some common ground between them. Fought harder to stay in real contact.

Rafe moved to perch on the table in front of her. 'If it's any consolation, I doubt she'd have known much about it. Ellie said she never regained consciousness.'

'The police said that too.' Lorna sipped her tea, struggling to swallow past the hard lump in her throat. 'They hoped I'd know who they should contact about the baby.'

'Don't you?'

She shook her head. 'I didn't even know she was pregnant.'

Rafe didn't react. 'So what happens now?' he asked quietly.

The million-dollar question. What *would* happen now? 'They seem to want me to take responsibility for the baby. Since I'm the only relative to have come forward so far.'

'You want that too, don't you?'

Lorna's hand shook as she picked up the teacup. 'No. No, I don't.' Deep inside her she felt a scream building. A mixture of panic, anger and pure fear. 'Why the...*hell* does everyone think I would?'

CHAPTER TWO

RAFE'S eyes narrowed, but other than that he schooled his features not to react. It was, after all, none of his business.

Even so, he couldn't help but have an opinion on a statement like that. It was repulsive.

And it was going to shock anyone who heard it. The general assumption was that she'd *want* to take on the care of her sister's baby. Even Ellie thought it…and she knew Lorna better than most.

But clearly not well enough.

The uptight blonde seemed to have no intention of doing anything that might conflict with the way she'd arranged her life. He might have some sympathy for her not wanting the responsibility of a child—he'd avoided it himself—but he couldn't like it.

Selfishness was unattractive. Always. And with a motherless baby girl needing someone to love and nurture her he thought it inexcusable. Family was everything. And anything else was always going to be a poor alternative.

'I don't know anything about babies.' She brushed a hand across her face, clearly defensive. 'I don't like them. And they don't like me.'

Rafe said nothing. What was there to say? He didn't know a great deal about babies himself. Time bombs waiting to explode, he thought them. But…

This was an exceptional situation. Under these circumstances, surely one would simply get on with it?

He looked at her curiously. Lorna had to be colder than ice to seriously contemplate putting her sister's daughter in foster care. Because that was what her refusal would mean. Did she realise that?

'I'm sorry,' Ellie said, returning and shutting the door. 'Everything's fine with Baby Benjamin. How are you feeling?'

'B-better. Much better.'

Lorna didn't look in Rafe's direction again. No doubt ashamed. And with reason.

'Good.'

Rafe took in his sister's warm smile, and the real concern in her face as she looked at her friend—he didn't understand it. Normally she valued kindness over and above any other virtue. If Lorna were that cold, why did Ellie like her so much? And she did. Lorna Drummond was one of the few people Ellie had conscientiously kept in touch with over the years.

He looked at the nervous twitch of Lorna's hands, the tight hold of her mouth. She was tighter than a bowstring. Beyond grief, he thought. *Frightened.*

'Why don't you slip your cardigan off?' Ellie suggested, sitting down and pulling a pile of papers towards her. 'It's kept very warm in here for the babies. Then…we'd better get the business side of this out of the way, so I can introduce you to your niece.'

Rafe stood up and held out his hand for Lorna's empty

teacup. She passed it over with the merest flick of a look in his direction.

'I'll wait downstairs in the Bistro for you,' he said, with a glance at his sister as he set the cup and saucer on the table. 'There's no hurry.'

He turned in time to see Lorna pull at the oyster-pink ribbon holding her cardigan together. Like her skirt, the cardigan shrieked money. Whatever else Ms Drummond was, she wasn't financially challenged. No reason there for her to refuse to care for her sister's baby.

Ellie was going to be disappointed. And he hated to see her rose-tinted view of humanity challenged.

'Thanks, Rafe.' His sister smiled, first at him and then at the woman opposite. 'My car is at the garage, and since Rafe has nothing to do…'

'But serve you,' he agreed smoothly, picking up his jacket.

Perhaps he was being too hasty in judging Lorna? She'd only said she didn't *want* to take on responsibility for her sister's baby, not that she wouldn't.

There was no doubt it would be a steep learning curve for her. Not that he imagined for one second much of the actual care would be done by her. Not exactly the 'yummy mummy' type, Ms Drummond.

'I'll see you later.' He nodded at Lorna. 'It was a pleasure to meet you. Again.'

The door clicked shut.

Ellie smiled. 'Rafe's been very good to me since Steve left. And it's so nice to have him near again rather than travelling all over. He's just bought a place on the outskirts of Framley…'

Lorna couldn't think what there was on the outskirts of

Framley, baring Priory Manor, but she wasn't particularly interested in where he'd bought a house. She was just glad he'd left and taken his disturbing presence with him.

Rafe McKinnion seemed to have the ability to fill a room simply by being in it. And it made her uncomfortable. He'd always made her feel uncomfortable. Right back when he'd been the boy every girl had secretly hoped would take them behind the bike sheds. A little bit bad…and a whole lot fascinating.

'I'm so sorry about Vikki. I know you two weren't close, but…' Ellie trailed off and reached for a brown file among the pile of papers on her desk. 'Had you spoken to her recently?'

Lorna shook her head. 'I sent her an e-mail last Christmas and she replied to it.' Lorna rubbed a hand up her arm. 'She must have been pregnant then, but she didn't tell me.'

'So you've no idea who the father might be?'

'I'd long since stopped asking if she was seeing anyone.' It had been too difficult. Vikki's life had been so different from anything she would ever want for herself. 'I should have tried harder. I could have helped her, perhaps.'

'You weren't to know she was expecting a baby. Not if she didn't tell you.'

But she *should* have known. Wasn't that the point? They'd been *sisters*. Sisters should share things, care about each other…

It was all too late now. Vikki was gone…and she felt numb about it. *Why hadn't she cried?* There must be something lacking in her that she couldn't cry for her own sister.

'I don't know how I feel.' The words were wrenched out of her. 'I haven't cried. Not once.'

Ellie reached out and touched her hand. 'Early days, hon.

There's no right or wrong way to feel, and there's no use pretending you feel something if you don't. Vikki was a difficult person to be close to.'

Lorna drew in a shaky breath. Glad beyond description that it was Ellie sitting the other side of the desk. Glad for the gentle touch on her hand and the understanding that shone from her eyes.

She sniffed—and she never sniffed. She looked round for her handbag, to find the small packet of tissues she always kept in the front zipped pocket. 'What do I have to do here?'

'Primarily, meet your niece. And I need some contact details from you…'

Lorna nodded. She felt so tired. Normally she was the type of woman who got things done, took control of situations, but here, now, she felt as if she was clawing through fog.

'Where are you staying?'

'Mum's old house. Vikki lives—lived—there.' She put her bag down on the floor. 'I dropped my things off there before talking to the police.'

Ellie wrote down the address. 'How much have the police been able to tell you about the accident?'

'They don't seem to know much about it yet. No other cars seem to have been involved. Vikki had no alcohol in her system.' Lorna put a hand up to her temple and tried to remember exactly what she had been told. 'They said one of the paramedics noticed Vikki was having contractions…'

Lorna felt her throat tighten. She couldn't bear to think of Vikki trapped in the wreckage. It was too difficult, too graphic.

'Vikki had an amniotic embolism,' Ellie began, after a moment. Her voice had become matter-of-fact, exactly what

Lorna needed. Facts appealed to the scientific part of her brain. She could deal with facts. Respond appropriately.

'It's rare—usually fatal for both mother and baby.'

'Wh-what is it, exactly?'

'It's where—' There was a hesitant knock at the door, and Ellie stopped. 'Yes?' It opened, and the student midwife entered carrying a plate of buttery toast. 'Ah, thank you. You'll probably feel much better when you've eaten something.'

Lorna smiled her thanks, even though she'd given up adding fat to her food more than three years ago. Future cholesterol issues seemed very insignificant right now.

The door shut and Ellie continued. 'An amniotic embolism is where the amniotic fluid is forced into the mother's bloodstream. As I've said, it's incredibly rare, and usually fatal for both mother and baby.'

But not this time. This time the baby had survived. Lorna picked up a triangle of toast and took a bite.

'Your niece is a little miracle. Baby Drummond, as we've been calling her, was born by emergency Caesarean section at 5:06 a.m. on the 26th. We've estimated her to be at about thirty-four weeks' gestation, but Vikki didn't seem to have had any antenatal care anywhere.' Ellie looked down at her notes. 'Baby scored three in the Apgar test—'

Lorna didn't even try and understand what that meant. Three out of what? Five? Ten? She could tell from her friend's expression that it wasn't good.

'But she's now holding her own beautifully, and I imagine she'll be discharged towards the end of the week. Maybe sooner. She really is doing that well.' Ellie looked up. 'Lorna?'

Lorna looked up too, with a start. 'I'm sorry. I was trying to work out if I knew where Vikki might have been thirty-four weeks ago.' She shook her head. 'I've got no idea. No use, am I?'

'Concentrate on what you can do.' Ellie smiled gently. 'I think you need to see baby. She's beautiful. You're going to love her.'

From a distance. That was all she was capable of. She was all cared out. Surely Ellie knew that?

'She's a really good birth weight for a prem baby. Her biggest difficulty has been that she suffered severe birth asphyxia.'

Lorna tried to concentrate on what Ellie was saying, but it was desperately difficult. She obediently washed her hands once more, and walked towards the small ward of maybe six incubators. Or were they called cots? Plastic cots.

And only two were filled. 'This is Benjamin. He weighed two pounds fourteen ounces at birth, and is a real fighter. And this,' she said moving along one, 'is your niece.'

Lorna looked down at Vikki's baby.

It was *unbelievable.* Her sister's baby. Tiny. Hands so perfect. Skin almost translucent.

'She wouldn't be in Neonatal now if Vikki was here to look after her. She really has done tremendously well.'

'Does she have to have the tube up her nose?' Lorna asked, feeling…overwhelmed. By everything.

'It's a nasogastric tube. A feeding tube. If there are no complications I expect it'll be removed in the next twenty-four hours. She's taking all her feeds by hand now.'

A sharp pain ripped through Lorna's head once more.

Vikki's baby. There were photographs of Vikki with the same mop of dark hair. A small bundle of potential.

'Do you know what Vikki wanted to call her?'

Lorna shook her head. She'd no idea. None. How awful was that? They'd never once discussed what they might call their children. Never talked about favourite names.

She couldn't even do that for Vikki. She felt tears prickle behind her eyes.

'No? Well, that was a silly question, really, if you didn't know she was pregnant. But she needs a name, all the same.' Ellie looked up from the sleeping baby. 'What are you going to call her?'

'Me?'

'She can't be Baby Drummond for ever.'

Lorna's hand moved to rest against her stomach. *A name?* Vikki would probably have chosen something slightly alternative. Maybe Delilah…or Lola? Or…?

Her mind was a complete blank. She might not be the earth mother figure everyone was hoping for, but she wanted to get this right. A name stayed with you for life.

'Choose something you like.'

'Katherine.' Her voice was husky. She'd no idea where that name had come from. Pulled from somewhere deep within her. 'I'll call her Katherine,' she said, more firmly.

'Nice.' Ellie reached for a pen and wrote 'Katherine' on the notes hanging off the end of the bed, then leant over the cot. 'Hello, Katherine. Your auntie is here, and you'll soon be going home.'

'She can't go home with me.' Lorna's voice rang out, overloud. She hadn't meant it to sound like that.

Ellie unbent and looked at her.

'I—I want to make everything lovely for her. I do. But she can't live with me.'

'Lorna—'

'I don't know anything about babies.' Her voice rose in a mixture of panic and desperation. 'I've never even held one, and—'

'There's nothing that needs to be decided this moment,' Ellie cut her off. 'Don't rush it. I'll put you in touch with all the interested parties. Decisions can come later. Much later. You've got a lot to adjust to.'

But Lorna knew better. You couldn't grow up with someone, share their secrets, and not know that if their situations had been reversed Ellie wouldn't have hesitated. Katherine would have had a home, been loved.

'There are lots of options for Katherine's future. You'll need to think carefully about them all. It's important we get it right. She's already lost her mum. That's a tough start for anyone.'

Lorna glanced back at Katherine. She was sleeping. Her right hand was curled into a fist and resting against her cheek. 'What will happen to her?'

'If she doesn't have a relative to take care of her, you mean?'

Lorna nodded.

'Most probably she'll be fostered while everyone makes every effort to find one.'

And if there aren't any? Lorna didn't need to ask the question out loud.

'Eventually she'll be put up for adoption. But not until everyone is certain her father isn't going to step forward and claim her. There's plenty of time.'

It was what she'd thought she wanted. All the way over on the plane. But it felt different when you were faced with a person not an 'it'. Lorna brushed her hair back off her face, feeling the heat and the stress. Pain thumped through her temples. If she could just sleep. She was sure everything would be clearer then.

'Did you come in by taxi?' Ellie asked, watching her.

'Yes.'

'Then Rafe and I will take you home.'

Home. It had never really felt like a home. Not like Ellie's. Ellie's and Rafe's. Their home had been full of comfy sofas, real coffee and walls of books. A wonderful, magical, warm place.

Their mother hadn't screamed for constant attention or taken a cocktail of pills to keep her alive. And, unlike Lorna's mum, she hadn't relied on either of her children to run the house for her.

'You don't need to—'

'We practically pass your front door.'

'Will Rafe mind?'

Ellie laughed. 'Why should he? I'll take that as a yes, then.'

CHAPTER THREE

RAFE looked up as Lorna Drummond walked into the Bistro. She stopped in the doorway and appeared to be scanning the tables, looking for someone.

He didn't like her much, but she was a stunning-looking woman. Ice-blonde hair cut in a tousled just-got-out-of bed style. Pencil-thin and expensively chic. High, high heels at the end of legs that seemed to stretch on and up for ever. He loved a good pair of legs.

Rafe sat back in his chair and admired the view. Who'd have thought Lorna Drummond would evolve into anything so glamorous? There'd been no suspicion of it a decade ago. Of the two sisters, Vikki had been the eye candy. A little too predatory for his taste, but undeniably a looker.

Lorna weaved her way through the melamine tables and queued at the self-service counter. He pulled his gaze away from the way the fabric of her cream skirt pulled tight across a neat bottom. Perhaps she'd had more in common with her flighty younger sister than anyone had imagined?

He sipped his black coffee and filled in the word 'Botticelli' for three down in his cryptic crossword. A shadow fell across his table.

Rafe looked up as Lorna sat down in the opposite chair. She put her coffee in front of her. 'Ellie asked me to find you here. I'm afraid you're taking me back to Little Mellingham. She'll be down in ten minutes.'

He folded his newspaper in half once more.

Lorna twisted the cup round so that she could pick up the handle. 'I meant to take a taxi, but…' She looked up, and he watched a red stain work across her cheek. 'Having fainted, Ellie won't hear of it.'

'Probably wise,' Rafe said easily, and stretched out his legs beneath the table.

She'd blushed. He'd have laid money on there not being a woman over sixteen who still did that. His attention was caught.

Vikki, certainly, had lost the ability to blush around the age of eleven. He couldn't make Lorna out at all. What kind of woman was she? Her words suggested one thing. Her blush something completely different.

Lorna picked up her coffee cup and took a sip. He watched as her face crumpled at the bitter taste. 'That's disgusting.'

'Like tar,' he agreed. 'It requires a strong constitution.'

She returned it to the table and splayed her hands out on the melamine tabletop. Nice hands. Long fingers with carefully manicured nails. He liked women with beautiful hands.

He rather liked the way her hair curled about her face, too. It emphasised her almond-shaped eyes. Deep, deep brown, with flecks of topaz.

Rafe pulled the newspaper onto his lap and picked up his mug, swigging down the last of his coffee. 'Have you seen the baby now?'

'Yes.' Her hands moved across the tabletop once more. 'I've called her Katherine. She needed a name.'

Lorna had a nice voice too. The faintest hint of an American twang laid over the top of a Home Counties accent. But it was the husky edge to it that made it so sexy.

If the circumstances had been different he might have been very interested in this new incarnation of Lorna Drummond.

Particularly because he remembered the old Lorna. She'd been the girl who was too bright to fit in easily with her peers, and she'd not been helped by a pair of unattractive glasses and some very unfashionable clothes. Mainly he remembered her as a blushing appendage to his more vivacious sister. Until today she probably hadn't managed more than three words in his company.

'Sorry. Really sorry.' Ellie arrived, clutching her handbag and a large plastic supermarket bag.

Rafe stood up, picking up his newspaper. And then he noticed Lorna hadn't drunk her coffee. 'Do you want to finish your drink?'

She shook her head and bent down to pick up her handbag.

'I stopped to ring the garage about my car—'

'"Car" being a loose term for what Ellie drives,' Rafe slid in, noticing the overly tight grip Lorna had on her handbag.

His sister glanced up at him and laughed. 'You might be right. It's going to be a six-hundred-pound bill. I said I'd let them know in the morning.'

'Not worth it. You should scrap it. Get something else.' Rafe took the shopping bag from her and led the way out across the car park. 'I'll help you if it's a problem. I'd rather see you in something safe.'

As soon as the words left his mouth he wished he hadn't

spoken. The safety of cars wasn't exactly the most tactful of conversation topics, and he'd been insensitive enough earlier. He wouldn't forget how awful he'd felt when Lorna had crumpled at his feet.

He glanced across at her. To a casual observer she looked as if she had everything together. It was only the vacant look in her brown eyes and that tight grip on her handbag that gave her away.

Maybe Ellie was right about her. She'd been certain Lorna would come back to the UK when she heard about the accident—and she had. She was equally certain her friend wouldn't walk away from her niece. Perhaps she wouldn't. And if she planned on staying around Sittiford that might be interesting.

'I'll get in the back,' Ellie said, as they approached his sleek vintage Jaguar.

Lorna slid into the seat next to him, and he couldn't help but notice the way her tight cream skirt rose up. She really did have the most amazing legs. Long and lean. Tempting to slide his hand up the creamy skin, feel the softness of her inner thigh…

Rafe set his key in the ignition and turned it. *What was the matter with him?* He must have been single too long, because his thoughts were entirely inappropriate.

Even so, he watched as she adjusted her skirt. Caught a waft of her light perfume as she bent forward to put her bag down by her feet. She probably had beautiful feet. Slender, like her hands. Hands and feet usually went together, in his experience.

'You know where we're going?' Ellie cut in to his X-rated thoughts.

'Little Mellingham,' he answered smoothly.

The village was barely three miles outside Sittiford. A small ribbon of a place. A mix of old and rather beautiful houses and bland council housing. He glanced over at his silent companion. Her face was mask-like, telling him nothing. But the hands in her lap were tense, and still clutched tightly together. She was barely coping.

'You'll need to tell me where to stop.'

Lorna looked over at him. Scared brown eyes. 'On the main road will be fine.'

'No.' Ellie leant forward in the back seat. 'I want to see you safely inside. I still think you should have come back to mine, really. For tonight anyway.'

'I'll be fine. You know I always manage.' Lorna looked over her shoulder. 'I might as well start clearing the house.' Then, 'It's the second on the left.'

Rafe swung the car round the left hand bend, towards a small close of council housing.

'It's number twenty-three. Just by the red van.'

Somehow this wasn't the kind of house he'd expected Lorna to have come from. Not this. She looked like a fully paid up member of the 'born with a silver spoon' club. Vikki, too, from the little he knew about her, had liked the high life. Interesting.

He pulled the car up outside the mid-terrace, pebble-dashed ex-council house. The door had been changed for one of those white double-glazed units, and a cheerful hanging basket hung outside.

'Thank you.' Lorna turned in her seat. 'Both of you. I'll speak to you tomorrow,' she said to Ellie.

'I'll speak to you tonight. Keep your mobile turned on.'

She nodded.

Rafe released his seat belt and went to get out of the car.
'I'm fine. Please.' Lorna stopped him. 'I'm fine.'

He climbed out anyway, and walked round to her door.
Lorna was already out, key in hand. Rafe glanced back into
the car at his sister. Her shake of the head was almost im-
perceptible, but it was enough to keep him still.

'Thank you. For the lift…' She half lifted her hand, and
then turned towards the house.

'No, I don't get it,' Rafe said, leaning against the worktop
in Ellie's kitchen.

Ellie handed him two pizzas to put away. 'In the freezer.'

Rafe obediently opened the freezer and searched for an
empty enough drawer to put them in. 'Explain to me again
how you two are friends.'

'Fridge,' she said, passing him six yoghurts. 'We met at
school. Don't you remember?'

'Yes,' he said, pulling out a barstool. 'But she's not like
your usual friends. And why aren't you more angry she isn't
keen to take on Vikki's baby? That's not like you.'

Ellie smiled. She rolled up the plastic carrier and stuffed
it into the holder on the back of a cupboard door. 'There are
things you have to know about Lorna.'

He waited.

'For example, do you remember when we first moved
here?' Ellie leant over to pick up the kettle and walked over
to the sink to fill it. 'You were fine. Girls salivating all
around you.'

Rafe smiled. He wouldn't quite have described it like
that, but overall, yes, he agreed his arrival in Little
Mellingham had been unstressful.

'It wasn't like that for me. I had a tough time those first few weeks.'

'I didn't know that.'

'Nothing too dreadful. Name-calling. That kind of thing.'

Rafe leant forward and picked a couple of brightly coloured mugs from the mug tree on the counter. He was listening.

'Lorna saw what was happening, and she came and sat by me one lunchtime. She said she could call for me, if I liked, and we could walk to school together.' Ellie set the kettle on to boil. 'And she did. Every day for something like seven years. She's got a good heart. If she makes a commitment she sticks to it.'

And baby Katherine? Did her good heart extend to her little niece?

As though she'd read his mind, Ellie said, 'Wait and see about the baby. When it comes to it I really don't think Lorna will walk away.'

'And if she does?'

'Then she's changed.' Ellie took milk out of the fridge and put a slurp in each mug. 'I wonder if she's got anything in the house to eat. I didn't think to ask her. Oh, *stuff.*'

Interesting that his outwardly confident sister had needed the more reserved Lorna Drummond. He pulled a hand through his hair and watched as his sister ferreted out a piece of paper from her handbag and walked over to the telephone on the kitchen worktop.

The kitchen door banged. 'Mum, I can't do my homework.'

Ellie held up her hand to silence her son. 'It's not ringing.' Then she sighed and returned the handset to its cradle. 'She's switched it off.'

'Is that a problem?'

His sister bit her lip. 'Rafe…?'

He knew what was coming next. 'Yes, I will. On my way home.' And it really didn't have anything to do with those incredible legs.

'Just check she's all right. You could take her some milk. Say I forgot to tell her the corner shop closed a couple of years back.'

'Mum…'

'In a minute.' Ellie shooed her son out of the kitchen. 'I'll have my cup of tea and then I'll come through.'

Rafe smiled. This whole set-up was his idea of hell. Never a moment to herself—but Ellie seemed to thrive on it. She reboiled the kettle and poured boiling water into the teapot.

'Lorna might not answer the door,' he said, thinking of how tired she'd looked. 'She looked ready to fall asleep to me.'

Ellie pulled open the drawer beside her. 'Don't use it unless you have to…but I've got a key.'

'How—?'

'Vikki.' She smiled sadly. 'I met her in Sittiford shopping centre shortly after she came back. I went round a few times, helped her get some things together for the baby.'

'Does Lorna know?'

'Not unless Vikki told her.'

Which meant no. Rafe wasn't sure what he thought about that. He slipped the key into his back pocket. 'I won't use it unless I think she's in trouble. And, if you take my advice, you'll tell her you've got it and offer to give it back.'

'I will.'

'No, really. I don't know Lorna anything like as well as you do, but I'd say she's a private person.'

'That's why I'm sending you rather than getting a baby-sitter and going myself. Lorna prefers to manage.' She set the milk on the counter. 'But this is just being friendly.'

Friendly. He thought about that as he stood on the doorstep, key burning in his pocket. He didn't feel particularly friendly towards her. Didn't know what he thought, really. His finger pressed against the doorbell.

Absolutely nothing.

Where was the woman?

Rafe stepped back and peered in at the window. Thick nets covered the glass, so he couldn't see through. And, being mid-terrace, there wasn't any way round to the back either.

And yet he felt certain she hadn't gone to bed. He lifted the letterbox and called out. 'Lorna? It's Rafe McKinnion. Ellie asked me to bring you some milk.' And then, feeling foolish, he pulled the key out of his back pocket.

If he was wrong, and she'd simply fallen into bed exhausted, he could quietly let himself out again. Maybe leave the milk in the fridge with a note…

The key turned easily. 'Lorna?'

The hallway was dark and narrow. He glanced up the stairs and saw that the hall curtains had been closed. Perhaps she *had* just gone to bed early? She'd looked tired enough.

'Lorna.'

He pushed open the door at the end of the hallway and walked into a small kitchen. The units were old, and well past their use-by date, and a bright, garish roller blind hung at the window, but it was all scrupulously clean.

Rafe opened the fridge door and put the milk inside.

There wasn't a lot in there. A little bit of cheese. A couple of jars of jam. He turned his head and located the bin beside the door—overflowing with jars and packets. The tangible results of a thorough clean-out. *Lorna? Or Vikki?*

'Lorna…?' He pushed the door to his left and walked through into a lounge/diner. Dark brown swirly carpet paired with heavy green velvet curtains.

And there in the corner was Lorna. Her face was buried in a cushion and he could hear her dry sobs. An empty bottle of sherry sat on the table.

'Lorna.' He walked forward and hunched down in front of her. 'Hey.' His fingers smoothed back her hair from her face and she looked up. Eyes shining, face flushed. She didn't even ask him how he'd got inside. Her hands snaked out to hold him, and he did just that. Wrapping his arms tightly round her and rocking her as though she were a child.

'I don't know what to do.'

He murmured comfort against her hair. Held her. And gradually her sobs quietened. She pulled a shaky hand across her face and hiccupped.

'If you've drunk as much as I think you have, you're going to have one hell of a hangover in the morning.' He set her back against the sofa and she automatically curled herself into a tight foetal ball.

He stood up and looked down at her finely boned face. The high cheekbones. The long, long lashes resting against the pale skin of her face. He pulled a hand across the back of his neck and turned away.

Water. Paracetamol. That was what she needed. Then a good night's sleep.

Only then, walking back to the kitchen, did he notice the

baby things that were stacked against the wall. The folded pram, the second-hand car seat, the pile of Babygros still in their plastic packets.

All tangible evidence of Vikki's preparation for her baby. And hard to see. If Ellie had known about this, no wonder she'd wanted him to check on her friend.

Rafe glanced back at Lorna, her body still curved into the arm of the sofa, then headed towards the kitchen. The glasses were easy to find. Tucked towards the back of one of the top cupboards.

The paracetamol was more difficult. Eventually he located a packet in an empty old ice cream tub. He filled the glass with tap water and headed back to the sitting room.

Lorna stirred as he came into the room. Her hand was tucked beneath her chin, her face peaceful. Rafe hunkered down beside her and smoothed back the hair falling over her face. 'Lorna? Sit up and drink some water. Lorna? Come on, honey.'

Her almond eyes opened sleepily and she looked at him, pupils dilated. 'I've got a baby. They want me to stay here and look after a baby.'

'I know that.' His fingers tucked in to her hair. It felt soft, smooth as silk. 'Sit up and drink some water for me.'

For a moment it looked as if she was going to defy him, and then her will crumpled. He sat beside her, supporting her body, feeling her warm beside him. Amazingly, what he wanted to do was to thread his hand through that glorious hair and pull her closer for a kiss. Feel her lips against his. Taste her.

Instead he handed her the water with a swift smile. 'Drink that down.'

'It's water.'

'You need to rehydrate,' he said, pulling the single sheet of foil-wrapped paracetamol out of his jeans pocket. 'And take a couple of these while you're at it.'

'I'm not thirsty.'

'Drink it anyway,' he said, sitting down beside her.

He coaxed her through most of the glass, and persuaded her to take the tablets. Her eyes kept closing, her head falling on his shoulder. Her hair smelt of lemons, or something equally bright and citrussy. He rested his cheek against it and let his fingers stroke the bare skin of her shoulder.

Ellie knew her friend well, he thought. Today Lorna's control had been hanging by a thread. He hadn't seen the real Lorna Drummond. Not yet.

And what *was* she going to do about her neice? He could even feel sorry for her now. Single parenthood was tough for anyone, but to be thrust into it when no part of the decision had been yours…

Rafe heard her breathing change and shifted in his seat. 'Don't go to sleep here.' He moved the hair back off her face. 'Let's get you upstairs.'

'I'm sleepy.' Her words were slurred and difficult to hear.

He smiled. There was absolutely no trace of the controlled ice maiden any more. He stood up and pulled her to her feet. 'Time for bed, then.'

It was a pity he hadn't been able to get her to drink more water, but at least she'd had a glass. Something was better than nothing. And without him she'd have ended up spending the night on the sofa and woken with a very stiff neck.

With his arm around her waist, she managed it up the stairs with only a couple of stumbles. She kept resting her head on his chest, her fingers bunched against the thin fabric of his T-shirt.

'Which room?' he asked at the top of the stairs, but her gaze was vacant. Rafe sucked in his breath. Ellie owed him for this. Big-time.

He pushed open the door nearest to him and found the bathroom. Useful, but not what he was looking for. Next to that was a box room which was clearly used for storage. To the right of that was a double room with built-in wardrobes around an unmade-up double bed.

Oh, grief! This was beginning to feel difficult. He settled Lorna in the Lloyd Loom-style bedroom chair and went to explore alone. The master bedroom was the third and final room. Make-up lay scattered on the built-in dressing table, and the duvet was crumpled from a night's sleep that could only have been Vikki's.

Damn.

Rafe pulled the door shut and ran a hand over his face. He wouldn't want to sleep in there, and he couldn't imagine Lorna would either. He shut the door and looked back towards the box room. These houses were standard, and somewhere there should be an airing cupboard...

Tucked in the corner of the box room, he found it. Inside there was a neat pile of towels, blankets and sheets. Rafe pulled out a selection and walked back to the second bedroom. 'It's back to the old-fashioned way of making beds,' he remarked, glancing across at her, slumped in the chair.

He smiled. There were probably few people, if any, who had seen her like this. He fancied she lived her life in a fiercely controlled way. The image she presented to the world was precise and carefully considered.

It had been years since he'd made a bed with blankets and sheets, but he made a good job of it and pulled back the top sheet. 'Lorna, let's get you tucked up.'

She allowed him to pull her out of the chair and cast him the sexiest of smiles. 'I'm a doctor of statistics, you know.'

'Are you?' Her shoes had long since disappeared, along with her cardigan. The silk camisole was fine to sleep in, but she'd do better without the skirt.

Just the thought of sliding it down past her hips spread warmth through his body. His smile became a little fixed as he decided she'd manage well enough. She lay down on the bed and he pulled the covers over her.

'Rafe…?'

His hands held onto the blanket, as though it would make it easier to deal with the effect of her sexy voice. 'Yes?'

'Stay with me.'

How easy would it be to slip in beside her, pull her beautiful body against his…?

'I'm scared.'

He made a snap decision. 'I'll be downstairs if you need me. Just shout.' His hand moved to push the fine strands of blonde hair off her cheek. He wasn't happy leaving her like this.

'You'll be here?'

'I will.' In the morning she probably wouldn't remember any of this, but he would. He'd never be fooled again by the icy image she presented to the world.

Her hand moved up to catch hold of his fingers. They felt cool, the palm of her hand warm as she wrapped her hand round his. Never had holding a woman's hand been so sexy.

'I can't think any more,' she said, letting her eyes close. 'I'm so tired.'

'Don't try. We can make plans in the morning.'

We. Somehow in the last hour or so he'd managed to become involved. This whole situation, though sad, had precisely nothing to do with him. But…

Her breathing altered and her hold on his hand loosened. Rafe slid his hand out of hers and took one last glance at her sleeping face. She was beautiful. Almost like a porcelain doll, but so much more interesting.

Her mouth was perhaps a little too wide, her eyes a seductive almond shape, her hair a million shades of gold and her skin unbelievably soft. Lorna Drummond had unconsciously cast a net and was inexorably pulling him in. *How the hell had that happened?*

Rafe walked back to the box room and pulled a couple more blankets out of the cupboard, along with a spare pillow. If he threw the sofa cushions on the floor he could make himself a tolerably comfortable bed for the night.

Blankets in hand, he paused. He ought to let Ellie know what he'd found. His leather jacket was thrown over the arm of the sofa, and he felt inside the top pocket for his mobile.

He knew from her voice that she'd been waiting for his call. 'What's happened?'

Rafe sat down on the sofa. 'Most of a bottle of sherry, I think.'

'She doesn't drink!'

'*Didn't* drink,' he corrected wryly. 'She's made a dramatic start. I've made up a bed for her, and I'm going to spend the night on the sofa.'

He closed his eyes and rested his head on the back of the

sofa as his sister peppered him with questions. Most he couldn't answer, because Lorna hadn't been in any state to explain what had happened.

Though if he had to hazard a guess it would be seeing the baby equipment scattered about the house, the spotty coat hanging on the peg in the hall, the bedroom waiting for its owner to return…

Rafe thought of the sleeping woman upstairs. Ellie might be apologetic she'd landed him in this situation, but he knew there wasn't anywhere else he'd rather be tonight. Though perhaps he might have made a slight adjustment to the sleeping arrangements…

CHAPTER FOUR

LORNA woke as light broke through a crack in the curtains. For a minute she wondered where she was and how she'd got there. Vague, fuzzy recollections filtered in, and she lifted a hand to cover her eyes, as though that would shut out the memories of the night before.

Or, more accurately, the embarrassment of the night before.

She remembered crying all over Rafe, and asking him to stay…and the warm, secure feeling when he'd said he would.

Stay.

How could she have said that? Everything cringed when she thought about it—from the inside out. And what if he *had* stayed?

She glanced over at the pillow next to her, as though she half expected to find him there. The only other room was Vikki's, and she doubted if he would have slept in there. Seeing her sister's things exactly as she'd left them had been more than she'd been able to take.

Lorna rubbed her hands across her face. How the heck had she ended up in here? She hadn't made up the bed. She was sure of that.

The blood that flew round her body suddenly turned cold, and Lorna lifted the sheet to check what she was wearing.

Her fantasies about Rafe McKinnion might have included something like this when she'd been a teenager, but no longer. She liked *safe*. And he wasn't that. Not at all.

But he had obviously helped her to get to bed without removing any of her clothing…and that was kind. Hopefully she'd not said or done anything too overwhelmingly embarrassing. Apart from the crying…and the clinging, of course.

Lorna gave a throaty groan and covered her face once more. *Why* had she drunk the sherry? She didn't like alcohol. Hated the bitter taste about as much as she hated the stupid way it made other people behave.

Nor could she see the point of nursing the hangover the next day. She sat up, feeling slightly smug that she'd escaped anything but a mild headache…before the full impact of the 'morning-after-the-night-before' hit her.

Her head spun and her stomach seemed to be trying to climb up a throat that felt as if she'd swallowed a mountain of sawdust.

Lorna gingerly lowered herself back down on to the pillow. *Did people really do this for fun?*

Forcing down the feeling of nausea, Lorna slowly rolled over and out of the bed. She needed water. Wasn't that what you were supposed to do? Drink lots and lots of water?

Slowly, as though any unconsidered movement would mean her head dropping off, Lorna made her way along the landing and down the stairs. Her hand tightly gripped the banister rail, and every step was an achievement.

'Lorna?'

Her head snapped round at the sound of Rafe's voice, and

she reached up with her hand, as though it were the only way to keep it in place.

He came to stand at the bottom of the stairs and his blue eyes took on a sinful glint. 'Bad?'

'I'm not used to sherry.'

The glimmer in his eyes intensified. 'So Ellie tells me.'

Ellie had told him? That could only mean he'd phoned his sister and told her he'd found her drunk. Lorna raised her chin in determination not to be intimidated by him. So what if he found her being drunk amusing?

He reached out a hand and guided her down the last two steps. His eyes had lost their gleam and they softened, almost as though he understood how difficult she was finding being laughed at. 'Go and sit on the sofa. I'll bring you the cure.'

Really? She wanted to believe that was possible. *Was* there a cure, other than instant decapitation? Lorna ran her hand along the hallway's woodchip paper. Whether there was anything that could stop her stomach rolling, she doubted.

In the sitting room she saw a pillow and blanket neatly stacked to one side and inwardly cringed. *Rafe must have spent the night on the sofa.* She stumbled forwards and sat down carefully. Never, in her entire thirty-one years, had anything like this ever happened to her.

'Here you go.' Rafe walked through from the kitchen, holding out a glass tumbler filled with something that didn't look like water.

'What's that?'

His smile twisted and he sat down on the chair opposite. 'It's probably better if you don't know.'

Lorna lifted the glass and sniffed. 'No, really. I want to know.'

'It's my special recipe, honed during my years at university…' He smiled and then gave in. 'Basically, it's whisky and egg yolk.'

Raw egg yolk. She looked down at the drink in her hand, completely disbelieving. 'You want me to drink something with raw egg yolk in it?'

'You committed the crime,' he teased, his eyes daring her to try it.

'And it works?'

He shrugged. 'It seems to. I'm sure there's some science attached to it, but I don't know what it is.'

Lorna closed her eyes and drank down as much as she could in one go. It was truly disgusting. The texture more than the taste. She put the almost empty glass down on the side table. 'I think I feel slightly worse.'

Rafe laughed. 'To be honest, I didn't think you'd do it.'

She tucked her bare feet in closer to the sofa and smoothed out her skirt. There was no reason for her to feel so pleased she'd bucked his expectations. It was irrational, but she felt as if she was back in school and the 'cool boy' had noticed her. Finally. And all it had taken was two-thirds of a bottle of sherry and a raw egg yolk.

'Now you need breakfast.'

Lorna shook her head. 'You've got to be kidding.'

'Trust me,' he said, his smile stretching.

There was something about Rafe's smile that made her feel all her carefully worked out five-year plans were irrelevant.

She'd never been *giddy*. Giddy was for girls who hadn't carried the kind of responsibilities she had. But Rafe made her feel that way with a smile.

And that scared her. How could a smile make you feel like that?

'What you need is bacon, eggs, fried bread…'

Lorna managed not to shudder, though her stomach revolted at the mere mention of anything so greasy. 'I don't eat breakfast.' She twisted the fine platinum bangle on her wrist. 'And there's nothing like that here anyway. I don't even have milk. I should have thought about that.'

'Ellie thought about it for you. That's why I'm here. Milk delivery,' Rafe said, standing up. 'Tea or coffee?'

'Tea. But I ought to be making it—' She went to stand up, but he waved her back down.

'I don't have the hangover. Sit down.'

Lorna sank down, grateful, as a feeling of nausea rushed through her once more. It seemed to come and go—but her head was a fairly constant pressure.

She picked up a cushion and hugged it against her stomach. In the kitchen she could hear him moving about. She heard the bang of a cupboard door, even the flick of the kettle turning off.

It was nice not to be alone.

Nice of him to have stayed.

Last night being in the house had felt overwhelming. For so many reasons.

Nothing much had changed since the day she'd left— same curtains, carpet, sofa… Lorna ran her fingers over the brown synthetic fabric. She'd almost forgotten. She closed her eyes against the single tear that welled up and tipped over onto her cheek.

Rafe touched her lightly on her shoulder. She opened her eyes and brushed at the trail of moisture.

'Tea.'

'Thanks.'

His knuckles rubbed against the bare skin of her upper arm. A simple gesture, but one that was more comforting than anything anyone had done since she'd heard the news about Vikki.

Rafe went to sit opposite her, and Lorna hugged the tea to herself. It was warm against her cold hands. She lifted the mug and sipped.

'I'm sorry about last night. You must think I'm awful,' she said huskily, glancing across at him.

'I don't.' He sat forward and rested his elbows on his knees.

She drew a shuddering breath. 'It's so weird, being here. I've not been back for such a long time.' Too long. Everywhere were echoes of the past. The photograph on the mantelpiece of Great-Aunt Edna that still had the piece of dried lavender her mum had tucked into the frame.

Nothing had been touched. She could almost imagine her mum would be shouting for her breakfast any moment.

'Why didn't you and Vikki sell up after your mother died?'

Lorna glanced over to where Rafe was sitting, legs outstretched, feet bare. He made even the simple act of drinking tea look sexy. His hand was looped round the mug, his thumb through the handle.

She swallowed. Selling this place would have required her to think about it, and she hadn't wanted to do that. She'd tucked it away in a part of her mind as something she would deal with later. Much later.

'I suppose it suited me to have a UK address still. And when I first went to the States I didn't know I'd settle. This was my safety net.'

'And Vikki?' he prompted, when she fell silent.

'Keeping this place meant she was on the property ladder. At least I think that's what she thought. We hadn't talked about it in years.'

Rafe sipped his tea. Lorna watched the movement of his Adam's apple as he swallowed. It was sensual. Her own hands tightened on the porcelain mug she was holding.

"Years ago we did think about renting this place out…but we'd have had to decorate. Change the carpets, curtains, fit a new kitchen and bathroom."

"Would have been worth doing."

"Probably." She shrugged. "It just seemed too complicated when I was so far away."

And Vikki had been too busy living her life to be interested. Lorna pulled at the chain around her neck. She'd resented that.

'What are you going to do with it now?'

Her eyes flicked up. 'Sell it. I've no plans to come back to England.'

Rafe nodded and then stood up, holding out his hand for her empty cup. 'Ellie said to say that she'll help you come and clear out Vikki's things. She doesn't want you doing that on your own.'

'She's lovely.' Lorna closed her eyes and sank back on the sofa.

Rafe paused a moment, watching her. It seemed she still had no intention of caring for her niece. Until it was clear Katherine's biological father wasn't going to claim her, it was unlikely Lorna would be able to take her to the States anyway—even if she wanted to.

He went back through to the kitchen and rinsed out the mugs. Lorna confused him. He wanted to dislike her, and he certainly disapproved of her attitude to family responsibility, but…something didn't sit right.

In fact, everything about her seemed to be contradictory. His sketchy memory of her as a teenager was at war with the elegance she exuded now, and, despite the tension that radiated from her, he knew she was strong.

Rafe rubbed a hand against the top of his head. Maybe it was the innate strength he believed she had which made it so difficult to accept her apparent intention not to take on the care of Katherine. If she *couldn't* do it, he would have been sympathetic. As it was…

He heard her behind him. Bare feet on vinyl flooring. He turned, feeling as though he'd been caught whispering.

'I forgot to say thank you for staying.'

'You're welcome.'

She wrapped her arms in front of her. 'You must have been incredibly uncomfortable, squashed up on that sofa.'

'I've slept in far worse places.' Rafe wiped his hands on a towel and threaded it back on the rail.

He watched her process that piece of information and come up with entirely the wrong interpretation. Lorna Drummond didn't seem to think a great deal of him. Perhaps she only dated men with a PhD? Men who wore black suits and were too predictable to challenge her.

He'd really like to kiss some sense into her beautiful blonde head. Yes, he'd really like to do that.

Her smile was shaky. 'Anyway, I just wanted you to know I appreciate you staying…'

Rafe thrust his hands into his jeans pockets. This was him being given his marching orders. He could hear it in her voice, see it in her face.

He'd have preferred to stay and help her. Every inch of this house was filled with reminders of her mum. Of Vikki. He didn't like the thought of her here alone.

'Are you sure you don't want me to make you some breakfast before I head for home? You'll feel better if you eat something.'

'I'll make some toast.' She smiled, her brown eyes holding the first hint of laughter he'd seen there, and his stomach flipped. 'Perhaps when my stomach has got over your cure.'

She had something, did Lorna Drummond. She really did. That mixture of vulnerability and strength was very potent. 'Fair enough. Is there anything else you'd like me to do?'

Lorna shook her head. 'I'll be fine. And I'm sure you've got things you should be doing.'

There was nothing else he could do but leave. Yesterday he'd not wanted to come. Today he didn't want to leave. He walked past her and picked up his jacket from where he'd left it, folded across one of the old-fashioned dining chairs.

'Rafe?' He turned to see she was frowning. 'I just thought…I mean… How did you get in? I hadn't left the front door open, had I?'

He reached into his pocket and pulled out the single key. 'Vikki gave it to Ellie. Do you want her to hang on to it in case you shut yourself out?'

'*Vikki* did?'

That was one conversation he didn't intend to get sucked into. 'Apparently.'

She lifted a hand and chewed absentmindedly at the edge of her nail. It was a curiously endearing thing for her to do. Her hands were beautifully manicured, every nail perfect, so it had to be rare.

'Should she hang on to it for the time being?'

Lorna nodded. And then, more slowly, 'Do you think anyone else has a key?'

'It's possible,' Rafe answered after a moment. He hadn't considered that aspect of it before. 'But, you know, I doubt it. Vikki doesn't seem to have kept up with anyone from here. Who could she have given one to?'

Perhaps Katherine's father?

He knew that thought had passed across Lorna's mind too. It was a flicker in her eyes. 'If you're worried, there's always a bed at Ellie's house. Mine, too, if you can't face the mayhem.'

And then he wished he hadn't said that, when he saw her instinctive recoil. Too close, too quickly.

'Though if you ended up at mine I'd hand you a paintbrush.'

She smiled, but he knew she wanted him gone.

CHAPTER FIVE

ELLIE laid a hand on the cot's side and looked at Lorna. 'Do you want to feed Katherine?'

'Feed her?'

'It's good for babies to have physical contact.'

Lorna hesitated. Saying yes would feel a little like jumping into a vat of lemonade. 'I don't know how to do it.'

'I'll show you.' Ellie turned and spoke to a more junior colleague. 'Nurse, would you fetch the milk? Now, sit down and get yourself comfortable.'

Lorna did as she was told. Her hands felt clammy, and her heart was pounding so hard it hurt. Katherine was so tiny. Fragile. She wondered if she moved too quickly whether she might do some terrible damage to such a tiny baby, but Ellie seemed confident.

'Put a towel over your lap. She has a bit of a habit of pos-setting. And that's not good for your dry cleaning bills.'

'Like this?' Lorna asked, spreading a piece of terry towelling over her lap.

'Perfect.'

Lorna watched as Ellie gently lifted Katherine out of her cot. Her tiny hands splayed out in a shocked gesture.

'Hold her nice and firmly. Like the rest of us, she needs to feel safe.'

Safe. Nothing about this felt safe. Lorna settled Katherine in the crook of her arm, feeling her heavy and warm. Her eyelashes were so dark against the pale skin of her cheeks and she felt a rush of…*love*.

It felt like love. Looking down at Katherine, she realised she wanted all the very best things for her. And not just because she was her sister's baby—although that was part of it. Maybe it was the helpless vulnerability of a new life.

'Keep the bottle tilted up, so there is always milk in the teat. You don't want her sucking in air.'

It was unbelievable that anyone would trust her to hold a new little person. And Katherine herself was so trusting. It didn't seem to matter to her that her aunt hadn't the faintest idea what she was doing.

After a short moment she started to feed. Her tiny mouth fastened tight round the silicone teat and she began to suck. Small contented little sounds emitting from her body.

'Beautiful,' Ellie said, standing up. 'You're doing really well.'

Lorna felt euphoric. *She was doing it*. Really doing it. Gradually her arms relaxed, but her focus never changed. Every ounce of her attention was fixed on this tiny, perfect human being. Lorna moved her fingers over the soft hair. *Baby*-soft. Katherine was oblivious.

'She's a good little feeder,' Ellie said. 'She's got a strong will on her.'

Lorna didn't turn her head. 'Like her mother.'

'And her aunt. You shared that, if not a lot else.' Ellie

picked up Katherine's notes. 'It was just that Vikki chose to use hers a little differently from you.'

That was true enough. Vikki had certainly been determined to pursue the life she'd wanted. She'd followed the beat of her own personal drum without a backward glance.

It was impossible to sit there and not wonder what kind of person Katherine would become. What kind of life would she want? There was such potential wrapped up in such a tiny frame.

Lorna bit at the side of her lip. Did she really want to lose the chance to see Katherine change and grow?

No, not really. It was like a whisper inside her head.

But it was complicated. Felt complicated, anyway. She had a life in the States. One she'd carefully carved out for herself. She had the respect of colleagues. The potential for advancement was there.

She wanted a professorship. Was that so wrong?

But…could she walk away? Really?

Lorna watched as Katherine's tiny fist bunched against the bottle. *She knew nothing about babies.* She didn't have the first idea what they needed, how you cared for them. Perhaps the least selfish decision would be to allow Katherine to be adopted into a warm and loving family.

'What do I do?' Lorna asked anxiously, watching the teat start to empty as the bottle drained dry.

'Just pull the bottle out. It's better if she doesn't suck on an empty bottle. It'll give her a stomach ache.' Ellie picked up a pen and wrote on Katherine's notes. 'That was a lovely feed. She's done so well. You both have.'

And it felt a lot like that. Lorna had achieved so much in her life, but none of it had felt as incredible as this. Finally she understood why friends became so boring once they had children. There *was* nothing else worth talking about.

'What do I do now?'

'Sit her up. Support her chin. That's it,' Ellie said as Lorna moved Katherine upright.

'Now, gently rub her back.'

Lorna moved her hand in small circles and heard a belch. She looked up at Ellie and smiled.

Her friend smiled back. 'Perfect.' Ellie moved round to take Katherine from her, and gently placed her on her back in the cot.

Lorna felt bereft. It was a strange feeling. She could have sat there for hours, just holding Katherine. She loved to hear her breathe, feel the softness of her skin, and smell that indefinable smell that was new baby. It was exciting. Really quite magical.

'Have you thought any more about what Katherine's future is going to be?' Ellie asked, without turning round.

Had she? She'd thought about nothing else. Round and round in circles, until her head hurt.

'There's really no medical reason for Katherine to still be in hospital,' Ellie said, turning and facing her. 'Time's running out for you to make a decision. We're going to need her bed.'

Rafe knew Lorna was the solitary figure sitting on the bench, but he hesitated to approach her. She looked…preoccupied, and he wasn't at all sure she'd want company.

He knew what she was thinking about too. *Katherine.* And that made him unusually hesitant. Every line of her body spoke tension—which told him she'd still not made her decision yet.

It mattered to him—God only knew why—in a way that his involvement with her, with Katherine, didn't warrant. He felt as if he was willing her to do the right thing. Make the right decision.

And it was none of his business.

He was on the point of walking away when she turned her head, a flash of gold in the sunlight. He saw the recognition, and her hesitant smile.

What was it about that smile? There was a sweetness about it that made him believe, all appearances to the contrary, that Ellie was right in her opinion of Lorna. Leastways he could feel the tug of attraction pulling him closer.

'Are you heading home?' he asked. 'Can I give you a lift?'

She smiled again. The same preoccupied, troubled smile that seemed to have him wanting to wrap his arms about her and tell her he'd keep her safe. *Crazy.* 'I don't think I'm ready to go back to the house yet.'

Not 'home', he noticed. That didn't surprise him. *Had her house ever felt like a home?* He'd not realised before how much time Lorna had spent at his own childhood home. Quiet, undemanding, she'd often been there. She'd joined them for tea, done her homework at the kitchen table, sat chatting to his mother…

'Ellie said I'd missed you.' He moved a little closer. 'Her car is finally mended and I've just dropped in her keys.'

'She paid the six hundred?'

'Six hundred and thirty-five in the end.' Rafe sat down beside her. 'But you know Ellie. Stubborn as they come. She likes to do things her way. And at least she's back on the road.'

Lorna laughed, but it was strained. 'She's not got things easy, has she?'

'Not since Steve left,' Rafe agreed. He moved his foot against a weed sticking out of the gravel. 'He wasn't cut out to be a dad. Found the day-to-day repetition of it difficult, I think.'

Incredibly selfish. Maybe that was why he was reacting so strongly to the possibility that Lorna might not choose to accept the care of her niece? And then Lorna turned to look at him. A fine strand of blonde hair had blown across her cheek, and he knew his interest had nothing to do with Steve.

He swallowed down the almost tangible awareness that sizzled between them.

Lorna rubbed her hands down her thighs, clearly uncomfortable. Then she tucked her hair behind her ear. 'Will he come back, do you think?'

'Ellie wouldn't have him. He's not spent enough time with the children, and she can't forgive him for that.'

'Doesn't he want to?'

Rafe squinted up against the mid-morning sun. 'Not noticeably. He likes his expensive cars and his foreign holidays.'

There was silence while Lorna thought about that.

Poor Ellie. The difficult life of a single mum hadn't been anywhere on her agenda. She'd always wanted to nurse, but she'd planned on travelling before having children. Maybe spending a couple of years in Australia, some time in Africa... Then she'd planned on marrying a doctor and settling down in one of those solid eighteenth-century houses in Upper Mellingham.

Life changed things.

'She seems happy, though.'

Rafe smiled. 'She is. Her children are her world.'

And that was the secret. Ellie loved her children. She'd

sacrifice anything for them because she loved them. And she was happy…

Katherine deserved that kind of love. But she couldn't give it. *Couldn't.* It wasn't in her.

'I wish I was more like that,' Lorna said quietly. Her hands fidgeted in her lap.

Slowly—so slowly that she knew it was going to happen—Rafe reached out and placed a hand over hers. The touch of his fingers was startling. Her eyes flew up to look at him.

'Being you is fine.' His thumb moved against the palm of her right hand, sending shivers through her entire body. 'Ellie's not perfect, you know. She still can't cook anything that doesn't come out of a tin or a packet. And she hides her ironing pile behind the sofa in the sitting room when anyone calls unexpectedly.'

A nervous laugh burst from Lorna. 'She's lovely.'

'Yes,' her brother agreed. 'But not perfect. No one is.'

'I wish I was more relaxed.' The movement of his thumb was beginning to make her feel light-headed. 'I have everything worked out to a timetable. I do my ironing on Mondays. Food shopping on Tuesdays. Wednesday I go to the gym. Thursday I—'

'Why?'

Why? It was like asking why she had brown eyes. It just was the way she'd been made. 'I like things to be organised. I have my clothes sorted by season and colour. I have the spices in my kitchen set out alphabetically. My DVD collection is catalogued—'

'But you wish you were more like Ellie?'

Lorna shrugged, a barely perceptible movement of her shoulders. 'I loved it at your house. When I was a teenager,' she clarified. 'I loved it that your mum was too busy painting pictures to have cleared the breakfast table, that she always had time to stop for a cup of tea and a chat, that whatever Ellie did was wonderful…'

Had she said that out loud? Lorna bit her lip. She hadn't meant to give so much away. But the kind of praise Ellie had enjoyed had been hard to come by in the Drummond house. Unconditional love impossible.

'What was your home-life like?'

Lorna stood up and smoothed down her black trousers. 'Let's just say we knew what day of the week it was by what we were eating.'

'We did have a great childhood. Can't deny it. Though sometimes it would have been nice if we hadn't always arrived late to everything.' Rafe stood up beside her. 'And sometimes I wished that my parents had conformed a little more. My mother dressed more conservatively.' He smiled.

Lorna felt the response tug at her own mouth. She effortlessly remembered her mum's scathing comments on Fi McKinnion's floating kaftans and low-necked halter tops, which she wore *without a bra*. It had all seemed so colourful. Glamorous.

'Well, my mum thought books made a room untidy, and that anything less than perfection was a failure.' She picked a fleck off her pink angora ballet cardigan. 'Vikki dealt with that by not trying…and I suppose I'm still trying.'

Ridiculous. She knew it with her head, but her emotions hadn't caught up.

'She must have been pleased with you? Didn't you get top marks for everything?'

'I worked hard.'

Rafe looked at her for a moment. He had the most unnerving stare. His eyes seemed to penetrate beyond the mask she liked to hold up to the world. He seemed to see *her*, and she responded with a shiver of excitement.

She knew it meant nothing. He'd always had an uncanny way of making the opposite sex feel special. She just hadn't been on the receiving end before.

It was in the way he focussed on you. Just you. And he listened as though you were the most fascinating woman he'd ever spoken to.

'Can you walk in those?' he asked, with a glance down at her three-inch stilettos.

'Yes.'

'Come on, then.'

'Wh—?'

Rafe took hold of her hand and threaded his fingers through hers. Her heart slammed against her ribcage.

'Let's get out of here. Wander down by the river.' It was on the tip of Lorna's tongue to ask why, but he forestalled her. 'This is a depressing place to sit.'

Lorna glanced behind her at the full car park and nodded. If she had to make the most important decision of her life by the end of today, she might as well do it somewhere beautiful.

And the river was stunning. Rafe led her through the back streets and out towards the embankment before letting go of her hand. Lorna pretended she hadn't noticed, and made a show of looking about her.

She remembered it all, but not well. And not looking like this. Like the hospital, it had seen huge investment in the past decade.

Now the wide walkways were lined with Victorian-style

lamp-posts, huge flower beds were filled with tulips and daf-
fodils, and there was a bridge she'd never seen before.

Rafe saw her looking. 'It's the Millennium Bridge. Unlike
the one in London, it experienced no difficulties—although
not everyone likes the contemporary design.'

It certainly was different from the Victorian bridge, further
along, and different again from the main town bridge, with
its thick stone pillars. 'In my head this place hadn't changed
at all,' she said, looking about her. 'But it's so different.'

'Everything changes. Except Carlos. He still makes the
best ice-cream within a sixty-mile radius.'

'Ellie and I used to cycle over here.' In the days before
she'd worried about the high calorific content of ice-cream.

They wandered over the older Victorian bridge, and along
the path between the boating lake and the bandstand. Lorna
glanced slyly over at Rafe, not wanting him to see that she
was looking at him.

He was still the sexiest of men. When they'd been at
school she'd not understood why that was. Now she knew
it came from his being so supremely confident in his own
skin. She envied him that.

'What?' he said, catching her.

Lorna looked down at her feet and back up again. 'I was
wondering how come you have so much time off. What is
it that you do?'

Almost true. She *did* want to know what it was he did.
But she also wanted to know how he managed to make her
feel so flustered all the time simply by being near her.

'It's being your own boss that does it. I set my own hours.'
He smiled, and then relented. 'And I'm at a bit of a crossroads. I own a travel consultancy.'

As soon as he said it she knew that it would suit him. The last time she'd seen him had been when he'd left to go back-packing round the world.

'But the wanderlust is dying. And sitting in an office isn't something I've ever wanted to do.'

'Oh.' Silently Lorna cringed. Surely she could think of something better than 'oh'. She was thirty-one. Successful in her own right.

'You?'

'I'm a statistician.'

'Oh.' He mimicked her.

Lorna looked across at him and his eyes were laughing. Sinfully laughing. She could feel her face heat and knew she was blushing.

He took pity on her. 'Actually, I already know. Ellie told me. Do you love it?'

'Yes. Yes, I do.' She brushed her hair back from her face. 'I've always loved numbers. And I like the teaching aspect of my work. I've got a great apartment…' Lorna sidestepped a child on a tricycle and smiled at the mum hurrying behind.

'A boyfriend?'

'No.' And then, because it suddenly seemed important that Rafe should know that it was by choice, 'I have male friends, of course.'

'Of course.'

And she knew from the inflection in his voice that Rafe was laughing at her again. 'Not like that. Just no one special.'

'Has there ever been anyone special?'

Lorna choked on a laugh. 'You do ask a lot of questions.'

His eyes glinted down. 'So, has there?'

It was tempting to say *you*.

But it wouldn't have been true. She'd always known Rafe hadn't noticed her beyond the fact that she was his younger sister's friend. He'd been carelessly kind, but he'd never noticed her.

Not like now. He'd never flirted with her before. And this felt a lot like flirting. She loved the way his eyes danced. The constant feeling of excitement in the pit of her stomach.

'No.' She pulled her bag higher on her shoulder. 'I made a decision fairly early on that I wanted to be financially independent. I didn't want to rely on a man to put a roof over my head, clothes on my back. So I made the choice that I'd concentrate on my career and not get sidetracked by anyone.'

They stopped at a small kiosk by the boating lake. The large hand-painted sign was still poorly done, and the white plastic chairs dotted around still tacky. But this was Carlos…

'Does that mean you don't want me to buy you an ice-cream?'

'I'm prepared to negotiate. You buy this time; I'll buy next.'

'Deal.'

Assuming, of course, there would ever be a next time.

'Chocolate-chip? Banana? Rhubarb Crumble? Toffee and Pecan?' Rafe pointed at a pink ice-cream. 'Strawberry? What's it to be?'

Lorna leant forward and looked at the plastic tubs and their handwritten labels. She shouldn't. Of course she shouldn't. It would mean an extra hour in the gym…

CHAPTER SIX

'BANANA, please.'

Carlos's wife, whose name no one had ever seemed to know, scooped out a large ball and set it on top of a twisting cone.

'Here you go.' Rafe passed it back to Lorna. 'And a Mint and Chocolate one, please.'

Lorna didn't have anyone she was serious about in the States. Rafe felt ridiculously pleased about that. He accepted his own cone and passed across the money.

'Do you want to sit here? Or walk?'

Lorna looked at the white plastic chairs and then back at him. 'Why don't we walk for a bit?'

It suited him. He just wanted to talk to her, find out what made her tick.

She licked her ice-cream and closed her eyes to savour the moment. 'There truly is no other ice-cream like this on the planet. I'd forgotten how fantastic it is.'

Rafe smiled. 'It's good, but I have to admit that some of the *gelato* in Sardinia and Sicily gives it a run for its money.'

'Didn't Carlos's family come from Sicily?'

'I don't know. Never asked.' Rafe watched as one of the

rowing boats was pushed out onto the boating lake. 'I used to love that,' he said, pointing.

'Never done it.'

'Never?' Rafe looked at her.

'I wasn't the kind of girl boys asked out onto the boating lake. More the sort they asked if they could copy my homework.'

'Want to go on now?'

She laughed. 'No. My desire to be rowed underneath a willow is completely gone. I bet there are millions of insects under there.'

'A fair few.' He smiled at her. Rafe licked his ice-cream and then pointed at the bridge. 'Let's walk back that way. Maybe we can stop for coffee at the other end.'

Lorna said nothing, but she followed him that way. She seemed to have relaxed with him. Even her voice had softened, and her eyes had lost their haunted look.

'So, once you had your career up and running, why no one serious then?' he asked, after a moment.

For a moment he wondered whether she'd answer, then she smiled 'I haven't made the time. At least I think that's the reason.'

'Time?'

'You have to invest time in a new relationship. Probably all relationships. But certainly a new one.' She smiled. 'You know—make time to go to dinner. Spend time talking, listening.'

'And you haven't done that?'

'I enjoy my job.'

She didn't sound as if she regretted it, but he had to ask. 'Has it been worth it?'

'Sometimes…' She brushed her hair back off her face. 'Sometimes I've wondered if maybe I've missed something…'

Lorna stroked her hand against the flat of her stomach. 'Mostly at other people's weddings. I think I must be the world's most experienced bridesmaid, and I've heard every possible variation of "you'll be next".'

They stopped on the bridge, and Rafe rested his elbows on the railing and looked out. 'And you've never been tempted?'

'No.' Then she smiled. 'Not enough to get married anyway.'

Rafe turned his head to look at her, his eyes gleaming with suppressed laughter.

Her mouth twitched in response, but she said, 'Marriage is a big commitment, and since I'm not maternal I've not really seen the point.'

'You think there's no point getting married if you're not going to have children?' Rafe asked with a sudden frown. He didn't agree with that.

'Not that, exactly. I just mean that lots of women settle because they can hear their body clock ticking and want a baby before it's too late. I don't have any particular drive to reproduce myself, so I thought if I meet someone—great. If not…'

And she hadn't.

But her saying she didn't want children reminded him of baby Katherine. Reminded Lorna of her too. He could see the tension return to her face. She took another lick of her ice-cream.

Rafe didn't want to have that conversation now. Not when he was enjoying her company so much. He watched a canal boat pass beneath them.

'What about you?' she asked after an awkward moment. 'Anyone special?'

'No.' He turned to look at her. 'No one special. I think you'd have to say I've invested the time, just spread it a little thinly.'

Lorna laughed—and it was a good sound.

'I spent practically all of my twenties travelling, the first half of my thirties doing the same. It's not a lifestyle that's conducive to long-term relationships.'

'I suppose not.' Lorna smiled. 'Nice to have traveled, though. It's on my list of things to do.'

'You keep a list?'

She nodded. 'Always. Things to do. Things to buy. Short-term goals. Longer-term ones. I like to tick them off. Makes me feel like I'm accomplishing things.'

Lorna bit into her ice-cream and winced at the cold against her teeth. 'Where is your favourite place?'

'Depends on the time of the year. And who I'm with.'

She thought about that for a moment. 'So where would you go in February? With a good friend?'

'Cuba.' Rafe said quickly, resting a foot on the lower rail. 'Havana is one of the funkiest cities. Great bars, fantastic music. But…if money is no object, I might take a private jet over to Nice, then be chauffered from the airport to an awaiting yacht.'

'Sounds expensive.'

'But worth it. Trust me. I'd anchor off the Cap d'Antibes for lunch, carry on down the coast for cocktails at St Tropez.'

'I'm sold.'

Rafe smiled at her. 'That's what I do. Build specific packages for people who want adventure and don't quite know where to begin. My misspent youth has been very profitable.'

And he'd done all the things he wanted to do. She hadn't. Lorna concentrated her attention on a rowing boat, and a cyclist shouting instructions from the bank. If she hadn't been so fixed on playing everything safe maybe *she* might have been to Havana or St Tropez.

'Where should I go for a long weekend? Somewhere I'd never forget?'

'From the UK?'

Lorna nodded, finishing off the last of her ice cream.

'Atla, in Norway. You could do that in a weekend. And it's certainly a place you should see before you die. I'd send you on a snowmobile safari inside the Artic Circle, take you swimming in the Barents Sea, spend a night in the Ice Hotel—'

'I've heard of that.' Lorna tried to keep her voice light, but somewhere along the line this had become a trip they might take together. Places *he'd* like to show her. She hadn't meant that.

Or had she? Every word was seduction.

'It's a hotel carved out of ice every year. Tables, chairs, beds…everything. Personally, I enjoy a spot of crab fishing after that. But I think for you…' He pretended to consider. 'I think it'd be a horse-drawn sleigh ride along the frozen river to see the Northern Lights.'

'I wish.' Her voice sounded husky.

'All possible.' Rafe let go of the railing. 'Of course lunch at Alexanders, with a table overlooking the River Cam, is very lovely too. Shall we?'

Lunch? With Rafe McKinnion? 'Do you have the time?'

'All day. I truly am at a crossroads with it all.'

Rafe cut across the grass towards the Millennium Bridge. 'The consultancy is too big, employs too many people…' He smiled. 'And, truthfully, I'm bored to death.'

Bored!

'I now employ a great team of people who can manage without me, and I need a new challenge. Something that'll make me feel like I'm really living.'

Lorna winced as her foot trod on something hard. 'Ouch.'

'What?' Rafe stopped, and turned to see her balancing on one foot.

'A stone, I think.'

'I forgot you didn't have quite the footwear for this. Hang on to me.'

She did that. Holding on to his arm and bending down to pick up her stiletto and give it a shake.

'Done?'

Lorna looked up and his face was so close. She could see each individual eyelash, the flecks of colour in his blue eyes, the faint stubble on his jaw. 'Y-yes.'

He took the shoe from her hand and bent down to put it on the pavement. 'Come on, Cinders.'

Everything he did was relaxed, easy, and so very sexy. She'd spent the past decade raising her self-esteem, clawing it back. She'd done it by discipline and hard work… And yet a few hours with Rafe McKinnion was starting to make her question whether she'd accomplished very much at all.

She pushed her foot into the shoe and tried to smile. The trouble was she felt so nervous around him. She wanted him to like her. Wanted it a lot.

Lorna swallowed the hard lump in her throat. 'Thanks.'

His hand moved on her arm. She could feel his fingers through the soft wool of her wrap-over jumper as though they were touching her skin. And his eyes seemed to be fixed on her…lips.

Rafe might kiss her.

It was like a cloudburst inside her head. *Please kiss me.* His sexy blue eyes moved up to look directly into her brown ones, and then flickered down to her lips again.

Kiss me. Please, kiss me.

The thought was so loud in her head it was a miracle he couldn't hear it.

Rafe took a step back, his smile as easy as before. 'It's not much further. Alexanders is the new name for Russells. New management, new style.'

He hadn't kissed her.

They crossed the road and walked along beside the open parkland with Lorna feeling a mixture of disappointment and relief that she hadn't given herself away. She wasn't used to feeling like this.

Of course Rafe hadn't kissed her. She was an idiot for thinking it had been a possibility. But, just for a moment she'd felt sure it had crossed his mind. His gaze had moved to her lips. She'd felt it as surely as any touch.

A few more steps and the large green awning of Alexanders was clearly visible. Black iron swirls in an art deco style marked out an outside eating area with a clear view across the River Cam.

'This is nice,' Lorna said, feeling that she needed to say something. 'Sittiford is becoming quite European.'

Rafe laughed. 'It's had a lot of money poured into it in recent years because of its proximity to London. This is considered prime commuter belt now, and house prices have rocketed. You'll be surprised what your mum's house is worth.'

Which immediately made her think of Vikki…and of Katherine. She lowered her eyes, not wanting Rafe to be able to read her expression. She was being asked to make an impossible choice, and everyone blamed her for taking time thinking about it.

Except perhaps Ellie.

Rafe stood back to allow her to walk in front of him. His hand hovered on the small of her back. Lorna closed her eyes to blink back the prickle of tears. She'd no idea why his kindness should affect her like this. Perhaps because she felt so alone…?

'Table for two, please.'

The waitress led them to a corner table. Parkland stretched out to the left, immediately in front was the tree-lined walk of the Embankment, and beyond that the River Cam.

Rafe took the chair which looked back towards the restaurant, leaving Lorna with the spectacular view. *No wonder women loved him.* It would be easy to be swept up into the fairytale of it all. But he was being kind. That was all.

And he'd probably be disappointed in her if she decided to go back to the States.

'Have I upset you?'

Lorna's eyes flew up to his blue ones. The laughter had gone from them. 'No. Of course not.' She hid her face by bending to tuck her handbag down by the legs of her chair. 'I was thinking about Katherine.'

'Ah.'

'Ellie says they will need her bed soon.'

The waitress walked over to hand them their menus. Rafe took his with a smile, and Lorna watched the younger woman's instinctive reaction to it. Whatever Rafe had was universally appealing. She was so out of her depth, being with him.

She was out of her depth with everything.

Lorna made a show of opening her menu. 'This is lovely.'

'I'm having the salmon bagel. You?'

'I think…the chicken and bacon salad,' she said, concentrating on the 'Lighter Bites' section of the menu. 'And a glass of mineral water with ice and lemon.'

Back in the States she had her life organised to perfection. She was good at her job. She had an apartment she loved. She had friends. Good friends. There were men she'd go out to dinner with occasionally…

She couldn't give all that up to take care of a baby.

And live where? Here? Back in Sittiford? Everything in her rebelled against that. It would be like going back into the dark times.

But Ellie was happy here. And Rafe had recently bought a house in the area. He was restless with his life and had chosen to buy a house in the most boring part of the world. Why had he done that?

Lorna sat back in her chair to allow the waitress to place a glass in front of her. She picked up the water and sipped.

'What now?' Rafe asked, a sudden glimmer lighting his blue eyes.

'Wh-wh—?' Her mouth formed the shape but no real sound came out.

'Your face gives you away when you're thinking. What have I done now?'

Lorna placed her drink down on the table and twisted it so the ice cubes knocked against the side. 'Didn't you want to get away from here? When you finished school?'

His hands played on the condensation on his beer glass. 'That's not what you were thinking.'

Lorna looked up and caught the understanding glimmer in his eyes.

'You want to know why I've come back.'

She lifted her chin slightly. 'If you like. It's the flipside of the question.'

'It's entirely different. You, me, Ellie…*Vikki*—we all wanted to leave here. Of course we did. It's part of growing up.' His smile twisted. 'Wanting independence, wanting to try new things, see new places.'

'But you came back.'

'Eventually. When I'd done enough to feel it was time I wanted to put down some roots. That's when I realised this is home. My roots are already here. The people I care about all live within a ten-mile radius of Sittiford.'

Lorna felt…disappointed. Without having consciously thought it, she'd hoped his answer might help—but it didn't. She had no roots. No family.

Except Katherine.

And Katherine wasn't so much family as *responsibility*—and that was what she'd run away from. She'd wrapped it up in all kinds of ambitions and dreams, but fundamentally she'd wanted to stop being the responsible sister. She'd wanted to go where no one had any preconceived ideas about who she was and what she should be doing. Freedom. That was what had driven her.

'That doesn't help you any, does it?' Rafe remarked, as soon as the waitress had left after bringing their food.

Lorna picked up her fork and pushed at a piece of chicken. 'No.'

He smiled. 'Do you want to talk about her?'

'Wh—?'

'Katherine?'

Lorna started to shake her head, and then she changed her mind. She was going to have to speak to someone or she was going to go out of her mind. The social worker she'd been assigned was too politically correct to be of any use. The only thing she'd said that had struck any chord had been that the decision was a personal one.

'That's who you're thinking about, isn't it?'

'Not just Katherine. Though Ellie says I'm running out of time to make a decision…' Lorna rested her fork on the side of her deep plate. 'But…'

'But what? Rafe prompted.

'I keep thinking about Vikki and who might be the father of her baby. If he's not here, why did she come back? Did Ellie tell you about her funeral?'

'A little.' Rafe picked up his beer. 'She said there were very few mourners.'

'There were five. Lots of flowers, but only five actual people. Me, Ellie, your mum, Mrs Randwell from next door, and Pippa Lewis.'

'The swimwear model who did that reality TV show?'

Lorna picked up her fork again. 'They shared a flat a couple of years back. But Vikki had *no* friends here…'

At least if Vikki had stayed in London she'd have been with the people she'd hung around with. Friends of a sort, even if they had all been too busy to make the one-hour drive out of London.

'Did Pippa know Vikki was pregnant?'

'No. I'd hoped… But, no. As far as Pippa knew Vikki wasn't seeing anyone either.'

Rafe finished his mouthful. 'Perhaps that's why she chose

to come back. Maybe she wanted anonymity. She was fairly well known in London. Here nobody would know, unless she told them.'

'I don't know. It's possible.' But doubtful. Vikki had never courted anonymity in her entire life. She'd only been really happy when she'd been the centre of attention.

'Does it matter?' Rafe picked up his beer. 'It doesn't change the decision you have to make.'

Lorna lifted up her fork and pushed her food around her plate. It did make no difference. But…

She frowned. The trouble was she felt like a puppet—with Vikki being the puppeteer, yanking on her strings. It stirred up all kinds of resentment.

And she'd thought she was free. But from beyond the grave it seemed her sister still had the power to control and change her life.

If she took on the care of Katherine she'd have to give up the life she'd worked so hard for. And that would hurt. Quite desperately.

But if she signed the papers that would let Katherine be adopted she wasn't sure whether she could live with the knowledge she'd done that. It was a lose-lose situation.

She felt as if she had a volcano rumbling inside her, just waiting to blow. 'I don't want to be trapped by a baby. I know it sounds awful of me, but if I'd wanted children I'd have had my own.'

Rafe sat back in his chair.

'And I'm so tired of picking up the pieces of other people's mistakes. Incredibly tired of assuming responsibilities for things that aren't really mine.

Lorna let her fork drop down on her plate. Rafe must think

she was a cold, cold woman. He couldn't know what her life had been like growing up…because she'd hidden it. She hadn't wanted anything else in her life to make her stand out. *Or had Ellie told him?*

'Lorna?' Rafe reached across the table and touched her hand. His voice was strong. Compassionate.

She looked across at him.

'Break the decision into smaller bits. You can't adopt Katherine tomorrow. I don't know what the legal procedure is, but I'm sure there'll be a time lag to give Katherine's biological father the chance to step forward.'

His hand looked dark against her skin. Long, strong fingers.

'Why don't you contact your employers in the States? Talk to them, explain the situation, and see if you can take some compassionate leave. Take it a day at a time.'

Her thoughts quietened. Lorna felt his words like a soothing balm.

'You know the best person to look after Katherine is the one who loves her. If you can't feel that for her, and her biological father can't be found, then, yes, the best thing for Katherine would be for you to let her go to adoptive parents who desperately want her.'

Rafe released her hand and picked up his knife and fork to continue eating.

Lorna was left feeling stunned. It seemed such an obvious thing to do now he'd said it.

She was still apprehensive about taking on the care of a baby, but how difficult could it be?

It made so much difference, though, to know she wasn't going to be signing the rest of her life away.

CHAPTER SEVEN

'TOLD you.' Ellie lifted her tired feet onto the leather foot-stool in front of her. 'I knew Lorna wouldn't be able to let Katherine go into foster care.'

Rafe sauntered into the Orangery which ran across the back of his house. 'It's only a temporary arrangement. You might be disappointed yet.' He handed over one of the two mugs of coffee he carried and sat down on the adjacent sofa.

Ellie's eyes sparkled over the rim of her mug. 'I won't be.'

'Why so sure? She seems to me to have taken on Katherine very grudgingly.'

'And you don't approve?'

Rafe rubbed a hand across his face. He wasn't sure what he felt about it.

Actually, he *was* sure. He had a real problem with it. Possibly because he felt such an attraction to Lorna, whilst finding it hard to like that apparent aspect of her character.

He found he kept thinking about her at odd times of the day. Kept wondering how she was doing. Whether there'd been any real bonding happening between her and Katherine.

And he kept remembering how it had felt to stand so

close to her he could feel her breath on his cheek. He wondered what would have happened if he'd kissed her…

'I suppose I don't,' he said brusquely. 'I saw so many unwanted children in the state-run orphanages I worked in during my first gap year. Babies who were so used to receiving no attention they'd given up crying. They just lay in their cots, hour after hour, day after day. It hits a nerve for me.'

Ellie put her mug down on the table. 'Even if Lorna does decide she can't keep going there are hundreds of couples in the UK desperate to adopt a baby like Katherine. She's not going to have a future like that. I'd adopt her myself first.'

'I know.' He shook his head, as though he didn't quite understand what he was trying to say. Something about emotional memories being difficult to control, maybe. 'But I find it difficult to hear that a child isn't wanted. It seems to be the ultimate act of selfishness. You can't put a career ahead of people.'

'That's easy for you to say. You have more money than you know what to do with.' Ellie sipped her coffee. 'And Lorna's not selfish. Not at all. You've spent time with her now. I'd have thought you'd have seen that for yourself.'

Rafe tried not to look too interested. The last thing he wanted was his sister to suspect quite how eager he was to talk about her friend. He'd tried to make his visits to Lorna seem a casual act of friendship.

Not that they were doing him much good. Lorna refused any help from him, and all her time was taken up with caring for Katherine. She seemed to have a need to prove something. Maybe she was over-compensating because she couldn't love her sister's baby? Rafe frowned.

'Don't frown.'

'Sorry—I was thinking. Do you think Lorna is trying too hard?' He pulled his hand through his hair. 'I don't know, but it's like she's playing out a part.'

'Hell, yes!' Ellie replied easily. 'What she's doing is not sustainable.'

'Can't you stop her?'

'Rafe, it's not that simple. Lorna had a really tough time growing up. *Really* tough. Her mother was…' Ellie searched for words. 'I suppose she was genuinely ill. But she was a very demanding woman.'

'And?' He hoped his question sounded only casually interested, but his sister's smile made him doubt it.

'Lorna was a carer for all of her teens. I think her father bailed out some time around her twelfth birthday. From then on Lorna was the primary carer.'

Rafe swore silently. He hadn't guessed that. He'd picked up very easily that Lorna didn't like being in Sittiford, but he hadn't really understood that it might be tied up with bad memories. He'd thought it probably had more to do with the contrast between life in a county town and life in a city.

'She bought the food, did the washing, cooking, cleaning. All the things you have to do to run a home and care for a sick mother. And she still managed to be an A grade student. I don't know how she did it.' Ellie sipped her coffee. 'Mum was really angry about the whole situation. She managed to get her a little bit of help, but Mrs Drummond didn't like "outsiders".'

'So she let Lorna do it all?'

Ellie nodded. 'Why do you think Mum was so keen to have Lorna with us?'

He hadn't thought. Lorna had simply been there, a quiet,

nervous figure in his home. He'd been too busy enjoying his life, planning his future…

'She used to try and get Lorna to talk about it.'

'Did she?'

'Rarely—because she's an incredibly private person. Lorna certainly didn't want anyone at school knowing. She didn't want to draw attention to herself any more than she had to. She was too clever, and she never wore the right clothes. In our year that was hard enough, without having a freak of a mum. And Mrs Drummond was a very strange lady.'

Rafe stood up and looked out over the long garden. Things were beginning to slot into place in his mind. Lorna had used the word 'trapped'. She didn't want to be '*trapped by a baby*'.

He let out his breath in one steady stream. Strange how, if you took the trouble to look beneath the surface, things were often very different than you might have imagined.

She'd simply meant she didn't want to be trapped in a situation she couldn't get out of. And who could blame her?

Ellie took another sip of her coffee. 'Vikki did absolutely nothing, of course.'

Rafe turned round and walked back to his seat.

'Vikki wanted out, and she left for London as soon as she hit sixteen. Within weeks she'd been "spotted", and had started earning really good money as a lingerie model.' Ellie put her empty mug down on the table.

'And Lorna?'

'Stayed and cared for her mum. She got a place at Oxford, you know, but didn't take it up. Instead she studied for her degree locally. Still got a first, but it's not quite the same, is it?'

'I didn't know any of that.'

'No reason you should have.' Ellie glanced at her watch and stood up. 'But I'm sure it's one of the things that make the situation now so difficult. It's like she's already had to put her life on hold, and now she's being asked to do it again.'

Rafe frowned as he worked through the full implications of what Ellie had just told him.

'She wouldn't thank me for telling you, so don't say anything. It's just…I don't want you thinking badly of her. She never has wanted children.'

'Why?'

'Perhaps she thought bringing Vikki up was enough? I don't know. Why don't you ask her? I ought to leave you something to talk to her about.' Ellie grinned, and Rafe knew he hadn't managed to fool his sister at all.

If Katherine would only stop crying.

Lorna bent down low to see whether the boiled water had reached the four-ounce mark in the feeding bottle, then she moved along to the second and third. She glanced over her shoulder at the source of the noise and rubbed a tired hand over her face.

'I'm doing it,' she muttered, as much to herself as Katherine. Then she reached out for the tin of formula milk and carefully measured out one scoop. 'I'm doing it. I'm doing it.'

One scoop per ounce of water. She tipped it into the bottle, only to notice that the steam from the boiled water had made the powder stick to the scoop.

Damn. She'd forgotten to cool the water first. So *stupid.* She couldn't do this. It was an impossible thing to ask her to do. And she *hated* it. She hated being trapped in this house with a baby who did nothing but scream.

Lorna placed both hands over her face and tried to fight back the tears as a wave of guilt hit her. She was so tired. Katherine had slept so little, and she felt completely out of her depth.

Why couldn't she do a simple, easy task like make up a bottle of formula milk? And Katherine wasn't going to wait patiently while the water cooled. Her mewing cries were beginning to increase in volume, and Lorna felt a level of desperation she hadn't known was possible.

The doorbell rang and she peeked out through her fingers. Part of her wanted to hide away and pretend she was out. But the other part of her hoped it might be Ellie on her way home from work.

Lorna glanced over at the clock. It was possible. She padded up the hall and pulled open the door. Her stomach dropped like a stone down a well. *Rafe.*

This wasn't his time. He stood, key in hand, looking almost as shocked as she did. And she knew exactly why that was. Lorna tugged at the front of her T-shirt pyjama top and resisted the temptation to pull her hand through her sleep-tousled hair.

'I thought you must be out.'

'No, I've been asleep.'

'Did I wake you?'

She tried to smile. 'That was Katherine. She's only slept a couple of hours since her last feed.'

Rafe, of course, looked completely gorgeous. He always did. Dark black jeans, white T-shirt, charcoal cotton overshirt. Lorna just wished for the floor to open up beneath her. She hadn't even got any make-up on. 'And now she thinks she's starving. And she's got a temperature from crying so much.'

Even to her own ears she sounded beaten. And she was. She'd sat in countless dentist's waiting rooms and read about sleep-deprived mothers, but she'd had no idea how intensely painful it was.

Rafe looked past her, up the hall and towards the crying noise coming from the depths of the carrycot. 'Can I help?'

'I'm fine. I can manage.'

'I could hold Katherine while you do…whatever it is you need to do.'

The piercing little cry rose another notch in intensity and Lorna's strength crumbled. What was the point in trying to pretend she could manage? It must be perfectly obvious to anyone within a ten-mile radius that she wasn't coping.

Lorna opened the door wider to let him in, but she just wanted to die. Curl up in a tight little ball and pretend none of this was happening. Rafe wasn't the kind of man you wanted to fail in front of.

In fact, she had a problem with failing in front of anyone. 'It's my fault. I should have boiled a kettle before I went to sleep, so I had some cool boiled water ready when I came down. But I was so tired and—'

'That sounds fixable.'

'Not to Katie,' Lorna replied. 'She's done nothing but cry for the last twenty-four hours.'

Rafe shrugged out of his jacket and threw it on the newel post. 'Ellie asked me to ask if you needed anything from the supermarket, by the way. She's going tomorrow, so if you want to give her a list she'll get the stuff and drop it in later.'

'Oh, right. Yes, I will.' She followed him down the hall. 'How long will it take for the water to cool?'

She shrugged and headed towards the kitchen. 'I don't know. I've never done this before. Up to now I've been using the ready-made-up cartons Ellie gave me.' She pushed her hair out of her eyes. 'I'm so tired I can't cope with joined-up thinking, and I swear I'm usually quite bright.'

'Stand a bottle in a jug of cold water.' Rafe stopped to pick Katherine up out of the carrycot. Her skin felt clammy to the touch, even though she was wearing nothing but a nappy. 'Is she feeling well?'

Lorna's eyes welled up.

'She just feels a little hot.' Then he sniffed. 'I think she needs a nappy change.'

'Really?' Lorna closed her eyes. 'I've only just done it. I can't believe how much waste product comes from someone so tiny. And it's all gone runny.' She rubbed a hand across her forehead, trying to smooth out the exhaustion headache. 'Okay, give her here.'

'You sort the bottles out. I'll change her.'

'You will?'

Rafe laughed. The total shock in her brown eyes was funny. 'I may be a little rusty, but I'm an experienced uncle. Just tell me where you're keeping her nappies.'

Lorna looked as if she might argue, but then she turned back to the bottles. It was a victory of sorts. The first time she'd been prepared to accept help from him. He watched as she pulled a teat through a white plastic ring.

'The nappy bag is on my bed,' she said, without turning. 'I've literally just done it.'

Rafe carried Katherine up the steep flight of stairs. He couldn't quite believe he'd offered to do this. He might have said that he was an experienced uncle, but he couldn't honestly remember whether he'd ever changed one of his nephews' nappies. And if he had he certainly wouldn't have volunteered for the task—particularly if they were 'runny'.

The only reason had to be the violet smudges under Lorna's eyes. If he'd had more of an idea what needed to be done he'd have packed her off to bed and given her the chance of some unbroken sleep. Maybe he should still do that.

Rafe pushed open the door to the spare bedroom. The duvet was pushed back and the nappy bag lay open on top of the mattress. Gingerly he laid Katherine out on the open changing mat, and set about finding the nappy, baby wipes and small tub of cream.

He braced himself. This was all about taking a deep breath and just getting on with it.

On the whole, he thought he managed fairly well. He popped the soiled nappy into a scented nappy sack and tied up the top, before turning his attention to opening out a new nappy.

'Rafe, do you want a cup of anything? Tea? Coffee?'

He turned his head for a moment as Lorna came to stand in the doorway. 'Coffee would be—'

'Rafe!' She cut across him as pale liquid spread out across the changing mat and seeped into Katherine's white Babygro.

Oh, damn! Rafe pulled away and tried to grab a muslin cloth to stop the urine trickling off the waterproof mat and onto the bed. *Damn, damn and damn.*

And then she laughed. A husky, sexy laugh that made him smile. It was lovely to see the haunted look vanish from her eyes.

'Don't say anything.'

'She's going to need a bath now.' Lorna's voice broke on

a chuckle, and her face had lost its look of broken exhaustion. It was almost worth it.

'That was all part of my plan to keep her occupied until the water was cooled. And she could probably do with one anyway. That was a corker of a nappy.' He picked Katherine up and held her out as though she would drip dry.

'If you hang on I'll fill the baby bath with some water.' She turned and padded barefooted towards the bathroom.

His eyes followed her—and more particularly the movement of her neat little bottom, hidden away beneath the thin jersey of her pyjama bottoms.

Rafe peeled off Katherine's wet Babygro and left it on the soiled mat. 'Do you want her now?'

'Hang on.' And then, 'Yes.'

Rafe carried her through, and Lorna met him at the door, holding out her hands for the baby.

'I'll do this. There's a knack.' He watched as she tucked her arm round Katherine's back and hooked her thumb underneath her armpit. 'Ellie came round and gave me a masterclass. I think this is something I'm getting right.'

Katherine looked a little shocked when Lorna first lowered her into the water, and then her face relaxed. Lorna scooped up a handful of water with her free hand and trickled it over the baby's tummy. 'She really seems to like this. Don't you, Katie?'

'You're calling her Katie now?'

'She doesn't seem quite big enough to be Katherine yet.' Lorna turned to look up at him, and the smile on her face had him feeling a little stunned by her. He wasn't just falling for her. He was falling *in love* with her. 'Could you hold out the towel for me?'

It took him a moment to respond. 'Sorry—yes.' He reached out and took hold of the white towel folded across the side of the bath.

Lorna wrapped Katherine up in it, drying her body at the same time. 'I love the smell of her when she's just been washed.' She looked up. 'Could you get me a clean Babygro out of the chest of drawers in my room? It's the top right-hand side.'

'Right.' He turned and walked back towards her bedroom.

Rafe picked out a pink Babygro and came back with it. 'This one?'

'Any one is fine.'

He watched as Lorna perched on the bed and dextrously fitted Katherine's limbs into the appropriate arms and legs of the Babygro. She looked as if she'd been doing it all her life. Then she scooped the baby up in her arms and pressed a light kiss on the dark mop of hair.

He'd wondered what it would be like to fall in love. His smile twisted. He'd imagined a very different setting from this—Bali, France, Austria…

'Do you want to take Katie while I clear this lot up?'

Now, that was quite obviously the more attractive option of the two, but…he couldn't do it. Rafe's smile twisted in self-derision. 'You take her down and check, and I'll do this.'

'Really?'

'I'm a saint.'

She laughed her rich chuckle. 'I don't know that I'd ever say that about you. There's some disinfectant spray on the side there,' she said, with a nod towards it. 'And don't worry about the bath water. I can tip that away later.'

Rafe rolled up the wet Babygro in the equally wet muslin cloth.

He had both the bedroom and bathroom looking spotless before he returned downstairs. 'Nearly done?'

She looked over her shoulder. 'Yes. If you want to put the nappy sack outside in the wheelie bin, that'd be great…'

Rafe couldn't quite believe the situation he'd got himself into. This kind of domestic set-up would normally have sent him running in the opposite direction… But somehow with Lorna it didn't feel so bad. In fact, it felt pretty great.

She shook up a bottle, and then flicked off the lid to check the temperature of the milk on the inside of her wrist. 'It's still a bit hot.'

Rafe dried his hands on a towel and threaded it back through the rail.

'Hopefully she'll sleep after this,' Lorna said, crossing her arms in front of her chest. 'Though she does seem to be a bit cranky in the evenings. And yesterday she was unbeliev-able. She just didn't stop.'

Half past seven on a Friday night—Rafe couldn't quite believe he was going to do what he was going to do. His life was changing.

He picked up the bottle and tested the milk on the inside of his wrist, as Lorna had done. 'Go back to bed. I'll do this.'

'But—'

'No buts.' He glanced down at his watch. 'I doubt she's down for the night, but at least you can get a few hours' sleep while I'm here.'

'I know I should say no, but I don't think I can.'

Rafe reached out for Katherine and tucked her in the crook of his arm. 'Go to bed, Lorna.'

CHAPTER EIGHT

'LORNA. Wake up.'

She woke to see Rafe's face a mere foot away. 'Wh—?'

'It's Katherine. She's not well.'

It was like pulling herself out of a deep, dark tunnel.

'I've already rung for the doctor, and he's on his way.'

The word 'doctor' had her eyes open. Lorna pushed back the duvet and swung her legs out of bed. But Rafe was already on his way back downstairs. Her heart was hammering against her ribcage as she followed him.

Rafe was holding Katherine and standing looking out of the window. 'It's some kind of central service, and they'll dispatch whichever doctor is on duty tonight.'

'What's happened?'

He turned, and his face softened as looked at her. 'Don't look so worried. I think she's got some kind of flu bug. But Ellie says she's so tiny we ought to have a doctor look at her.'

Lorna pushed her hair up off her forehead. 'You spoke to Ellie?'

'Do you mind?'

Of course she didn't mind. 'I should have done it myself. I nearly did, but then Katherine seemed a little better. Happier.'

Which was nonsense. She wasn't happy, and her cries were difficult to talk over.

'You might want to put on some clothes. The woman on the phone said someone would be with us within twenty minutes. Oh, and you need to have her red book handy. Do you have it?'

Lorna nodded. She felt scared. What if she'd done something wrong? What if it was *her* fault Katherine was ill? But until yesterday she'd seemed to be doing fine...

She walked through to the kitchen and opened the top drawer, pulling out the red book the health visitor had given her. Katherine's cries were piercing. They seemed to get into her head and reverberate.

'How long has she been like this?' Lorna asked, returning to the sitting room.

Rafe let the curtain drop back into place. 'About three hours like this.'

'I can't believe I didn't hear her.'

'You were tired.'

Lorna bit her lip. 'But what if you hadn't been here?'

His smile was caressing. It almost felt as if he'd touched her. 'I doubt you'd have slept so deeply. You knew you could relax because I was here, that's all.' Rafe walked forward and pressed a light kiss to the top of her head. 'None of this is your fault. Babies get ill.'

Babies get ill. Babies sometimes die. Lorna felt as though all the blood had drained from her face. *Please, God, no.*

'Is that the red book they were talking about?'

Lorna nodded and held it out. Her hand was shaking. 'Yes. It's got her birth weight, and a graph which shows how much weight she's put on each time I've had her weighed.'

'Great.' Rafe tossed it on the coffee table. 'I'll be glad when the doctor gets here, though. This crying is beginning to get to me.'

But you couldn't tell that it was. Rafe looked so calm. He always looked calm. Every time she'd seen him he looked like someone who was completely in control of what they were doing.

What would it be like now if she was alone? If Rafe hadn't offered to look after Katherine? She probably would have phoned the doctor herself by now, but she'd have been a nervous wreck waiting for him to arrive.

'You really ought to go and put some clothes on,' Rafe said with a smile, breaking in on her thoughts.

Lorna looked down and caught sight of her nipples, standing proud against the thin jersey fabric of her top. She was too worried to care what Rafe thought of her. Just pleased he was here.

She ran back up the stairs and threw on a pair of denim jeans and a thicker T-shirt. Below, she could hear the shrill cries of her baby girl.

Her baby girl. It was the first time she'd ever thought about Katie like that. A large tear flipped over the edge of her eye and ran down her cheek. More followed, and she swiped a hand across her face.

She didn't cry.

But she was crying now. Somewhere over the past couple of weeks she'd really fallen in love with Katie. She felt as passionate and protective towards her as any mother could.

Her hands shook as she covered her face, desperate to regain some kind of control. *Oh, God,* what a time to discover how she felt.

'Lorna?' Rafe called up the stairs. 'I think this might be the doctor. A car has stopped outside.'

She gave her face one final swipe and then ran down the stairs. Rafe was waiting at the bottom, poised to open the front door. He glanced back at her and then moved nearer. 'Oh, Lorna, honey.' His free hand moved up to cup her cheek. 'I'm sure it'll be fine.'

She gave a tremulous nod. His blue eyes weren't glinting down at her tonight. They were solid and trustworthy. Eyes belonging to a man she could depend on.

The doorbell rang and Rafe turned away to answer it. Lorna walked through into the sitting room and waited for them to join her. She picked up the red book and leafed through the pages. So far there was very little information in there, but there were pages and pages waiting to be filled in, right up to the age of five.

'Mrs McKinnion?' The attractive-looking Asian doctor walked forward and held out his hand.

Lorna held out her own. 'I'm not… We're not married. I'm Lorna Drummond.'

Rafe came in behind, holding a still crying Katherine. 'Lorna's the baby's guardian. I merely made the phone call.'

The doctor nodded, not particularly interested in the domestic arrangements of the people he'd come to see. He wasted no time in looking at Katherine.

Cowardly, Lorna left Rafe to answer most of the questions. Her arms wrapped tightly around her body as she waited to hear what was that matter with Katie and what she was expected to do about it.

In just her disposable nappy she looked so vulnerable,

so tiny. Having lost so much already in her short life this didn't seem fair.

'I'm tempted to admit her,' the doctor said. 'But since there are the two of you with her…'

Lorna moved closer, about to explain that she was alone. But Rafe stood up and moved to hold her hand, his fingers squeezing gently. She looked up, and he shook his head.

'…and you need to keep her hydrated. No milk.'

His instructions were difficult to follow, but Lorna knew it was panic that was making it hard for her to take in what was being said. The doctor seemed to have made a judgement early on in the proceedings, and was addressing almost all of his remarks to Rafe.

She was given Katie to hold. Lorna ran her finger gently over her heated skin. She should have called a doctor sooner. If Rafe hadn't been here they'd have certainly been on their way to Sittiford Hospital now.

'Miss Drummond.' The doctor nodded his farewell. In her other life she'd have corrected him, insisted on the use of her own title of Dr. But…not now. Now all that mattered was Katie.

Rafe came back into the room and smiled. 'You look spaced out.'

'I feel like that. This isn't your problem. It's mine.'

He shook his head. 'Actually, it's Katie's. And if you think I'm about to leave you to deal with this on your own, you don't think very much of me,' he said with a flash of anger.

'Rafe, I—'

'Don't. I understand you like to manage everything by yourself, and that you're usually totally capable of doing so. But not this time, Lorna.'

It was a relief to be able to give in. She stroked the side of Katie's flushed face. Totally exhausted, she'd dropped into an uneasy sleep. It wouldn't last long, but it was a welcome break from the crying.

'We've got to get her to drink salty water. Every hour if possible.' Rafe moved into the kitchen and filled the kettle with fresh water. 'You'd better do the bottles as I don't know how this steriliser works.' He held out his hands to take Katie.

Lorna handed her over and took the three bottles she'd already made up out of the fridge. She tipped the milk out into the sink. 'What happens if she won't drink salty water?'

'Then she'll have to be admitted to hospital. Considering she was born prematurely, it's amazing she doesn't have to go in now. He was very definite about that.' Rafe carried Katie out of the kitchen.

Lorna took the bottle brush and carefully washed out the bottles, salted the teats and arranged everything in the steriliser. She felt like such a failure. The emotions of the last hour welled up inside her and she began to cry quietly.

'I've put her in the carrycot. She's all right for a while, but I don't think we'll have long,' Rafe said, returning. Then he came up behind Lorna and spun her round to face him. 'Oh, Lorna.'

His shirt felt cold against her hot cheek, his arms strong and his body warm. Lorna hadn't been held for the longest time, and this felt like heaven. Like coming home.

'She's going to be fine. If she really can't cope with taking the water then they'll put her on a drip.'

Lorna lifted a hand up to her face, smoothing away the tears. 'I know. It's just I've tried so hard—'

Rafe held her away from him. 'This is just one of those

things. Not something you've done wrong.' He let his fingers run down her arm. 'Where does all this come from?' he asked, holding her hand and leading her towards the sofa. 'Do you want to tell me?'

She shook her head. It was complicated. And it was in the past. And, no, she didn't want to tell him. He would tell her it wasn't her fault, and she wouldn't believe him.

Rafe sat her down on the sofa. 'I'm going to make us some coffee with the water I've boiled. I can put another lot on for Katie.'

Lorna nodded. It would take a few minutes for the steriliser to run through anyway.

She looked around the sitting room of her old home. She'd been so unhappy here for the longest time. Always feeling that she wasn't doing quite enough, and that if only she could do more everything would be better.

It was like a tape running through her head. Guilt writ large, and an insidious sense of failure. Lorna reached up her sleeve, looking for a tissue, and then swivelled round to reach behind the sofa.

She was being ridiculous. For someone who hadn't cried in years, she was beginning to make a habit of it.

'Here you go.' Rafe passed across a mug and then pulled the footstool closer with his foot, so he could sit opposite her.

'Thanks.' Lorna took a sip of coffee.

Rafe settled himself down on the footstool. 'While I try and get Katie to take some of the salty water, I suggest you pack up some things for you and her.'

She looked up. 'Do you think she'll have to go to hospital, then?'

'No. I think we'll manage to get her to drink the water.

There are two of us; we can work in shifts. If necessary we can give her something to drink every few minutes.'

Lorna started to shake her head. 'This isn't your—'

'It is now. And, assuming we can get Katie to drink, I suggest we move everything to my house for the duration.'

'I can't do that.'

'You're not contemplating a night squashed on the sofa.'

From the hallway came the unmistakable sounds of Katie waking. Lorna put her coffee down on a side-table and stood up. 'I'll get her.'

'And I'll make up the feed.' He tipped some packets out onto the table. 'The doctor has given us these to use tonight, and we've got a prescription for tomorrow.'

Lorna picked one up and tried to read the name on it. 'Does it taste revolting?'

'Apparently.'

Katherine still felt warm to the touch. Lorna lifted her up and carried her through to the sitting room, and waited for Rafe to return with a small bottle filled with the salty liquid.

'After an hour we have to discard this and make up a fresh lot,' he said, setting it down on the side-table and walking over to take Katherine from Lorna. 'Ready?'

Lorna nodded. She knew exactly what Rafe meant by that. It felt as if they were at the beginning of a difficult mission. It felt as if they were a team.

It was the strangest sensation. She'd never been part of a team. She'd never had any one person she could rely on.

Rafe put the bottle to Katherine's mouth as he would have done her milk feed. Her little mouth opened with energy and she sucked hard on the teat.

'She's doing it!'

'Hang on,' Rafe said softly. 'She's not to know it's not milk yet.'

Lorna almost didn't dare breathe. She hadn't prayed since she was twelve, but she prayed now. And Katherine kept on sucking. 'I think she likes it.'

'She must be incredibly thirsty.'

Lorna looked up to meet Rafe's eyes. His were suspiciously moist. 'It's going to be fine, isn't it?'

He nodded. 'Just tiring. Go and pack up what you and Katie need for tonight. We can come back tomorrow to get the rest. We might as well leave as soon as she's had this.'

She ran a hand through her hair, still feeling very uncomfortable with that as an idea. It was hard enough for her to accept that she really couldn't manage this without his help. But to live in his house…

Lorna looked back up at him and found he was watching her, a curious smile hovering about his mouth. 'This is a depressing house to be in, Lorna. It's dark, it's old-fashioned in a bad sense, and it's full of difficult memories. If we're going to suffer, let's do it in comfort.'

He knew.

Ellie must have told him. Strangely, she didn't feel any anger about that. All those years ago she'd sworn her friend to absolute secrecy—and Ellie had honoured that. She couldn't have borne there being something else that would have marked her out as being different.

She bit her lip now, and watched as Rafe made himself more comfortable. He held Katie's head in the palm of his hand and he was smiling down at her, pleased to see the baby was still sucking hard.

'Hopefully she'll be able to keep this down. You should have seen what happened to her last feed.'

Guilt sliced through her yet again. She knew what must have happened because it had happened the feed before. Only she'd assumed it was one of those things…and had been grateful when Katie had fallen asleep.

'It's not your fault.'

Her eyes flew up to meet his again. It seemed he was a mind-reader.

'Why do you always think you're to blame when things go wrong?'

This time she felt it possible to answer him. Maybe it was her relief that Katie was drinking. Maybe it was the warmth in his voice that made her believe he'd understand how she'd felt.

'I think you already know that.' Her voice broke. 'Did Ellie tell you?'

Rafe hesitated, and then nodded. 'Only that you'd been a carer. She wanted me to understand that taking on Katie was a big decision for you. Bigger than most.'

'Did…did you…?' She felt like a small child, asking to be loved. Vulnerable, and very scared. 'Did you blame me for not wanting her?'

'In the beginning.' His eyes went to hers. 'I didn't understand how you could contemplate abandoning her to the state system.'

She'd known that really. Right from the first time they'd spoken together she'd seen his instinctive recoil from her harsh words. But she'd meant them. And she still wasn't sure whether the best place for Katie was with her.

Lorna moistened her lips and dared to voice the thoughts

in her head. 'I'm still thinking about it. She ought to be with a family.'

'You're her family.'

'No.' Lorna shook her head. 'Brothers and sisters type of family. Uncles, aunts, cousins. If she stays with me, I'm it.'

He paused, as though he were searching out his words. 'There's time for you to give her that.'

'It's not very likely.' Lorna stood up and gathered together the sachets the doctor had left. She tapped them on the table so the edges lined up. 'After Mum died I felt so fantastically free. I did love her,' she said quickly. 'But I was so tired—'

'There's no blame in that.'

Lorna glanced over. 'It's hard being the emotional support for other people. You know when you asked about relationships…? Well, that's why I haven't wanted anything serious. I don't want to be responsible for anyone but myself.'

'And now?' His question was asked softly.

'I still don't.' *But it was all too late.* Her eyes fixed on Katie's little face, her eyes closed and her eyelashes dark against her skin. She loved her. Really loved her.

It was as if a splinter had been lodged in her head and a larger wedge had come in after it. The channels for loving had been reopened. And, yes, there was pain. The prospect of sacrificial caring…but there was no choice.

Rafe was watching her closely. He drew his eyes away for a moment and removed the teat from Katie's relaxed mouth. Her breathing seemed steady and her body sated.

'I still think the best place for Katie is to be with someone who loves her.' He looked up, his blue eyes more blue than she'd ever seen them. 'And that's you.'

And inside her heart she heard a resounding yes.

CHAPTER NINE

RAFE could see the look of revelation on her face. She must have been shut down to the possibility of loving for the longest time.

There were issues for her to sort—of course there were. Not least was the fact that she had a career she loved and she was going to have to find a way of blending that together with being a mum.

And he had every intention of being around to help with that.

Rafe settled the half-empty bottle on the table. Maybe it was going to take her time before she was ready to add him to the very select group of people she loved. He'd wait. She was absolutely worth waiting for. And in the meantime he'd do what he could to make her life easier. Starting now.

'Have you got her car seat? We might as well put her straight into it.'

'Oh.' Lorna dropped the sachets back on the table. 'I'll get it.'

She returned moments later with a blue-checked car seat. Rafe settled Katie into it and adjusted the headrest round her small head so she looked comfortable.

'Do you want me to tip that away?' Lorna asked, pointing at the bottle.

'Let's do it as we're about to leave—in case she wakes up while we're getting ready.'

Lorna didn't take long gathering together what she thought she needed for one night away, but the pile in the hallway looked quite terrifying. It quickly became obvious that it all belonged to Katie.

'Do you think we should take the steriliser now?' Lorna asked, appearing from the kitchen with it in her arms. 'Seems safer, doesn't it?'

He nodded, and carried the carrycot out to his vintage Jaguar. She followed with the sterilizer, and stood by and watched as he tucked it down the side and wedged it in against a rocking seat.

'Have you got yourself some fresh clothes? Toothbrush?'

'I think that's it. I've put in some Babygros for Katie, even though I don't think she'll wear them.'

'Just the lady herself, then,' Rafe said, stepping back from the car.

Lorna stayed outside while Rafe returned for Katie. She took in a deep breath of night air, loving the silence and the huge expanse of sky. Leaving this house felt good. Accepting help felt better. It all felt as if a huge burden had been lifted from her shoulders.

And Rafe didn't seem to think any less of her because she couldn't manage alone. There were moments when she'd caught him watching her… She looked over as he walked out of the house.

'Have you got your keys?'

She laid a hand on her jeans pocket and nodded. 'Shall I

get in the back? This car must be pre-airbags, so Katie can go in the front.'

Rafe came up alongside and his arm brushed against hers. She felt a frisson of awareness pass between them. At least she thought it was mutual. Another glance at him and she wasn't so sure. He was frowning. 'I think I might need you to fit the car seat.'

'Why don't I drive my hire car?' she suggested, after a cursory look at the front seat of Rafe's Jaguar. 'I know how it fits in that, and it makes sense anyway—if I need to come back for some more things in the morning.'

It was a real palaver to get Katie's car seat firmly anchored in the middle of the rear seats in her two-door hire car. Lorna was grateful Katie didn't wake up and begin crying again. It couldn't be long before she would. The salty solution might keep her hydrated, but it wouldn't make her stomach feel full.

'Done it.' Lorna unbent and backed out of the car, stumbling as her heels caught on the side of the pavement.

'Careful.' Rafe's hands reached out to catch her, the warmth of his hands on her bare arms.

Lorna drew a sharp intake of breath. She was so aware of this man. It was as if she was hot-wired to respond to everything he did.

'Follow me,' Rafe said, pulling down the driver's seat. 'It's the second turning on the right to Framley.'

'I remember.'

'Straight through the village, and Priory Manor is round the second bend.'

'Priory Manor?'

'It's where I live.' Rafe held the door open and Lorna climbed in. Then he turned and walked back to his own car.

Priory Manor. Her hands gripped the padded steering wheel. Priory Manor was a Grade Two listed former gentleman's residence. It was serious money. When Ellie had mentioned he'd bought a house on the outskirts of Framley she'd disregarded it as impossible.

It seemed incredible that she should be going there now. Even more incredible that Rafe should own it. Lorna swallowed down the hard lump in her throat. It also underlined how ridiculous it was that she'd been imagining Rafe might be attracted to her.

Why would he be?

The taillights of his car shone brightly, and Lorna had no difficulty following them as they drove down the country lanes. Behind her she could hear Katie beginning to stir. She glanced over her shoulder, and then back at the road.

Framley was what was known as an 'executive' village. Almost all the properties were detached period homes, and Priory Manor was a little on the outside of it.

Rafe swept up the drive and parked by the front door. Lorna pulled up behind him.

'She's waking up,' Lorna said, as soon as Rafe had walked level with her window.

'Let's get her in quickly.'

Lorna climbed into the tight space at the rear and unclipped the seat belt. Then she stood back and allowed Rafe to reach in and carry the seat out.

Katie's head was turning this way and that, her mouth searching for food. Rafe held up his car key. 'You'd better bring the bottles and changing bag in. I think we're going to need them quickly.'

She followed him up the wide stone steps, feeling completely out of her depth. Rafe pushed open the door to the left and carried Katie in, setting her down on the cream-coloured carpet.

The room's perfect proportions, high ceilings and elegant cornices, marked this house as being one of quality. *And Rafe owned it.*

'It's a beautiful house,' Lorna said awkwardly.

Rafe unclipped Katie from her car seat. 'Yes, it is.' He looked up and his eyes softened. 'It's just a house, Lorna. I told you my misspent youth had served me well.'

But it was the house of a man who'd never be interested in a woman like her. Never in a million years.

He passed Katie across to her and felt inside the changing bag for one of the bottles they'd brought with them. 'I'll take the cold edge off this and be right back.'

Lorna sat down in one of the comfortable sofas and let her eyes wander around the room, slightly stunned by it all. Rafe had to be worth millions to own a house like this.

Katie's soft whimpering raised in volume, so Lorna stood up again and started to pace along by the window, hoping the movement would calm her.

'Just in time,' Rafe remarked, returning with the warmed bottle. 'Let's hope she wants to drink it this time as much as she did the last.'

Lorna sat down again and settled the baby against her. Katie fairly grabbed at the teat, and her suck was as hard as before. 'Ellie told me babies born as early as Katie some-times haven't got a very strongly developed suck reflex. It's not true for her, is it?' she said, looking up and smiling into Rafe's blue eyes.

He shook his head. 'She's certainly got the hang of it.'

Rafe sat down next to them and turned his head so he could look at Lorna. 'I suggest that I take the first shift and you the second. I'll go and make up a bed for you, and then come down to keep a watch on Katie. Does that suit you?'

'I don't mind which way round.'

'I'd rather keep going for a bit. How about four hours on, four hours off?'

Lorna nodded. Rafe yawned, and then stood up. 'And before you go up to sleep I'd better show you around the kitchen, so you can help yourself to things.' He paused, his hand resting on the doorframe. 'Oh, and I'd better unload the car, too.'

It was the start of a peculiar few days. During the first twenty-four hours it didn't matter what day of the week it was, or whether it was light or dark outside. As soon as Lorna appeared downstairs it was the signal for Rafe to go up.

But Lorna knew he was there. For the first time in her entire life she found she could really trust someone to be there for her. He made her feel as if she was one half of a team—that they were working together for a joint aim. And that aim was Katie's wellbeing.

As they passed into the second twenty-four hours Lorna found she could relax. Katie continued to be unwell, but it didn't feel quite so desperate. She was taking the saline solution with ease, and the doctor was very encouraging about her progress.

The four-hour shifts became less necessary as Katie no longer needed liquid on the hour, every hour. They'd even managed to introduce a weak milky feed, and although Katie had lost weight, it wasn't too scary an amount. Gradually

Rafe and Lorna had more than the odd snatched conversation…and Lorna found she liked it.

Really liked it. She loved the way Rafe smiled when he saw her for the first time each day, loved the way he casually touched her as he passed, and she loved the way his eyes seemed to look at her with approval. She felt liked. Special. For the absolute first time she felt as though she had someone on her side. And that was such a novelty.

For so long she'd felt unlovely because she was unloveable. Her mother had been critical and demanding, her sister self-absorbed and her father absent. But here, with Rafe, she felt accepted and valued. *Loved.* Almost.

The look in his eyes warmed her every time they rested on her, and she felt as though she could achieve anything. *Be* anything.

Surely that was what being part of a family should be like? And for the first time Lorna wanted that. She wanted to feel as if she belonged to a strong, fighting unit. She didn't want to go back to doing the best she could on her own.

She'd manage. She would. Because she was incapable of not sticking out her chin and taking whatever life threw at her. But life with Rafe would be better. Of course it would be better—it would be wonderful.

Only she couldn't quite take the leap of faith needed to believe *his* life would be better with *her*.

Lorna stretched out in bed and then rolled over to look at the luminous hands of the ugly alarm clock she'd brought with her. There were still fifteen minutes before she was due to relieve Rafe from his shift. Time enough to shower and dress.

She pushed back the duvet and swung her legs down to the floor. Rafe had to be exhausted. Somehow the shifts had fallen so that he was the one sitting up through the night. This had to be the last time. If Katie was beginning to take a milky feed she would start to sleep longer…and she wouldn't need someone sitting up with her.

Which would also mean it was time to leave Rafe's house.

The thought of returning to her childhood home wasn't a good one. And she was going to miss him. Miss him as she'd never missed anyone before.

Lorna grabbed a quick shower and threw on a long white linen skirt and a simple pink T-shirt. She hurried down-stairs…but to find the entire floor in darkness. Curtains drawn and lights switched off.

'Rafe?' She pushed open the door to the kitchen and scanned it. Nothing. Next was the informal sitting room.

There was just enough light to see Rafe sitting on the sofa, head back and legs outstretched. Katie was curled up on his chest and both were fast asleep.

Lorna bit down on a smile. She didn't think she'd ever seen anything quite so sexy or touching as Rafe McKinnion with a sleeping baby on his chest.

She walked over to him and laid a gentle hand on his arm. 'Rafe?'

He didn't stir.

'Rafe?' Lorna sat down beside them. She leant back on the sofa and studied his profile.

He'd not shaved in over twenty-four hours, and the stubble on his face was rough. It was tempting to stretch out a finger and run it across his jawline.

She was going to miss him when she had to leave. She'd got used to this feeling of connection.

Katherine made a small grunting sound and Lorna leant

in closer, to see if she was waking. Her tiny mouth pursed, and it looked as if she might be dreaming about her next feed. She also looked relaxed, and Lorna felt a wave of gratitude.

She looked up at the man who was holding Katie and found…he was no longer asleep. His blue eyes were watching her, the expression in them making her breath catch.

'Morning.' His voice was husky and full of sleep. Slowly, quite deliberately, he wrapped his spare hand around the back of her head and pulled her in towards him. His breath brushed her lips and his eyes seemed to actually touch them.

He was going to kiss her.

Rafe McKinnion was going to kiss her.

Lorna closed her eyes and let it happen. She heard him murmur her name, felt the fingers of his right hand bury deep in her hair.

His lips were warm, and they were skilful. She didn't have a vast amount of experience, but she knew she was being kissed by an expert. Every touch of his lips coaxed a response from her, and left her feeling a mass of quivering sensation.

Then his tongue snaked out. Light, suggestive. She felt her own mouth open to receive him. His name seemed to resound in her head as her body became pliant. She'd never responded to a kiss like this before. Never wanted anything quite so much.

And it went on and on. Every touch of his tongue sent her nerve-endings into spasm.

Rafe pulled back, his breathing a little laboured, his eyes searching her face as though gauging her reaction. 'Lorna.' He rested his forehead on hers, and the hand that had been in her hair stroked down her cheek.

Then he smiled. She was almost too shy to meet his eyes, but she did.

Rafe glinted down at her. 'That's a perfect way of starting the day.'

Lorna bit her lip and tried to sit up. Rafe stopped her, and pulled her in for another kiss. 'I think I could go on kissing you for hours.'

And she knew she'd let him. If he wanted to. Kissing him was everything she'd ever imagined it might be. Her insides seemed to have become liquid, and a dull ache had settled low in her body. His thumb brushed across her bottom lip and she felt her mouth part, heard the small shaky intake of breath.

'Did you sleep well?'

Lorna nodded, not trusting her voice to answer him. She didn't really understand what was going on—only that Rafe was touching her and she felt *whole*.

And a little frightened. Because this mattered so much to her. *He mattered*. Realisation hit her like a thunderbolt. He mattered, *this* mattered—because she loved him as she'd never intended to love anyone.

CHAPTER TEN

RAFE put down the telephone and went to find Lorna in the kitchen. His hand hesitated on the door handle, and then he took a deep breath and walked in.

Quite suddenly he'd run out of time to tell Lorna how he felt about her. Despite the kisses they'd shared, he'd never been quite sure she was ready to hear it…and now he was going to lose her. He couldn't fool himself that he wasn't.

It had been hard enough to persuade her to stay in his house after Katie had begun to recover. Now she *would* leave…and he felt as if she was being ripped from him.

'Who was that?' Lorna looked across at him, bottle brush poised over a bowl of soapy water.

'The police.'

'Police. Why—?' And then she stopped, and the colour drained from her face. 'Oh, God, no.'

Rafe walked further into the room. 'Katie's father has made contact. He'd like to meet with us.'

He saw the pulse beat at the base of her neck, and then she turned to continue with what she'd been doing. Calm. Controlled. And it felt as if she'd shut him out. 'When?'

'He's available today. If that suits us.'

'Best to get it out of the way,' she said quietly.

In a way, she was right. If someone was about to be ripped out of your life it was better that it happened quickly—like a sticking plaster being pulled from skin.

He stood for a moment, watching the movement of her back as she washed the bottles. Could he tell her now? Just say, *Lorna, I love you. I need you.*

He's always been so glib around women. Always known how to charm and to captivate. But…

If she looked at him and said she couldn't love him back, that sharing his life wasn't what she wanted, he didn't think he would be able to cope with that.

And he knew that by asking her to love him he was asking her to take a step towards something she'd never known. She'd been so hurt in the past—undermined and taken advantage of by all the people who should have loved her best.

She'd return to the States.

Rafe's hands balled into fists and he had to consciously relax them. He felt…impotent, for want of a better word. There was nothing, absolutely nothing he could do, to make meeting Katie's father easier for her. And he could do absolutely nothing to make her stay if she wanted to leave.

'I'll call them back and let them know.' His voice was toneless.

For a brief moment Lorna rested her hands on the edge of the sink. 'Yes.'

'Lorna—' he began, her name dragged from deep within.

'Don't!' She carried on cleaning the bottles. 'I—I can't…'

If she'd only turned round he might have managed the step that separated them. But she didn't. Her hands moved in the soapy water and then she carefully placed one of the bottles on the draining board.

Rafe quietly shut the door.

Lorna sat looking at Katie in the bouncing seat. A few short weeks, one tiny baby and her life had changed beyond imagination. It had been shattered and rebuilt—better than it had ever been before.

She watched as Katie's little eyes started to close. Once they fluttered open and then shut again, her breathing even and steady. Asleep. She looked so beautiful when she was asleep.

Her heart welled up with love for her little girl. Not hers, exactly, but hers by virtue of love. This mystery father could never love Katie the way she did. He hadn't seen her with a tube up her nose. He'd not taken a share of the hourly saline feeds. He'd not come the minute he'd heard the news that his daughter was motherless...

But Katie was his—if he wanted her. And how could anyone not want her? Lorna stroked a finger over the back of Katie's soft hand.

It seemed a lifetime ago that she hadn't. Or hadn't believed she had the capacity to love Vikki's child the way she deserved to be loved. It had taken Rafe to show her that she wasn't irrevocably damaged by her childhood.

Lorna stood up and looked down at the sleeping little girl. She loved her. And she loved Rafe.

Losing either one would hurt her as nothing ever had. But she was about to lose both. Without Katie there was no reason for her to stay in England—unless Rafe asked her to.

She felt a hot tear run down her cheek and brushed it angrily away. A few kisses and snatched conversations wasn't enough to build dreams upon. She had a life in Texas waiting for her—a job being held open for her. Only she didn't want that any more.

Lorna walked out of the sitting room, meaning to go to her bedroom and cry in private, but she had to walk past Rafe's study, and the door was a little ajar.

He was sitting perfectly still, staring out of the window that looked over the front driveway. Silent. Sad.

Lorna hesitated. *Rafe loved Katie, too.*

As though he sensed her standing there, he looked round. 'Are you busy?'

'No.' He shut his laptop and turned to face her. 'I can't concentrate.' His face had a gaunt, haunted look she'd never dreamed she'd see on it.

Lorna throat felt as if it had been stripped with razor-blades it was so sore.

'Is Katie—'

'Asleep.'

He stood up and flexed his fingers. 'Good. That's good.'

'Yes.' Lorna rubbed a hand up her bare arm. 'D-do you think he'll want her?'

Rafe didn't ask her who she meant by 'he'. 'It depends why he didn't come forward at the beginning. Katie's eleven weeks old—just over.'

Nearly three months.

That did seem quite a long time for a man to decide to come forward to claim his baby. And he hadn't been at the funeral either…

'What will you do?' Rafe's voice grated, and her eyes flew up to look into bleak blue ones. 'If he does want her? Will you go straight back to the States?'

Lorna smoothed her hand across the flat of her stomach. 'I suppose I'll have to. But I'd like to keep in contact with Katie.'

'Of course.'

Rafe turned and picked up his mobile phone from the table. 'I think I'm going for a walk. I can't bear this waiting.'

Her eyes wandered over to the window and she looked out at the light summer drizzle. 'In this?'

'It won't kill me.' He moved to walk past her and his arm brushed against hers. He stopped and looked down at her, his blue eyes holding hers captive. 'Lorna, I didn't think this would happen. I'd have never encouraged you to love her if—'

She reached out and touched his forearm. 'I'm glad.' The sensitive pads of her fingertips could feel the light sun-bleached hair. 'If you'd not been around I don't think I'd have had the courage to spend time with her. I'd have gone on thinking that I was better off alone, but now I know…'

Her voice cracked. She didn't know how to tell him what she'd discovered about herself. In a few short weeks everything she'd thought she'd wanted had been tipped upside down.

She wanted people to love her. She wanted to have children of her own that she could worry about and care for. She wanted…him.

'Lorna.' His hands moved of their own volition to cradle her face. 'Oh, God, Lorna.' Then he kissed her.

Her mouth opened beneath his and her fingers clutched at the back of his shirt, pulling him closer. She didn't have the confidence to say the words that were bubbling up inside her. *I love you. Please ask me to stay. I love you.* Everything she felt was poured into that kiss. She let her tongue flick out to battle with his. It was primeval. Desperate.

His hand moved to push the hair back off her face and

he looked down into her eyes, his own suspiciously moist. 'I love you.'

'You l-love…?'

'You. I love you.' His strong mouth twisted. 'If we lose Katie I'm going to hurt. But if I lose you I'm going to die. I know this isn't the life you want, but—' his voice became deeper '—stay with me.'

She felt a little stupid. 'You want me to stay here?'

'Or let me come to the States with you. I want to know everything about you. I want to build a life with you. I want to sit on some balcony somewhere beautiful in our old age and look back on a life we've shared together.'

A sob ripped through her.

His thumb moved across her full and throbbing lips. 'Lorna,' he breathed. 'Will you stay? Even if you don't need me?'

Lorna heard the uncertainty in his voice and forced herself to answer. 'I'll always need you.' She felt the emotion pulse through his body and smiled. 'I love you.'

'You…?'

Her smile widened as she saw the relief flood his eyes, the warmth and the shock too. 'I love you. I—'

Rafe's mouth cut off the words, and for a few minutes all she could think about was how happy she was. Then she remembered Katie. He seemed to sense it, because he pulled back.

'I want Katie,' she said softly, her face buried against his chest.

'I know.' Rafe kissed the top of her head. Then he stepped back and threaded his fingers through hers. 'She feels like ours, doesn't she? Yours and mine?'

She nodded, unable to speak. He led her back into the

sitting room and they sat together waiting as the minutes ticked by.

'I'd never thought about having children,' he said into the silence. 'But now building a family with you is all I want.'

It was what she wanted too. God willing, beginning with Katie. But after that she wanted more children. She wanted to be surrounded by people she could love. Now she'd started it seemed to be an unstoppable force within her.

Katie stirred at a little before three. Lorna picked her up and cradled her on her knee. Rafe stood and walked across to the window to look down the drive.

But there was nothing.

At ten minutes past there was a ring on the doorbell. Lorna felt her stomach quiver with nerves, then Rafe leant across and lightly kissed her lips. 'I love you.'

She smiled, but she knew it wavered. He walked out to answer the door, and she listened to the low-voiced conversation happening in the hallway. Then the door opened.

Lorna looked up to see a man—a boy, rather, no more than twenty. Her eyes looked behind him, as though there might be someone standing there more obviously the person they were waiting for.

'This is Callum Waugh.'

The young man put his backpack down on the carpet and stepped forward, holding out his hand. 'Viks and I...' His eyes became transfixed by the baby. He thrust a hand through his hair. 'We...I...erm. *Oh, God, a baby.* I didn't expect... We...'

It was later, much later, after Callum had left, and Lorna had put Katie to sleep in her carrycot.

'She's ours,' Lorna said brokenly. She reached in to adjust the blanket that covered her. 'I didn't think that would be the outcome of today.'

Rafe put his arm around her waist. 'He's young, and a long way from his family in Australia. It'd be nice to think we could encourage him to stay a little in contact with her.'

'Yes.'

Rafe's fingers turned her so that she faced him. His eyes were so full of love…for *her*. It made her feel breathless, and a little scared that now she had so much she might lose it all.

Rafe lowered his head and kissed her. 'Marry me?' he said, against the long column of her throat.

The temptation was to say yes. Actually, the temptation was to scream it. But something held her back. Marriage was serious. It was a lifelong commitment…

'Rafe, we can adopt Katie together without our being married.'

His hands cradled her face. 'We can. But I don't want you to marry me because of Katie. Or because of the other children we might have together. I don't want you to marry me because of a million other reasons. I want you to marry me because I love you. And because I want the world to know that. I want to marry you because anything else isn't quite enough…'

Lorna swallowed. Then she reached up to touch his mouth. 'In that case…my answer is yes.'

THEIR BABY BOND

by
Amy Andrews

As a twelve-year-old, **Amy Andrews** used to sneak off with her mother's romance novels and devour every page. She was the type of kid who daydreamed a lot and carried a cast of thousands around in her head, and from quite an early age knew that it was her destiny to write. So, in between her duties as wife and mother, her paid job as Paediatric Intensive Care Nurse and her compulsive habit to volunteer, she did just that!

Amy Andrews lives in Brisbane's beautiful Samford Valley, with her very wonderful and patient husband, two gorgeous kids, a couple of black Labradors and six chooks.

Don't miss Amy Andrews's latest novel,
An Unexpected Proposal, **out in March from Mills & Boon Medical Romance™!**

To Sandra Baxter, my mother.
You lift me up so I can walk on mountains.
I am truly blessed.

CHAPTER ONE

DR WILLIAM GALLIGHER knew he'd been fooling himself the minute he saw Louise Marsden again. *Damn it.* He wasn't as over her as he'd thought! One year apart had obviously not managed to erase five years of the best relationship he'd ever had. He paused at the entry to Ward Two, his hand on the swing doors, and took a deep breath, his heart pounding in anticipation. He watched her through the glass panels, the familiar pull of attraction flaring to life.

Even a good ten metres away, and with her back to him, he knew it was her. Her thick, golden, rope-like plait brushed the gentle curve of her bottom, revealing her identity at any distance. That plait and the cute package attached to it were known the width and breadth of the hospital.

His groin tightened as, unbidden, images stormed his mind. Lou naked with her hair loose, flowing over her shoulders and down her back. He still had far too vivid recall of how great it felt trailing over his body. How thick and heavy it felt against his fingers when they were buried in it. How he had spent many an hour brushing it, until the streaks of blonde, honey and gold blended together to form a shiny silken curtain of glorious colour. He had missed her hair.

She was leaning against the raised return of the central nurses' desk, her elbow resting against the smooth surface. Her petite body as slender as he remembered. Her derrière as cute as ever. She was chatting to Lydia, and he could hear her wicked laughter drift towards him. Lou had a fantastic laugh. He had missed her laugh too.

He sighed. Louise Marsden had been an easy woman to love. Generous, loyal, uncomplicated—the complete opposite of his ex-wife. She had known how messed up he'd been over Delvine and the demise of his marriage, and she had been a soothing balm for his battered soul. Lou had been just what he'd needed.

Damn it. He could feel himself being seduced by the past and put the brakes on. He wasn't here for this. For her. His work had bought him back. And that was it. Because for the first time in years he had a chance to start a fresh page with his daughter. And he wouldn't complicate it by rekindling the flame with Lou.

Okay, Candy adored Louise, but after years of Delvine muddying the waters with his daughter he finally had the opportunity to reconnect with her, and he needed to devote all his time and energy to that. Not chase after something that he had ended a year ago. No matter how tempting it was.

Louise Marsden felt like hell. She gripped her stomach as the baby did a somersault. *Come on, little guy, give me a break.* Her back ached, her legs ached, her ribs ached and her stomach growled as the little commandant inside her demanded a sugar-hit. She felt shaky and nauseated as she pulled a packet of Fruit Tingles out of her pocket and crammed one quickly into her mouth.

Her tongue tingled as the sweet fizzed in her mouth, the effect almost instantaneous. The trembling ceased and her stomach stopped feeling as if it was imminently in danger of losing its contents.

'You okay, Lou?'

Louise nodded, easing her grip on the desk. 'Am now,' she smiled weakly at her second-in-charge and good friend Lydia Clarke.

'Fruit Tingle time?' Lydia asked.

Louise smiled and nodded. 'Little dictator,' she said.

'Hah! If you think this is bad, just wait. You're going to be dancing attendance on that little tyke for the rest of your life.'

Lydia had four kids, so Lou figured she could speak with reasonable authority. 'Oh, goody,' she grumbled good-naturedly.

'Still sleeping badly?'

She nodded. 'I just can't get comfortable. I feel like I'm an elephant sleeping in a hammock.'

Lydia laughed. 'You aren't exactly small.'

'Gee, thanks…why are we friends again?'

'Because I've known you since first grade and I keep you supplied with Fruit Tingles.'

'I can buy my own Fruit Tingles,' Lou protested, but couldn't deny that Lydia's multiple stashes had got her out of many a baby-induced hypoglycaemic attack.

The phone rang and Lydia answered it. Peter Booth, a nurse on Ward Two, steamed into the nurses' station, baby on hip. 'I can't get anyone else to do the shave. I just need one more, come on guys—Lou…people are going to pay big money to see all that gorgeous hair come off.'

'No, no, no and no. It's all right for you,' laughed Lou, staring at Pete's bald pate. 'You're used to it.'

'You could just get it cut short or even coloured. You don't have to go the whole hog.'

'Out,' Lydia ordered, replacing the phone, picking up a chart and whacking him playfully. 'That would be a sin.'

'True,' he sighed. 'But still…'

'Out,' said Lydia, grinning. They watched him leave. 'So, what have you got planned for the weekend?'

'Anything and everything I can to keep my mind off Will's return.' A month had passed since the memo from the Medical Director had announced Will's appointment, and she wasn't any closer to indifference.

Kristy Freeman, a newly graduated nurse, bustled into the station along with Lynne Oliver, the ward clerk. The phone rang again and Lynne answered it. Lynne was efficient and practically indispensable to Ward Two, but loved to gossip. Lydia took her friend's arm and steered her out of the nurses' station—too much activity, too much noise, too many flapping ears.

They parked themselves just on the other side of all the activity, in the main thoroughfare, leaning their elbows against the raised return. 'It's been a year, Lou. Don't tell me you still love him?' Lydia asked.

'Oh, God, no. I'm over him. Really.' *Really.*

'So, what's the problem?' Lydia demanded.

'I don't know. Will took up every part of my life for a long time, and…'

'You loved him?' Lydia finished.

Lou nodded miserably. She was over him. *Really.* But suddenly a year's separation didn't seem like enough distance.

'Tell me, Lou,' Lydia said gently, 'how long were you unhappy in that relationship?'

'I was happy most of the time,' she protested.

'Sure. But did he ever ask you to marry him? Did he ever give you any indication or promise of anything other than living for the moment?'

'No.'

'No,' said Lydia, touching her friend's arm, 'he didn't.'

'It wasn't his fault. His life is complicated. Delvine made everything so difficult. You know that, Lydia. He's your friend too.'

'Sure.' Lydia nodded. 'And you were more than understanding, Lou. In fact I don't know of any other woman who would have been quite so understanding for quite so long. But he ended it, and vacated your life, and you've moved on,' she said, indicating Lou's round bump. 'And you have this baby to think about now. And Will may have been my friend too, but my loyalty will always be with you.' She grinned. 'Always. Now, repeat after me: Will Galligher is in my past. I am over him.'

Lou rolled her eyes. 'Will Galligher is in my past. I am over him,' she said dutifully.

'Now repeat it over and over until you believe it. All weekend if necessary.' Lydia laughed.

Lou laughed too. She felt empowered by talking to Lydia. Her friend always had the knack of cutting through the layers to the crux of the matter. 'You're right, Lydia. Besides, the only room I have in my heart these days is for this little guy,' she said, patting her stomach.

'Atta girl! You'll be fine, Lou,' said Lydia, hugging her

reassuringly. 'Really. You'll be cool. You'll be calm. You'll be collected. And if he puts one foot wrong, I'll beat him to a pulp.'

Will hesitated a little before pushing open the doors and approaching. He hadn't expected to feel this churned up, and part of him urged retreat. Maybe this meeting would be better on Monday morning? At least she'd be expecting him then, and it would be business as usual. Lou and Lydia looked deep in conversation. *Don't be stupid, man. She won't bite. Get it over and done with.*

He swung the doors open defiantly and ordered his legs to move. *I am over her. Candy is my priority. Only Candy.* He strode towards his goal, his eyes planted firmly on his target. Her long plait like a homing beacon. He noticed a crawling child with bilateral leg plasters also making its way to Lou from the opposite direction. Except he wasn't looking at her with grim determination, but absolute glee. As if she was the best thing in the whole ward. *Good taste, kid.*

He saw her look down as the little one touched her leg, and he heard her laugh again, the noise carrying to him, evoking myriad memories from their five years together. She bent and hauled the babe up on to her hip, still chatting to Lydia. The child snuggled his head into Lou's breast and Will's heart skipped a beat as Lou cuddled the little boy close, her chin rubbing absently against his downy hair. He remembered how she had held Candy just like that. *I am over you. I am over you.*

'Hell, Lou, don't look now, but Will's coming up right behind you,' murmured Lydia.

Lou froze and cuddled little Terry closer. Today? He

wasn't due to start till Monday. She wasn't ready for this. She was supposed to have the weekend to prepare. How was he going to react to her news?

'Hello, Lou.'

Louise bugged her eyes at Lydia. *Help.*

Lydia bugged hers back, and nodded ever so slightly. *It's okay. I've got your back.*

Will smiled at Lydia, who gave him a cool look. *Oh, dear.* He had counted Lydia as one of his friends. He and Lou had been out with Lydia and her husband, Gerry, many times, had been to dinner at their house on numerous occasions. Candy counted Rilla, Lydia's third child, as one of her closest friends. But Lou and Lydia had always been really tight, and he'd known that Lou had been hurt when he'd left. And women stuck together.

He felt his heartbeat kick up a notch as Lou slowly turned. What would he see when she finally faced him? Would she still look as hurt as the day he had told her they couldn't go on as they were? Or had she moved past that? To anger? Or contempt? Or maybe she'd be happy to see him? She'd smile at him and throw her arms around his neck?

Lou took a deep breath and slowly turned, bracing herself for his reaction, pulling Terry closer to her chest. 'Hello, Will.'

Will's thoughts stuttered to a halt. For a few seconds he wondered if he was having some kind of absent seizure. Or stroke. It took a few moments for the wiring in his brain to reconnect. He had heard about people being struck dumb and knew he was living their nightmare.

How naive had he been? The look on her face didn't register. The amazingly large bosom where the little boy was snuggled didn't register. He leant against the counter and took a deep breath. The only thing that registered was her enormous stomach. Pregnant? She was pregnant? He was completely speechless. In fact he was fairly certain he had his mouth open and was gaping like an idiot.

'Close your mouth, Will,' said Lydia, saccharine-sweet. 'Don't want to catch any flies.'

He glanced at her and saw the amusement and triumph in her eyes. *Oh, yeah. Lydia definitely wasn't keen on him.* He ignored her, and struggled for a moment for something to say. The initial shock was waning, and he could feel the first spurt of a darker, stronger emotion. Anger? Jealousy? Possession?

Lydia's smugness goaded him. 'Jeez, Lou. You sure didn't waste any time,' he said, staring pointedly at Lou's belly.

Lou gripped Terry even closer as she heard Lydia's shocked gasp. She stared at him for a moment, stung by his words. 'My office,' she said, through clenched teeth.

Lou passed Terry to Lydia, feeling her friend's hostility as a palpable force. If she didn't get Will out of harm's way Lydia was going to tear him to shreds. And the way she felt at the moment, with his insulting remark hanging between them, she might well let her.

He followed her, watching her plait sway and glide against her shirt. The urge to pull on it, flip her around, kiss her mouth and refamiliarise himself with those lips was strong, and he suppressed it with difficulty. Even if his life hadn't been complicated, and there hadn't been Candy to consider, Lou had obviously replaced him.

Lou pulled out her chair and glared at him as he sat opposite. How dared he? She was mad as hell, and battled to bring her temper under control. The very fact that being in this office reminded her of the number of times he had dragged her in here and kissed her made her madder.

'I'm sorry. Was I supposed to sit around and pine for you all this time? Was I?'

He knew he had no right to feel so outraged. But he did. 'Of course not,' he snapped. 'But, jeez, Lou. Did you even let my side of the bed get cold? Just how pregnant are you?'

'I'm thirty weeks. And I don't owe you an explanation, Will. You ended it. You left. You said you didn't know when you'd be back. So I got on with my life. You were too involved with your own stuff for a baby. So I found someone who wasn't.'

The baby chose that moment to give her a hefty kick, as if objecting to the lie. She placed her hand over the spot and rubbed it absently. *Sorry, baby, but if he's going to accuse me of being easy when he should know me better, then he can suffer for a bit.*

Will followed the movement and felt another irrational streak of jealousy. She was carrying another man's baby. He hadn't been prepared for that. Her anger, her hostility—yes. But not how much it was going to sting knowing she had traded him in for someone else so quickly.

He shook his head to clear it. 'Since when did you want a baby?'

'I've always wanted one,' she snapped.

'You never told me,' he said indignantly.

'When was it ever the right time to tell you, Will? I'm a thirty-five-year-old woman. What makes you think I wouldn't want one?'

He blinked. *Good question.* She was a paediatric nurse. A

damn good one at that. She'd been wonderful with Candy. He sighed. 'Who's the father?' *Please, God, don't let me know him.* 'Are you going to marry him?'

Lou felt herself getting sucked in to the lie further, and searched for a half-truth to assuage her guilt. 'He's…not on the scene any more.' *It's complicated.* She thought about Jan and Martin and clutched her swollen belly harder.

Will blinked. The surprises just kept on coming. 'What do you mean? Doesn't he know you're pregnant?'

'It's not like that,' she dodged, hoping she could keep the lies straight. 'It was just a casual thing.'

Will narrowed his eyes and looked at her closely. *Rubbish.* There was something she wasn't telling him. How badly had she wanted a baby? Had she used some poor, unsuspecting guy to accomplish her goal?

'Lou, you didn't just use some guy to get pregnant, did you?'

The baby kicked again. Did he really think her capable of such a cold-blooded plan? Anger simmered through her veins. 'This is none of your business, Will. All you need to know is that I'm pregnant and I'll be out of your hair in a month. I'm sure you and I can manage to be civil to each other in that time, right? Or is that going to be a problem?'

Four weeks. He'd been looking forward to coming back to his old job, knowing he'd get to see Lou every day. Because apart from their history she was the best damn nurse unit manager he'd ever worked with. Efficient, knowledgeable and resourceful. 'No problem,' he said emphatically, staring into her pretty face and blue eyes. 'Who's filling in for you?' he asked.

'Lydia.'

Oh. Great. Just what he needed. The friend from hell. 'Excellent,' he said.

There was a moment of awkward silence. 'I suppose you're here to familiarise yourself with the new computer system?' she said, not seeing any point in continuing hostilities when they had to work together.

'No, I have some other stuff to attend to first. I'm coming back this afternoon to get myself orientated with that. I actually came to see you. Check that we were…okay.'

'And?'

'I don't know, Lou.' He raked his hands through his hair. 'You've thrown me for a bit of a loop, actually.'

Welcome to my life. 'Well, back at you,' she said.

The phone rang and Lou was grateful for the interruption. 'Ward Two, Louise Marsden speaking.'

'Everything okay?' demanded Lydia.

Lou smiled. 'Fine.'

'Do you want me to come in and kick his butt?'

This time she laughed. Lydia would, she had no doubt. 'Thanks, I have it under control.' She hung up, still smiling.

'Lydia?'

She nodded.

'She doesn't like me much these days.'

'No.'

'I wasn't aware I'd done anything to upset her.'

Lou shrugged. 'You didn't. You left. You upset me. It's enough.'

'What else could I have done, Lou? Delvine was making it impossible. You were miserable. I wasn't…we weren't making you happy any more.'

'You did what you had to do, Will. I understand that. But it still hurt.'

'So I do the only decent thing and I'm the big bad wolf? That's hardly fair,' he grumbled. *Women!*

Lou nodded. 'That's what friends are for.'

'Do they all hate me?' he asked, feeling slightly apprehensive about working with a hostile staff.

She shook her head. 'Only about seventy-five percent.'

The phone rang again, and it was the pharmacy checking on supplies. She replaced the phone and felt more on an even keel now the initial hostilities were over and they'd settled into polite chit-chat.

Will shook his head. 'Candy's going to flip when I tell her you're having a baby. She was just lamenting only yesterday how she didn't have a little brother or sister to play with. You're going to be her favourite person…but then I guess you always were.'

Lou smiled, thinking about Will's gorgeous eight-year-old daughter. 'How is Candy?'

'Good,' he said. 'Surprisingly so. I thought she might be more upset…withdrawn… But she's amazed me. I'm lucky she's so resilient.'

Lou loved the way his mouth, his entire face softened when he talked about Candice. *Just as well I'm over you.* 'How long will Delvine be gone for?' Harold Yates, the Medical Director, had filled Lou in on Will's new circumstances. Delvine had found herself a rich property developer and had decided to relocate to Italy with him.

'At least two years. Probably more.'

Lou shook her head. *How could she?* How could she walk out on her daughter, a sweetie like Candice, for such a long time? But then Delvine had always had the maternal instincts of a spider. And it wasn't the first time Delvine had done a runner. She had taken off for two and a half years when Candy had been one, leaving Will a single dad.

Lou felt the bulge of her belly and knew that although the baby inside her had never been a part of her future plans, it was her responsibility and she could no more walk away from that than fly to the moon. And the baby wasn't even hers.

Lucky for Candice she had a father who doted on her and was one hundred per cent committed. Hell, despite the custody arrangements, he had practically raised her. When Lou thought about the interference and stress Delvine had caused in Will's life, their life, she wanted to spit.

'She signed over custody to you?'

He nodded. 'I think she was looking for an out. Again. She was relieved I wouldn't sign the passport application. To be honest, I don't think she'll ever return.'

Lou nodded. 'Are you back in the house?' Will had a beautiful federation-style Queenslander, in the trendy suburb of Paddington.

He nodded. 'Why don't you come over this weekend? She's dying to see you.'

Lou swallowed. She'd do anything for that little girl. But this? So soon? 'I'm kind of busy.' She fobbed him off. 'I'll see how things pan out.'

There was another awkward silence. He looked so good. A year had been too long. The things she'd wanted to do with this man…to be with this man. Her tiredness was making her sentimental and emotional. She suddenly felt like crawling into his lap and bawling all over his chest. She'd missed him. *Curse hormones! I'm over you, damn it.*

'Anyway, I'd better get back. Peter's out there causing havoc, no doubt,' she said, rising and crossing to the door like a spooked filly. She'd worked too hard to put him behind her to falter at the first real challenge. *I will not cry.*

'Wait. Lou…'

Lou stopped at the door, her hand on the knob. 'Yes?' she said, a tremble husking her voice, refusing to look back at him.

'I'm sorry about before,' he said, joining her at the door. Her body was so close, and his burned hot with memories of how good it had felt to hold her.

'It's fine,' she said briskly, turning the knob and pulling before she gave in to the urge to lean back into him.

'No,' he said, pushing the door shut with his hand up high on the frame, keeping it there, his other hand automatically reaching for her hip. He could feel the unfamiliar flare of her abdomen where once had been the jut of bone. 'It's not. I was shocked. I acted like a Neanderthal.'

'Yes, you did.'

There was a moment of silence, of stillness, full of things unsaid. His hand at what used to be her waist was burning a hole in her side.

'Lou…'

'Don't,' she begged him quietly.

Her hair smelt fantastic, as always, and he wanted to touch it so badly his fingers itched. 'I missed you,' he whispered. 'I missed this,' he said, removing his hand from her hip and giving in to the urge to feel her hair.

The skin at the nape of her neck broke out in goosebumps as his fingers lingered there a little, before moving down the length of her plait.

'I've dreamt about touching it again. I'd forgotten how heavy it is. How glorious.'

She couldn't do this. She was going to have a baby in a couple of months. It was no longer just about her. The baby deserved a stable home life. Not some male figure who had too much of his own baggage to commit to them. She had to think even harder about who she let in.

'Let me out,' she said, holding on to the last shred of her sanity.

Will sighed, releasing her hair, and stepped away from her.

'Thank you,' she said, opening the door hastily and walking out into the cool air outside.

Her office was suddenly hot. Stuffy. She couldn't breathe. Lydia was hovering outside, and looked relieved when Lou appeared intact. Will took a moment to collect himself, and then stepped out of Lou's office.

'Help! I need help in here!' came a raised voice from one of the bays.

The voice held just the right note of panic, and they ran. Lou, Lydia, Peter and Will, with Lou reaching the bedside first. 'What's wrong, Kristy?'

'I think she's having an allergic reaction to the penicillin,' said Kristy, her face pale.

'Stop it,' Will ordered as he looked down at the very frightened-looking child in question. The little girl was naked but for a nappy, and had large red welts forming all over her body before their eyes. Her lips were looking very puffy, and Will didn't need a stethoscope to hear the wheezes coming from the lungs. *Anaphylaxis.*

'I'll get the resus trolley,' said Peter.

'Oxygen, adrenaline, phenergan, hydrocortisone and

some ventolin,' Will directed, as everyone sprang into action around him.

Lou drew up and administered the drugs, Lydia attached a sats probe, Peter assembled the ventolin and Kristy took care of the oxygen.

'How old is she? What's her diagnosis?' Will asked.

'Erica's eighteen months,' Lou told him. 'Cellulitis from a possum bite.'

'Is this Erica's first dose?'

'Second,' said Kristy.

He nodded. That made sense. Often anaphylactic reactions weren't seen until the second or subsequent exposure to the particular allergen. Will looked around for a stethoscope and found one being thrust into his hand by Lou. *Efficient.* He smiled at her gratefully.

The wheezes had reduced markedly, and Will breathed a sigh of relief that they had halted the rapid progress of a condition that could have been fatal in minutes.

'Let's get her into the high dependency bay. We'll special her for the next little while,' said Lou.

Her hands shook slightly as she helped push the cot to the bay opposite the nurse's station. Thank God Will had been here. Having an experienced paediatrician in an emergency on Ward Two was a definite bonus.

Will hung around while the nursing team got the little girl settled in her temporary locale.

'Possum bite?' he asked as they trooped back into the nurses' station.

'Camping with the family,' explained Peter. 'Tried to pat one of the friendly possums. It bit her arm.'

'Ouch.' Will winced.

'Hey, Pete,' said Lydia casually. 'I've an idea. Why don't you ask our new colleague about the shave?' She nodded towards Will.

Pete's eyes lit up. 'Good idea, Lydia. Brilliant. Just brilliant.'

Pete smiled at Will and rubbed his hands together.

Lydia gave him a baleful smile. 'What?' Will said warily.

'Dr Galligher,' said Pete, narrowing his eyes speculatively. 'You do know what they say about bald men, don't you?'

Will nodded, still wary. 'Ah, but is it true, Pete?'

'Never had any complaints.' Pete winked. 'But seriously, Shave for a Cure is on in a few weeks, and I just need one more person to agree to have their hair cut.'

'That's for the Leukaemia Foundation?' Will asked.

Pete nodded. 'I've been trying to convince Lou.'

Will looked at Lou and her beautiful hair, completely horrified by Pete's suggestion. *Over my dead body!* 'That's the dumbest idea I've ever heard,' he said dismissively.

'No, no,' Pete said, shaking his head emphatically. 'Think about it. That plait is famous in this hospital. It's been part of the history here for years. We'd raise a fortune. People would come from all over the hospital to finally see Lou lose the plait.'

'Sacrilege.' Lydia shook her head.

'Hear, hear,' agreed Will, suddenly warming to Lydia again.

'Yes, I can see the signs around the hospital now. "Come see our Lou lose her plait",' Pete said, staring at a point in mid-air and flicking his hands to emphasise each word.

'Are you insane?' asked Will incredulously. How could the man even *think* of cutting off Lou's gorgeous locks?

Lou listened to their conversation about herself and her hair, feeling suddenly invisible. Like a life support system for a head of hair.

'Oh, come on, there wouldn't be one person who hadn't thought about snipping it off as she's walked past all these years. And it would make such a glorious wig,' Pete said, lifting Lou's plait and examining the blend of colours.

'Ah, excuse me—I am actually standing here in the same room,' said Lou, bemused by their in-depth discussion.

'The plait stays,' Will said firmly.

'Lou?' Pete entreated, appealing to his boss one last time.

Lou opened her mouth to graciously decline.

'No, Pete,' said Will, even more firmly this time. 'Absolutely not.'

Lou turned and raised her eyebrow at Will. She knew he'd always been obsessed with her hair, but this was ridiculous. He was looking at her as if he owned her hair. As if he owned her. She felt the early simmer of her blood pick up to a slow boil. Did he really think he actually had a say over what she did with her hair? Or any other part of her body? Did he think he could walk back in after a year and she'd just fall back into her old Will-worshipping ways?

If she was going to hold on to herself and her sanity now Will was back, he had to know that their old dynamic was dead. No more following meekly wherever he led. *I am over you, buddy boy.* Time to draw a line in the sand.

'I'll do it,' she said, talking to Pete, but looking point-edly at Will.

'Oh, no,' gasped Kristy.

'Lou,' warned Lydia.

'Yes!' Pete rubbed his hands together with glee and picked up a pen.

'No. Don't put her down. I'll do it,' Will instructed, still holding Lou's gaze.

Lou broke eye contact. 'Do not listen to him. Long hair with a baby is not a good combination. I'm doing it.'

'He doesn't need you now,' said Will, placing a stilling hand on Pete's, hovering above an official form, pen poised. 'I've already volunteered.'

Everyone in the nurses' station looked at Lou. She felt as if she was in a tennis match, her colleagues looking left and right as they lobbed the bone of contention between them.

She shrugged. 'You want to as well—fine. But I'm not changing my mind. He can have both of us,' she said.

'Lou,' said Will, looking at the stubborn set of her chin, 'you're just trying to prove a point now. You don't have to do this.' Will realised his fatal error. By disagreeing, he had goaded her into it.

'No, my mind is made up. It's for kids with cancer. I'm the kids' ward nurse unit manager. It's a good cause. I normally go along, sponsor everyone, sell raffle tickets, do my bit. But this year I'm going to lead by example.'

Will shook his head, not really able to believe that she was seriously going to go through with it.

'Are you really going bald?' asked a mystified Kristy.

'No.' Lou laughed, not quite indignant enough to agree to that. 'But shaved all over. Like Lydia's Matt. How short does he have his?' she asked her friend. Lydia's ten-year-old son always got a crew cut.

'He usually gets a number four blade,' Lydia said, almost as horrified as Kristy.

'Good.' Lou nodded emphatically. 'A number four it is.'

Will still couldn't believe the direction of the conversation. He searched around for something to deter her, one last-ditch effort.

'Jan will have a fit,' he said. Lou's sister probably coveted Lou's hair even more than he did. Jan had always bemoaned her thin, stringy, can't-do-anything-with-it hair, especially as Lou's was the exact opposite.

Lou blinked, and braced herself for the inevitable pain. She heard a slight gasp come from Kristy, and felt rather than saw the sudden tension emanating from Lydia and Pete. It was suddenly deathly quiet, as if the entire ward had chosen that moment to cease all noise and activity.

'Hardly,' she said, keeping the gut-wrenching sorrow from her voice. 'Jan's dead.' And she pushed herself off the desk and calmly walked away, before she did something awful—like burst into tears at the unexpected reminder of her sister's tragic death.

CHAPTER TWO

WILL watched her go, completely dumbfounded. That was twice today she had utterly shocked him. His head rejected the information instantly, but one look at the faces of the others in the nurses' station and he knew it was true.

'Lydia?'

She nodded. 'Jan and Martin died in a light plane crash just over five months ago.'

'Oh, God, how terrible,' he said, remembering all the good times he and Lou had had with Jan and Martin. Remembering how close Lou had been to her big sister. And how the couple had doted on Candy. 'Why didn't somebody tell me?'

'Maybe if you'd bothered to check on her at any time during the last year you may have found out,' Lydia chided.

He looked at Lydia and knew he deserved the criticism. He had deliberately avoided any contact, believing it was best for both of them. And poor Lou had gone through this all alone. No, not alone, he thought, as he looked at her fiercely loyal staff. But still… If he'd only known, he could have… Could have what? Rung? Sent her some flowers? A sympathy card? How trite. He could have come back and comforted her. Gone to the funeral at least.

He left the station and headed directly for her office. He knocked on her door and didn't wait for her to reply, opening it straight away. Empty. He thumped his hand against the door in frustration. He needed to talk to her about it. To let her know how very, very sorry he was. She might have dropped the bombshell calmly, but he knew her well enough—or at least he had—to know it hid a whole heap of anguish.

He looked at his watch. He was due at Human Resources five minutes ago. But he was coming back this afternoon, for an in-service with Lynne on the computer system. He was torn between what he had to do and what he needed to do, but her disappearing act left him with little choice. Talking with Lou was just going to have to wait until then.

A couple of hours later, after sorting out payroll and rostering issues and lunching with Harold, the Medical Director, Will walked back onto Ward Two. He tried Lou's office first. *Damn it!* Not there. He entered the nurses' station and found Lynne waiting for him, so he sat down with her, completely distracted, while she tried to impart the intricacies of the computer system.

He toyed with the idea of pumping Lynne for information about Lou. There probably wasn't anything the ward clerk didn't know about the goings-on at the hospital, and he'd bet his last cent that Lynne knew all there was to know about Jan and Martin. But he restrained himself. Lynne was good at her job, but he abhorred gossip—had been on the nasty end of it, thanks to Delvine—and he would not encourage her.

Will was passing time waiting for Lou's return, performing some dummy tasks Lynne had set him, when Pete entered the nurses' station with an inconsolable child. It was a little boy who looked about five, and he was sobbing broken-heartedly.

'Oh, my,' said Will, looking up, pleased for any respite from the screen. 'What do we have here?' he asked.

'Josh's mum has just left to go and pick up his sister from school. He's a little upset,' Pete said, sitting on the chair next to Will.

Will raised his eyebrows at Pete's understatement. The kid looked as if he'd lost a million bucks. 'Oh, dear,' said Will. 'Never mind, mate. She'll be back soon.'

Josh buried his head in Pete's shoulder and sobbed louder.

'So, Pete? Does Josh like magic?' Will asked, raising his voice a notch and winking at Pete.

'Ah, no, Will. I don't think so.'

Josh's cries started to wane, and he peeked out at Will.

'Are you sure? Because you do know I'm a magician *and* a doctor, right?'

'Really?' said Pete, fake incredulity dripping from his words. 'I didn't know you were a magician as well, Dr Galligher.'

Josh's sobs were slowly quieting. Lou peeked her head around the corner. She had heard Pete and Will's efforts to placate the child from halfway down the corridor.

'Sure.' Will nodded. 'In my spare time I'm Captain Incredible.'

Josh's crying had stopped, and he watched the two men's magic discussion solemnly. Lou felt a lump rise in her throat. Will was so good with kids. His doctoring method was incredibly unique. He was the kind of doctor who really understood how kids ticked. Maybe it was having a child of his own? But he always had a magic trick up his sleeve, and a dozen different jokes on the tip of his tongue. And it worked—his patients loved him. And so did their parents.

'Ohhhh. *You're* Captain Incredible? I heard he hung around the hospital a lot.'

'Shh,' said Will, and winked at Josh. 'It's a secret. Can you keep a secret, Josh?'

The little boy looked at Will with starstruck eyes and nodded seriously. 'Can you really do magic?' he asked, his voice hushed with awe.

Will grinned at him and moved closer to the little boy. 'I sure can,' he said, and pulled a coin out from behind Josh's ear.

The little boy gasped, and looked at Will as if he was Santa Claus. Lou stifled a laugh at the look of complete hero-worship on Josh's face as Will made the coin disappear into thin air. Then he held out his two downwards-facing fists and got Josh to choose one, and the coin was miraculously back again.

'Cool!' said an excited Josh.

Will laughed. 'Hey, you want to come over here with me and help me with this computer thing? Captain Incredible isn't so good with computers. My magic computer wand broke.'

Josh giggled and went eagerly, jumping off Pete's lap and launching himself onto Will's. Will swivelled his chair back to the screen and showed Josh a few different things to try. He did have a vaguely horrible thought that if Josh pushed the wrong button the entire hospital computer system could go down, but what were the chances? Josh was happy. And Lynne wasn't here to mind.

Lou watched Will a little longer. He'd taken a crying, fretting child and turned his fears around in minutes. If ever there was someone born to their field it was him. Josh obviously thought he was the bee's knees. She remembered a time when she'd thought that too.

'Hey, Lou,' said Stuart Myers, coming up behind her and almost scaring her half to death. She noticed Will turn and spot her as she greeted the registrar.

'Hi, Stu,' she said, 'what brings you down to Ward Two?' She tried to keep her voice casual, and not betray the fact that she'd been spying on Will.

'The boss,' he said, and nodded towards Will.

Lou glanced over at Will as he nodded back. She looked back at Stu, ignoring Will's heavy gaze. 'You're doing the paed rotation now?' she asked. Lou had spoken with Stuart quite frequently not long after she and Will had split regarding surrogacy, as he'd been working an IVF rotation at the time.

'Yep. More my cup of tea,' he said.

'I agree.' She grinned. Stu was up there with Will as far as rapport with kids went.

'I just wanted to say that I'm really happy you went ahead with the surrogacy idea. I'm pleased it was successful. It was such a marvellous gift for your sister,' he said, placing his hand on her stomach. 'I'm so sorry to hear that she's since died.'

Lou saw Will out of the corner of her eye and knew instantly he had heard the conversation. *Hell. Damn Stu!* She monitored Will's reaction as if it was happening in slow motion. His back stiffened, he stopped swivelling idly on the chair and his eyes narrowed.

'Pete,' Will said, 'can you keep on eye on Josh, please? Lou and I need to talk.'

Pete looked at Lou, then back at Will, then at Lou again. She sighed and nodded at him.

'Come on, matey,' Pete said, hauling Josh off Will's lap.

'Mummy will be back soon.' The boy didn't protest, waving at Will as Pete walked him back to his bed.

'Stuart. Would you mind if I spoke to Lou before we get to our business?' he asked.

'Not at all,' said Stu. 'I have to go to Accident and Emergency to insert an IV. Can you page me when you're ready?'

Will nodded, and they both watched Stu leave the ward. He brushed past her, opened the door to her office and indicated for her to precede him. Will waited for the door to click shut behind him before he said a word.

'Why didn't you tell me?'

Lou wasn't fooled by his calmly delivered question. He was mad. She could tell by the whiteness of his knuckles as he leant against the desk, and the rigidity of his facial muscles, and the way a little nerve jumped spasmodically near his left eye.

She sighed. 'Will—'

'Why, Lou? Why lead me to believe that you'd been involved with someone else?'

'Actually, Will, I didn't. If you remember correctly, you jumped to a certain conclusion because my pregnancy came as a shock and you were angry that I'd replaced you.'

He opened his mouth to deny it, and then closed it again. She'd pretty much hit the nail right on the head with her quick summation.

'You didn't disabuse me,' he pointed out.

'Why should I have? The first time I see you again after a year you accuse me of hopping from your bed to someone else's. I wasn't exactly feeling very friendly towards you.'

'I'm sorry, Lou,' he said, sitting down in a chair and pulling his tie a little looser. 'I was a jerk.'

'Damn right you were,' she said, lowering herself into her chair too.

'I was…gobsmacked. I engaged my mouth before my brain caught up.'

'You should have known I'm not capable of doing that. You were my everything for five years. You ending it was the hardest thing I've ever been through. Other than burying my sister, of course. You really think I could just jump into bed with somebody else? You know I abhor casual sex.'

Will heard the frustration and sadness in her voice, and her supreme disappointment in him. 'I must admit it didn't quite ring true about the Louise Marsden that I knew.'

'And yet still you believed?'

He shrugged. 'I'm really sorry, Lou.'

'You know, the crazy thing is that you could have known all along about my surrogacy and about Jan if you'd just bothered to keep in contact with anyone from here. Neither is exactly a secret in this place. I mean, we agreed to make a clean break, but cutting yourself off completely wasn't entirely necessary.'

'I didn't,' he protested. 'I kept up with your news. Candy read me your letters. They were the highlight of my week, actually.'

Lou suppressed the impulse to laugh hysterically, because a part of her was touched that her chipper newsy ravings, targeted for eight-year-old eyes, had meant something to him. But they'd hardly been representative of her life.

She had written to Candy every week because she had promised her she would. She had written no matter how wretched she had felt. When her heart had been aching for Will, she'd written. When she'd barely been able to move from the toilet with morning sickness, she'd written. When her sister was dead and she'd been unable to see the lines on the paper through her tears, she'd written. And she hadn't missed a week, despite the state of her emotions. In fact, her letters to Candy had been just about the only thing at times that had kept her focused on putting one foot in front of the other. They had been chatty and bright, even when things were falling apart.

Lou's life in the year since their split had been like a rollercoaster ride. After the break-up she'd drifted along for a while on the flat, trying to pretend that everything was okay. And then there'd been the steep but exciting ascent as IVF and fertility treatments resulted in a pregnancy for Jan and Martin. Their pure and utter joy at finally becoming parents had had her flying high.

And then the horrible stomach-dropping plummet when news of the plane crash had reached her and she'd realised not only had she lost her darling sister, but the baby would never know its real parents.

'Well, I did censor them quite a bit,' she said sarcastically.

'Obviously.'

'Did you seriously expect me to tell your daughter that Jan was dead in a letter? Or that I was having a baby? My sister's baby?'

'No,' he said, raking his hand through his hair. 'Of course not.'

Lou felt the familiar burn under her ribcage start up and stretched herself out, her elbow resting on the back of her chair to make a little more room. She absently rubbed the curve of her ribs where bump met bone. Sometimes she could have sworn she felt a foot up there.

'You okay?' he asked, indicating where she was rubbing.

'Yes,' she dismissed. 'There's just not a lot of room for movement these days.' The burning sensation eased, and she removed her arm and sat up straight again.

'Tell me about the surrogacy,' he said. 'They were still trying IVF when I left.'

She nodded. 'Jan had a hysterectomy the week after you took up the remote paediatrician position. It was a hard decision for them to come to, but after years of crippling pain and bleeding, with her endometriosis and regular blood transfusions due to her chronic anaemia, she couldn't take it any more. She was forty, with three failed IVF attempts and two miscarriages. She just couldn't go through another period from hell.

'They spoke to me before they went ahead with the op and asked if I would be interested in being a surrogate for them. They still had fertilised embryos, and they thought I might be interested in helping them achieve their goal.'

'And you said yes?'

'Of course.' Lou nodded. 'Without hesitation. At thirty-five I was pretty sure I was never going to have my own...' Lou deliberately didn't look at Will. 'And...she was my sister. She would have done it for me.'

'And so...you were okay with having the baby inside you for nine months, growing it, nurturing it, and then just handing it over at the end?'

'Absolutely one hundred per cent okay. It wasn't my baby to keep.'

'Is it really that simplistic?'

Lou nodded emphatically. 'It's her egg and his sperm. It's *their* baby. It's their genetic material. I'm just incubating it for them. Could I have done it if it had had my own genetic material? No. But to be able to give them their own baby after all their problems—nothing has ever been simpler.'

'And how does that work legally?'

'Grey area,' she said. 'Legally I'm recognised as the mother, so Jan and Martin would have had to have officially adopted the baby.'

'And now? Now they're gone? You didn't exactly sign up for this, did you?'

Lou gave him a sad smile. 'No. Not really. But you know, this is my sister's baby, and whether I like it or not the law recognises me as its mother. And,' she said firmly, daring him with her eyes to argue, 'I'm going to give it the best damn life I can.'

Will felt his heart swell with pride at her selfless generosity. He'd always been proud to know Louise Marsden, but this was the icing on the cake. She was doing something completely selfless. Completely worthy. Lou had been through so much in the time he'd been away. Such a momentous year. And then an awful thought struck him. 'Did they know you were pregnant before the accident?'

Lou felt the impact of her sister's death again at his quiet question. The same picture that always haunted her came back again. The despair Jan and Martin must have felt as the plane spiralled towards the ground, knowing they wouldn't ever see their baby. Hold it in their arms. She swallowed a sudden lump of emotion blocking her throat. She nodded. 'I was eight weeks when they died. They'd known for a month.'

Will shut his eyes briefly as he, too, thought about Jan and Martin's last earthly moments. He could see the mist in Lou's eyes. 'I'm so sorry,' he said.

'I know,' she said. 'I know.' The sincerity in his voice was too much. Revisiting the nightmare was too much. Having him here to confide in again was too much. How often had she wanted him to lean on this last year? She felt the pool of tears brim in her eyes and one splash down her cheek.

'Lou,' he said, his voice a low growl as he got out of his seat, came around the desk and crouched down in front of her. 'Don't cry.' He reached up and wiped the tear away gently with his thumb.

'I'm sorry. I can't help it. It was just so awful, and I wanted to pick up the phone so often and talk to you, and—' her voice cracked '—and I hated that I couldn't.'

Will got to his feet and pulled her up with him. 'You could have,' he said, hauling her into his embrace and rocking her while she silently cried. 'I wish you had.'

He felt the strange intrusion of her bump between them and held her awkwardly at first. But knowing that it was Jan's baby and not some other man's made him less wary of it. And when she relaxed he did too, and it felt as right as it always had in the circle of her arms.

'It's just not fair,' Lou sobbed into his shirt. 'Why? Why them? They had so much to look forward to.'

'I don't know, Lou. I just don't know.'

Lou knew she shouldn't be doing this. That this was crossing a boundary that shouldn't be crossed any more. That she was over him. But he felt so good, and he smelled so wonderful, just as she remembered, and sharing her grief with someone who knew her as intimately as Will was such a relief.

'And now I've got to look after this baby. I'm scared, Will,' she said, pulling away and looking up into his beautiful face. 'What if I suck at it?'

He chuckled and kissed her forehead out of habit, snuggling her close to his chest again. 'You'll be fantastic, Lou. You've been marvellous with Candice, and all the kids at work. And, trust me, we all suck at it from time to time.'

Lou had an ear pressed to his chest, and could hear the deep rumble of his voice vibrate through the layers of skin and bone. A delicious shiver puckered her skin. 'You don't. You've always been a fantastic parent.'

He laughed again, and the vibrations tickled her ear, causing her stomach to flop. 'No, Lou. I've tried to make the best of a really sucky situation. But there have been times when my parenting has been pretty average.'

She pulled away and looked into his serious face. 'Maybe. But, you know, you never once put down Delvine in front of Candy—and God knows you had plenty of reason to. You never called Delvine on any of her outrageous monetary claims, you always paid your child support and rearranged your life at a moment's notice when she got herself another hot date. You took everything Delvine dished out just so Candy knew she was the most important thing in your life. I think you deserve a medal.'

He shrugged. 'That's what you do when you're a parent.'

'Exactly,' she said. 'I hadn't planned for this to happen but…it did, and I want to be the best. Give this baby the best start in life I can. It's all I have left of Jan,' she said, her hand rubbing her stomach. 'It's too important to stuff up.'

'You're going to be great,' he said firmly. 'What about financially? Are you going to be able to afford to take time off?'

She nodded. 'A year. Jan and Martin changed their will the minute the preg test was positive. I have legal guardianship, and they left me well looked after. Money won't be an issue.'

He hugged her close again, and they were silent for a few moments.

'Are you okay now?' he asked. Will was starting to have less than pure thoughts now Lou's tears had dried up, and the familiar scent of her perfume was taking him back to days when holding her had usually led to something else. Time to get the hell out of her office.

Lou nodded, feeling similar temptations. 'Do I look like I've been crying?' she asked, as she reluctantly pulled out of his arms and patted around her eyes with her index finger.

'Yep,' he said, his hand on the doorknob.

She laughed through her tears. 'Thank you, Will,' she said softly.

'Any time,' he said, and stepped out of her office before he did something crazy—like turn back and kiss her.

Lou braked outside Will's house Saturday morning and switched the engine off. She looked up at the old Queenslander, with its beautiful wrought-iron lacework and wide verandah, and recalled how many times she had whiled away a sunny afternoon there in the shade, sipping wine with Will. She had missed that.

In fact there were very few things she *didn't* miss about her life with Will. She missed his devilish sense of humour and his smooth baritone when he sang in the shower, and having Sunday lunch at his mother's. She missed waking before him and just staring into his face, coveting his incredibly long eyelashes and waiting for that slow, sexy smile to warm his face when he woke to discover her staring at him.

She missed how goofy he was with the kids at work, and how he would go to any lengths to get a smile from them.

She missed his practical jokes. She even missed his knock-knock jokes. She missed the sound of his voice. And his whispers. And his silences. She missed his razor next to hers in the shower. The smell of his aftershave in the morning. She missed being wrapped up in his arms. And feeling him deep inside her. She missed him. Period.

The baby moved, and for a moment she fantasised that it was hers and Will's. But it kicked her again, as if to snap her out of it, and she realised that if she'd stayed with Will she would never have been pregnant. She'd known all about Will's history when they'd become involved. Working with him on and off through the years she'd been a witness to a lot of it. She'd known he'd been badly burned by Delvine.

He'd been up-front about that, but when they'd moved in together she had begun to hope he would be able to get past it one day and fully commit to her. Maybe have a baby of their own one day. And they'd had a full year of uninterrupted bliss together, the three of them—Will, Candy and her.

She remembered that time with bittersweet fondness. The flowering of her and Will's relationship, the bond she had formed with Candy, and the high of knowing that Will was the only man for her. Watching Will's cautiousness slowly abating, starting to hope that the wounds his ex-wife had inflicted were healing under the influence of her love.

But the abrupt intrusion of Delvine's return had thrown everything into chaos. She had decided, after deserting Candy for two and a half years, that she wanted to play mummy again and damn the consequences. And her demands that she be allowed a place in her daughter's life, and hence in theirs, had slowly eroded their perfect time together.

And Lou had watched with dismay as Will had retreated,

and with it her dreams of babies and happily-ever-afters. Oh, he had loved her, she had no doubt about that, but Delvine had made their situation untenable. The emotional trauma of being separated from his daughter on Delvine's days, and the time and energy he'd had to devote to battling his bitter, litigious ex-wife on every little nit-picking aspect had put such a strain on them. Whoever had said that sometimes love wasn't enough, had been a wise person indeed.

A stray foot kicked her, protesting the squished confines. Her belly was jammed against the steering wheel and she wondered how much longer she'd be able to drive without impinging the baby's circulation. If only she'd been taller, she wouldn't have needed to sit so close to the wheel to reach the pedals, and the rapidly growing baby would have had more room.

She looked down at her tummy and felt apprehensive. How was this supposed to get out again? Logistically it just didn't seem possible. Well, that was what she got for agreeing to be a surrogate for two giants! Jan had been one inch off six foot, and Martin had been four inches over. At a petite five-two, Lou had often coveted her sister's height. But then Jan had coveted Lou's hair…so the grass was always greener.

Lou unbuckled the restrictive seat belt, and was climbing out of the car when Candice came running out of the house, screaming excitedly, her arms flung wide. Candy! God, how she had missed her too. She had known Will's child since she'd been a charming two-year-old toddler with a gappy smile. Losing Candy had been as much of a wrench as losing Will.

Tears welled in Lou's eyes as a miniature version of Will threw herself at her. She braced her body for the impact and caught Candy up in her arms before the little girl could permanently maim her or the baby. Lou expected the baby to protest the sudden weight of an eight-year-old pressing into it, as it had the steering wheel, but it was curiously silent.

'Lou, Lou, Lou,' said Candy into Lou's neck. 'I've missed you!' She pulled back and looked earnestly at Lou. 'Did you miss me? I loved your letters. Thank you, thank you for writing to me.'

Lou looked into Will's daughter's face. 'Of course I missed you. It's so good to see you!' And she hugged the little girl into her neck again, squeezing her tight.

Lou's back started to protest, so she put Candy down, taking her hand and walking towards the house. 'What about Daddy?' Candy asked, looking up at Lou and shading her eyes from the midday sun with her hand. 'Did you miss him too?'

More than anything, baby doll. Lou looked down into Candy's dear little face. She had her father's brown wavy hair, and his brown eyes, and those incredible lashes. She also had his smile and his quick wit and his sense of humour. But her chin was all Delvine, and Lou had seen it jut determinedly on more than one occasion—just like her mother's.

'Not as much as you,' laughed Lou.

'Hey!' Will protested good-naturedly. 'I heard that.'

Lou looked up and saw him lounging against a verandah post at the top of the wide staircase, his hands thrust into the pockets of his cargo-style shorts. He looked all warm and happy and relaxed, just like the Will she remembered, and she was thankful there were only five steps. Her knees were shaking so badly she doubted she could climb any more.

'We're round the back,' said Candy, tugging on Lou's

hand once they drew level with Will. 'We made lasagne 'cos I remembered how much you like it.'

Lou didn't have time to greet Will as she responded to the pull of Candy's hand. Which was just as well. What would she say? Sorry for dropping two bombshells on you yesterday and then crying all over you?

'Oh, Lou! It's so good to see you again,' said Candy as she walked along and held Lou's hand. She put her skinny arm around Lou's expanding waist and giggled. 'Daddy was right. He said you had a big fat tummy.' She giggled again.

'Candy!' said a horrified Will, who was following the two girls. 'You weren't supposed to tell Lou that.'

Lou laughed and squeezed Candy's shoulders. 'It's okay, sweetie. It is pretty big.'

'Sit here next to me,' said Candy, stopping at the solid wooden table Lou and Will had bought together, and pulling out a heavy wooden chair.

'I'll get us a drink,' said Will. 'We made some ice tea. I didn't think you'd want wine?'

'Ice tea would be lovely, thanks.' She smiled at him.

Will escaped into the kitchen gratefully as a surge of feeling overwhelmed him. She looked lovelier than ever today. Her hair was down, a slight crinkle effect from wearing it in a plait rippling through the streaks of blonde. Just thinking about her losing her glorious mane made him crazy. If he'd only kept his trap shut yesterday she would never have agreed to having her hair shorn. Good cause or not.

He could hear Candy's excited chatter, and was reminded of how many good times they'd all had together on his back deck. In this house. It seemed like a million years ago now. He picked up the tray and went to join them.

'How long till the baby comes, Lou?' asked Candy as Will plonked the drinks on the table and distributed them.

Lou looked at Will questioningly. 'It's okay, I told her about the surrogacy,' he said.

She nodded, and hoped it wasn't too complicated for an eight-year-old to grasp. It certainly was difficult enough for some adults! 'Another ten weeks,' Lou said, smiling at Will's daughter.

'What are you going to call it?'

Will sat opposite her and took a long swig from a bottle of beer. Lou was caught unawares by how distracting watching him drink was, and swallowed, finding it hard to concentrate on the question.

'Olivia for a girl. Charlie for a boy.' Jan and Martin had at least decided that before the plane crash.

'What about middle names?' Candy asked.

Lou took a deep breath as memories of her older sister were stirred. 'I thought it might be nice to have Jan or Martin.'

'Daddy told me about the plane crash. It's so awful, Lou,' she said, her dear little innocent face marred with sorrow. 'I really liked them. Martin gave the best piggy-backs.'

Lou laughed, and could feel the prick of tears as she remembered how much Martin had made Candy giggle when she had ridden on his back. Jan and Martin had adored Will's daughter, a decade of infertility causing them to spoil her rotten.

'What exactly happened?' asked Will. 'I meant to ask you about it yesterday, but the whole surrogacy thing threw me a bit.'

He could see a faint trace of moisture in her eyes and realised that five months wasn't a lot of time to have elapsed. 'Oh, Lou,' he said, reaching across the table and touching her hand with his. 'I'm sorry. You don't have to talk about it if you'd rather not.'

Lou smiled at him, touched by his concern. 'No, it's okay. It just feels a bit raw still sometimes.'

'Of course,' he said gently. 'She was your big sister and you loved her.'

Lou swallowed a sudden lump in her throat and nodded as she shifted her hand out from under his. *I'm over you.*

'It was just over five months ago. Jan and Martin were holidaying in the Northern Territory, where friends of theirs have ten thousand acres. They took them up in one of the property's light planes to get a bird's eye view, and there were some engine difficulties. It crashed about twenty minutes into the flight. It exploded on impact. All four passengers were killed.'

Will suppressed the urge to say something inane—useless phrases such as *at least they didn't suffer.* Words were so trite in such tragic circumstances, and nothing anyone could say would take away the fact that two really nice people had met a grisly end, well before their time.

'I'm so sorry, Lou. That's just not fair, is it?'

She shook her head and blinked back the moisture in her eyes. 'No,' she agreed, 'it isn't. And they were so happy too. They were over the moon about finally having a baby.'

Lou could only hope in those last few terrifying seconds that Jan and Martin had known she'd love their baby like her own.

'Are they in heaven?' Candy asked, breaking into Lou's thoughts.

Lou hesitated. Typical kid question. She might as well have asked her for the quantum physics theory. Years of nursing hadn't left her with much faith, and her sister being killed had destroyed the rest.

'I'm sure wherever they are now they're watching over us,' said Will.

Lou smiled gratefully at him. *I hope so, Will, I really do.* She placed her hand on her swollen stomach, absently seeking assurance from the one remaining connection to her sister.

The conversation moved on to other topics, and Lou found herself relaxing and enjoying the afternoon, just like old times. Hearing Will's deep chuckle and Candy's high, sweet giggle, it was as if nothing had ever changed. She was where she'd always wanted to be—a part of Will's life.

'Daddy said you're shaving all your hair off,' said Candy.

Lou smiled. Even at eight, Candice sounded more outraged than anyone so far. 'Almost all, sweetie. But don't worry. It'll grow back.'

'But it's so beautiful,' said Candy. 'Won't you please at least think about it?' The little girl had such a melodramatic look of pleading and lament it was hard to keep a straight face.

'Nope. My mind's made up,' she said, staring defiantly at Will, who she suspected might have had something to do with this line of conversation. 'Besides, it's about time. Long hair and a baby don't mix. Look at how many times you used to grab hold and pull, young madam,' she teased, looking back at Candice.

Candy giggled. 'I remember going to sleep all curled up in your lap and twirling my finger in it,' she said wistfully.

Lou smiled, remembering those times too. Holding a younger Candy in her arms, looking down into her sweet baby doll face as she wrapped a lock of hair around one finger and sucked her thumb as she went to sleep. She remembered the soap and powder smell of Candy's skin, and the way her little bow mouth pouted prettily in sleep. She remembered how full of love for Will's child her heart had been.

She roused herself from memory lane. 'Anyway, your dad's getting his done too. Did he tell you that?'

'Coloured,' Will corrected. 'I think I'll just go for getting it sprayed red.'

Lou looked from Will to Candy and then back again. 'Chicken,' she laughed, and flapped her arms and made a clucking noise. Candy laughed and joined in.

'Cluck all you want—Kojak,' he teased. 'I'd rather be red than bald.'

'Nearly bald,' Lou corrected, still laughing.

The phone rang, interrupting their hilarity, and Lou was grateful when Will excused himself. Her heart ached at the perfectness of the day, because it wasn't real. Shortly she'd get in her car and drive back to her apartment, go back to her life without Will or Candy. She'd had a glimpse again today of how great it could be, which only made it harder. There was too much water under the bridge, and she mustn't be distracted by perfect days such as these.

She had Jan's baby to think about, and he had Candy. They both had to concentrate on being parents: there wasn't time for each other and the demands of starting over.

'You want to see my new computer?' Candy asked.

'Sure,' said Lou, shuffling out of the chair and taking Candy's outstretched hand.

'Mummy got it for me,' the little girl said, leading the way into her fairy wonderland bedroom. Lou's hand lingered on the doorjamb. She had helped Will paint the room, and had taken Candy to choose the curtains and bedspread. 'Isn't it cool?' Candy asked.

Lou saw the excited sparkle in her eyes. 'Way cool.' She nodded, admiring the slick piece of machinery on the yellow desk she had lovingly stenciled a swirly border on.

'Dad has it hooked up to broadband, and Mum and I talk to each other on MSN a few nights a week.'

Lou looked down at Candy as she showed off her expensive laptop. Will was right. She did seem to be taking the separation from her mother better than expected. But Candy had always had a resilience that belied her years. Thanks to Will's love and devotion, Candy's world had always had stability and security—even if it had come at a personal cost to him.

'Do you miss her, sweetie?' she asked gently.

'A little.' Candy shrugged. 'But I would have missed Brisbane and Rilla and all my friends too much, and I didn't really want to go to Europe and be so far away from Daddy. And with this—' she tapped the keyboard '—it's just like having her in the next room. She sends me pictures and stuff all the time. I can even go on holidays to Italy when I'm older.'

Lou nodded, and again wondered how it was possible for a mother to leave her child. She knew as sure as her next breath that Jan would never have abandoned her baby through choice. She absently rubbed her stomach.

'Can I come and visit you and the baby?' Candy asked.

Lou returned her attention to Candy and noticed her watching Lou's involuntary belly-stroking. 'Of course.' Lou smiled.

Candy sighed. 'I wish you and Daddy would get back together, so you and the baby could live with us. I'd be able to help you.'

Lou felt her breath catch in her throat at the rosy picture painted by the eight-year-old child. It was terribly seductive, but she knew one thing for sure—she couldn't get involved with Will again. She was over him, and even if she hadn't been she had a baby to think about now.

It was funny how things worked out, she thought. She'd always tried really hard to understand Will's position. His initial caution before throwing himself fully into their relationship, and then his retreat as Delvine threw a spanner in the works. But it was only now she had a child to think about also that she truly understood his actions.

The urge to protect your child was very strong and that included protecting it from people who could come and go with devastating consequences. But it had been more than that for Will. He had also been protecting himself. And she understood that as well—that Delvine had scarred him. But his emotional wariness had hurt. And she wouldn't do that again. Not to her or the baby.

'I'm sure you'd be a tremendous help, sweetie. So you'll have to come and visit…a lot.' Lou grinned and ruffled Candy's hair to soften the subtle rejection.

Just then the baby stomped on her cervix, and Lou let out a yelp as she clutched underneath her bump.

'Ooh! Did it kick?' asked Candy. 'Can I feel it? Please, Lou?'

'Sure,' she said, grimacing as the pain eased. 'Here.' She picked Candy's hand off the desk and placed it on the spot where the baby was now looping the loop.

'I can't feel it,' said a disappointed Candy after a few moments.

'Just wait,' said Lou, willing the now still baby to move. 'It can be tricky sometimes.'

They waited a few more moments, and then Lou felt

the baby give a hefty kick to the spot where Candy's hand was resting.

Candy squealed excitedly. 'It kicked! It kicked!'

Lou laughed. 'Ouch. I know.'

Will chose that moment to enter the room. What he saw stopped him in his tracks. Candy gazing wondrously up into Lou's face, her hand pressed to Lou's swollen stomach. Lou looking down in shared awe. The bond between the two girls was obviously as strong as ever. He felt his heart stop. It could be like this again.

But even as he watched them he knew it wasn't possible. Lou's pregnancy was a timely reminder of how much such a huge life-changing event could put relationships at risk. As it had with him and Delvine. And how much a new baby would impact on their lives. Candy had to come first. She deserved that. His daughter had to be uppermost in his mind. She'd been to'd and fro'd enough in her eight years. And Jan's baby would be Lou's priority. Neither of them was free to commit fully to the other. Bad timing—as usual.

Will's eyes met Lou's, and their gazes locked for a brief moment in time. *God, I missed you.* 'Here you both are,' he said, injecting a light note into his voice. 'Dessert's up.'

'Okay, then,' Lou said, and was the first one out of the room.

She didn't linger after dessert. The look on Will's face in Candy's room had been so conflicted she'd wanted to run a mile. He'd looked as if he wanted to push her away and pull her close all at once, and she knew exactly how he felt.

CHAPTER THREE

MONDAY morning rocked around, and Lou was as ready as she was ever going to be for Dr Galligher. She couldn't think of him as anything else. If she thought of him as Will then her legs turned to jelly and she started to shake. Will was personal. Will was the last six years of her life all rolled into one. The good and the bad.

Dr Galligher, on the other hand, was work. Dr Galligher was professional. He was charts and sick children, and medication and tests and examinations. He was nine to five. He was five days a week. Dr Galligher was business as usual.

'Hey, Lou,' said Pete, putting the phone down, 'it's all organised now. You can't back out. The hospital liaison lady is thrilled you're participating. She's going to do a big hospital-wide advertising campaign. She reckons your hair's going to make them a mint. She's going to try and raise ten grand from you alone.'

'What?' Lou almost spluttered her coffee over the desk.

'She thinks it'll be a piece of cake.'

Lou looked at him dubiously. 'If she says so,' she said, putting her mug down so she could check an antibiotic with Kristy.

It was for little Erica, the possum bite patient. They'd changed her from penicillin and the cellulitis was clearing nicely. Lou suspected she'd only need a couple more days' worth.

'Can I get a sponsorship list happening here? I'll stick it to the wall and people can sign up to sponsor you and Will.'

Will. *Oh, God, Will was going to be here soon.* She thought of that look he had given her in Candy's room, and wanted to go into her office and lock the door.

'Dr Galligher,' she corrected, and Pete gave her a puzzled look. Why would he call Will Dr Galligher? He certainly hadn't in the past. Most of the older staff on Ward Two had known Will since he'd been a junior doctor.

'You okay, Lou?' Lydia asked, catching the conversation and Pete's look as she walked into the nurses' station with a grizzling Terry on her hip. 'You run out of Fruit Tingles? There are some in the third drawer down, under the staples,' she said, handing the babe to Lou.

Lou automatically took the child, skilfully avoiding the heavily plastered legs as they flailed around excitedly. Terry loved Lou. He grinned up at her and she kissed the top of his head. 'I'm fine,' she said, amazed at the number of places Lydia had sweets stashed.

That she managed to keep them hidden from the rest of the staff, who had pretty good noses for all things sweet, was pretty amazing also. Although no one was stupid enough to dare risk the wrath of Lydia and eat one of Lou's sweets. They had been given strict instructions that all Fruit Tingles were Lou's property, and for emergency baby use only.

'What's up with you, grizzle-bum?' Lou asked Terry as he used Lou's bump to bounce his plastered legs off. He had a sniffly nose, and Lou hoped he wasn't getting a nosocomial infection. Having a perfectly healthy child in hospital with a million bad bugs floating around wasn't optimal. The last thing this little boy needed was a hospital-acquired infection.

'Nothing,' said Lydia briskly. 'You've just spoilt him rotten.'

'Lou? Spoil a baby? Never.' A familiar male voice drawled in her ear.

Will… Her grip tightened on Terry. No. Dr Galligher. She turned and gave him a tight smile. It slipped slightly as she took him in. She'd forgotten how impressive he was in a suit and tie, and the desire to run her hand up his chest, over his crisp shirt and under his lapel, was so, so tempting. *I'm over you. I'm over you.*

Will crowded into the nurses' station with his entourage of residents and registrars, most of whom Lou already knew.

'Who do we have here?' he asked, as he stretched out his hand to Terry.

Lou watched with dismay as the little traitor grabbed hold of Will's hand and giggled. Terry never took an instant like to anyone.

'This is Terry. He has bilateral talipes,' she said.

'Poor little guy,' he crooned, looking down at the little boy and getting another dribbly smile for his effort. 'Club feet are no fun.' He turned to Lou, his hand still trapped by Terry. 'How come he's been hospitalised? Surely this can be managed at home?'

'His parents have mild intellectual disabilities, and couldn't cope with the routine plastering regime. He kept coming into ortho clinic with wet plasters. They love him, and can take care of his basic needs, but this is just a bit much for them. They also have three other children. We had a multi-disciplinary meeting with the parents and decided admitting him for the duration of his treatment was the only option. So he's with us for a little longer.'

'What about surgery?' Will asked.

'Not severe enough.'

'How long has he been in for?'

'Two months,' she said, and smiled at the little boy as he gave her a gappy grin.

'Cute,' he said.

Lou looked at him, startled. Did he mean her or Terry? He held her gaze with an amused look.

'Do you think we can get this round started now? Tweedle-Dum and Tweedle-Dee have been holding up that wall for half an hour. They're getting in Lydia's way.'

Will looked over to where Lou had indicated with her head. Two of his med students, with white coats and matching glasses, had propped themselves against a wall in the corridor and were drumming their fingers.

Will chuckled. 'Sorry 'bout that. I'm surprised she didn't give them something to do.'

'Are you kidding? They don't look much older than babies themselves,' she said.

Will laughed again, and indicated that she lead the way.

She handed Terry to Lydia, who kept the ward running while Lou went round with Will and his band of merry followers. The ward held thirty beds, and was rarely under capacity. It was a general paeds ward, part of a busy Brisbane inner-city general hospital, and therefore catered to all ages from birth to sixteen, and all conditions, medical and surgical.

Just over half of Ward Two's patients were under Will's care. One quarter were surgical, and under various surgeons, and the other quarter were under different private paediatricians. Today's round was particularly lengthy as this was the first time Will had met any of the patients, and he wanted to hear a complete history from his junior doctors.

Despite having a zillion other things she could be doing, with only one month left until she handed over to Lydia, Lou patiently followed them around. She knew that Will was just being thorough, and that subsequent rounds would be nowhere near as tedious.

Brian Billham, Will's resident, did most of the histories with Will, who stopped him occasionally to confirm things with Lou or ask her a question or opinion. Will was a doctor who recognised and respected input from the nursing side of things, and understood they were valuable members of a multi-disciplinary team. Unfortunately Lou had to contradict Brian a couple of times, and hoped it was just because the young doctor was nervous rather than incompetent.

Will also used the round to test the calibre of his minions, as Lydia called them. He bombarded his juniors with questions, teaching without conscious effort as he went. Lou could feel the vibe in the group. It was always dynamic working with Will, and she felt sorry on a professional level that she only had a few short weeks to go.

By the time they got to Terry, Lou had a page of notes to pass on to the appropriate staff members. Things to check on, tests to organise, referrals to chase. She had a busy morning ahead. Normally on a day shift Lou did four hours' clinical in the morning and four hours' management, depending on staff levels and skill mix. With Lydia on today and good staffing she should definitely be able to retire to her office a little later.

'Twelve-month-old Terry,' said Brian, flipping open a reasonably thick chart for such a young child.

Terry, who had been grizzling in his cot, stopped the minute he spied Lou amongst the coats and gave her a grin. Lou let down the side and hauled him out as she listened to Brian's background story.

Will watched them intently. The little boy stuck his thumb in his mouth and snuggled into Lou's chest, just as Candy used to do. Terry pulled his thumb out and placed his hand against a breast. He squished it innocently as he jiggled around like a baby monkey, and then decided to play with the top button of her polo shirt.

Will's gaze lingered on Lou's chest. What had been a very generous C-cup had swelled considerably since the last time he'd seen her—thanks, no doubt, to the pregnancy. He wondered absently whether Lou was going to breastfeed, and then realised he hadn't heard a word that Brian had been saying.

He tuned back in for a moment, but was instantly distracted again as Terry propped one plastered leg on top of her bump and swung the other one lazily against her side. He looked in baby heaven, oblivious to the discussion about his feet. And Lou looked the epitome of maternal, gazing at the floor as she unconsciously rubbed her cheek through his hair and swayed back and forth with Terry on her hip.

'Callum and Tristan,' he said, addressing the med students, suppressing the urge to use Lou's most apt nicknames, 'who can tell me about talipes?'

'There are four types,' said Callum, jumping in eagerly. 'This patient—'

'Terry,' interrupted Will. Doctors who didn't know their

patients had names other than their conditions had always irritated him. Best to get it through to them young.

'Terry…' Callum faltered '…has the most common type, talipes equinovarus, also known as club foot. It's often associated with other deformities, but this…Terry's…seems to fall into the idiopathic bracket.'

Lou smiled to herself. She loved the medical euphemism for don't-have-a-clue.

'Like to add anything, Tristan?' Will asked.

'Terry's foot is typical of most cases of equinovarus,' said Tristan. 'The front parts of his feet are turned in and down, giving them a kidney bean shape. Both ankle joints are quite stiff, and he has atrophy of his calf muscles, which is also typical.'

'What happens if we leave it uncorrected?' Will shot back.

'The patient…Terry,' said Callum, 'will be unable to mobilise.'

'Very good,' said Will, risking a look back at Lou. 'Any concerns?' he asked her.

Lou thought Terry felt quite warm, and checked the chart hanging at the end of his cot. His temp had been up this morning—night staff hadn't handed that over. She checked his med chart. They'd given him some paracetamol.

'He's febrile at the moment,' said Lou, again hoping he wasn't coming down with something.

'Get a ward urine test,' said Will, seeing Lou's concern. 'Just to be sure.'

Terry chose that moment to sneeze, and show all and sundry some nice green nasal discharge. Lou dodged his attempt at rubbing his face into her shirt. The group laughed at her quick reflexes.

'Hmm,' said Will, grinning broadly, 'and maybe an NPA as well.'

Lou pulled a tissue from her pocket and wiped, much to Terry's disgust. He grizzled at her, and then grinned when she stopped. He didn't look his usual happy self. His eyes looked a little dull, and he was already rubbing at them—an indication he was ready for his morning sleep, which he wouldn't normally be for at least another hour.

The round broke up, and Lou hurried away to alert her different staff members to the changes that Will had instigated for any of their patients. She was pleased to see Will go. She'd been conscious of his stare as she'd held Terry, and had been pleased with the distraction when the little one had almost slimed her. Between Will's stare today and the memory of his look yesterday, it wasn't quite the way she'd planned to restart their professional relationship. *And I'm over him!*

'Kristy, have you done a naso-pharyngeal aspirate before?' she asked, tracking the grad nurse down to the medication room.

Kristy shook her head. 'Not yet. It's on my checklist, though.'

Lou nodded. Grad nurses had to achieve proficiency in certain procedures during their ward rotations. 'Good. Will wants one on Terry, and as he's your patient you can do it. I'll show you when you've finished there. He's ready for his nap, so we'll get the unpleasantries over, then he can have his bottle and go to sleep.'

Five minutes later a grizzly Terry was lying on his back in his cot, looking at them suspiciously.

'We'll do the urine bag first,' Lou said. 'Then the NPA.'

Kristy gooed at Terry as she undid his nappy, and Lou helped keep him still as Kristy secured the small, sterile urine-collecting bag. It was a tricky job and the bag needed to be fixed in the right spot or the urine could leak out everywhere. A wriggly, grizzly baby made it trickier still.

'Much easier with a boy,' Kristy commented as she checked her handiwork, folding the excess plastic into his nappy and refastening it.

'Yes,' Lou laughed. 'Much.'

Terry had taken it reasonably well, for which Lou was pleased—because she knew there was no way on earth he was going to take the next bit well at all.

Lou talked to him soothingly as Kristy assembled the specimen collector into the suction line. Kristy turned it on at the wall, and Terry looked at her and started to grizzle.

'It's okay, baby,' Lou crooned. 'It's only horrible for a few seconds.'

'So I just put the catheter in his nose, advance it to the back of his throat and suck, right?' asked Kristy.

'Yep,' Lou confirmed. 'Are you ready?'

Kristy nodded, and Lou laid her chest across the little boy's legs and torso so he couldn't kick her, and held his head firmly between her hands. Terry started to cry and squirm his head, and Lou increased her grip. He really complained when the thin clear catheter was introduced to his nose, and then coughed and gagged through his cries while Kristy completed the job.

They watched as thick green discharge tracked up the catheter, and Kristy withdrew it quickly, satisfied they had enough for a specimen. Lou quickly picked the protesting babe off the bed and gave him a big hug as Kristy sucked a bit of sterile saline into the suction catheter to move the exudate into the collection canister at the end of the catheter.

'Oh, no—real tears,' Lou crooned as she sat with Terry on the chair beside his cot and wiped away a little tear from his face. 'Will this help?' she asked, and picked up his bottle.

Terry looked slightly mollified and reached for it. She handed it to him and he lay back, snuggling into the crook of her elbow and placing it in his mouth.

'And then there was peace.' Kristy laughed as she labelled the specimen.

Lou laughed too, and even earned a half-smile from Terry before he closed his eyes and drank himself to sleep.

A knock interrupted Lou after lunch, and she welcomed it gratefully. She'd been getting nowhere with her work. The policy review she wanted to finish before going on maternity leave sat untouched in front of her. All she could think about sitting in her chair was how good it had been, hanging with Will and Candy on the weekend.

'Lou—sorry to interrupt, but can you come here, please? Lydia's on a tea break, and the bloody doctor won't listen to me.'

Lou jumped up from her desk immediately at the tone of Kristy's voice and her obvious annoyance. She might be only new to the job, but she had the makings of an excellent nurse and Lou trusted her judgement.

'What's wrong?' she asked, hurrying after Kristy.

'It's that Dr Billham—Brian. Thinks he's God's gift to the medical fraternity. He's had two goes to get Erica's IV back in, and he's trying for a third. I told him it was enough, but he's doing it anyway.'

'What happened to the other one?' asked Lou as she followed Kristy to the treatment room, where all IVs were inserted.

'It tissued,' the nurse said. 'I paged him to come and put another one in. I think I interrupted his lunch.'

'Oh, what a pity.' Lou frowned. 'It only had to hold out for another day.'

Lou could hear baby Erica screaming from halfway down the corridor—and so could her mother, who was bawling her eyes out by Erica's bed on the ward. Lou felt her ire rising.

'It's all right, Mrs Jessop,' Lou said reassuringly, stopping momentarily to calm the distressed mother. 'The doctor's obviously having a bit of trouble getting the new IV in. We'll give Erica a breather for a little while. You wait here, and I'll bring her out to you in a moment.'

Lou squeezed the mother's shoulder, and she and Kristy continued on their way. They reached the treatment room, and burst through the door in time to witness Brian take another jab.

'Hold still, kid,' he said, an edge of frustration tainting his voice.

'Excuse me,' Lou said firmly, walking over to the baby, pushing the doctor's poised hand aside, snapping off the tourniquet that was clamped to Erica's little arm and picking her up off the bed. The little girl was red in the face and hiccupping, she was so upset.

'I nearly had it,' Brian protested.

Lou bounced Erica as she shot a look of pure disdain the doctor's way. Brian Billham wasn't much taller than Lou, and quite weedy-looking, with a thin, snarly mouth. Lou hadn't though much of him on rounds, and she'd certainly seen nothing here to change her mind.

Lou turned to Kristy. 'Go and page Will, please,' she said pleasantly.

'I can manage,' said Brian.

Moron. Lou took a while to soothe Erica. She was not going to have this conversation over a screaming child. Finally the child's cries settled to a heart-wrenching hiccup.

'Do you see that sign up there?' Lou asked, indicating the handwritten, laminated card stuck to the front of the IV supplies cupboard. '"Two strikes and you're out,"' she said. 'Do you think that doesn't apply to you, Doctor?'

'Kids have difficult veins. Sometimes it takes more than two goes,' he said sulkily.

'Indeed it does,' Lou agreed. 'And that's when you take a break and try again in a couple of hours' time. All you've succeeding in doing is making her and her mother hysterical, and yourself so angry you were never going to get that drip in.'

The door opened, and Will, Kristy and Lydia entered the fray.

'Everything okay here?' Will asked. He looked from his resident to Lou and back again. Brian was clearly fuming. Lou looked calmer, but he knew her well enough to know a calm Lou could be lethal. He pitied Brian, he really did. Lou took her job as advocate very seriously.

'Your resident seems to have problems reading signs,' Lou said, clutching Erica to her.

'I was trying to insert an IV,' Brian said, ignoring Lou, looking at his boss for support.

'Oh, dear.' Will whistled. 'You didn't break the two strikes rule, did you?'

'The kid has difficult veins,' Brian said defiantly.

'Did you have some local anaesthetic cream on?' Will enquired.

'Yes,' Kristy piped in. 'But he hadn't given it long enough to work.'

'Brian, Brian, Brian.' Will tutted, looking at the three hostile women and knowing the green young doctor didn't stand a chance. 'What were you thinking? The nurses here know their stuff. Trust me, you don't want to get on their bad side. Isn't that right, Lydia?'

Lydia gave him a grudging smile. 'No way.'

Lou almost felt sorry for Brian now that Erica had calmed down. Everything Brian ever did from this moment forward would be treated sceptically. It was a hard way to learn a valuable lesson. *Don't annoy the nurses.*

'If you can't get an IV in after two goes, trust me—it's not going to happen,' Will said to his junior. 'Because then you get frustrated and put yourself under all kinds of pressure. Time to take a breather after two. And always, *always,* wait for the magic cream to work. Are we clear?'

'Sorry. I was just in a hurry.'

'That's fine,' said Will pleasantly. 'Why don't you go and do what you need to do, and I'll see to Erica in a little while?'

Brian didn't need any further encouragement, leaving the room as fast as he could. Lydia and Kristy followed him out. Will smiled at Lou, who had managed to get Erica to sleep. She was cradling the baby close, still protecting her, as she gently rocked from side to side.

He loved how passionate Lou was when minding her charges. She took her job and her role as patient advocate very seriously indeed. Looking at her now, her cheeks still

flushed from her confrontation with Brian, her belly emphasised by the way she was holding Erica, he couldn't
remember a time when she'd looked sexier. When he had
loved her more.

Loved her more? No. No, no, no! *I'm over her, damn it.*
And then Erica stirred, and Lou clucked softly and kissed
her little forehead gently. She looked up at him and smiled
a serene, satisfied smile. And he knew with dreadful clarity
that he'd been wrong. That he wasn't over her. That he loved
her. That he hadn't stopped loving her.

He stared at her stupidly. How foolish had he been?
Detaching himself from his true feelings to make their
break easier. But he'd been lying to himself all along. His
feelings hadn't changed in the last four days. He was just
finally allowing the truth to surface. He'd been living in
complete denial.

Will became aware of the silence in the room, broken only
by the ticking clock. Thankfully Lou was too engrossed in
Erica to notice his dazed look. He had to get out of here.

'I'm sorry…I have to go…I was in the middle of clinic,'
he muttered, his brain operating on autopilot as he opened
the fridge door and found some local anaesthetic cream.

'But I'll be back in an hour,' he said, inspecting the
sleeping child's foot, grateful for something to do with his
hands. He found a nice blue vein and covered it with a daub
of the cream.

Erica stirred a little in her sleep, but didn't wake as Will
covered the cream with a transparent sticky dressing. 'I'll
insert the IV when I come back.'

'I'll be in my office. Kristy can help you,' she said.

Kristy. Good. 'Excellent,' he said, backing out through the door, needing to be away from her. *Too much.* It was too much. He needed to get away from her. Before he said something silly. Like, *I love you.*

'Thank you,' she mouthed to him as he left the room.

Will nodded and swallowed, and shut the door behind him. *Hell!* Being back had been hard enough without this. He loved her. How could he have not known? How could he have ignored his feelings for so long? More importantly, how could he work with her for the next few weeks and not tell her? Because their circumstances still hadn't changed. He had Candy, and a whole heap of baggage, and she had Jan's baby. Loving her just complicated it further.

Will was as good as his word, and an hour later, through the glass panel in the treatment room door, Lou watched him insert the IV into Erica's foot. Kristy was helping him, and the whole procedure was accomplished in a few minutes.

Lou couldn't hear what he was saying, but his body language was easy to read. He was a natural around kids. His low, crooning voice and his slow, gentle movements were calming to little Erica, who barely protested at all. He was like some kind of baby whisperer, and as she watched his skilful movements, saw the smile Erica gave him, her heart filled with love for this extraordinary doctor. For his kindness, his compassion, his gentleness.

Oh, no. A sinking feeling enveloped her as she pulled sharply away from the glass. She was still in love with him? Her heart thundered in her ears. She'd been lying to herself. Going to bed every night pretending she was over him. Reciting all the reasons why she'd be stupid to fall for him again. Shutting her eyes, completely satisfied that her heart was intact.

But she'd been wrong. She should have known that her love for Will could survive anything. She had known five years ago he was her guy, and despite enormous upheaval, nothing had changed. She risked a look through the glass again—the plain truth was right there in front of her. She pulled back and leaned against the wall, grateful for its support as she sighed heavily. She was still in love with Dr William Galligher.

And no amount of fooling herself she didn't love him was going to make up for the fact that she did.

CHAPTER FOUR

WILL shut and locked the door behind him, sat at the desk and slowly thumped his head against the wood several times. He wanted to bellow out loud, but figured the relatively thin walls in the clinic wouldn't keep his frustration a secret.

Three weeks into his job and Will couldn't stand it any more. His heart, his body, were telling him he loved Lou and wanted her back. But his head knew it was insane to go there again. *He wouldn't, damn it all.* He just wouldn't. Things with Candy were going amazingly well. It had been a long time since they'd had such an uninterrupted bond, and he was determined to nurture that at any cost. He would not divide his time.

One more week to go. Just one, and things should become a lot easier around here. Because with every day he saw Lou it got harder to deny himself. Despite her pregnancy becoming more and more pronounced, he wanted her. Which was crazy, because her swollen belly, more than anything, should have been a big neon flashing light telling him to forget it. They both had kids to think about now.

His external circumstances had already ruined their relationship once. Putting his heart on the line again was not an option. Despite his feelings, it had been too traumatic, and with Lou being pregnant their situation was further complicated.

He was tired of 'complicated'. Wary of it. He thought back to his marriage and shuddered. Learning about Delvine's affair when Candy had been six months old had knocked the stuffing out of him. He had known Delvine hadn't been thrilled about the pregnancy, had worried about her figure and how much a baby would tie her down, but he had never doubted their love or commitment. The affair had been totally unexpected and completely soul-destroying.

But the worst blow had been Delvine leaving shortly after and taking Candy with her. Those first six months of Candy's life had been the most amazing time. She was simply the most precious thing he'd ever seen. One look at his bawling, wet newborn daughter had had him totally entranced.

He'd been completely caught up in the wonder of Candice—her smiles and her squeals, and her sweet, clean smell. And all the mornings he had gone and picked her up out of her cot and watched the sunrise with his little early bird. It had been magical.

The separation from Candy had been terrible. He'd taken it for granted that she would always be there, and when she was gone he'd felt as if his heart had been ripped from his chest. Those next six months had been the worst of his life. He'd seen Candy a few days a week, but it hadn't been enough. So when Delvine had decided out of the blue, just before Candy's first birthday, that she didn't want to be a mother any more, and had dumped their daughter on him, he had been ecstatic.

And then a year later it had got even better, as his relationship with Lou had budded into something amazing. Lou had been marvellous. Had adored Candy and never griped or moaned about the fact that she'd got herself involved with a man who came with a child in tow and all the restrictions that placed on their courtship. Six months after that she'd moved in, and things had been almost perfect.

For one fabulous year they'd had Candy all to themselves, and Will had just started to think a future for him and Lou was possible. Then Delvine had returned, with a vengeance. Interfering and undermining and calculating—but being granted access in the courts, nonetheless.

Sharing custody with Delvine, having her back in his life, had been messy and stressful, and he had run himself ragged, trying to keep up with her latest legal whim and looking after Candy and not neglecting Lou. Sure, Lou had understood, but he'd known she was unhappy. They'd stuck it out over the years because they'd both known how good it could be. But it hadn't been fair to her. She'd deserved to be happy, and external problems had made it almost impossible.

And today, a year after their split, their situation was still complicated. More than before. Okay, Delvine was off the scene, but there were now two children in the mix. Hell, Lou had a baby on the way. What sort of stress would that put on any relationship he might be foolish enough to consider? It had been the breaking point in his marriage. And Candy had to come first.

The doorknob rattled suddenly, bringing him out of the past, and he looked up, startled by the noise in the quiet room. It jiggled a few more times before the person on the other side obviously realised it was locked and knocked instead. He looked at his watch. Probably Lydia, wanting to check if he was ready for the first patient. For his sins, he was stuck with Lydia for three hours on clinic afternoon. Still, at least it wasn't Lou.

He leaned forward, flipped the lock and opened the door. *Damn.* It was Lou.

'Oh, you're in here,' she said. 'I thought it mustn't have been unlocked yet. I was just about to get the key.'

What the hell was she doing here? 'Yes, sorry about that.' He grimaced. 'Where's Lydia?'

'She had to go home. The school called. Rilla is sick.'

'Oh, that's no good. I suppose you're taking her place?' he said gloomily.

Lou laughed. 'Yes. Sorry to depress you.'

What was she so happy about? He nodded tersely. 'Give me five, then send the first one in.'

Lou walked away, peeved. *What was his problem?* Honestly, he'd been getting more and more impossible to deal with over the last couple of weeks. Lucky she already knew him quite well, because if she'd only just met him for the first time she'd think him a right arrogant so-and-so. He'd been short and irritable. And today he'd been like a bear with a sore head on rounds.

She stopped short and back-tracked determinedly. If he thought she was going to work with him all afternoon in this grumpy mood then he could think again. She barged back into his office without knocking.

'What?' he demanded, startled by her vigorous entry.

'What's up? Spit it out, Will.'

'I don't know what you're talking about,' he said.

'You've been grumpy for ages, and I'm not going to put up with it this afternoon.'

He looked at her, standing in front of him, all gorgeous

and pregnant and indignant, and he wanted to kiss her. 'Nothing's wrong,' he said tersely. 'I was expecting Lydia, that's all.'

'Lydia gives you hell every day, Will. I'd have thought you'd appreciate the reprieve.'

'Well, she's growing on me,' he snapped. 'Do you think we could get on with this? We've only got three hours.'

Lou stared at him, torn between belting him over the head with a chart and yanking him up by his lapels and kissing him. She heard the harshness of her breathing and knew it wasn't all anger.

'Please?' she snapped, sounding like a demented kindergarten teacher and not caring.

'Please,' he parroted in an exaggerated fashion, and bugged his eyes at her, then returned to the stack of lab results on the desk.

Dismissed, huh? So this is the way it's going to be, Will Galligher? Well, two can play at this game. Resolving to be as unhelpful as she possibly could, she put her hand on the first chart and smiled. Bailey Hillgate. Eight years old. Nice kid. Chronic constipation. MFH. *Mother From Hell.*

'Bailey,' she said, smiling sweetly at Will as she ushered patient and mother into the room.

'Hey, there, champ,' said Will, ignoring Lou and her fake smile. 'Pull up a chair,' he said, patting the one near him. 'Hi, Mrs Hillgate? I'm Will,' he said, holding out his hand.

'Will?' She sniffed. 'Are you a proper doctor? I'm supposed to be seeing the paediatrician.'

Will looked at Lou, and narrowed his eyes slightly at her innocent look. He smiled at Mrs Hillgate. 'Yes, I'm the paediatrican. I just don't believe in too much formality.'

'Why on earth not?' she asked, peering down her nose at him. 'Surely your parents didn't spend hundreds of thousands of dollars on your education so you could go around calling yourself anything other than Doctor?'

Will looked at Bailey, who was staring at the floor and generally looking as if he wished the ground would swallow him whole. 'Hey, Bailey,' he said, 'knock-knock.'

'Who's there?' the boy mumbled.

'Annie.'

'Annie who?'

'Annie one you like.'

The joke barely raised a smile. 'Okay, not a knock-knock fan? How about this? Why did cavemen draw pictures of hippopotamuses and rhinoceroses on their walls?'

Bailey shrugged.

'Because they couldn't spell their names.'

Lou covered her mouth as both mother and son looked at Will, completely unamused.

'Tough room,' he said to Lou.

She bit on the inside of her cheek and gave him her best unamused look as well. *This is just the beginning, William.*

'So,' he said, abandoning all hope of a laugh, 'how goes it with the bowels?'

'Still bunged up to the eyeballs,' said Mrs Hillgate, and proceeded to give Will all the gory details of Bailey's bowel habits.

'Did you have an X-ray before coming here, Bailey?' Will asked.

Bailey nodded.

'Say, Yes, Doctor, Bailey,' his mother nagged.

'Yes, Doctor,' said the boy.

'I'll just get it up on the screen,' said Will, logging in to the X-ray department and loading the latest image of Bailey's abdomen. 'Nice bones.' He whistled. 'Hey, Bailey, where does a skeleton plug in his toaster?'

'Don't know,' he mumbled.

'His eye socket,' said Will, laughing at his own joke. This time Bailey did laugh, which made Will laugh harder still.

'Are you sure you're not one of those clown doctors?' Mrs Hillgate asked in disgust.

Will laughed at Mrs Hillgate, amazed that the woman had actually cracked a joke—even though she'd obviously intended it as an insult. Bailey laughed too.

'That was not funny, Bailey,' his mother said.

Will watched the laughter die from the boy's face. *Jeez, lady, I'd be constipated if I lived with you.* 'Sure it was,' said Will. 'You're a funny lady, Mrs Hillgate.'

'Hmph,' she said coldly.

'Seriously, I think you should do stand-up.'

Lou rolled her eyes at him. If Mrs Hillgate had to make a living from comedy she'd starve to death. She tapped her watch impatiently. They had thirty patients to see, and she would be the one to cop the flak if they ran late—not him.

'The X-ray, Doctor?' said the unimpressed mother.

Will sighed and winked at Bailey, earning a quick grin from the boy. 'Well, it's much improved since the last one,' said Will, pulling up Bailey's previous X-ray and comparing them. The older one had significant distended loops of bowel, but today's looked almost normal. 'I think the current therapy of stool softeners and diet seems to be having an effect.'

'But he only goes two or three times a week,' said Mrs Hillgate, not bothering to hide her annoyance.

Will ignored her. 'Bailey, does it hurt when you open your bowels?'

'No,' he said.

'I think this may just be Bailey's body finding its own natural rhythm,' Will said, looking at Mrs Hillgate. 'As long as Bailey continues to grow and be healthy I think we may need to accept that for Bailey this pattern is normal.'

'The Hillgates have always had regular bowels,' the woman said indignantly.

Will almost laughed—until he realised Mrs Hillgate was absolutely serious. Obviously irregular bowel habits were a grave sin.

'I want a second opinion. I want him to see a specialist.'

Will felt sorry for poor Bailey. Being stuck with a mother who was obsessed with your bowels was tough. He had thought it bad enough that *his* mother had been obsessed with his grades. Looking back, maybe that hadn't been too bad.

'You're perfectly entitled, of course,' said Will, 'I think you'll be wasting your money, though.'

'Money is not an issue,' she sniffed.

Will reached into the top drawer for a writing pad and scribbled a quick note to a private gastroenterologist. He put it in an envelope and handed it to Bailey's mother.

'Thank you…Doctor,' she said, gathering her stuff. 'Come along, Bailey.'

Will watched as the poor kid sighed and rose with slumped shoulders. 'Hey, Bailey, what does a skeleton order at a restaurant?'

Bailey grinned and straightened up, a twinkle entering his eye. 'I don't know,' he said.

'Spare ribs,' said Will, and was rewarded with a giggle.

'I said come along, Bailey,' his mother said, grabbing her son by the arm and pulling him out of the room—but not before he gave Will a little wave, and Will winked back at him.

Will looked at Lou and narrowed his eyes. 'You could have warned me she was MFH.'

'And ruin the surprise?'

'Lydia always warns me about the mothers from hell.'

'Well, I'm not Lydia, and that's what you get for being in a crank for weeks.'

'So Mrs Hillgate was payback?'

'No, Mrs Hillgate was just the beginning,' she said, giving him a saccharine smile.

He looked at her assessingly. Oh, great, he'd violated the most important rule, learnt very quickly by newbie doctors everywhere—except Brian. *Don't annoy the nurses.* Fortunately Lou Marsden didn't scare him. 'Well, bring it on, Lou. I can hardly wait.'

'That's Sister Marsden to you,' she said, turning abruptly and leaving the room.

Her long plait swished behind her, and he'd never been more tempted to give it a good hard yank and lay her across his knees and spank her bottom. Didn't she realise her being so near and his not being able to touch was torture? That he was grumpy because being around her constantly reminded him of things he couldn't have?

'Sarah Montgomery, *Dr* Galligher,' said Lou.

'Thank you, *Sister* Marsden,' he said.

And so the afternoon progressed, in polite formality. Lou saw the patients in, but refused to hold his hand like most nurses would normally do in a clinic situation.

'Can you get me the tendon hammer please, Sister Marsden?' Will asked at one stage.

'Bottom right-hand drawer,' she said, smiling serenely at him as she left the room.

Will sighed, stopped his neuro assessment and swivelled on his chair to retrieve it.

'I need a ward test urine,' he said to her a little later.

Lou pulled a packaged sterile urine bag out of her pocket and slapped it in his hand. 'All yours,' she said, with another deceptively nice smile.

'Right,' said Will watching her go, her plait swishing.

By the time the last patient was leaving he had a headache, and his mood was not good. Between her unhelpfulness, glimpses of her cleavage and that damn tempting flick of her plait as she turned her back on him, he was ready to throttle her.

Lydia hadn't ever been this hard on him, and at least *she* brought him a cup of coffee between patients. He hadn't dared even ask Lou, for fear he would end up with third-degree burns in a very delicate area of his body. *Only one more week.*

Lou had finished sorting through the charts, and was contemplating going back to Ward Two without even telling Will, when a very familiar wave of nausea struck. She checked her pocket for Fruit Tingles, but wasn't surprised to find none. She had left them on her desk. Her hand started to shake, and she knew if she didn't get something sweet into her mouth she was going to vomit. Or faint. Or possibly both.

Her wobbly legs kicked into action. Maybe Lydia had a stash in the clinic office? God knew she had them everywhere else Lou was likely to be in the entire hospital.

Will was still writing in a chart when she opened the door.

'What are you doing?' he asked, as he quickly shifted a leg to save it from being amputated by her swift opening of a desk drawer.

She ignored him, her single-minded pursuit of a sweet making her oblivious to everything.

'Lou, this cold shoulder thing is getting a bit ridiculous, don't you think?'

Her hand shook as she searched through all three drawers on one side, then moved around Will to hunt through the drawers on the other side. She could feel sweat beading on her upper lip at the effort it took to concentrate on not vomiting. She could hear his voice, but the words weren't registering.

'Lou!' he said, grabbing her arm. 'For God's sake, what are you looking for?'

She straightened up and felt the world tilt. 'Some sugar, okay? For God's sake just shut up for a minute,' she snapped.

'Sugar? What the hell—?'

Lou didn't hear the rest of what he said. Her vision blackened from the outside edges in, and a loud ringing in her ears obliterated everything coming from his mouth. She could see his lips moving, but that was it. And then it all went black, and she could feel herself letting go and falling, falling, falling.

Will caught her as she slumped against him. 'Lou? Lou!' he said, shaking her slightly, his heart thundering in his chest as at least six worst-case scenarios stormed through his head. He swept her up in his arms and placed her on the examination couch in the office. Even seven months pregnant and all baby she weighed less than some people pumped at the gym.

'Lou?' he said again, shaking her shoulder, pulling the BP

cuff off the wall and almost sagging in relief when he heard a faint murmur escape her lips.

Her blood pressure was seventy-five on forty-five. He felt the fist that had rammed into his gut and squeezed his stomach relax its hold. Hypotensive vagal episode. Probably exacerbated by a hypoglycaemic episode. For an awful moment, despite all his medical training, he'd thought she had stopped breathing, and he never wanted to go through that blind dread again as long as he lived.

Lou's eyes fluttered open and shut a couple of times, and Will fell even more in love with her. 'Lou?' he said again, stroking her forehead gently, giving his heart-rate time to settle.

'Will?' she murmured. Lou took a moment for her eyes to focus. Will and the room swam before her, and it was a full minute before her confusion cleared and her recall returned. 'Oh, God, what happened? Did I faint?'

'Yes,' he said. 'Yes, you did. You scared the hell out of me, actually.'

She had? Lou moved, trying to sit up and flailing about like a beached whale. Her low sugar level had left her feeling irritable. 'Are you just going to watch me get nowhere or help?' she grumbled.

Will snapped out of his grateful stupor, locking forearms with her and pulling her upright slowly. 'Easy,' he said. 'You're quite hypotensive.'

The room swam again, and she kept hold of his arm as she struggled to focus. A fresh wave of nausea hit as her surroundings became clear and sharp again.

'You okay?'

She shook her head, her arms and legs shaking. 'I need to eat something. Now. The sweeter the better.'

'I have some Tic-Tacs,' he said, fishing them out of his pocket.

'Perfect,' she said, snatching them out of his hands, flipping the lid, opening her mouth and pouring in half of the container. The little bullets of sugar practically dissolved on her tongue, and she shut her eyes as the spearmint flavour exploded in her mouth—and, more importantly, revived her flagging blood glucose, dispelling her trembling and nausea in one magical minute.

She opened her eyes as the last one melted on her tongue, to find him looking at her.

'Better?' he asked.

She sighed heavily as the residual wooziness subsided. 'Much.' She handed him back his Tic-Tacs.

He put his hands up in protest. 'No, no. You have them. You obviously need them more than I do.'

'No, I'll be fine now. I just got caught without my Fruit Tingles. Didn't expect to be here today. It can be a demanding little critter,' she said, rubbing her bump.

The baby disliked the weight of her hand and kicked at it. 'Ow!' she yelped, still amazed at the power of a five-pound foetus. 'I swear this kid's going to be a line rower, like his dad.'

Will laughed. 'Where?' he asked. 'Is it here?' He placed his hand next to hers and she shook her head, picking his hand up and moving it over slightly, getting an immediate response. 'Maybe he'll kick for Australia?' he grinned.

'Maybe *she'll* kick butts in the courtroom? Or parliament?'

He laughed as she continued to cover his hand and steer it around, trying to follow the movements of the baby. 'Do you know the sex?'

She shook her head. 'We were going to find out. Jan and Martin wanted to be able to name the baby and talk about it as a real person instead of *the baby*. But after the accident…I just wanted something out of all of this to look forward to, you know? A nice surprise after all the bad ones.'

He nodded, moving his hand up high on her bump as the baby frolicked there. It looped the loop a couple more times, and he grinned at her, remembering the times he had felt Candy's foetal contortions and how endlessly fascinating they'd been. For one brief moment as they shared this intimate experience, her hand on his, he wished the baby was theirs. His and Lou's.

The baby stopped moving, and they waited for it to start up again. After a minute it became apparent that the show was over. By then Will was more conscious of how close they were. How, from his vantage point, he could see down her cleavage to the creamy rise of her breasts. How her neck smelt like flowers and her breath like mint and her hair like coconut. How her lips shimmered with some gloss stuff she had on, and her breath was raspy and uneven.

She removed her hand from his. 'I think it's stopped now,' she said quietly.

She stared at his nicely tanned hand against the white of her polo shirt, because his head was so close to hers she didn't dare look up into his eyes. His mouth, his lips, were somewhere in the vicinity of her forehead; she could almost feel the heat from them searing into her flesh. As the silence grew to a loud roar she wanted him to remove his hands and step back. But she needed to feel his arms around her more.

'Will,' she pleaded softly, her resolve to not go back crumbling by the second.

I can't. 'I missed you,' he said huskily, feeling the strength of his connection to her not just through the intimacy of his touch but through a thousand rekindled memories.

She nodded, and felt a lump of emotion clog her throat. 'I missed you too,' she admitted, and looked up into his face.

'Lou,' he groaned, as a shimmer of moisture glimmered in her beautiful blue eyes. He moved his hands to cradle her face, and before he could analyse it, or she could protest, or they could both think better of it, he kissed her.

Lou felt the soft touch of his lips and a groan of sheer unadulterated lust escaped her mouth, and then she was kissing him back as if it was her last moment on earth. Her hands crept up his arms, revelling in the feel of his strength beneath them, and linked at the back of his neck, her fingers playing with the hair at his collar.

She felt heat flare to life deep down low inside, and she wanted to push herself closer. Be nearer. Feel his heat and his hardness. Be one. It wasn't enough. She wanted to tear off his shirt and feel his chest, the hard ridges of his back. She wanted to run her hands over his warmth, feel the smooth glide of his flesh. As if nothing had changed.

She heard him groan and pressed her lips closer, opened her mouth wider, held him tighter. He was right in front of her, but it wasn't enough. She wanted more. She wanted him everywhere. She wanted to be wrapped up in his body, part of him. Part of them.

Will, too, was totally lost in the moment. It didn't matter that this was what he shouldn't be doing. The simple matter was that it was *exactly* what he wanted to do. And something so wrong had never felt so right. She was soft and female, and her minty breath and coconut hair were driving him

crazy. He was being blown to a tropical island on a pepper-
mint breeze and it was bliss. But he wanted more. He wanted
all of her.

And then his pager beeped, and startled the hell out of
both of them. Lydia might as well have come in and thrown
a bucket of cold water over them. They broke apart, and he
stared at her for a few moments, her chest heaving, her lips
moist and swollen from their passion. They didn't speak—
they didn't have to.

He teetered on the edge for those few precarious moments,
achingly close to claiming her mouth again. She wanted
him to. He could see it in her eyes, hear it in the rasp of her
breath. He swayed closer and watched as she shut her eyes
and parted her lips, and he couldn't stop the groan that
rushed out from inside him.

And then the pager beeped again, and he stopped. She
opened her eyes and stared at him, and then stared at his lips.

'You'd better get that,' she said huskily.

He sighed and nodded, pushing himself away from the
couch and turning to the phone on the desk. His hand shook
slightly as he dialled the extension number displayed on his
pager. He cleared his throat and shut his eyes, and waited
for the other end to pick up.

Lou took a few deep breaths while Will spoke, making a
conscious effort to settle her breathing and her heart-rate.
She wiped her lips and tried not to think about how close
they had come to losing perspective. *Saved by the bell.*

'That was the ward. The new admission with the metabo-
lic disorder has arrived,' he said, replacing the phone, his
back to her.

Lou nodded, staring at his back, noting the slump of his

shoulders and the slight gravelly remnant still husking his voice. She waited for him to leave, the silence between them growing.

'I'm sorry,' he said, finally turning to face her. 'I shouldn't have done that.'

Lou shrugged. 'You weren't exactly in it alone,' she said.

'Still…' he said. 'It was wrong. It's just that…' He sat down on the desk and raked his hand through his hair. 'I've been going mad these last few weeks…it's harder than I thought it was going to be…'

'Working together again?'

He nodded and looked at her, frustration mirrored in his brown gaze, and she almost forgave him his recent grouchiness.

'Look, of course it's hard, working with someone you were once involved with. There's a lot of baggage that makes being professional difficult sometimes. I understand that,' she said. 'Don't worry about the kiss. I've only got another week, and it's not likely to happen again.' What was the point in Will beating himself up over one little slip-up?

'No, Lou… It's not just the kiss… It's…it's…it's everything.'

'Everything?' she asked. *What on earth was he talking about?*

'Everything about you. Your perfume…and your lipgloss… and your damn plait…' She was staring at him as if he was speaking another language or had just grown another head, and he wanted to shake her. He couldn't stand it any more.

Walking around pretending he wasn't in love with her was giving him hypertension. So too bad if she couldn't handle it. At least if he got it off his chest and could talk about it a bit it wouldn't be bottled up inside him, making him crazy.

He stared at her, exasperated by her blank look but not quite ready to blurt his secret out despite the potential for catharsis.

'What?' she demanded. 'I swear to God, Will, just say what you have to say. I'm not spending my last week on Ward Two with you carrying on like you have been.'

She couldn't see it? 'God, Lou,' he said. 'I'm still in love with you.'

Lou blinked, the words impacting into her body as if he had reached over and pushed her backwards. Her mind went blank for a moment, before it rebooted and his words sank in. Well, they were a right pair of fools, weren't they?

'I really thought I was over you, but I'm not.' She opened her mouth to talk, but he shushed her. 'I know it's impossible. We're impossible… But there it is.' And he did feel better. As if a weight had been lifted.

'There it is,' she said. The words she'd never thought she'd ever hear coming from his mouth again.

'Nothing to add?' he asked a few moments later, when she was still staring and blinking at him.

'Only that I'm in love with you too,' she said, depressed beyond words.

Oh, no. It was his turn to blink now, quashing the shot of triumph that streaked through him. 'Really?' he asked, despite knowing that the answer mattered little to the outcome.

She nodded, and they stared at each other miserably for a few moments.

'We can't do it,' Will said, in an effort to convince himself as much as her. 'I have Candy to think about. I finally have a chance to be a full-time dad to her. I need to concentrate on that.'

'And I have Jan's baby to bring up, and I'm terrified I'm

going to stuff it up, and I know I will if I allow us to happen again. This baby has to come first. There's too much water under the bridge for us.'

He nodded. 'I can't have another failed relationship, Lou. I can't risk it.'

Lou felt tears prick her eyes and nodded. Delvine's legacy lived on. For a while in the beginning she had thought he would risk it, but he had retreated from the brink when Delvine had arrived back on the scene. Sure, he had loved her, but she knew that until he learnt to give himself up to someone else totally, put his injured heart in her hands and trust her with it, they could never make it work.

'I'm thirty-five years old, Will, and this is me. What you see is what you get. All I want, all I've ever wanted, is for you to let me in. All the way. Not ninety per cent or even ninety-nine per cent. But all the way, Will. I can't risk it either.'

Fair enough. 'Which is another reason why this would never work, Lou. Our kids need a hundred per cent of us too.'

'I know,' she said, taking a deep breath. 'I know. So…now we go back to the beginning. We can't do it.'

'It's the timing, Lou. Maybe later, when the kids are older…'

Lou swallowed a lump. 'Yes, our timing does suck. But it's not just that, Will. It's you. It's in here,' she said, tapping his chest. 'You guard your heart too closely.' She dropped her hand and walked to the door. 'But it's okay. Only one week left, and we won't have to see each other every day. That'll make it easier, right?' she asked, as she put her hand on the doorknob and gave him a sad smile.

'Right,' he agreed half-heartedly, and watched her turn the knob and walk out the door.

Wrong!

CHAPTER FIVE

A WEEK later, Lou got up from her desk for the last time. Everything was neat, everything was completed, ready for Lydia to take the helm on Monday. But for now she could hear her farewell party had started without her.

She stood gingerly, her thirty-four-week pregnant abdomen making the task difficult. She felt a Braxton Hicks contraction tighten her uterus and took a couple of deep breaths. She'd been getting them irregularly for a few weeks now, but today they were really quite painful, each set lasting for about ten minutes at a time.

'Come on, Lou,' said Lydia, bursting through her office door. 'The party's nearly over!'

Lou smiled, and then held her breath as another contraction squeezed through her. She forced herself to breathe out. 'Just a second,' she said, holding up her hand.

'What?' said a concerned Lydia. 'What's happening? Another Braxton Hicks?'

Lou nodded. She put her hand under her bump and supported it. 'Bloody…things.' She grimaced.

Lydia shut the door and walked over, closer to her friend. 'Hey, look at the bright side. Your uterus isn't sitting around idly, it's practising. When you do go into labour it'll be an old hand.'

'It'd better be,' Lou said through clenched teeth.

Lydia laughed. 'We brought Terry in to the tearoom to help us celebrate,' Lydia said conversationally, as she rubbed Lou's back and waited with her for the Braxton Hicks to settle.

'And you say *I* spoil him!'

'It wouldn't be a party without the ward mascot.' Lydia grinned.

Lou started to breathe a little easier as the contractions waned. 'I guess he is part of the furniture here now.'

'You'll miss him. You'll miss us all.'

'Of course.' She smiled at her friend. *Except Will.* Not being around him was going to be a welcome change.

'Come on,' she said, forcing her legs to move now the contractions were just niggly remnants. 'My party awaits.'

When Lou entered the tearoom everyone cheered. The room was decorated with balloons and streamers, and the posters of Lou that the Shave for a Cure people had plastered all around the hospital. The table groaned with food. Terry, who had been perfectly happy devouring a lamington finger on Pete's lap, saw her and held his arms out to her. Pete got up from his chair and Lou took his place, a very happy Terry in her arms.

Lou was humbled by the attendance. Nurses had come in on their day off. There were physios, social workers, doctors who had worked with Lou over the years, and even Harold, the Medical Director, had made it. And Evelyn Mason, the domestic who had been cleaning Ward Two for longer than Lou had been around and was currently on long service leave, was there also.

There was laughter and chatting and a farewell cake. And lots of presents—baby clothes and toys, and nursery stuff, and some novelty things just for her.

And then, as a surprise, three clown doctors arrived. Lou had embraced the Humour Foundation, and had opened Ward Two's doors to the clown doctors when they'd just been a crazy fledgling idea. And the kids had adored them. Now three days a week they visited, with their balloons and magic tricks and off-key singing, and made the kids laugh and the nurses' job a little easier.

They performed a very adult hilarious routine, and twisted some very unconventional balloon figures to take home with her. They'd composed a special tribute to her, and one of them sang it while the other two provided the backing music—on a toy guitar and a plastic harmonica.

Lou was in fits of laughter by the end of it, and jumped when a spray of water sprinkled her face from a plastic lapel flower. 'Thanks so much, you guys. That was terrific,' she said, as she wiped away droplets of water with her hand.

'I propose a toast.'

Even over the noise of all the laughter, and several different conversations happening at once, Will's voice broke through. Lou felt her heart slam against her ribs as she looked up to see him standing in the doorway, and she thanked God this was her last day. Knowing how he felt about her had made their situation even more hopeless, and it would be good to be away from the constant reminder of him and what they couldn't have.

He looked all tall and broad and masculine, and she felt her body respond to him, despite the hopelessness. He smiled at her, and she swallowed the lump in her throat and smiled back.

'Everyone got a glass?' he asked. Will looked around the room at the assortment of Styrofoam cups, mugs and hospital-issue tumblers. *Classy.*

'You got the French champagne?' someone piped up, and everyone laughed.

'French champagne in paper cups? Sacrilege!' he scoffed. 'Lemonade's gonna have to do,' he said, holding his cup out for Pete to pour him some.

The bottle went round, and people charged their glasses. Will waited patiently, thinking about his words carefully, until everyone was ready. When they were all looking at him expectantly, and the murmuring had died down, he cleared his throat. He wanted to get this right. Putting aside his own feelings, few staff members embodied the spirit of the hospital like Lou. Normally this would be a speech that Harold would make, but Will had wanted it to come from him.

'To Lou,' he said, holding his paper cup up. 'For her years of dedication to Ward Two and this hospital. Those of us who know you well know you always go above and beyond the call of duty. You've given this hospital seventeen years— Ward Two, ten. And in this day and age that is indeed remarkable. You are efficient and resourceful, and what you don't know about paediatric nursing isn't worth knowing.

'But probably the one attribute that distinguishes you the most is how seriously you take your advocacy role. I'm sure, had Brian been here, he would agree whole-heartedly.'

Everyone laughed. Lou's confrontation with Brian over the IV was already the stuff of legend on the hospital grapevine.

'He sends his apologies. He's too busy sticking pins in a doll with a long blonde plait to come,' Pete joked, and there was more laughter.

Will joined in. 'Having been on the nasty end of Lou's "two strikes and you're out" rule once as a junior doctor, I can relate.'

Lou laughed too. She remembered that showdown. She'd just taken the helm as NUM and had read him the Riot Act very firmly. But it had cemented a fabulous working relationship, and she knew that not backing down that day had earned her his undying respect.

'But seriously, Lou,' he said, and waited for her downward gaze to meet his, 'this thing you're doing, the surrogacy, is typical of your selflessness. We know how close you and Jan were, but this goes above and beyond sisterly duty. We hope you know how very sorry we all are over Jan and Martin's tragic death, and that if you ever need anything to just holler.'

Will paused as a round of hear-hears broke out. Lou had dropped her gaze again, and was absently rubbing her cheek against a sleeping Terry's head.

'To Lou,' he said again. 'May you be blessed with an easy labour and a good sleeper. We love you.'

Lou looked at Will as her colleagues toasted her. Their gazes locked and it was as if they were the only two people in the room. If only... He blurred before her as tears pooled in her eyes, and she blinked them away rapidly before smiling around at her friends and accepting their good wishes.

'Speech, speech!' Lydia cried, and soon everyone was joining in.

Lou cleared her throat. 'Jeez, guys, I'm only going on maternity leave. I'm not dying. You know how weepy we pregnant women are, and I refuse to have my mascara run on my last day. And anyway, I'll be seeing you all in two days' time for the shave.'

'I still can't believe you're going to go through with it,' said Kristy wistfully, as others murmured their disbelief too.

'Speaking of Shave for a Cure,' said Harold, addressing the group, 'I thought you might like to know that the consultants and I have banded together and are putting in five hundred dollars each. That's twelve thousand dollars just for Lou alone.'

Cheers and whistles broke out, and everyone clapped.

Lou could hardly believe what she was hearing. What an incredible amount of money! She looked at Kristy and laughed. 'See, I can't back out now.'

The party broke up a little while later. There was still a ward to run and sick kids to help. Lou gathered all her stuff together, trying to ignore how heavy her heart felt over leaving. It seemed disloyal to be turning her back on Ward Two after so many years. It had been her life, her second home for ten years. And then there was the big, scary unknown future. She pulled her office door shut behind her, balancing bags and packages in her arms, said another round of goodbyes and walked on wobbly legs into the unknown.

Will was coming into the ward as she was going out, and opened the doors for her. 'Good, I was hoping you hadn't left yet,' he said. He saw her juggling act and relieved her of some of the packages.

'You just caught me,' she said, forcing her voice to sound casual as her heart beat a mad tattoo in her chest. 'Can you walk and talk?'

They traversed the distance to the car park in silence. Lou popped the boot and Will helped her load it up.

'You're going to be missed,' he said, after she'd shut the boot and looked up at him, shading her eyes in the afternoon sun.

'Lydia will have everything under control.' She shrugged, feeling more than a little fragile over her departure.

'Ah, yes, Lydia.' He grimaced. 'Goody.'

Lou laughed. 'Lydia's damn good, and you know it.' She shifted slightly, so her head was in the shadow cast by his body. The sun framed his head, bathing his hair in a golden glow and throwing his face into shadow.

Will nodded. They gazed at each other for a few moments, and then he realised she was looking at him expectantly. 'I bought you something…a gift…for the baby, really.' He reached into his briefcase and pulled out a small, beautifully gift-wrapped package.

'Oh, Will,' she said, touched by his thoughtfulness. 'You didn't have to do that.'

He shrugged. 'I was walking past this antique shop and saw it in the window and thought of you.'

Lou's fingers were shaking as she carefully undid the yellow tissue paper. The wrapping was like a work of art, several layers of yellow artfully blended together, and it seemed almost a crime to disturb it.

Nestled amongst the paper was a little silver box. It was quite heavy for its size and Lou picked it up, loving the feel of its weight as it fitted snugly into her palm. She rubbed her finger over the decorative engraving. 'Oh, Will,' she said, tears burning her eyes, 'it's lovely.'

'Open the lid,' he said.

Lou flipped it open gingerly with her thumb, and gasped as a row of tiny ducklings moved along a conveyer belt, disappearing at the end and then reappearing at the beginning again one at a time, to the strains of 'The Blue Danube'. She shut the lid and then opened it again, fascinated by the antique handiwork.

'I thought you'd like it,' he said.

She smiled up at him, stood on her tiptoes and kissed his cheek, avoiding the temptation of his mouth. 'I love it,' she said. 'Thank you. I'll treasure it.' She looked at it one last time, and then slipped it into her handbag.

He nodded and smiled. 'I'm sorry, Lou...about everything.'

'I know,' she said, hearing the genuine despair in his voice. She felt her Braxton Hicks start again, and unconsciously rubbed her belly. 'It's better this way. For the kids.'

A really strong one cramped her uterus, and Lou gasped at the impact, grabbing onto the roof of her car as it squeezed tight.

'What?' Will asked. 'What's wrong?'

She held up her hand to shush him as she breathed her way through it. 'Just a Braxton Hicks,' she assured him, when she could finally talk.

'Are you sure?' he asked. The pain had looked really strong. 'You're not going into labour, are you?'

'Will!' she said, glaring at him as another squeeze began its grip. 'It's nothing. I'm paranoid enough about this. You're not helping.'

'What can I do?' he asked, as her increasingly white-knuckled hold on the car alarmed him.

Lou bit her lip and struggled to breathe through another one. 'Just shut up for a moment. They'll pass in a few minutes.'

Will wanted to do more. He wanted to touch her belly and relieve her of the pain instantly. But he held out his hand instead, and was pleased when Lou took her hand off her belly and placed it in his. She gripped his hand hard, and he waited until her grip had eased off completely before he checked how she was again.

'Fine now, thanks,' she said, releasing Will's hand and the car.

'Are you going to be all right to drive?' he asked as she opened her car door.

She laughed. 'I'm pregnant, Will, not disabled.' Although as her bump squashed against the steering wheel she did think she wasn't going to be able to fit in very much longer.

'Tight squeeze,' he said.

She looked up at him to find him grinning. She admired his flat belly enviously, and ran her hands over her own expanse, barely able to remember her body before the baby. 'I'll remember that in twenty years' time, when you've got a beer gut,' she said.

He chuckled and shut her door for her. 'See you Sunday?'

She nodded. 'Sunday.'

And then she drove out of the car park and away from Will and the hospital as fast as she could. She could see the collection of buildings in her rearview mirror, and Will standing there staring after her.

Tears blurred her eyes as she drove further and further away, until the hospital and Will were a speck in the distance. She had just left everything from her past behind and embarked upon a bright new future—she hoped.

Sunday morning dawned and Lou felt terrible. If there hadn't been so much money riding on her plait she would have pulled the covers over her head and stayed in bed all day. Her back ached, and she'd been up intermittently all night with mild diarrhoea. As it was she didn't drag herself out of bed until nine, and the shaving ceremony was starting at ten.

She took her time in the shower, washing her hair. The plait was being donated to a charity wig place after, so she wanted it to be clean. She supposed absently that she was going to save a heap on shampoo and conditioner. She leaned heavily against the glass in the shower as her first Braxton Hicks kicked in for the day.

The cascade of warm water running over her bump and back lessened the severity, and she made a mental note to add the use of a shower to her birth plan. And then she made another mental note to actually get on with *writing* her birth plan. That was what maternity leave was for, after all. Getting ready for the birth and bringing the baby home.

Her grand plans to attack the nursery this weekend had died a quick death with her back pain and the tiredness that had hit her from out of the blue. She turned the taps off and resolved to start preparations tomorrow. *Please, Jan, if you're out there, let me get this right.*

There was a hive of activity in the hospital canteen when she arrived. A stage had been set up down at the far end, and crowds of people were milling around. Patients in their pyjamas, some of the kids from Ward Two with their parents, nurses, doctors, domestics, physios, reps from the local leukaemia foundation and even some local media. The clown doctors were there too, spreading their cheer, twisting balloons and pulling coins out of the air for the kids.

Somebody spied her and started to cheer, and everyone turned and looked and then joined in. She blushed and made her way to the Ward Two crowd, who were waving madly at her.

'Goodness,' she said. 'Is anyone manning the ward?'

Lydia laughed. 'We're covered. Don't worry.'

'Are you ready?' Pete asked, holding up the clippers and turning them on so they buzzed threateningly.

'Is it too late to change my mind?'

Pete laughed. 'Yes.'

A low voice growled in her ear, 'No.'

Lou felt the kick in her chest a second before she registered that the words had come from Will. She turned to look at him. He looked gorgeous. 'Hello, Will,' she said, going for a teasing, friendly tone. They were friends, after all, right? 'Are *you* ready?'

'Piece of cake,' he grinned.

'Where's Candy?'

'Over getting a balloon animal,' he said, turning to watch his daughter patiently waiting in a short line.

Lou watched her too. She was so much like Will. She wondered what a daughter of theirs would look like. Would she be the spitting image of her big sister? More Will than her? Or would she be a perfect blend of them both—Will's brown eyes and her honey-blonde hair? Will's height but her petiteness?

Candy spotted Lou and she waved excitedly. 'She looks like she's having a ball,' Lou said.

He grinned. 'She loves the clown doctors. She's decided she wants to be one when she grows up.'

'Really?' Lou laughed. 'There are worse things she could be.'

Candy dashed over to them a few moments later. 'Lou, Lou,' she said, 'look at what the clown doctors twisted me. It's a green and pink zebra.'

'So it is,' said Lou, looking at the bizarrely garish animal. 'Very…talented.'

'Ladies and gentlemen,' said Harold into the microphone from up on the stage. It broke through the chatter in the room, 'if you could all please be seated, we can get the Shave for a Cure under way.'

It was great entertainment. There were six stools on the stage. They brought up the willing victims in sixes, caped them, and then six eager apprentice cutters either shaved or coloured. The audience cheered and clapped and wolf-whistled. Raffle tickets were sold and then drawn at intervals throughout the morning. Pete had set a twenty thousand dollar fundraising target which, thanks to Lou, they were going to achieve easily.

It kept Lou's mind off her backache and rib-ache and the Braxton Hicks that kept coming with monotonous irregularity. Candy chattered to her excitedly and her enthusiasm was infectious. And, before she knew it, it was their turn. Will and herself. And as they were the two star attractions, Harold got them up on the stage together.

'Okay, folks, a lot of interest has been raised in the hospital over these two heads. Dr William Galligher, our staff paediatrician, and Sister Louise Marsden, Ward Two's Nurse Unit Manager. Or at least she was until Friday.'

There was general cheering, and Harold smiled enthusiastically and waited for it to die down. 'Now, Will has decided to go for a colour—' The crowd interjected, booing good-naturedly and clucking at him like a henhouse full of chooks. 'So we're going to do him first and leave the real draw card to last.'

There was more cheering as Will sat on a stool and a

pretty hairdresser apprentice picked up a can of red hairspray and shook it. Lou spied Candy, sitting with Rilla and the Ward Two staff, looking at her father with such pride and love in her eight-year-old eyes. Would Jan's baby look at her like that too?

Will signalled he was ready, and shut his eyes as his hair went from mid-brown to bright red in thirty seconds. The crowd went wild and Lou joined in with them. It was amazing how changing hair colour could transform someone. He looked so fake—comical, almost. Like one of the clown doctors. She looked at Candy, who kept standing and clapping, and then sitting, and then standing again, she was so excited.

Will got off the stool after his cape had been removed, and did a theatrical bow—to the absolute delight of the crowd.

'Please join with me and give Will a round of applause,' said Harold.

Will joined Lou where she was standing as the clapping continued. 'How bad does it look?' he asked in a low voice.

'Bad.' She grinned, smothering her laughter. Up close, he looked even stranger.

'Laugh all you like, Lou. This is gonna wash out in a few days. You're going to be shorn for much longer.'

'I'm looking forward to it,' she said, and looked away from his sexy grin as Harold beckoned her over and introduced her.

'And then there was one,' he said to Lou. 'Turn around, Lou, let everyone see just what you're losing here today.'

Lou obliged, turning so the crowd could see the plait that fell down her back, the tip brushing the rise of her buttocks. Someone yelled out, 'Don't do it!' and everyone laughed.

'How long have you been growing your hair, Lou?' Harold asked her.

'Since I was seventeen,' she said, turning back and speaking into the microphone.

The crowd ooh-ed. 'So that's about eighteen years?' he said. And the crowd ooh-ed again.

'That's right,' she said, appreciating Harold's theatre, aware that he was building up to the moment not just for the sake of the television cameras but for the audience as well.

'For those of you who have known Lou for as long as some of us, you'll know that this plait is a legend in this hospital. It's followed Lou through her training, and all her years on Ward Two. But today the plait is coming off!'

There was clapping again, and Lou's smile dented slightly as the Braxton Hicks started up again. *Great timing, kid.*

'Twelve thousand dollars,' Howard continued, 'and that's just the doctors. Lou's generosity will help the hospital achieve its goal of twenty thousand dollars, so let's hear it again for Lou.'

'She hasn't done it yet,' came a voice from the crowd.

Lou laughed. 'Well, let's get this show on the road, then.'

Sitting on the high stool was difficult for someone who was as short and as pregnant as Lou. She was wearing a strappy black T-shirt that moulded her breasts and stretched right over her bump, and a purple tie-dyed skirt that came to just above her knees. Slip-on chunky-heeled sandals completed the outfit. She decided to just prop herself against it, and not treat all and sundry to a rather inelegant display.

The cape went around her and she relaxed a little. The Braxton Hicks had stopped as abruptly as they had started, so things were definitely looking up. Now that she was here, she was eager to get it over with. Cutting off her hair was strangely symbolic, and she couldn't wait to have it done.

The plait represented the old Lou and everything that had come before, including Will. From today she would be purged, able to start anew. Just her and the baby.

A male apprentice held up a pair of sharp-looking scissors to the crowd and everyone ahh-ed.

'Any last words?' Harold joked, putting the microphone in her face.

'Hurry.'

The crowd clapped, and Lou scanned the faces for Candy. The little girl gave her the thumbs-up and she winked back. Then, with swift precision, the hairdresser grasped her plait and chopped it off.

There was an audible gasp as the crowd reacted to Lou's plait, separated from her head and held triumphantly aloft. Lou looked at it dispassionately, more than ready to let it go.

She put her hand up to her hair and felt the soft thick fall of hair around her ears. It felt good. Unfamiliar, but good. The hairdresser held up a pair of clippers next, and brandished them to the crowd. Someone in the audience started to slow-clap, gradually picking up momentum until everyone joined in, so that the noise was almost deafening.

He held Lou's head very still and then, with a number four blade, ploughed a line of near baldness down the middle of her head. Lou almost laughed into the sudden silence. The joviality had gone, just looks of horror were left. It was quite comical.

But suddenly a huge, intense pain ripped through her abdomen, voiding the audience's reaction. She clutched at it convulsively, and then she felt something like a tearing inside her and, to her absolute horror, her membranes ruptured right there, up onstage in front of everyone—

including the six p.m. news. Buckets of the warm sticky fluid oozed down her legs and soaked into the material of her slip-ons. It pooled at her feet in an ever-widening puddle.

Despite the fact that they were in the middle of a hospital, and the medical to non-medical staff ratio was at least five to one, no one seemed capable of any movement for a few split seconds. Until Will rushed to her side and that seemed to be the signal for everyone else to put their brains into gear.

'Will—Will,' she wailed, clutching at his shirt, his ridiculous red hair not even registering through her panic. 'This can't be happening. It just can't. It's too early Will. Please, I can't lose this baby.' Lou hadn't come this far for anything to happen to Jan's baby now.

'You won't. I promise,' he said authoritatively, sweeping her up into his arms and striding off the stage. 'For God's sake,' he snapped to the immobile audience, 'Don't just stand there—someone get her a wheelchair.'

Lou clung to his neck, and he could feel her trembling. Lou needed him. And it felt good.

CHAPTER SIX

'DADDY, Daddy,' called Candy, rushing over to them as Will lowered Lou into a wheelchair. 'Is Lou okay?'

'I'm fine, sweetie,' said Lou, hearing the worry in Candy's voice. She smiled at the child and squeezed her hand. She tried to project a calm, confident exterior, but inside she was thinking the worst. 'The baby's just decided to come a little early.'

'She'll be fine,' agreed Lydia, also joining them, and giving Candy a reassuring smile. 'Get her to Maternity,' she said to Will over the top of Lou's head. 'Now.'

Will heard the underlying urgency in Lydia's otherwise light tone. 'Can you…?' he asked, nodding at his daughter.

She nodded. 'Candy, sweetie, Daddy's going to go with Lou. You want to come home with me and play with Rilla for a while?'

'Sure,' Candy said. 'You will phone me straight away when the baby's born, won't you, Daddy? And I can come and visit you, can't I, Lou?'

'Of course, sweetie,' Lou said, gritting her teeth as the contractions came in wave upon relentless wave.

Lydia took Candy's hand. 'Good luck,' she said, squeezing her best friend's shoulder as she ushered Candy quickly away.

'Go!' Lou said urgently as soon as they'd left.

Will didn't need to be told twice. 'Are you having contractions?' he asked as he strode along.

'Yes.'

'How far apart are they?' he asked.

'They aren't,' she said, gripping the arms of the chair for dear life, pushing down through her legs and feet to raise her bottom slightly off the chair. Her back felt on fire, and sitting was aggravating the pain. 'They just keep coming. I'm not getting a break between them at all.'

Bloody hell. Will pushed faster. 'Are you breathing?' he asked, concerned about her white-knuckled grip.

'Of course I am,' she snapped. 'I'd hardly be talking to you if I weren't.'

Will ignored her testiness and stopped the chair at the lifts, pushing the up button several times. *Come on, damn it.*

'It's going to be fine,' he told her, as he pushed the button three more times.

'It's supposed to be six more weeks,' she wailed. 'It'll be tiny, and its lungs won't be developed enough.'

Will banged the button harder this time at her distress. 'Nonsense—look at you. You're huge. This baby is going to be a goliath. Anyway, it's only six weeks,' he dismissed firmly, pushing the button continuously now. 'That hardly even registers as prem.'

Ordinarily the female inside her would have been insulted by his blunt summation of her size. But right now she couldn't have cared less. 'Sometimes the not so prem ones fare the worst,' she said, biting her lip to stop the threatening tears. Crying was not going to help Jan's baby.

The lift arrived, and Will could have kissed the opening doors. 'The baby's gonna be fine,' he said again.

The four other occupants in the lift stared open-mouthed as Will pushed Lou inside. They did look a sight. Will with his clown doctor hair, and Lou with hers half shorn, a near bald strip down the middle like a reverse mowhawk, panting and puffing and clutching her tummy, her clothes soaked.

Still their expressions didn't register. Lou didn't even notice. Between the bite of contractions and worrying that the baby was too early, her brain was full. All that mattered was that the baby was okay. The baby that Jan and Martin had wanted so badly. Her niece or nephew. She'd been scared all along that she'd muck this up, and now her worst nightmares were coming true.

Will burst through Maternity's doors a couple of minutes later. 'I need some help here,' he called, as he pushed her down the corridor.

'Dr Galligher?' a nurse said to him as he reached the nurses' station, looking at his scary hair. 'Lou?' she said, her eyes widening even further as she came around the counter and saw Lou and her half-hacked hair.

'Bree,' Lou said, holding out her hand and squeezing the midwife's fingers when she took it. 'It's the baby. It's coming. It's too early, Bree. You have to stop it.'

Bree looked at Will and raised her eyebrows.

'Her membranes ruptured about ten minutes ago. She's having continual contractions.'

'How far along are you now?' Bree asked calmly, crouching in front of Lou.

'Thirty-four weeks. I mean it, Bree. You have to help me.'

'Let's check you out,' said Bree gently, rising from her squat.

Will followed Bree into a birth suite and helped Lou out of the chair and onto the bed. Bree snapped on some gloves and started to help Lou undress. 'Ah…I'll go, then… I don't want to…I'll hang around for a while outside.' He didn't want to go and leave Lou with no one, but he was unsure of his role or what she wanted from him.

'No,' said Lou, looking up from derobing in a panic. *Please don't leave me.* A contraction hit her and she stopped, breathing through it, needing him with her. Needing his strength to get her through the next harrowing hours. 'I want you…to stay…please…please stay.'

Will's heart swelled with love. 'Of course,' he said, coming over to the bed and taking the hand that was gripping the side of the mattress. 'Squeeze this instead.'

Bree helped Lou into a gown, and then did an exam. Will held her hand and kissed it absently, stroking her forehead soothingly. He was totally oblivious to her bad-hair-day appearance. He only saw Lou, the girl he loved. Not the bizarre half-done haircut, but the woman who was having her sister's baby, trying to be brave, but scared out of her mind.

'Maybe if I'm not dilated they can give me some ventolin to stop the labour?' Lou said to him, trying not to tense up.

Will knew full-blown labour when he saw it, and he knew this baby was coming now. But he just smiled at her and kissed her hand and said, 'Maybe.'

'You're six centimetres,' Bree announced, pulling off her gloves.

Will shut his eyes and shook his head. He had so wanted to be wrong.

'What?' said Lou, pushing herself up onto her elbows so

she was half sitting. 'No.' She shook her head. 'Check again. That can't be right.'

'Lou,' said Bree quietly, 'it's right.'

Lou struggled to get all the way up, and Will helped her. 'But I need you to be able to stop it, Bree,' she said, trying to not let the hysteria bubble to the surface.

'I'm sorry, Lou,' the midwife said gently. 'This baby wants out.'

'But my membranes only just ruptured,' Lou said incredulously.

'Have you been having contractions before this?' asked Bree.

Lou shook her head. 'Just Braxton Hicks.'

'Regularly?'

'They've been getting more constant.'

'Any backache or diarrhoea?'

Lou nodded. 'Both, over the weekend.'

'I'd say you've been grumbling along in labour for a couple of days.'

Lou couldn't believe what she was hearing. The baby was coming now? *Now!* No, she wasn't ready for this. The nursery wasn't done, and the clothes weren't bought, and she hadn't read the books on labour and child-rearing, or written a birth plan.

'But I haven't even written a birth plan,' she said to Bree, as if that would make all the difference. As if Bree would say, Oh, well, that's different. You're not in labour any more. Go home.

'Most people's plans usually go straight out the window anyway,' said Bree, unfazed.

A contraction tore through Lou, and she sat on the edge

of the bed, wanting to scream it hurt so much. *Birth plan—get through birth without going insane.*

'So what happens now?' Lou asked when the grip had eased, pushing herself off the bed.

Bree laughed. 'The fun part. You push the baby out.'

Lou looked at Bree, then at Will. 'No.' She shook her head wildly. 'I can't do this. I can't.'

'Lou,' said Will quietly, 'you are the strongest woman I know. You can do this.' He walked towards her slowly. She looked like a scared animal, sitting in the headlights of a truck, waiting for the inevitable. He didn't want to spook her. He closed in and gently held her shoulders.

She shook her head, not quite able to comprehend what he was saying or that she was actually in labour. 'I'm not ready,' she said to him, her expression dazed.

'Sorry, babe,' Bree said. 'You don't get to choose. Babies are like that. I'm going to call your obstetrician, and alert the resus team.'

Bree left the room and Lou shivered. Will pulled her into his arms and she was grateful for the warmth. The resus team? Of course. They would attend in case the six-week premi baby needed help with its breathing. *Please, no. Please let it be okay.*

She leaned into him, and then tensed in his arms as another contraction took hold. He murmured softly into her hair, rocking her, and rubbed her back until it eased. It felt like heaven to be this close, even in the middle of labour. She'd always felt safe in the circle of his arms, his chest warm and hard beneath her ear, the reassuring thud of his heart booming to a primal beat.

Bree came back in again with some paperwork, and sat

quietly and unobtrusively filling it out. After she'd completed it she orientated both of them with the room. 'There's a shower through here,' she said, opening a door. 'Would you like to use it, Lou? The heat on your back or under your bump is good for the contractions. They sound like they're getting worse,' Bree added.

Lou nodded. They were. And she had planned on using the shower at some stage. 'I don't know…not yet.' Lou didn't know what she wanted. The contractions were really biting and lengthening, lasting for quite a while.

'We haven't talked pain relief,' Bree said. 'Have you thought about that?'

Lou shook her head and held on to Will's shoulder as a contraction swamped her. She breathed hard and dug her fingers into the flesh of Will's arm. 'I thought I had another six weeks to think about it,' she gasped out.

Thoughts of Jan flashed into her mind, and Lou wondered what her beloved sister would say. The sudden pain in her chest almost contended with those dilating her cervix. Jan's baby was about to come into the world, and she was never going to see its precious, darling face. The despair she had felt on hearing about Jan's death swamped her, and the unfairness of life almost brought Lou to her knees.

Will felt her grip on his arm ease. 'What do you reckon, Lou?' he asked. 'You can't go on like this.'

'I don't know,' she said wretchedly. 'I want to do what's best for the baby.' She looked up into his face, feeling more desolate now than she had that terrible day the police had been on her doorstep. *Jan. I miss you.*

She pushed away from him, feeling as if she was failing Jan, but a contraction rocked her and she stopped, clutching at his just-in-reach shirt. It eased slowly and she released him, wandering around the room, too churned up to stay still. *Help me, Jan. Please help me. I'm scared. I want to do the right thing and give your baby the best start in life. But it hurts so much. Not just in my body, but in my heart, and I wish you were here. I hope you know I'm going to look after your precious baby.*

Memories of Jan flooded her. Like the time she had taught Lou to ride her bike, and then patched her knee with a plaster when she'd fallen off the first time. And Wendy, her favourite doll, and Mittens, Jan's tabby kitten, who had slept with her every night. And the day Jan had got her braces. And her driver's licence. And her graduation.

And the day she'd met Martin for the first time. And their wedding. And how excited Jan had been when she'd first fallen pregnant. And the devastation of the miscarriage. And the utter wonder in Jan's eyes when she had said yes to the surrogacy. And her sister's tears when the pregnancy was confirmed.

As Lou paced the room, stopping every couple of minutes, interrupted by a contraction, she could feel the lump of emotion in her chest getting bigger and bigger. It just wasn't fair. Jan and Martin were good people. *Had been good people.* It wasn't right that they couldn't be here to see their baby being born as they'd planned on doing. Or that they weren't going to take him or her home from hospital. Lou wanted to kick the wall. She'd trade her soul at that moment to have them here in the room with her.

She felt a sob choke in the back of her throat at the same time as the most forceful contraction to date surged through her womb, and she bellowed in despair, leaning against the wall, tears streaming down her face as she railed against the fates and the pain cramping her belly.

Will had been watching her pace, feeling about as useful as udders on a bull. Every time he'd tried to comfort her she'd shaken her head and moved away. He wished he knew what to do. She didn't seem that content, walking back and forth, in fact she looked miserable, but she seemed to want to be alone as well. But the bellow was just too much.

'Lou,' he said, rushing to her side. 'Let me help you. What? Tell me what I can do.'

Lou felt the hot burn of tears trekking down her face, and she squeezed her eyes shut as she tried to cry and breathe at the same time. 'Nothing,' she said.

Will heard her voice, thick with emotion. 'Do you want me to rub your back?'

'No,' she said, choking on a sob that she couldn't hold back.

Will saw her slim shoulders shaking and felt as if a knife was stabbing him in the heart as he put his arms around her shoulders. 'You want an epidural?'

'No,' she wailed, disintegrating further into tears.

'Pethidine?'

'No,' she sobbed, and shook her head, shrugging her shoulders so his hands fell away.

'Lou, they don't give out medals for bravery, here. Tell me—I must be able to do something! What do you want?'

Lou felt rage and impotence and worry and physical exhaustion rise inside her like a tidal wave. She turned to him, her blue eyes burning fiercely, tears brimming and then spilling down her face. 'I…' she took a deep breath '…want…' and another '…my…' She swallowed a sob and plunged on, her voice cracking, '…sister!' And she didn't bother holding back the tears or the emotion, sobs racking her body along with another contraction as she grunted her despair and grief.

Will felt as if he had been punched. He hadn't seen her grief this raw, and he pulled her in close, whether she wanted it or not, and held her while she unburdened.

'Jan was supposed to be here…' Lou sobbed into his shoulder. 'She was going to deliver her baby…' Her breath caught on a sob and she coughed and spluttered briefly. 'Martin was going to cut the cord…'

Will rocked her, at a loss for something to say. What could he say to make it better? To take away her grief? The birthing process was always an emotional journey, but for Lou it was bittersweet in the most poignant way possible.

'I'm so sorry, Lou,' he crooned.

'Oh, Will,' she sobbed. 'I— Oh, no! Here comes another one. I want it to stop, Will,' she said, looking at him with her face screwed up in agony, her hands clutching his shirt and her chest heaving with the effort to stop the convulsive sobs and breathe through the contraction. 'I don't want to do this any more.'

'I know,' he said, rubbing her back as he supported her weight and absently kissing her forehead. 'I know.'

Try as she might, Lou just couldn't stop the tears. She felt weak and useless and powerless against the contractions. Her grief magnified her misery tenfold. Not even Will's solid presence, the feel of his chest beneath her hand, the hard ridge of his collarbone beneath her forehead, could quiet her cries. 'Make it stop,' she begged, her voice muffled by his chest. 'Make it stop, Will.'

Will had never felt so impotent in his life. He didn't know

what to do. Delvine had had an elective Caesar, so he was at a loss. Anything. Anything that would take away Lou's suffering.

'Bree?' He looked at the unruffled midwife questioningly. *Stop writing in that stupid chart and do something, damn it!*

'She's in transition,' she said quietly over Lou's cries. 'Feeling that you can't go on is perfectly normal at this stage.'

'How do I help?'

Bree smiled at the helpless-male look written all over the very competent Dr Galligher's face. She put down her pen and walked towards them.

'Lou,' she said, 'you need to stop crying and concentrate.' Her voice was stern, devoid of emotion.

'I can't,' said Lou, sobbing harder.

'Nonsense,' Bree said briskly. 'There's no such thing as can't. Right, Will?'

'Er…' said Will, looking at Bree doubtfully.

'She needs you to snap her out of this,' Bree said quietly in Will's ear. 'She's going to have to push this baby out soon, and she needs to be strong and focused for that.'

'But…'

'No buts, Will. You gotta play bad cop for a while.'

Will looked down at Lou's downcast head, rubbing his chin against her hair, the shorn strip prickly against his face. She felt so good in his arms. So right. She belonged there, and the fact that she was leaning on him, that she needed him, was an acknowledgement of their special bond. He didn't want to be the bad guy again.

He looked at Bree. *Don't make me do this.* But he saw the determination in her eyes, and as a doctor he knew she was right. Lou had the hardest part ahead of her.

'Lou,' he said, kissing her forehead, his hands on her shoulders, pushing her back slightly. 'Come on, Lou. Time to stop crying.'

Lou eased her grip on his shirt as a contraction passed. 'It's so unfair, Will,' she cried, not caring that her eyes were red or her nose was running, and she was sniffling and snorting like a toddler with the flu.

'I know, I know,' he said.

'I just want to curl up in a ball and cry for ever,' she wailed.

'I know. But you can't. You've got a job to do,' he said gently, smoothing her damp fringe off her face.

She shook her head, more tears spilling down her cheeks. 'I don't want the job any more. I just want to wallow for a while. Please?'

He chuckled. 'No, Lou, you can't. Baby first,' he said firmly.

Lou heard the chuckle and felt irrationally annoyed that he found this remotely funny. That he found *her* funny. She pushed herself away from him and paced to the other end of the room. 'Go to hell,' she said. 'Last time I checked you weren't the one pushing out your dead sister's baby.'

Will blinked. Her anger was palpable. He looked at Bree, and she urged him on with a nod. 'No. I'm not,' he said. 'But you are.'

'Oh, really?' she snapped, staring down at her very large abdomen. 'Is *that* what this is doing here? I hadn't noticed.'

'Lou—' he said, stepping closer.

'Don't come near me,' she said, holding her hand up to prevent him coming closer. She wiped angrily at the tears on her cheeks.

Anger—that was good. Better than tears, right? 'I'm sorry, darling,' he said. 'But you need to stay focused.'

'Don't darling me,' she sneered. 'Since when have I ever been your darling?'

Will looked at Bree, who nodded some more to encourage him to keep going. 'You're doing well,' she mouthed.

I damn well hope so, now that we're airing all our dirty laundry in front of you!

Lou stared at him, waiting for his answer. He looked as if he'd rather be anywhere but here. *Well, get in line. Darling.* 'I mean, did you really ever love me?' Lou demanded.

Suddenly she wasn't sure. He'd told her last week that he still did, but now, with his chin-up-darling routine, she was forced to confront the fact that maybe he'd only told her what she'd wanted to hear.

It was Will's turn to feel caught in the headlights. He didn't want to have to defend his feelings for her like this. He sighed. 'You know I did Lou. I still do.'

'Well, you've got a funny way of showing it,' she said. She felt another contraction building and braced herself. 'Damn it,' she wailed, leaning forward over the bed, centring her weight on her rigid outstretched arms. She was too angry to cry over the vice-like grip cramping her abdomen.

Will moved forward automatically, but halted abruptly at her vehement, '*No!* Don't you dare come near me.'

Will looked at Lou, isolated in her pain, and then at Bree, miserably. *Thanks a lot.*

'I'll give you guys some privacy,' the midwife said. 'I'll be just outside if you need me.'

'Why don't you join her?' Lou panted as the door shut behind Bree and the contraction ebbed.

Will hardened his armour against her barbs. 'I'm not leaving you,' he said.

Lou straightened, rubbing her back. 'Well, you're sure as hell not helping me.'

'I do love you, Lou,' he said. 'It's just complicated. You know that.'

'Right. Complicated,' she said bitterly. *Ain't that the truth!* 'Lou—'

She held up her hand. If she hadn't been in the middle of giving birth, she might have felt sorry for him. She knew what he was saying was right, but knowing that they loved each other only worsened her predicament.

'Save it,' she said, as her uterine muscles began to tighten again. She mewed in pain and resumed her leaning-over-the-bed position, rocking back and forth through her arms and the balls of her feet.

She felt as if she was going to die as she squeezed her eyes shut and tried to ride the crest of the wave without crying out. This contraction was significantly worse, and she moaned loudly despite her clamped lips.

'Will!' she gasped, as the pain built to a crescendo, and she held out her arm to him, eyes still squeezed shut. She couldn't do it alone. It was too painful, and she didn't want to be all alone should the pain actually kill her. The same part of her that rejected him also wanted to cling to him for dear life, like her anchor.

Will didn't need to be asked twice. He was by her side in two seconds and stood behind her, rubbing her back in rhythm with her pelvic rocking.

'Thank you,' she murmured, opening her eyes and straightening slowly as the pain disappeared. She turned to face him. 'Will, I'm sorry for what I said. I do understand. Now probably more than ever.' She looked down at the soon-to-be-here baby and rubbed her tummy. 'This pain is just wearing me down.'

'Of course,' he said, pulling her into his arms and kissing her forehead. 'It's okay.'

Lou inhaled deeply and smelt his pure male essence. She was grateful to have him there. He felt solid and male and strong, and she could lean on him—thank God. Her back was screaming at her, and Lou felt so tired she doubted she could stand or walk another second.

'I'm exhausted,' she said, pulling out of his embrace, looking for an alternative position.

'You want to sit? Or lie?' he asked.

Lou didn't know what she wanted. All she knew was that she was about to fall over. She spied some exercise balls over in a corner, and it was like manna from heaven. She knew some women swore by them for labour.

'A ball,' she said.

Will retrieved one. 'How about if I sit on the edge of the bed and put the ball between my legs and then you sit on the ball with your back to me and lean against me while you sit?'

Lou nodded. 'Sounds divine,' she said. 'Thanks, Will.' She touched his arm, and he smiled a smile of such gentleness it broke her heart.

Will helped her get into position, and for the next twenty minutes they didn't talk. Bree popped in and out. Her contractions were coming a minute apart now, and lasting for about ninety seconds. During the contractions she leant forward, her elbows on her knees, breathing heavily, rocking back and forth on the ball while Will rubbed her back. In between she leant back against Will and recovered.

'I'm scared, Will,' she said, after a particularly nasty one.

'I know. I'm here.'

'I'm not talking about the labour,' she said. 'I mean after. I have to get this right, Will. I don't know the first thing about raising a child.'

'You're a paediatric nurse,' he said, his low voice rumbling in her ear, his chin resting lightly on her shoulder. 'Of course you do.'

'It's not the same as having your own,' she said.

He shrugged. 'You'll be fine. And I'll be here to help you.'

Lou shut her eyes and fantasised for a few brief seconds. Will and her together, with Candy and the baby. A family. Him being there for her. Helping her. But she knew that wasn't what he'd meant.

She shook her head sadly. 'No, Will. I don't want you to be there but *not* be there. I'm scared at the moment, but I'm sure I'll muddle through. For Jan's sake. For the sake of my little niece or nephew. But I can't do it with you hanging around in the background. It has to be all or nothing for us. Having you around and knowing it can never be is too hard.'

Will knew what she was saying. And he understood where she was coming from. She was right. Being friendly would be torture. 'I know,' he said miserably, kissing her shoulder. 'I know.'

Lou felt a sudden incredible pressure inside, and pushed herself away from him, flailing her arms until she grabbed Will's knees to balance herself.

'What?' Will asked. 'What's the matter Lou?'

'I need to push,' she said. *'Now!'*

'I'll get Bree,' he said, moving out from behind her quickly, his long stride reaching the door in seconds.

And then it was action stations. Lou clutched Will's hands, worried again, now that the arrival was imminent, about the babe's prematurity. She pushed all the dreadful worst-case scenario thoughts to the back of her mind as she concentrated everything she had on pushing the baby out. But still the dread persisted.

Was the baby going to be all right? Six weeks early… It was going to be small. Would it breathe okay when it finally emerged? Would its premi lungs be able to cope? Would it have to be intubated or spend time in the NICU or the special care nursery? Her bond with Jan's baby was already so strong that the mere thought that she might have to be separated from her niece or nephew was too horrible to think about.

Lou found it impossible to lie on her back, the pressure of the mattress causing excruciating pain in her lower lumbar region. So Bree placed a bean bag in the middle of the bed, threw a sheet over it, and Lou knelt in front of it, settled her bump into the soft cushion of beans and hugged her arms around the bag in a supported kneeling position.

Will also knelt on the bed, on the other side of the bean bag, opposite Lou, holding her hand, crooning encouragement and brushing her hair off her face. Bree was behind Lou, gloved, ready for the head to crown.

'Nearly there. I can just see the head now,' she said to Lou. 'You're doing so well.'

'Tell me the baby's going to be okay,' Lou panted to Will, as one contraction eased and she waited for another to push some more.

'The baby's going to be perfect,' Will said, wiping her face with a cool cloth.

'No tube, no oxygen, brilliant apgars,' Lou chanted, trying to calm herself with positive thinking.

'Quick suction, quick once-over, apgars ten out of ten,' he assured her, kissing her forehead.

'Oh, God,' Lou wailed, 'here comes another one.'

'One step closer,' Will said, rallying her, his forehead against hers, preparing himself for her vice-like grip on his hand. She looked exhausted. 'You can do it, Lou. Not long now. Big, big push.'

She looked at him mutinously until the pain forced her eyes shut. She gripped his hand and obeyed. Just as well they weren't married, she thought as she drummed her feet against the mattress. Because at the moment she never wanted to see his peppy, you-can-do-it expression ever again.

After three more pushes the baby's head had almost stretched Lou's birth canal to the maximum. In one more push the head would be crowning, and, barring any complications, the baby would be here in less than two minutes.

'Page the resus team,' Bree said to the other midwife in the room.

She looked over the top of Lou's head and nodded at Will. 'Lou, the baby's about to crown. I've paged the team and they'll be here shortly. With the next contraction I want you to just pant—don't push, okay?'

Lou heard her words and nodded wearily. She'd do anything if it meant the pain would be over soon. But, despite her exhaustion, her fears for the baby were uppermost. 'The team *is* going to be here in time?' she asked anxiously.

'Any second,' Bree assured her.

The team arrived thirty seconds later, just as the next contraction hit, and as soon as Lou heard their arrival she knew it was safe for the baby to come out. She shut her eyes as the pain built to a crescendo and concentrated on the impossible—not pushing.

'Don't push, Lou, pant,' Bree demanded, her hand on the baby's head, trying to slow the delivery a little to prevent any tearing.

Lou felt as if she was splitting in two. The stretching was unbearable, and there was a fierce burning sensation. *I'm going to die here on this bed.* At least Will would be with her at the end.

'Easy, Lou, easy. Don't push.'

'I'm not,' she groaned. 'It's just happening.'

'Pant, Lou. Pant,' Bree instructed.

'Pant,' Will parroted.

The pain was too much. 'I can't,' she wailed, overwhelmed.

'Yes, you can,' Bree and Will both demanded, in unison.

Lou choked on a sob and reached deep inside her for the last skerrick of control she had left, and she forced herself to pant as her body tore in two.

'Good girl, Lou,' Will whispered in her ear. 'Good girl. You can do it. Good panting.'

'Shut…up,' she ground out through gritted teeth.

And then, miraculously, the pain was gone. Lou heard a huge grunt escape her mouth as the head slipped out, and she collapsed against the bean bag, gasping in relief. It was over—the pain and the pressure and the burning.

'You did it!' Bree exclaimed. 'We'll wait for the next contraction to deliver the shoulders,' she said.

Lou was too caught up in the bliss of relief to register that the job wasn't quite done yet. She vaguely heard suction happening, and Will congratulating her on a job well done.

The next contraction started down low, and Lou squeezed Will's hand in anticipation.

'Okay, last push,' he said quietly into her ear. 'Then you're all done.'

Lou nodded, and squeezed her eyes shut one last time. The burning and the pressure were there again, but not as bad as last time, and she sagged gratefully against the bean bag and Will's shoulder as she felt the baby slip out completely. And for a few seconds nothing else mattered other than the fact that it was over. Not whether the baby was all right. Or its sex. Or whether she was still in one piece. Just that miraculously, after seven and half months, and five hours of the worst pain she'd ever been through, it was over.

'You did it. You did it.' Will was whispering in her ear and kissing her face, and still the overwhelming sense of relief fogged her thought processes. And then the baby cried, and the fog disappeared instantly. The baby. How was the baby?

'The baby?' she said to Will.

She felt frantic suddenly that it had taken her this long to focus on the most important part of all this. She looked behind her at the bawling newborn lying on the mattress between her legs. His lusty cries were a salve for her fears.

'He looks fine,' said Bree, preparing to cut the cord. 'Do you want to do it?' she asked Will.

Will blinked. Did he? The baby wasn't his. Hell, it wasn't even Lou's. Yet, strangely, he did want to. He'd been a part of the birth, totally helpless for most of it, but this was something he could do. He looked at Lou.

Lou looked into his face, his ridiculous Clown Doctor hair not even registering. Whether she wanted to admit it or not, they'd just been through a deeply intimate experience.

Together. And now the pain was gone, and her thinking was clear, she didn't want him to ever forget this bond.

She nodded. 'Set him free,' she whispered.

Will's hand shook as he took the scissors. Jan's little boy was the hugest thirty-four-weeker he had ever seen. His unimpressed face screwed up, his powerful lungs bellowing his displeasure. If this baby needed any form of assistance he'd be amazed.

He paused before making the final cut, totally transfixed. Apart from Candy he was simply the most beautiful baby Will had ever seen. Bree touched his elbow.

'Come on, Will,' she joked. 'Do the deed. The team's getting bored.'

Will had done this many times before, and cut quickly and efficiently through the thick tissue of cord between where Bree had clamped. Will instinctively went to pick up the still crying infant, to comfort him, soothe his cries, but an impatient resus team member scooped the baby up before he had a chance.

'Is he okay?' Lou asked, turning her body around so she was facing the activity, leaning back against the bean bag, the pain in her back miraculously gone.

'He's perfect,' said Will.

Lou felt tears well in her eyes and reached out her hand to him. Will took it and squeezed it and smiled at her, and she loved him so much there was an actual ache in her chest.

Lou smiled back for a few seconds. 'Thank you, Will,' she said.

'Thank you,' he said.

They gazed at each other for a few moments, and then Lou became aware of the noises the resus team was making.

'What are his apgars?' she demanded, dropping Will's hand and sitting forward.

'Nine and ten,' said the doctor, tending to Jan's baby in a prepared warmed resus cot. 'He seems fine. Fighting fit.'

Lou smiled and breathed a sigh of relief. Her nephew's cries were evidence of his good condition.

'Six pounds, ten ounces,' a midwife said, picking the baby up off the scales and wrapping him quickly in warmed blankets.

'Jeez, Lou,' said Bree. 'Just as well he was prem. Imagine how much he would have weighed in another six weeks.' The room erupted into laughter, and Lou joined them. What a whopping boy! No wonder her ribs had been so sore!

And a few minutes later her nephew was pronounced fit and put in her arms. He quietened instantly, as if he knew she was the one he'd just come from, and stared at his aunty with his mother's eyes.

'Oh, look, Will,' she said, her voice full of wonder. 'He's just like Jan.' And he was. He had Jan's eyes, and cute little upturned nose, and her chin, and her high cheekbones.

'Hello, baby,' she crooned. 'I'm your aunty. Welcome to the world.' Lou pulled back the blanket from his head a little, and gasped as tufts of red hair became evident.

'He has Martin's hair,' she exclaimed. How perfect for this little treasure to have a legacy from both his parents. 'Oh, Will, I wish they were here,' she murmured, feeling the tears prick her eyes.

He sat on the bed beside her. 'I know,' he said gently. 'I know.'

Will had never seen her looking lovelier. With her hair half shorn, her face still flushed from the exertion, tears glistening in her eyes and a look of complete and utter adoration on her face, he couldn't remember ever loving her more. And he knew in that instant that he never wanted to be apart from her ever again.

What kind of a fool had he been? Everything he wanted, needed, was right in front of him. Who had he been kidding? He had made another mistake. The first one had been thinking he was over her. That he could ever be over her. But the second one was worse. He was allowing the past, with all its emotional trauma and baggage and the present complications in their lives, ruin the best thing that had ever happened to him.

The baby stirred in her arms and Lou hushed it. Sitting before him was the woman he loved. Through this amazing act of complete selflessness she had proved to him again her endless devotion. And not just to Jan. He had seen it in her determination to lose her hair for leukaemia research, and the way she was with Terry and Candy, and her dedication to Ward Two. And he had certainly seen it in their relationship.

How long had she stayed the first time around, when others would have left the minute Delvine had started putting her oar in? He was in love with a woman whose capacity for dedication and commitment knew no bounds. Surely they weren't going to let stuff from their past and their perceived complications now stand in the way of something truly beautiful?

Yes, it was complicated. Yes, they both had kids to think about now. But how much better could they provide for and nurture their children if they were together? As they wanted to be. Yearned to be. Deserved to be. Could he be the best father he could be to Candy when he was denying himself a chance at adult love? At true happiness? Could she mother Jan's baby while denying she needed to be fulfilled and loved as woman as well?

Through being here to witness Lou's special journey, he was part of her life again. How could he have fooled himself otherwise? They were joined, always had been, and trying to deny it was insane. And witnessing the last weeks of her pregnancy, being here for the birth and cutting the cord, had just drawn him in deeper, closer.

Despite fighting it, he was already in over his head. Why had it taken this tiny, or not so tiny baby to make him see that some commitments, some bonds were never broken? Were there whether you wanted them to be or not. And that pretending they didn't exist, or that you could do without them, didn't make them go away.

'Oh, Lou,' he said, watching her watch the baby, a tear rolling down her cheek. 'I've been such an idiot.'

Lou heard his words, and her finger tracing the soft down of the baby's cheek stilled. What exactly did that mean? She took a moment to steady her heart before she looked at him. 'What are you talking about?'

'You. And me. And Candy and the baby. I love you. I've tried to pretend I can do without that for the sake of the kids, but I don't want to. I don't ever want to be without you again.'

Lou took a deep breath. 'What does that mean, Will?'

'It means I want us to be together. I want to wake up to you every morning.'

Lou nodded, seeing her wonderful fantasy tantalisingly close, just out of reach.

'We can't, Will. The kids… I have a baby to think about. To commit my time to. One hundred per cent. I won't have time to commit to us. That's not fair to either of us.'

'I know that, Lou. But we can make it work. We're not new to this. We'll have to skip a lot, I know.'

She shook her head sadly. 'Even rekindled relationships need time, Will.'

Will understood what she was saying, and in normal circumstances he would agree. But this wasn't normal. It was complicated—as they were both fond of pointing out. But that was just being defeatist. 'None of that matters as long as we're dedicated to each other and to making it work,' he said.

'It's not that simple,' she protested.

'Of course it is, Lou. It's only complicated if we let it be. All that matters is that we love each other. Do you love me, Lou?'

'Of course.'

'You're one of the most dedicated people I know. You have this great capacity for devotion. Don't tell me you don't have enough for me? The man you love? For us?'

Lou looked at him. He was asking her to risk everything again and give them another try. 'It's too—'

'Complicated.' He smiled, interrupting her. 'I know. But I love you. I want this. I need this. So does Candy, and so does this baby. We'll both be better for them when we're happy. And you, my darling, make me happier than I've ever been. I'll be miserable without you.'

He was right. She knew he was right. The temptation was overwhelming. But could it really be as simple as he said, after denying themselves for so long?

'There'll be no time for romantic dinners and walks down the beach and sunsets.'

'We've had that.' He shrugged.

'There'll be two a.m. feeds and dirty nappies and sleepless nights.'

He grinned. 'We've had plenty of sleepless nights.

Lou suppressed the urge to grin back. He needed to realise that getting back together wasn't going to be remotely intimate, with an eight-year-old and a baby demanding their attention.

'There's probably not going to be time for sex, even,' she pointed out.

'I don't need it,' he dismissed quickly.

'You don't?' she asked dubiously. *I sure as hell do.*

He shook his head. 'We've done that too, Lou. A lot. And, as much as I've wanted you badly these last few weeks, it can take a back seat—because nothing is more important than us becoming a family.'

Lou heard the magic word and felt tears prick her eyes. It was all she'd ever wanted—to be part of a family with Will. She'd almost had it in the beginning, and then Delvine had come back and the sense that she belonged as part of a unit with Will and Candy had disappeared. And Will had been too distracted and busy and stressed to give her the assurances she needed.

'A family, Will? Are you sure? You know you've never really considered me part of your family.'

What? 'How can you say that?' he asked, trying to keep the rejection from his voice. 'I loved you. We lived under the same roof for five years.'

She nodded, swallowing the lump of emotion lodged in her throat. 'Sure, you loved me—and I was really starting to feel like I belonged in your family. But then Delvine came back, and a part of you kept me on the outside.'

He went to interrupt, and she hushed him by placing a finger on his lips. 'I understand why, Will. She'd hurt you, and her coming back opened the wounds, and her meddling made them bigger, reminded you of the pain and trouble relationships can cause. But I never felt that sense of family again. So I can't go through that again. I want to be part of your family, Will. And I know that you love me. But you've got to let down your guard and embrace me fully. I won't be an honorary member in your family any more. I want to be a fully fledged, card-carrying Galligher.'

Will hadn't realised how excluded Lou had felt by his guardedness. 'Oh, God, Lou. I'm so sorry. I never meant to make you feel that way,' he said, running his fingers through his red hair and staining his hands in the process. 'I want you to be a fully fledged Galligher too. Okay, we're going to have to re-invent the wheel, I know that. But living a moment longer without you by my side is not an option. I want us to get married.'

Lou blinked and tightened her grip on the now sleeping baby. *Married?* 'What?' she asked faintly.

'I. Want. To. Marry. You,' he said, grinning at her incredulous expression.

Lou stared at the man she loved. Inside she was screaming—*yes*. Yes, yes, yes. A thousand times yes. But she'd been hurt by him in the past, and she needed to make sure he was for real. She suddenly felt disorientated and foggy again, as if she was back in labour without the excruciating pain.

'Lou, please,' he said, tipping up her face with a gentle finger under her chin until he was looking into her beautiful eyes. He saw the doubt there. 'I need you. Let's do something for *us*, for once. Let's take control of our situation instead of being overwhelmed by it. Let's decide right now that we're going to be together for ever and spend the rest of our lives dedicated to making it work.'

Lou's heart pounded in her chest. Was she really hearing what she was hearing? 'Will…are you sure about this? I mean…'

'Just say yes, my darling. We've wasted too much time already. Make me the happiest man on this planet.'

The baby squirmed, and she looked at her nephew and knew she had enough love in her heart for him and for Will. And that to be truly happy, and do the best job she could, she needed Will in her life.

'Oh, Will,' she said, her voice wobbling, tears brimming in her eyes. 'Yes. Of course yes. I love you. I'll dedicate my life to making it work. You're right. We belong together. You, me, Candy and Charlie.'

Will pulled the two of them into his embrace, elated. He kissed her. 'A family,' he said.

She smiled. 'That's all I've ever wanted to be with you, Will.'

'I know, Lou. Can you ever forgive me for being such a fool?'

'Oh, Will.' She sighed as she leaned her head into his shoulder and gazed down at her sister's baby, her heart bursting with joy. She couldn't believe that after so much upheaval and misery she could be this lucky. She could be this happy. 'Of course, you fool. I love you.'

And they stared at Charlie together for a very long time, content to bask quietly in their love, safe in the knowledge that today was the first day of the rest of their lives. As a family.

Queens of Romance

The Marriage Risk

Sensible secretary Lucy transforms her prim image to catch her sexy boss's interest and is thrilled when he sweeps her into an intense affair. But when passion leads to pregnancy…dare she risk marriage?

The Hot-Blooded Groom

When Bryce Templar meets Sunny, the attraction is like a bolt of electricity – business is forgotten and passion takes over… But even more stunning is Bryce's proposal the very next morning! Will she be his convenient bride?

Available 16th March 2007

Collect all 4 superb books in the collection!

In 1875, a row of tiny cottages stands by the tracks of the newly built York – Doncaster railway…

Railwayman Tom Swales, with his wife and five daughters, takes the end cottage. But with no room to spare in the loving Swales household, eldest daughter Mary accepts a position as housemaid to the nearby stationmaster. There she battles the daily grime from the passing trains – and the stationmaster's brutal, lustful nature. In the end, it's a fight she cannot win.

In shame and despair, Mary flees to York. But the pious couple who take her in know nothing of true Christian charity. They work Mary like a slave – despite her heavy pregnancy. Can she find the strength to return home to her family? Will they accept her? And what of her first love, farmer's son Nathaniel? Mary hopes with all her heart that he will still be waiting…

Available 16th March 2007

www.millsandboon.co.uk

M&B